Pride & Passion
Sarah Roberts

By Sarah Roberts

His Sugar Baby
IT Specialist
Pride & Passion

By Kate Anthony

Action Hero Junkie

By Harper Lewis

Hunted, Beware

Prologue

The door crashed open. The viscount staggered into her bedchamber and kicked the door shut again. Sucking in an alarmed breath, Lady Ogden whirled. He advanced menacingly on her. His face was contorted by rage. He shouted, slurring his words, "Wife! I demand my husbandly rights!"

"You're drunk, Henry! You disgust me! Leave me!" She spoke sharply, backing away, her heart beating hard with dread. He hit her, the blow knocking her down onto the bed. She cried out, more frightened than she had ever been, and scrambled away. He pounced on her, clawing and tearing the lawn nightgown from her shoulders. Breathing heavily, blowing inebriated fumes hot in her face, he snarled, "*Bitch!* I'll bring you to heel!" He fell on top of her. She screamed once before all of her breathe was for her frantic struggle.

Before the monster could finish the violent assault, he passed out in her bed. Sobbing, panting from horror, she fixated on escape. Terror gave her the strength to wriggle out from under the heavy weight of his supine body. She snatched up a long shawl, stumbling in her haste. She ran to lock herself inside the darkness of her sitting room. Trapped and trembling, her face smarting from his heavy blow, her body badly bruised, she wrapped the large woolen shawl tight around herself and curled up on the settee. The fire had died down, with little more than red embers glowing behind the grate, but the seeping cold was infinitely preferable to remaining in her bedchamber with the mean-spirited brute who was her husband.

She slept fitfully, spending much of the wretched night listening for the approach of heavy footsteps or the rattling of the doorknob. Waking with the approach of dawn, she regarded the pale light with apprehension. She dared not return to her own chamber so early, where the monster might still be in her bed. She fled again and sped through the impenetrable dark shadows of the hallway, making for the safety of her aunt's bedchamber. The eddying air wrapped cold fingers over her ankles and the floor was chill under her bare feet. She tightened the large woolen shawl closer around her shoulders and hurried faster. The umbra was slowly giving way to the indistinct light of day as it peeked through the panes of the tall window at the end of the hallway. Suddenly, a huge black figure loomed up before her and she recoiled, gasping in fright.

"Well, well, Lady Ogden."

She recognized the gentleman's voice. "Sir William!" She should not be so shocked to run into one or other of the gentlemen, climbing the stairs to the upper floor where their bedchambers awaited. The late-night card parties always lasted well into the early-morning hours. Yet her heart gave a jump of fright.

As Sir William Talley came closer, she began to make out his face in the slowly gathering light. He was smiling. His heavy-lidded, bleared gaze traveled from her face to the hair tumbled down over her shoulders. A heated gleam lit his eyes and he made a leisurely, thorough perusal of her state of *dishabille*.

Heat scorched her cheeks. It felt as though he had stripped her. Apprehension poured over her. She pulled the long shawl closer over her nightgown. "My aunt needs me," she said abruptly, coldly.

Sir William considered her statement for a moment before he moved aside. She hastily passed him. At her back, he called softly, "Shall I see you at breakfast, my lady?"

"No, you shall not!" She heard the gentleman's chuckle behind her as she hurried on to her aunt's door.

He raised his voice slightly. "Perhaps at tea, then."

Lady Ogden knocked urgently at her aunt's door. She sent a blazing glance of contempt down the lightening hallway at the mocking gentleman. He merely laughed. Then the door opened and she whisked herself through it.

Some hours later, she and her aunt were seated comfortably in the upper sitting-room, where they had breakfasted. The orange flames of a fire blazed behind the metal grate to stave off the season's cold. A thin blanket of silent snow had fallen during the night. The ladies had accordingly dressed in merino wool gowns and each had arranged a neat shawl over her shoulders.

Sipping at her sweetened morning tea, Lady Ogden unwillingly recalled her dismaying encounter with Sir William. *One of Henry's drunken, loutish friends.* It still covered her with shame, and a peculiar distaste, reanimating her feeling of dread, and she shivered. *The way he looked at me!*

Lady Ogden never, at any time, wanted to find herself in the company of the viscount's friends. She thought them to be an unmannerly, contemptible lot, barely suitable to share the table with any respectable lady. All of the gentlemen were well-born enough, of course, but their amusements and proclivities often put them beyond what was pleasing. An old saying fleeted into her mind. *A man is known by the company he keeps.*

She would not think about her husband the viscount. The nightmarish night still had the power to evoke abject wretchedness. Neither her dresser nor her aunt had remarked on the bruised swelling on one side of her face. They had seen such tokens of her lord's affection before.

The butler brought word to the ladies that the viscount and his friends had left the manor house, shouting cheerful quips amongst themselves, before bowling off in their smart conveyances to watch a bout of fisticuffs in the next village.

"There, my dear! We may be comfortable for the rest of the day," said Mrs. Merriweather, pointing out the happy fact. "Surely that must lift your frown."

"Yes, we may be comfortable. They'll not return for hours," agreed Lady Ogden with rising spirits. She smiled up at the hovering butler. "My aunt and I shall take luncheon in the front parlor, Somerset."

"What a perfectly splendid notion!" exclaimed Mrs. Merriweather in quick approval.

With a faint smile, the butler bowed. "Yes, my lady."

"It will be a rare day, aunt," said Lady Ogden cheerfully, with not an inkling of premonition.

At dusk, under a sullen scurry of wind-whipped clouds, Lord Henry Ogden was brought home on a wood plank. The tale was swiftly told: the fisticuff bout, luncheon at an inn with flowing ale, an impromptu bet. In the mad, drunken race, his lordship had smashed his curricle wheel on a snow-shrouded rock. Thrown from his sporting carriage, he had landed on his head. Senseless, bleeding from nose and mouth, and obviously suffering some broken bones, his lordship was carefully laid down in his own bed. The physician was sent for at once.

The viscount's friends were shocked into sobriety. They waited in morbid dread, along with the rest of the apprehensive household. Lady Ogden had never seen the smart London gentlemen either so sober or somber. She quietly instructed the servants to see to the gentlemen's requirements for drink and food. Much as she detested their intemperate invasion of her home, she was nevertheless scrupulous in her duties as hostess in the trying circumstance.

Sir William Talley watched her ladyship and he felt a faint stir admiration for her calm authority. *I must give the creature her due. She is a lady,* he thought. Her shadowed gaze chanced to meet his bold stare. He inclined his head. He expected to see self-consciousness form in her eyes, given their pre-dawn encounter, but there was not. She merely turned away.

His lordship never regained consciousness. As the wind howled outside and rain battered at the window panes, the scene illuminated by the feeble light cast by flickering candles, her husband lay dying. Lady Ogden remained faithfully at his bedside. She was a dutiful wife, though there was little of respect or affection left between herself and her lord. It was a long, long vigil that lasted into the black night, into the next day and the next. Later, she would have a muddled recollection of conversations. The physician, saying, "There is no hope of his lordship coming out of coma. The viscount is bleeding to death internally." Someone else – the viscount's steward? One of the viscount's friends? – advising her that his heir presumptive must be sent for, and her weary agreement.

1

*J*an.1813

It was late winter, a bleak ugly day. Against the frosted window panes, icy rain pattered. The chill in the high-ceilinged room, what had at one time been a cramped second parlor, was made barely tolerable by the heat from the large fire burning behind the ornate metal grate. The flickering candlelight from the several branched candelabras, which had been placed on top of the high fireplace mantel and elsewhere, barely kept at bay gloomy shadows in the deepest corners of the ground-floor study.

There were only three occupants in the room, the lady and the gentleman each occupying a faded wingback chair, with the solicitor facing them from behind the expanse of an impressive mahogany desk. The lady pulled the folds of her black shawl closer about her shoulders, but the gentleman was immobile, seemingly unaffected by either the cold or the solemnity of the occasion.

The widow waited tensely to hear what the future held in store for her. It was common knowledge the late viscount had flung his fortune to the four winds. Lady Ogden clung tight to the hope that there was something left, something upon which she might live, even if it was to be in an impoverished manner; indeed, it would be a minor miracle to learn that her husband had thought much at all about her welfare. That conviction was actually the basis of her meager hope. Without a jointure being settled on her at the time of marriage, she was entitled to support arising out of one-third of whatever was left of the late viscount's squandered estate.

The will was read, the solicitor's dry voice making the particulars of the legal document sound all the more horrible, the hateful words

ringing in her ears: *The Right Honorable Charlotte Viscountess Ogden,
my wife, an annuity of one hundred pounds for services rendered.* The
revelation shocked her, battered at her stunned wits, over and over. He
had left her only a hundred pounds a year! A faithful servant might
be left such an amount as an honorarium. It was more than insult. It
destroyed her world. She could scarcely take it in.

"*But what shall I do? How shall I live?*" she uttered. Even though Lady
Ogden spoke in scarcely more than a whisper, she was heard by the two
others in the room.

The new viscount had no decipherable expression on his
sun-browned face. He got up from his chair and turned away to look
out through the tall, leaded window at the darkened sky. The weak light
silhouetted his head, the breadth of his shoulders; the close cut of his
plain brown coat emphasized his stiffened back.

The solicitor was unable to meet her ladyship's appalled expression.
He uncomfortably cleared his throat. "It is unusual, certainly."

"It is monstrous!" she exclaimed. "Surely, there is some mistake. Are
you certain there is nothing else?"

The solicitor slowly shook his head. His reply held a note of pity.
"Quite certain, my lady."

Without another word, white-faced, the widow jumped to her feet
and swiftly quitted the room; behind her fluttering black skirt the door
slammed. In the abrupt silence, a log cracked and fell into the fire,
sending up a burst of yellow sparks.

The solicitor meticulously gathered his papers. He shot a sidelong
glance at the stern profile of the new peer. He had himself sent word
to the gentleman of the late viscount's expected, imminent death and a
request for his immediate return to England.

The former Major Vincent Crawford had resigned his commission
in the Army, the decision made to leave his military career due to his
unexpected elevation to the peerage. The last viscount, a dissolute
gamester and a bad whipster, had died lingeringly of internal injuries, the
outcome of a senseless curricle race. Mr. Digsby knew next to nothing
about this Lord Ogden, but he hoped that his lordship was a better man
than the one whose shoes he had inherited.

The brutal lack of provision for Lady Ogden pointed up the unfortunate stamp of the late viscount's character. Such an appalling omission was surely to be condemned by any gentleman worthy of the name. Hesitatingly, Mr. Digsby ventured to give voice to his most prominent thought. "It is difficult for her ladyship."

"Quite." The single syllable was clipped. The new viscount did not look around.

Suddenly feeling very ill-at-ease, the solicitor stood. "The most important items I am leaving for your later perusal, my lord. If there is nothing else, I shall take my leave."

Lord Ogden turned. His expression was calm, as was his voice. "It is sleeting, Digsby, and already late in the day. You must stay the night."

The solicitor was astonished and gratified. Such consideration had never before come his way at Delincourt Manor. The late viscount had not been a hospitable man, nor an easy employer. The solicitor's opinion of the new peer rose a few increments. Mr. Digsby bowed. "Thank you, my lord. That is most kind."

"Have one of the footmen show you to a room."

The solicitor thanked the viscount again and quietly quit the study, closing the door.

Lord Ogden turned again to the window, clasping his hands tight behind him. Frowning deeply, he stared through the frosted panes at the sheets of icy rain. He stood thus for several minutes. In his mind's eye, he could see her lovely face. She had not changed overmuch in the intervening years. Subdued, yes, and pale, with the light all but extinguished from her green eyes, but otherwise the same. Even the bruise on her cheek – he could have throttled his cousin for that alone – had not detracted from her loveliness. The instant he had seen her again, at the gravesite, everything had faded away and once again he had become a young fool desperately in love.

The painful memories of five years ago came rushing back, churning in his mind. He'd spoken too late. Almost on the eve of rejoining his regiment, before departing to the war on the Peninsular, he'd pressed his suit. His sudden declaration had startled her. He had not had time to fix his interest with her, and so he had ridden off with a heavy heart.

Bitter regret tinged his recollections. She had been persuaded to make her choice elsewhere. He'd had his cousin's letter crowing of their marriage. In all the time since, he'd seen her only once and that but fleetingly, during his short furlough upon the death of his father. It had been an awkward meeting, one unexpected and fraught with inarticulate emotion on his part. He had suddenly come upon her in the church, where she had brought flowers. She had stared at him, a strange expression flickering across her face. She had said not a word but turned and hurried away. In public and under the watchful eyes of his cousin, there had been nothing but stilted civilities exchanged between them. He had gone away again, grimly eager to return to duty.

Though he had returned unscathed from the war and rich in prize money, though he had gained a peerage, he knew as certainly as his heart beat that she would still not have him. Her pride would not let her forget. It would not let her bend. It would not allow her to accept from him anything but his charity.

Of course, as a man of honor and his cousin's heir, he must do something for her, he thought. That was without question. The late viscount's deliberate cruelty in failing to provide a proper dower for the widow was criminal, in his opinion. He had been left incredulous by it. All of his sympathies had been roused, and, yes, perhaps some feelings relic of the past. Those conflicted emotions must be set aside. He must regard the settlement as only another of the late viscount's many debts, which he was obligated to discharge.

I shall never see her again.

"Nonsense! Of course, I shall." He mocked himself savagely. "At some ball or *soirée*, where we shall exchange distant nods of civility!" The new viscount could not tolerate any longer his unpleasant reflections. With barely suppressed violence, he cursed his dead cousin.

Lord Ogden turned from the window. He strode across the faded carpet, as much to leave behind his recollections as to take himself over to the desk. His gaze fell on the stack of documents which the solicitor had left and he uneasily eyed the number of them. It had always been the military for him. He had not been bred to the management of estates. First his blighted hopes, now to be saddled with this burden. Under his breath, he muttered, "Damn your eyes, Henry! Perdition is too good for you!"

2

When Lady Ogden so precipitately fled the ground-floor study, she had rushed upstairs, her unhappy emotions threatening to swamp her. The tightness in her chest made it difficult to breathe except in small gasps. Her feet must have flown because before she was properly aware of it, she had rounded the turn of the stairs, and reached the upper landing. A housemaid came out of a room. Lady Ogden swiftly turned aside, without voicing her usual quietly-worded acknowledgement of the servant's presence. She heard another door open somewhere near but paid it no heed. She needed and sought privacy before she was overborne by her agitation. Her turbulent mind was fixed on her objective; only a few steps more, to the refuge of her apartment. Outside her sitting room door, however, she was intercepted by her aunt.

"You were not long closeted with the solicitor." The older woman's pleasant, wrinkled face was puckered by an anxious frown. She had put out a detaining hand to impede her niece's passage. "Pray, will you not tell me anything?"

Lady Ogden burst out, distraught, her words disjointed. "Nothing, nothing! A paltry hundred pounds, aunt! A hundred pounds, nothing more!"

Mrs. Merriweather stood frozen for a long second before she let go of her niece's arm. Slowly, she folded her hands in a tight clasp at her waist. In a low, troubled voice, she said, "His lordship barely tolerated me. Naturally, I didn't expect – but you! My *dear*, dear Charlotte! What are we to do?"

"I know not, aunt! Pray-*pray* let me be! I must be alone!"

"Of course, child."

Brushing past her aunt, Lady Ogden rushed into the sanctuary of her private sitting room. She shut the door and turned the heavy key, clicking the lock into place. As she moved away from the door, a hitching sob broke from her. She pressed one agitated hand against the base of her throat, where her pulse was tumultuous

"I cannot believe it! I cannot! The bastard, *the bastard*!" The violent exclamations seemed to relieve the worst of her outraged feelings, as well as the rigidity of her thickened throat. She did not go altogether to pieces, as she feared she would. She dashed a hand across her eyes, clearing them of the threatening tears. "I will not weep! No! I shall not!"

Lady Ogden paced the sitting room. She was aware of a chill, despite the small fire on the hearth, and she drew her shawl closer about her shoulders. She was trembling, and she knew it had nothing to do with the physical temperature in the room, but rather, the cold fist which clutched her heart. With the viscount's death, Delincourt Manor was no longer her home. She had no other place to go. She had no funds except what was left of the last quarter's pin money and her meagre annuity. *A hundred pounds! My God, how cruel!*

Of necessity, she was well-versed in the household accounts. Salaries alone – the butler, L35 a year; the housekeeper, L25 pounds; the cook another L25. Her own dresser earned L35, and all were entitled to their own rooms and board as part of their support at Delincourt Manor. There were the additional costs for food, heating coal, candles, and all the rest that must be taken into account besides...she couldn't possibly set up household. "A hundred pounds a year! I cannot afford even a rat-infested garret room!" Her lord might as well have condemned her to a vagabond's starving existence or, if she was so foolish as to get into the clutches of the moneylenders, to debtor's prison

The viscount had been laid in the cold, muddy ground only hours ago. She'd had the fortitude to uphold her dignity during the service in the shadowed, echoing church and to accept the condolences of the few mourners attending from the neighborhood. She had been surprised even that small number had come; her husband had not been a gentleman popular with his neighbors. The late viscount's London friends had taken abbreviated leave of her and had posted immediately back to town. Sir William Talley alone had the courtesy to offer some solace. His mocking manner uncharacteristically muted, he had lingered for a moment. "If you should ever have need of my services, my lady, call upon me. I have left my direction with your butler." Despite her deadened sensibilities she had felt a flicker of warmth and she had been grateful, conveying it with a small nod and the trace of a smile.

Of course, Major Crawford, the heir presumptive, had been in attendance. She'd been strong enough to bear seeing him, to watch him approach through the dreary, gray rain after the service was concluded, to hearing his deep voice utter the empty polite phrases. She had steeled herself when he had taken her gloved hand and bowed to her. She had accepted with melancholy resignation that he had succeeded to the title and estate.

However, when those hateful words had been read aloud in front of him, it had been too much for her to bear. She could not look at him again. *She could not.* She couldn't force herself to meet whatever expression might be found lurking in his cold, dark eyes, and so she had fled.

"He has stepped into his cousin's shoes." Lady Ogden uttered a sharp, bitter laugh, but her heart bled. "How ironic!"

It had been three years since she had last seen Major Crawford, this cousin-in-law of hers. He had been on furlough to settle his late father's affairs. The viscount had not liked his heir presumptive. Her hand lifted to touch her marred cheek. But Henry had not much liked her, either, which went far in explaining how it was that she had not produced an heir during the brief period of their marriage.

The marriage had been difficult, sometimes almost insupportable. However, she had made her choice. It had seemed the sensible one to make at the time and it was the cruelty of hindsight which showed her how wrong she had been. Now the consequences had to be dealt with.

The insidious panic crept up inside of her once more, nearly overpowering her. She had no family left to speak of nor to turn to in her extremity – except her father. Even if she made an appeal to Sir Martin and he acquiesced, it would not be a happy homecoming; indeed, a place at his table would be grudgingly given. The spiral of genteel poverty was a difficult thing to break, and another mouth to feed and another back to clothe would not be welcome. "There is my aunt, too. My father will not want his sister-in-law back at his hearth, any more than a widowed daughter!" No, she could not apply to her father, for she knew very well that even if he allowed her to return to his roof, his grudging charity would never stretch to include her aunt also. She and her maternal aunt, Mrs. Merriweather, shared the strongest of bonds, one established during her girlhood even before the sad, lingering death of her mother and which had only strengthened with the passing years. "I cannot abandon my dearest of companions! No, I shall not!"

Her spirit sank under its burden, though she valiantly fought against it. She had nothing but her own wits and a stubborn will. It had to be enough. It *must* be enough. The pall of despair that mired her thoughts was suddenly rent by a desperate possibility. *Vincent – if he wished to help me –*

Lady Ogden shook her head in quick agitation. "Cold charity! No, no, I cannot ask for it! Not from him!" She breathed unevenly as her thoughts revolved, over and over. She struck the heels of her hands together, raging impotently, but she could not hide from the unhappy truth. "What choice have I? What other choice *is* there? None, none!" She must ask for his lordship's charity. If it was offered, she would accept because she had no alternative.

Lady Ogden abruptly turned, looking up into the large gilded mirror hung above the fireplace, which reflected a good portion of the sitting room and where she stood in the middle of the worn rug. In the glass, she critically inspected herself. *Vincent once believed me beautiful.* Her hair was covered by a newly-acquired black widow's cap, with the black satin ribbons tied under her chin, and she was attired in full mourning. The black shawl had also been a necessary purchase. Her funds had not stretched to the cost of a whole wardrobe; the daydress she wore was one that had been picked apart, dyed and sewn back up. She did not look her best in black, she decided. The severity of the mourning clothes accentuated the bluish circles under her eyes, the hollows in her cheeks, and her skin appeared sallow. The bruise on her face had faded to a mottled purple and yellow. She would be attired in full mourning for six months before her widow's weeds could be put off, before she could wear half-mourning of gray or lavender.

She squeezed shut her eyes at the foolish trend of her dismal thoughts. Her appearance, her wardrobe...none of it mattered. "Oh, why am I wasting time? Why am I such a coward? I did not used to be! I must go down, before I lose heart altogether!"

3

On the echo of her knock, Lady Ogden entered the ground-floor study. All was just as it had been several minutes ago, the shadows held at bay by flickering candlelight, the chill countered by the blaze in the fireplace. Yet she fancied the atmosphere was turned oppressive.

The viscount was sitting behind the desk, but as her eyes met his dark gaze, he rose to his feet. If he was surprised she had sought him out, he gave no indication of it. His expression was inscrutable. He gave a civil nod. "Lady Ogden."

She closed the door behind her. Her heart was pounding. She felt almost physically ill. For the barest second, she hesitated, uncertain that she could carry through with her pitiable petition. *There is no other choice.* She squared her shoulders. She was glad, when she addressed the viscount, to hear the command she had over her voice. "Forgive my intrusion, my lord. I should like a word with you, if I may."

Lord Ogden gestured politely toward the wingback chairs which were still situated in front of the massive desk. At a glance, he had taken in her set, proud expression and her rigid posture, which at once made him wary. The iciness of her tone did not escape him, either. He replied with chilly civility. "Of course, my lady. Pray be seated."

Lady Ogden sank down in one of the chairs and sat stiffly erect. She waited for him to sit back down behind the desk before she spoke again. "I have come to solicit your help, my lord." The enigmatic expression on his face did not alter. If she had hoped for a flicker of surprise or some sign of sympathy, it was not forthcoming. She swallowed the bile in her throat; her voice began to quiver. "The-the behest in his lordship's will is-is inadequate for my needs. Indeed, I do not state it baldly enough. I have nothing – nothing whatsoever – to live on, so I beg of you, my lord!

I beg of you to find it in your heart to grant me some-some sort of annum for my support."

He leaned back in the chair, one wiry hand lying on top of the desk. His gaze half-hooded, he looked at her. The dark gaze was piercing. It struck her forcibly that he had the look of a fierce falcon, sighting its prey. A disdainful smile flickered across his lean face. "Forgive me, my dear lady. The irony does not escape me. You – come to beg from me!"

All of the wretchedness, all of the fear, crashed up against her barely-shored defenses. Lady Ogden felt something crumble and give way inside of her. She leaned forward, her desperation pouring forth in her unwisely-worded plea. "You swore you loved me! Was it all a lie? Ah, Vincent, Vincent! For the sake of the love which you once held for me!"

"A lie, madam!" Incredulity and fury came into his dark eyes. Under the permanent sun-bronzed tan, his cheekbones reddened. His aquiline nostrils flared. "You dare!"

She was past caring for her pride. "I must! For pity's sake, Vincent, please!"

He regarded her in stony silence. His lips were tightly compressed. The control he exerted over himself was patent. She did not allow her gaze to drop, but she could not stop the way her hands twisted in her lap. Behind her, she heard the loud ticking away of the mantel clock. Her heart beat time more rapidly than the clock. It seemed a lifetime before he spoke and his grating reply astonished her.

"If you had delivered an heir, by law you would have been granted tenure at Delincourt and a stipend."

Lady Ogden felt the sudden, tight constriction under her breastbone. It was a dulled pain now but still capable of hurt. She would not deign to let him see how his words wounded. "I failed in my duty."

"Is there any chance you might be breeding?"

A flush sprang into her cheeks. She tightened her clasped fingers until her knuckles turned white. She couldn't imagine what conceivable business it could be of his – *but of course!* In a flash, she understood. He'd still be the heir presumptive if she was with child, and not entitled to the chair in which he was now sitting. For a wild moment, she thought of lying, of saying that there was a chance of it, if only to gain some time in hopes of making another way for herself; but she could not sacrifice her honor, after all. It was the only thing left to her besides her tattered pride. Her husband had not lain with her in the several weeks before the accident, and as for the last time... She lifted her chin. "None, my lord."

"Then there is nothing to be done for you."

The viscount's flat statement fell harshly on her ears. Whatever fragile hope she had nourished withered. In dull despair, she looked at his angered, set face. The slow tick of the clock sounded unbearably loud. Some odd quality gathered in his expression, suddenly frightening her. His hard gaze bored into her own. He spoke slowly, very deliberately. "Unless, my lady, you were brought to bed of a child within the year of your mourning."

Lady Ogden stared into his unreadable eyes. *But I have just informed him* – At first, she did not understand. Then – when the incredible import dawned on her – she went hot and weak. The echo of his words taunted her through the chambers of her astonished mind. The air shuttled in and out of her lungs in rapid, shallow breaths. She wondered why she did not faint. But he waited, still watching her. *Falcon's cruel eyes.* Hating him, hating herself, she was sickeningly aware of the traitorous tempo of her heartbeat. She made herself answer him. "Y-yes, that is true."

"Then you know what you must do."

With a muffled exclamation, Lady Ogden leaped up from the chair, shoving it back in her haste. She quickly crossed to the fireplace and stared down into the red-yellow flames, her breath coming much too rapidly. *Beasts – beasts...they were all beasts.* She clutched the hard edge of the high mantel. Her other hand fisted tight to her waist, pressing in against her knotted stomach. She flung the words over her shoulder. "You are hateful, as hateful as he was!"

She heard his swift boot steps. Then he was standing behind her, so close that she could sense the leashed power of his taut body. His detested voice spoke nearly at her ear. "It must be a kinsman, one who bears a strong resemblance to the late viscount."

The pulse beat heavier in her throat. *No, no, no!* But the last shreds of her integrity could not withstand the powerful battering ram of her desperation. She uttered her surrender. Her low voice sounded strangled even in her own ears. "Yes."

His warm breath stirred the tiny hairs at the nape of her neck. She shuddered. Appalled, yet held spell-bound, her brain comprehended sharply the next insidious words. "It must be as soon as possible. As often as possible."

Her face burned when she felt the suggestive bunching of the fabric of her skirt on her thighs. He was letting her know that he would not delay in coming to her bed. Horror blanketed her; she felt suffocated. "Yes."

Then his hands were on her, a boot kicked her feet apart, a muscular thigh parted her legs. His hard, blunt head probed her delicate flesh; finding her intimate opening, his full organ thrust up inside of her, the fiery invasion arching her spine. A sharp cry broke from her throat. One of his calloused hands came down heavily over her mouth, smothering the sound. He breathed shallowly in her ear. "Soft now, my lady, or the servants will be in on us." He wrapped an arm tight around her waist and held her for the vigorous transaction. There were only the sounds of her shallow, hitched breathing, his harsher breath, the dull sucking noises of their coupling.

The ugly business was swiftly concluded.

It didn't take long, a few heavy thrusts, before he was shuddering. In the convulsive, rushing release, he uttered a hoarse-throated groan of spiked pleasure. His heart raced. He felt as though camp fever burned his flesh. When he was finished, he pulled himself free of her heated pith and dropped her black skirt and petticoat back down to cover her trembling nether limbs. He stepped back. Mechanically, he began to make himself presentable. His mind was curiously suspended, on some distant plain flooded with self-loathing, yet wholly absorbed with the ramifications of the infamous bargain that had been struck.

Lady Ogden clung to the mantel for support, stunned and reeling. Before she had a complete comprehension of what was happening, it was over. Shudders afflicted her body. She could barely keep herself from collapsing. She kept desperate hold of the mantel as she turned. Shocked, staring, she watched as he took out a fine linen handkerchief to dry his veined, thickened member. Numbly, she watched as he tucked it away inside his unmentionables and buttoned up the fall of his pantaloons.

The full, horrid reality finally burst upon her.

Lady Ogden staggered forward, making for the wingback chair she had quitted. He caught her elbow in steely fingers. His voice was roughened but cool. "No, do not sit down. You will dampen your skirt. The servants will notice." He dropped his hand from her arm and moved away. She clutched the high back of the chair, swaying on her feet. She felt the drainage of his cold seed trickling down the inside of her thighs.

She started to cry. With her free hand, she covered her eyes so that he couldn't see her but she couldn't tamp down the wretched sound of her weeping.

"You are overwrought." He did not know how he spoke so impassively. Yet in his mind he knew it had to do with the seething, conflicting emotions that still roiled inside of him. Her words had incensed him; she had basely sought to manipulate him. He had been caught fast in the grip of a white-hot fury, seemingly powerless before the onslaught of all he had so ruthlessly suppressed, and it had come uncaged all at once. The wicked stratagem had sprung full-blown into his brain.

The viscount yanked the bell pull and waited, his hands clasped tightly behind him. There was a harsh cast to his aquiline features. The suspension of his faculties had vanished. He grappled with guilt and fury. He had been out of his senses. It was the only explanation. Yet...*the bargain was struck*. The heavy pound of his heart underscored that fact.

Lord Ogden did not glance in her ladyship's direction, but he tightened the grim set of his mouth. He wished he could close his ears to her distress. It seemed an eternity to him, but was actually only moments before the door opened and a footman stepped in. The servant's gaze flickered briefly at the sound of weeping before settling firmly upon the viscount. "My lord?"

He spoke in a clipped, sharp tone. "Lady Ogden is overwrought. Send down her ladyship's dresser to her."

"Yes, my lord." The footman exited and shut the door again.

Lord Ogden addressed her ladyship brusquely. "I have taken my cousin's room." *The bargain has been struck.* The viscount watched her, wondering if she was in a state capable of comprehension. He wanted her to take his meaning. He baldly stated his intention. "I will bed you tonight."

Lady Ogden drew in her breath sharply. She shot up her head. Her swimming, tragic gaze fastened on him, a dawning horror on her face.

The viscount smiled, pleased that he had not underestimated her intellect, after all. He softly reminded her. "As often as possible." He saw her stricken face go even whiter and her eyelids fluttered. For an alarmed second, he thought she might faint. However, she was made of stern stuff. She merely leaned heavier on the chair back and averted her gaze. Tears continued to drip down her face. She didn't wipe them away. With deliberate detachment, he wondered if she had gone into hysterical shock and was no longer aware of them.

Lord Ogden waited with stiffened posture, his hands clasped behind him. Finally, with an anxious expression, the dresser came into the study. The tiring woman dipped a curtsy, then slipped a supporting arm around her ladyship's waist and led the softly weeping, bowed figure of the viscountess out of the room. The door shut. It was only then that the rigidity left his lordship's frame.

Lord Ogden swung around and stalked to the window. He drew back the heavy drapery with one hand, so that he could stare fiercely out into the cold gathering night. His breathing moved harshly in and out of his chest. He'd fought in bloody battles, but nothing had rattled him like what he had just done. *"I have damned my honor. It is a wretched course I have set."*

4

Upon entering her bedchamber, Lady Ogden colorlessly asked that the back of her dress be unbuttoned. The dresser quickly did so, casting several concerned glances at her mistress, which her ladyship ignored. She held herself rigid, but she was keenly aware that she was visibly shaking. The breath rasped in her throat. It was all she could do to retain a measure of control. Every bit of her energy was expended in keeping herself from flying apart. As soon as she could, Lady Ogden sent her woman away. "I will lie down, Mills."

"Yes, my lady." With a last worried, backward glance, the dresser exited and quietly shut the door.

Her ladyship's gorge rose. She bolted for the chamber pot. Dropping to her knees, she retched violently. When it was over, she wiped the sticky wet from her mouth with the back of a palsied hand, but she could still taste the sour vomit.

Lady Ogden forced herself back up to her feet and walked leadenly across the bedchamber. She ached, as though she was suffering from an ague.

Earlier in the day, before her departure for the church, in what now seemed an eternity ago, her dresser had brought in a small glass of sweet wine for her. She had ignored the cordial then, leaving it untouched on her bedside table; now, she was grateful to have it available to her.

When she picked up the half-filled glass, her hand was trembling so much that the glass clicked against her teeth as she set it to her lips. She drank the contents all down at once. She coughed and covered her mouth with the back of her hand, the empty wineglass hanging from between her fingers.

The wine cleansed the sourness from her palate. When it hit her rebellious stomach, however, she had to press a flattened hand tight against her middle. She breathed deeply, willing herself to keep the wine down. She set aside the wineglass and placed that palm, too, hard against her stomach.

Once she was certain that she wasn't going to vomit again, she took off her dress and petticoat. She left on her corset and chemise, her hose and shoes. The air was too chilly to bathe, but she couldn't bear not getting clean. She poured cold water out of the pitcher into the washbasin, wet a washcloth, and scrubbed away the sticky evidence of what had happened. *He was a monster, a beast! So very like his cousin!*

As often as possible...Yes.

The enormity of her rashness, the baseness of her assent, suddenly smote her, and she staggered. Anguished, she cried, "What have I done?" She bowed her head over the washbasin, straight-armed, her damp hands gripping the hard edge of the wooden stand. She had been so foolish – *no, incredibly stupid!* A wave of dark despair washed over her, yet hiccoughs of hysteria escaped her throat. To her own ears, her laughter sounded demented.

The viscountess abruptly lifted her head. Above the washstand, hanging on the wall, was a small mirror. It captured the reflection of a woman unknown to her, with bruised blankness in her eyes and the splotchy evidence of tears on her whitened face. Lady Ogden slapped herself so hard that her cheek burned. The red imprint stood out starkly against the abnormal paleness of her skin. Her deep-set eyes glittered back at her.

Pride put strength back into her spine and she straightened up. Hysteria was pointless. She'd compromised her honor. She'd thrown it away with a single, ill-advised word and she couldn't call it back. *Yes...*Minutes, and her world had irrevocably altered; he had shuddered to completion, spewing his seed deep into her womb. Her stomach pitched. She sucked in a deep breath, slapped herself again "No, I *will* not be ill! I must think! I must decide – what's best to be done."

The viscount had said he would come to her that night...the specter of another rape loomed before her inner vision, and her heart thudded fearfully. Unless she ran from the manor, with no place to go, and froze to death in the hedgerows, she could not see any way of avoiding his brutish attentions. A cold, hard inner voice interjected. She needed what he could give her, moreover. *One who bears a strong resemblance...* Her stomach twisted itself in knots again. She tried to calm herself, but her tortured reasoning was a goad to her afflicted spirit. Her mind cast this way and that, seeking an alternative, a way out of the maze. But there was none. That practical voice intruded again. She would have to suffer him, until it was impossible for the birthing of a full-term babe to be accepted as that of her late husband.

*...his arm tight around her, his hard hand close over her open mouth, his scorching length thrusting high up inside of her...*she started to shake again, so she cut off that perilous memory.

The jumble of her frantic thoughts went around and around. She recognized that she was still too numbed, too shocked out of her senses. There wasn't a prayer of being able to behave normally, of going downstairs at the dinner hour, of sitting calmly at the table across from her ravisher.

Lady Ogden was inordinately relieved. The disorder of her senses was not permanent. She'd been able to make one rational decision. It was a momentous one. She tugged the bell-pull, summoning back her personal servant. When the dresser came to her door, she said, "I shall take a tray in my room."

AFTER SEVERAL MINUTES of restless striding, from fireplace to desk and back again, Lord Ogden called for a footman. "Take a message up to Mr. Digsby. I wish him to come down to me at once."

"Aye, milord." The footman left and quietly shut the door.

Lord Ogden awaited the solicitor with impatience. When the man entered, he said, "Ah, Digsby! There you are. Close the door."

"Yes, my lord." The solicitor did as he was bid and advanced toward the desk, at the corner of which his lordship was standing. He was naturally curious as to why he had been summoned back. "How may I serve you, my lord?"

Lord Ogden pointed. "Sit there, at the desk. I want you to draw up some papers. They concern the financial affairs of my cousin-in-law, Lady Ogden. I wish to redress the late viscount's inadequate support of her ladyship."

"My lord, this is very good news, indeed." Mr. Digsby was more than glad to be of service. He thoroughly approved of the viscount's wishes. He dipped a pen in the inkwell and waited with it poised over the blank white sheet.

"The year of mourning for a woman exists to prove posthumous live issue to be that of her husband. I wish to address that possibility." Lord Ogden moved slowly around the candle-lit study, his head half-bowed in an attitude of thought, his hands loosely clasped behind his back. In an unemotional voice, he dictated what he wanted for several minutes. He stopped before the fireplace, allowing his arms to drop to his sides, and he toed a smoldering log toward the back. Over his shoulder, he added, "If at the end of the period of mourning, and there is no issue, she is to receive an annuity of L750."

"This is most generous of you, my lord," said the solicitor with obvious satisfaction, carefully making the appropriate notes. "Most generous, indeed. Her ladyship must count herself fortunate."

The viscount turned, resting one hand on the high mantel. A roil of unpleasant emotion filled his brain. He sent what he felt to be a queer smile in the solicitor's direction. "Do you think so, Digsby?"

"Oh, definitely, my lord."

Lord Ogden shrugged. *It's but a sop against my guilt.* The evenness of his voice hinted at nothing of his feelings. "When the time comes and we know for a certainty what terms will be in effect, you will have two copies drawn up and readied for signature, one for me and one for her ladyship. In the meantime, you will have my signature on my statement of intent."

"Certainly, my lord." The solicitor returned the pen to the inkwell and carefully sanded what he had written. He perused it, nodding to himself. With the sheet held in his hand, he stood up. "I shall not retire until I have completed an initial draft. I will have it ready in the morning for your approval, my lord."

Lord Ogden stirred restlessly. He angled himself a little more to face the hearth, staring down into the flames. The fire's light threw his cheekbones into prominence. His expression was pensive. "I should like you to delay your departure tomorrow, Digsby. I wish you to explain my intentions to Lady Ogden."

"Of course, my lord. I will be most happy to do so." The solicitor bowed and quietly let himself out of the room, leaving the viscount alone again.

With a sigh, Lord Ogden turned from his contemplation of the fire. He crossed behind the desk and sat down in the chair. His brooding gaze traveled back to the cheerful flames sheltered within the fireplace. In his imagination, he watched the lady rush over and clutch the mantel. *You are hateful, hateful!* There was a grim set to his mouth. Regret, sorrow, self-disgust, all tumbled about inside of him. He did not know how long he was trapped in unpleasant reverie until he heard the dinner gong.

Reluctantly, he rose and left the study to make his way to the drawing-room. He was unsurprised to find only one lady waiting to go in to dinner. The viscountess' emotional overset was explanation enough but, of course, he must pretend to know nothing of its cause. He made a slight bow. "Good evening, Mrs. Merriweather. I hope you are well."

The elderly lady curtsied. "I am well, my lord, thank you."

He glanced around. "I do not see your niece. I trust she is well, also?" As he listened to his own bland inquiry, he felt quite sickened by his hypocrisy. *I was mad, mad!* Self-recrimination was of no use, of course. The foul deed was done. A hellish bargain had been struck. And, God help him, he could not bring himself to withdraw from it now.

Mrs. Merriweather hesitated. She said, on a troubled note, "My niece is indisposed, my lord. She has bespoken a tray in her sitting room."

Lord Ogden inclined his head. "Perhaps she will feel more the thing on the morrow." He offered to escort the elderly lady. Mrs. Merriweather smiled, nodded in acquiescence, and took his arm. He savagely wondered what the lady would say of him if she ever discovered what he had done to her niece. "Shall we go in to dinner, ma'am?"

5

Through the connecting door, he entered the bedchamber. Warmth reached him from the fire crackling quietly on the hearth. The flickering flames made for shifting shadows, but he could see well enough. She was sitting up in the wide bed, the covers drawn tight up to her shoulders, her fingers clutching the heavy folds against her. Even in the dim firelight he could see the pulse beating wildly in her throat. Her eyes were twin pools of darkened fear.

He had put that fear in her. He had done it downstairs when he had taken her like a low-minded soldier would have taken a baggage whore – a quick toss-up of the skirt – fast, hard, dry. *By God, she'd been tight.* Her hot, narrow sleeve had fitted him like a supple kid glove. With the memory, his balls drew up. His heavy prick was already readying for action.

He couldn't do it again like that. He'd already hurt her, but he'd done it that once out of a reasoned calculation. *No, not true. Let me have brutal honesty.* There had been nothing cold-blooded about the fury which had blazed to life in him, suspending every decent tenet of honor. He had been as a madman, carried away on a tide of rage and bitterness. He had known he couldn't give her time to think about what he was proposing. In that moment, when her faculties were overbalanced by her desperate fear of destitution, she'd been vulnerable, and he had taken despicable advantage.

She had screwed up her courage and battened down her pride to plead her case. If she had but known it, he had already decided to provide her with a comfortable income. Then she had said – God, her words had flicked like the tip of a whiplash, lacerating his sensibilities, inflaming him - she had tried to manipulate him in such a way! Even now, he

28

burned with anger in recalling how she had flung what he had once declared for her at his head. She had spurned him then. She could not reject him now. The bargain was well and truly struck. *She's mine, for as long as she pleases me.*

His gaze never leaving her stiff, still face, he opened his dressing-gown and pushed it off of his broad shoulders. He was naked beneath it.

Lady Ogden watched while he disrobed, where he stood silhouetted against the banked fire. Terrible and magnificent, his figure loomed large before her. The firelight played along roped muscles in his arms and his chest, made a shadowed plain of his flat abdomen, limned the long muscular length of his legs. Her gaze was inevitably drawn to the thickly-haired dark juncture of his corded thighs. She caught her breath. He was fully aroused. His heavy organ jutted out from his body.

Without a word, he advanced on the bed.

Blind panic exploded within her. *I cannot! I cannot!* Throwing back the bed linens, she scrambled wildly for the other side of the bed. As soon as her bare feet touched, she took wing, fleeing away from him like a small, cornered animal.

She did not welcome him, but then, that was to be expected. What he did not expect was for her to bolt. He merely caught her up into his arms and tossed her back onto the bed and followed her down. He pinned her thighs with one leg. She was trembling violently. "There, there." He soothed her as he might have a wild thing. "It shall go better, I promise you."

He pulled her nightcap off and lightly stroked her hair. He heard how shallow her breathing was, coming through her open mouth, and felt the rapid puffs of air against his face. She was terrified of him and he regretted it, but it didn't matter, not yet at any rate. "Show me some willingness and I shall not hurt you. You may keep your nightgown on for now."

He saw the flicker of startled gratitude in her eyes and despised himself. The concession meant nothing. It was a sop to her modesty to ease her fear. She'd be rid of the nightgown soon enough.

Lady Ogden was still greatly afraid, but the slow caress of his hand on her hair was reassuring. He had not ripped her nightgown from her shoulders or pinned her at once beneath him, like her late unlamented husband had done. A tiny sigh escaped her lips. It was dawning on her that he did not intend to ravish her as he had in the ground-floor study. She blinked back the spring of silly tears. She had not much experience of the marriage bed. It had not led her to expect much. Her husband had taken possession of her body; so would this man. She had only to endure as she had before. *It will be no different.*

When the viscount looked down into her frightened, lovely face, his instinctive desire to comfort her had to be fought. He hardened his intemperate emotions against her; the intimacies of arousal and the satiation of passion were altogether different, however. He would sate himself on her, but he would also teach her to take pleasure of him. She would willingly yield to him. If not this first night, then the next, or the next. He would bind her to him, soul and body. That he was determined upon. It would be a fine revenge, he told himself, upon her and his cousin for betrayal.

Despite his heavy, throbbing erection, he spent time learning her body. He stroked her leisurely, her face and neck and shoulders, her soft belly and slender limbs. He suckled her through her nightgown, until the fine fabric was wetly plastered to her breasts, until the twin peaks beaded and she arched up under the suction of his hot mouth.

The rigidity of her body slowly left her. Though she was still trembling, he intuited that she had forgotten part of her fear. When he judged her ripe, he moved over her and settled between her parted thighs. In one stroke, he sank his shaft deep inside her snug quim. He expended his breath, reveling in agreeable sensation. A little gasp caught his ear; he discerned a tensing of her limbs beneath him. *No matter. The tiff will be speedily finished.*

He rode her at a brisk pace. It wasn't long before he grunted his satisfaction. He rolled off of her, breathing easily. He'd hardly broken a sweat. He'd anticipated the first time he possessed her in the bed would come to swift conclusion. After all, he'd been exerting great self-control to ready her enough so that when he took her it would not be a brutal ravishment all over again.

She hadn't convulsed in a paroxysm of pleasure. But neither had she dissolved into a weeping puddle.

Lady Ogden stared up into the shadows of the bed-hangings, amazed. Such strange sensations. The act had not been...entirely unpleasant. She breathed more freely. *The dread deed is done.* He had coupled with her. Now he would leave her bed, as her lord always had.

He sat up and pulled her up beside him. While his fingers nimbly undid the collar button of her nightgown, he said matter-of-factly, "You won't need this any longer." He tugged the nightgown up and over her head and tossed it aside.

She stared at him, baffled, as her hands flew up to cover her bare breasts. The firelight threw his strongly-cast features into stark relief. His dark, heated eyes gleamed. The significance of his expression evaded her. Then he drew her close against his warm, naked body, and she sucked in her breath.

Catching her chin in his fingers, Lord Ogden lowered his head and kissed her for the first time. Her mouth was neither soft nor yielding, but she didn't try to draw away. He threaded his fingers through her thick hair and pulled her head back, slanting his mouth more firmly over hers. Her lips trembled, softened, tentatively responded to his slow exploration.

When he lifted his head, he smiled down at her. "You haven't much experience at love-making, have you?"

Her reply was barely audible. "N-no."

He was inordinately pleased. His cousin had not been much of a man. With another kiss, he eased her down onto her back. "I shall teach you. We have all night." She made no answer, but he didn't expect one.

Utterly shocked, her brain tumbled with surprise. Surely, he did not mean to remain! Her husband the viscount had never done so. When he was finished, without a word, he had simply gotten up and left her. Abruptly, she felt a sharp flash of old emotional pain.

Lord Ogden began to touch her again. Lips, tongue, hands, he quickened her flesh. By the time she let out a low moan of pleasure, his prick was eager and he mounted her. The flexing of his flanks, the driving of his throbbing shaft into her warm quim, elicited response from her, and over and over, her hips tilted to meet his rhythmic thrusts. "That's it, puss. Give the bull a good screw."

She shivered under him. "Filthy, filthy."

He laughed and nipped her shoulder with his teeth. It surprised him that his obscenity seemed to excite her. He experimented by murmuring a few choice vulgarities into her ear. She shivered again and her hands fiercely gripped his shoulders. It was a good omen of things to come.

He began to thrust faster, finally losing himself in her tight heat. "Fuck, fuck, fuck," he panted, laboring towards the crowning point. His muscles drew taut. The whole of his body suddenly stiffened. He crested, the pleasurable convulsions of his prick spurting hot seed deep in her womb.

He lay atop of her, resting, feeling her lying quiescent beneath him. He was still anchored between her slender thighs. Her hands slipped away from his shoulders. He had not taken her to the heights with him.

He coolly admitted to himself that she might not fall into frenzy in their nighttime of rogering; but before he was done with her, before their illicit affair was over, she would learn to lust after his carnal possession. *It will be a sweet victory, that.*

In the dark hours that slipped by, he took her four more times. She finally slid into exhausted sleep and, ignoring her incoherent protests, he grimly pushed himself back into her for a fifth time. They were lying on their sides, his arms wrapped around her body for leverage, her knee cocked over his thighs. The lovemaking was no longer pleasurable. He was driving himself as much as he was her. The release was long in coming, and was disappointing, the seed quitting him in meager spurts. *I am fucked dry.* Without withdrawing from the warmth of her snug body, he fell into deep slumber.

Dawn was breaking when he finally left the bed. Honed by years of military discipline, his inner clock had abruptly wakened him, bringing with it instant mental clarity. Some of the servants would be stirring, beginning to go about their duties. He could not be found in her bedchamber. It was no part of his revenge to brand her a whore.

Lord Ogden slipped his arms into his silk brocaded dressing-gown, letting it fall loosely around his body. He glanced down at her. She was curled on her side just as he had left her. But her eyes had opened and she was watching him. His lazy gaze caressed her naked body. She didn't lift a hand to try to cover herself. He smiled down at her. It was indeed too late for false modesty. The past hours had been energetic ones. "I've used you hard. In the morning, order a warm bath."

He espied the white crumpled folds of her discarded nightgown and tossed the garment at her. "You'll want to put it back on before the chambermaid comes in to build up the fire. We don't want the servants to gossip."

Scarlet flooded her cheeks. She lowered her lids, hiding the expression in her eyes. She pulled the nightgown to her bosom, shielding the rose-tipped, soft mounds from his sight. Her gesture of tardy modesty struck him as highly amusing and he laughed.

Without a backward glance, he left his cousin's widow, quitting the bedchamber and firmly closing the connecting door behind him. Then he crossed to his own undisturbed bed and pulled back the heavy coverlet and the bed linens. Shedding his dressing-gown, he got between the chilly sheets and pulled all of the bedclothes up over his naked shoulders.

He felt the physical tiredness of his sexually-satisfied body and silently congratulated himself on a difficult task well done. *It was a good beginning. A very, very good beginning.*

He closed his eyes and allowed his limbs to sink more heavily into the thick mattress. Soon he began gently to snore.

HUMILIATION CLOSED over her. Weak tears burned her eyes, trickled down her burning cheeks. *Hateful! Spiteful!* The misery made her turn her face into the down-filled pillow. The viscount's heartless laughter was a cruel taunt. *He mocked me! He used me and mocked me!*

She cried awhile, letting the drain from emotional and physical exhaustion have its way. But then a muffled footstep, sounding from outside her bedchamber door, quickly made her sit up. *I can't be discovered like...like this!* She yanked the voluminous nightgown down over her head and thrust her arms through the long sleeves. She looked wildly around for her night cap but didn't find it. She just had time to slide under the covers, turning on her side so that her back was to the door as it opened.

She pretended to be asleep as the chambermaid crept across the bedchamber to the fireplace, but as the girl bent to her work, she gave a false yawn, trying to sound as though she had just awakened. The tears she shed had left her voice hoarsened, which was all to the good. "What time is it? Never mind, it doesn't matter. Send Mills to me."

Lady Ogden rolled over and rubbed her eyes, disguising the evidence of her weeping. As she half-sat up, she felt the strain and stiffness in her muscles, and unusual tenderness in the most intimate part of her body. She thinned her lips, helpless against her anger that he had known how it would be. "I want a bath brought up."

Not long after, submerged in the bath, Lady Ogden closed her eyes. With her thick locks pinned at her crown, she rested her head on the folded towel covering the metal lip of the brass bath. On the one side of the bath was the quietly-crackling fire on the hearth; on the other, a tall wooden screen was placed to reflect the fire's warmth back over her. She soaked for several minutes, the warmth doing her tight muscles and assorted aches good.

Her brain began to function again, rational thought finally taking precedence over her tumultuous emotions. Of course, the natural bent of her mind gravitated to all that had happened, since the reading of the will, and the terrible gentleman who had so prominently figured in it all.

Her mind uneasily skipped over his unspeakable conduct in the ground-floor study but dwelled rather longer on what had taken place in her bed. Lord Ogden had shown two sides of the same coin in his intimate treatment of her: the cruel brute and the lusty lover. She wondered which was the real man. She'd glimpsed the brute again when the viscount had so mockingly laughed as he left her. The dichotomy was unsettling, striking uneasy apprehension in her. She must always be on her guard. She could not let herself become complacent in her dealings with such a changeling. *My dealings...dear God.*

Lady Ogden abruptly stood up in the bath, sending the cooling water splashing over the side. She grabbed a towel from a nearby rack, where it was warmed by the fire's heat, and briskly dried. "I'm done, Mills." The dresser came around the screen with a frilly robe and wrapped it around her mistress's slender body.

Lady Ogden moved out from behind the screen and her gaze fell on the bed. While she had been in the bath, her dresser had laid out for her a merino wool daydress and the requisite undergarments, consisting of a long petticoat, a short corset, the chemise to go under it, her open drawers, a pair of ribbon garters and stockings. But she wasn't seeing the clothing on her bed. Scalding memories, vignettes of twining limbs, ran rampant through her brain. She felt suddenly breathless. She perfectly recalled his low, deep voice. *As often as possible.* She averted her gaze from the bed, a light flush mounting to her cheeks.

6

When Lady Ogden entered the breakfast-room, she glanced swiftly around, but she found only her aunt seated at the table. Profound, anti-climactic relief made her feel weak in the knees. She had steeled herself to face the viscount that morning, not such an easy matter with the past night's amorous frolics centered at the forefront of her brain.

As she seated herself, she told an attentive footman what she wanted from the sideboard before turning her attention to her sole table companion. With what she hoped was the right touch of indifference, she asked, "Where is his lordship, aunt?"

"I understand Lord Ogden is shut up with Mr. Digsby." Mrs. Merriweather eyed her niece. "Is there something amiss, my dear? You appear rather pale."

Lady Ogden felt her pulse flutter in her throat. "Am I?" She managed to smile. "I slept very ill. The-the news given me yesterday by Mr. Digsby was unexpected. I-I sustained quite a shock."

"Yes, as I well know. Is that all you are having, Charlotte? That bit of toast and tea?"

"My appetite is rather indifferent this morning, aunt." Lady Ogden picked up a piece of dry toast and bit into it. Mrs. Merriweather silently watched, incredulous, while she slowly consumed the toast and took a sip of her tea.

"We shall do now, thank you." Mrs. Merriweather waved the butler and footman from the breakfast-room. When the door had closed, she turned a thoughtful gaze back to her niece. "My dear girl, this is unlike you. I have never known you to be so out of sorts."

Lady Ogden didn't feel up to the task of soothing her aunt's concerns. She propped an elbow on the table, elevating her hand so that she could lay her cheek in her open palm. She said wearily, "Leave it, aunt."

"What happened between you and Lord Ogden?"

"What?" Lady Ogden popped up her head to stare at her aunt, her eyes widening to their fullest extent. Shock electrified her system; her heart skipped a beat. "What-whatever can you mean?"

"Why, it was all over the house. My woman told me last night. You had a private interview with Lord Ogden, from which you emerged visibly distraught." Mrs. Merriweather observed her niece's fluctuating color with gathering worry. "Did you quarrel with the viscount, my dear? That was surely unwise of you. We are entirely dependent upon his lordship's generosity."

"I did not *quarrel!*" Lady Ogden was awash in shame and an agony of alarm. The hideous possibility – that her aunt would guess the truth – reared its ugly head, leaving her panic-stricken. *No, no! Aunt must never know!*

"Well, if you did not quarrel –"

Lady Ogden broke in, anxious to derail speculation, afraid that her face had already betrayed her. She hurried into an explanation. "After I spoke with you and spent some time in reflection, I-I sought an interview." She dropped her hands into her lap, twining her fingers together and drawing strength from her tight clasp. All of the evils of her situation struck her anew. Her riotous emotions were all in a snarl, like a tangled skein of yarn. It was all she could do to control the timbre of her voice. "I begged for a show of charity from the viscount. I pleaded for him to bestow a small annum upon me."

"My dear!" Mrs. Merriweather was taken aback but she swiftly recovered. "I know only our extremity of circumstance could have driven you to be so forward. The viscount did not take heed of your pleas, then?"

Lady Ogden shook her head. "I made wretched work of it." Her stomach pitched as she recalled how badly it had gone. She attempted to bring her suddenly-shortened breath under control. "I did not realize...I did not realize how *angered* he would become when-when I reminded him that he had once sworn his love for me."

"Oh, my dear! You could not have known. But what a pity! Now I can understand why you were so upset. Surely, simple generosity would dictate –!" Mrs. Merriweather caught herself up and composed herself. "It is hard to believe Lord Ogden is behaving so shabbily. You have no claim on him, of course, but still, I had always thought him to be a gentleman."

Lady Ogden let loose a rather hysterical-sounding laugh. She was fortunate her aunt's attention was not centered on her, for she would have been hard-pressed to explain herself.

Mrs. Merriweather's expression was troubled. She sighed heavily. "I am very much to blame. I'm so sorry, Charlotte."

Lady Ogden was confused by her aunt's response. "No, no, how can you say so? It has nothing to do with you, ma'am!"

Mrs. Merriweather slowly shook her head. "No, I am deeply at fault. I knew you were beginning to form a partiality for Vincent Crawford. When I recall how I advised you against accepting his suit – but *then* he was a mere line officer! There was also Lord Henry Ogden's so very unexpected offer! All this as your father was putting the house and grounds up for rent, determined to break household and make for London! There was so little time! The young man was already leaving the country. Such a scrambling affair it would have been – you couldn't have been married until you reached port in Portugal. Oh, my dear! How could one have known it would turn out in *such* a disagreeable way?"

"No one could have predicted it, aunt," responded Lady Ogden, more bitterly than she liked. Certainly, her thoughts had dwelled more than once on her aunt's persuasive role, but allotting blame was destructive and pointless. She was just as much at fault for that long-ago decision as her aunt. And her aunt had nothing to do with the disastrous impulse which had formed her decision last night in the ground-floor study. A shudder ran through her. She still shied from memory of the cataclysmic repercussions.

"I *am* sorry, Charlotte. If I had only known, I would never have advised you as I did." Her aunt's anxious expression nearly overset her. It was enough to warn her of how close she skated to self-betrayal.

Lady Ogden quickly lifted her tea cup to her lips, taking a swallow the mild brew to give herself a moment. By the time she set down her cup, she had managed to bring herself under better control. With a lightness she was far from feeling, she said, "Believe me, I also have railed against the caprice of fate. Hindsight is always perfect, is it not?"

There was a discreet scratch at the door before it was pushed open by the butler. The ladies turned their heads, their gazes inquiring. The butler bowed, addressing Lady Ogden. "Begging your pardon, my lady. His lordship has requested your presence in the study."

Lady Ogden and Mrs. Merriweather exchanged a swift, questioning glance. Lady Ogden set aside her napkin beside the plate of crumbs from her meager repast. "Thank you, Somerset. I shall come at once." She stood up and moved toward the door, which the butler was holding open for her. As she was passing out of the breakfast-room, she heard her aunt say, "I shall be in the upper drawing-room working on my needlework, my dear."

"Of course. I shall join you presently, aunt."

Lady Ogden presented a cool front, but she broke out in a clammy sweat as she obeyed the summons. She drew her black shawl further up onto her shoulders. She told herself there would not be a repeat of what had happened in the ground-floor study. *He will not ravish me. No, he will not ravish me again.* It had been going on for evening, then. The viscount would not be so rash as to risk discovery in full day while the staff was busy going about their household duties. However, her rational assurances to herself could not completely quell the riddling anxiety besetting her. She knocked on the panel of the study door. *"Enter."*

Lady Ogden twisted the knob and opened the door. Upon entering the ground-floor study, her heart literally leaped in her chest, and she scolded herself. *Stupid, stupid!* She met the enigmatic gaze of the viscount. who was seated behind the broad expanse of the desk. She was relieved to see that his lordship was not alone. The solicitor, Mr. Digsby, was also present in the room. She immediately felt the tension easing from between her shoulders. "Good morning."

"Pray close the door, my lady," said Lord Ogden, his tone one of impersonal civility. She was astonished; it would not have surprised her to have been addressed with a repugnant familiarity after the sordid night's passage. His gaze was clear, direct. She could discover no sign of tiredness from a sleepless night in either his countenance or his appearance. He was attired neatly in a dull bottle-green coat and dark waistcoat. The black crepe armband around one sleeve was his only concession to mourning his cousin. "Digsby has a private matter to discuss."

"Of course, my lord," she murmured.

Lady Ogden shut the door. As she advanced into the room, she averted her gaze away from the fireplace, where the rape had occurred. Her raw emotions were too close to the surface. She was afraid she might disgrace herself, perhaps by screaming. The whole affair seemed something out of a surreal nightmare. It had begun here, violently, but had been furthered more thoroughly in the shifting dark shadows of her bed.

With a pretended calm which she was far from feeling, she approached the nearest wingback chair and gracefully seated herself. She looked across at the viscount, at the inscrutability of his expression, before she turned her gaze to the solicitor, who was standing beside the desk. She was surprised when the man actually smiled.

Mr. Digsby bowed. In his dry voice, he informed her, "We are here on a somewhat happier occasion than yesterday. His lordship wishes to provide for you, my lady."

Lady Ogden's brain was set awhirl by conjecture. She couldn't imagine what the solicitor meant. His lordship had already made it quite plain to her what she had to do for support; naturally, it was not a conversation which she could enter into with the solicitor. A queer, unnatural amusement caused her insides to quiver. Around the feather-touch of hysteria, she managed to speak with credible calm, inquiring politely, "Indeed?"

Mr. Digsby gravely nodded. "His lordship wishes you to remain at Delincourt Manor for the duration of your mourning period. He will naturally provide for your support. Contingent upon the posthumous birth of an heir before the end of the year of mourning, you are to have a permanent place at Delincourt Manor and an annual stipend. There are other particulars, but we need not go into those details at this time. The actual amount of your support, in the event of a birth, is yet to be determined." The solicitor discreetly cleared his throat. "Is there a possibility you might be able to take advantage of this remarkable charity, Lady Ogden?"

Lady Ogden glanced at the silent viscount, briefly meeting his unreadable dark gaze. She quickly looked away again. Vividly, the night's activities flashed across her mind. *As often as possible.* Shame heated her face. Bowing her head, she said, very low, "Yes."

"My pardon, Lady Ogden. I did not quite hear that."

She raised her head and tilted up her chin. The fragile thread of her control slipped. She replied in a clear, well-modulated voice. "I said yes, there is a chance!"

The solicitor shot a glance at the viscount's expressionless face. He rather thought he could guess the thoughts that must be running through the other man's mind. With Lady Ogden's declaration, Lord Ogden's inheritance still remained in question. He remained the heir presumptive until a direct heir was no longer a possibility. Mr. Digsby's gaze traveled back to the widow. The solicitor pursed his lips. As for Lady Ogden, her ladyship was exhibiting every sign of the natural embarrassment inherent in the situation; she had completely turned her head away, so that she could not possibly meet the enigmatic stare which Lord Ogden had leveled on her.

Mr. Digsby believed the gathering tension between the two in the room would not be dissipated until Lady Ogden became certain whether or not she was going to bear a possible heir. He was glad he was leaving within the quarter hour. He cleared his throat and addressed the viscount. "Well. Then that is all that must be discussed at present on the matter, my lord. You will, of course, be able to fully function in your present position."

Lord Ogden briefly bowed his head. "Of course."

"I am glad this amicable business is concluded, my lord. I thank you for your hospitality but I must now take my leave. The gig is waiting to carry me to the posting house, where I'm scheduled to take a place on the mail coach." Mr. Digsby turned and bowed. "Lady Ogden, my compliments."

Her ladyship murmured a polite good-bye.

"I will see you out, Digsby." The viscount stood and moved out from behind the desk. He glanced at the viscountess. "Lady Ogden, pray do me the courtesy and await my return."

Lady Ogden cast a somewhat wild look around. A sudden pall of claustrophobia oppressed her. There was nothing that could persuade her to stay. "The atmosphere is rather close in this room." The pulse beat uncomfortably in her throat. "I generally take exercise at this hour. Perhaps you will join me, my lord, in a turn on the terrace?"

For a moment, Lord Ogden regarded her, his expression unreadable. He nodded. "Certainly. A quarter hour then, Lady Ogden."

She stood up. "I shall leave you, then, my lord." The viscount and Mr. Digsby courteously bowed. The solicitor was quick to leap forward to open the door for her. With a nod of thanks to him, she swept out. Lady Ogden walked across the entrance hall to the wide staircase that swept up into the upper reaches of the manor. She lifted her skirt with one hand and trod swiftly upstairs. She felt as though she had been reprieved. Exclaiming under her breath, she said with intense loathing, "I cannot abide that room!"

Belowstairs, Lord Ogden exited the study with Mr. Digsby and paused outside it in the entrance hall, where he exchanged a few more words with the solicitor. "I shall send you word, Digsby, when it's time to return and draw up the final documents." He was aware that his conversation was overheard, as the butler stood but a few paces away, giving quiet instructions to the footman who was at his station in the hall. Naturally, after the will-reading, the solicitor's continued presence had generated curiosity among the servants, he thought. It would not go amiss to satisfy some part of that curiosity.

"Very good, my lord."

After seeing the solicitor off, Lord Ogden addressed the butler. "Somerset, pray attend me for a moment."

"Of course, my lord."

Lord Ogden returned to the study, followed by the butler. "Close the door, Somerset." He waited until the butler had obeyed. He believed it was important that he made plain how things stood. "Somerset, I shall speak frankly to you of what closely concerns Lady Ogden. The late viscount did not provide support for her ladyship. At my request, there will be legal documents drawn up to rectify that oversight."

The butler gave a nod. "I am honored by the confidence, my lord."

"Lady Ogden will continue to reside here, of course. I wish you to convey my wishes to the entire household. Lady Ogden has been mistress of Delincourt Manor since her marriage to my cousin. I wish her ladyship to continue in that capacity. In short, you will let the staff know that all matters related to Delincourt Manor and its proper management will continue to be referred to my cousin-in-law, Lady Ogden."

"Very good, my lord."

"You may go."

The butler bowed and exited. He approved of the new viscount's decision. Lady Ogden was a good mistress, well-liked, a pleasant lady with a kind word for everyone. Her ladyship had not had an easy time of it with the late viscount. Her continued status as mistress of Delincourt Manor would please the whole house.

7

Lady Ogden had a few minutes to wonder, with an anxious flutter under her breast, what the viscount could possibly have to say to her. Her courage wavered. She did not want at all to be private with his lordship; but reluctantly, she decided it was wisest to humor him. *Better on the terrace than in that horrible room.*

Lady Ogden buttoned up warmly in a fur-trimmed black pelisse over her merino daydress. She placed a velvet bonnet trimmed in black ribands over her head and tied the black satin ribbons in a bow under her chin, then picked up a large fur muff. She returned downstairs, turning aside when she reached the entrance hall to enter one of the parlors, which had the advantage of letting on to the back terrace and the gardens beyond.

Unlatching the door, she stepped outside onto the terrace, which ran almost the entire length of the manor house. The cold struck her cheeks and she tipped her head, taking delight in inhaling the pure, chilly air; it was a blessed relief. She had not realized how stultifying she had found the atmosphere inside. The oppression she had labored under was not all emotional, she found. Her mental clarity seemed to sharpen in the freshness of the open. She pushed her gloved hands into the warmth of the muff.

The viscount was already there before her, standing near the stone-hewn balustrade. He was wearing a drab greatcoat, but she wondered at it that his head was bare to the cold. His hair was clipped fairly short yet sprang up in natural curls; she had intimate knowledge of the crispness of those locks. Her cheeks burned, warning her to keep a better guard over her wayward thoughts.

Lady Ogden resolutely approached the author of her ruination. At the sound of her firm booted tread on the wide flagstones, the viscount turned, putting up a black-gloved hand to caution her. "Be careful, ma'am. There are patches of frozen sleet here and there."

"I will be careful." When Lady Ogden had come close enough, he offered his arm. She accepted his escort with a gracious nod, slipping her arm through the angle of his elbow before placing her gloved hand back into her fur muff. "Thank you, my lord."

They paced slowly up and down the length of the broad terrace. The pale morning sky was threaded with high, gray cloud. Below their vantage point, a long, browned lawn, glossed over with snow and ice, sloped a fair distance before disappearing into the thick dark woods that formed a distant boundary.

"I spent much of my boyhood here. My uncle had a great fondness for me," remarked the viscount.

"It is a beautiful place."

She might as well not have spoken; he seemed not to hear her through his own retrospection. "It was remarkable, the closeness between those brothers, my father and my uncle. They were twins, you see, and never desired to live more than a stone's-throw from one another. My father had the living at Delincourt, do you recall?"

"Yes, of course. My family regularly attended the parish church. The Rt. Reverend Crawford was a wonderful gentleman." Lady Ogden wondered where these polite reminiscences were leading. She was perfectly willing to promote them, however. It was a relief to have a civil conversation with her companion, one not fraught with fearful animosity on her side, or undercut by illicit passion. "We often had the reverend to tea at the Grange, at least in the earlier years. He was much missed by the neighborhood when he passed away."

Before the broadest sweep of terrace, marked at either end by gigantic stone urns, the viscount stopped; there, before them, was the panorama of the park. He turned his stern profile to her, fixing his gaze on the wintery vista. "I was sincerely attached to my father. He was a good parent, to me and my three sisters, after the death of our mother. He was also an erudite scholar. He made an excellent tutor for me and my cousin, until Henry was sent to Eton and I went to Harrow." Lord Ogden turned his head to look down into her uplifted, interested face. "The Rt. Rev. Crawford, my father, my mentor, would not have approved of our alliance."

Lady Ogden lowered her gaze. She stared blindly across the terrace balustrade. She felt as though she had been slapped. "No, of course he would not."

"I'm glad he is not here," he said quietly.

She cast up a surprised glance. His lean features were set in a stern mold, but it seemed to her that he was looking particularly grim. His brows had lowered over the bridge of his aquiline nose. His narrowed eyes, fixed on some point in the distance, held a decidedly unpleasant expression, while his firm mouth was set in uncompromising lines. As she watched, his lips thinned even more. Her heart beat a little quicker. Surely this was the very embodiment of the beast who had ravished her: cold, remote, implacable.

Lady Ogden did not dare break into his lordship's thoughts. She had a fervent wish to be gone; if only she could think of a civil way to escape from their tête-à-tête. Perhaps she communicated her inward anxiety to him by some small movement. After a moment, his expression relaxed and he glanced back down at her. "Forgive me. I was momentarily caught up in my reflections. Let us walk a few more turns."

Lady Ogden inclined her head. "Certainly, my lord." She preserved her silence as they paced together. So far as she knew, her companion was still in thrall to his unpleasant meditation. She was feeling decidedly uneasy in his company and had no wish to antagonize the viscount by making some remark at which he might take offense. She already had experience enough of his lordship's temper that she was wary of incurring his displeasure.

They had half-traversed the long terrace before the viscount spoke again. "Digsby rather sketchily outlined my intent." He cast down a glance at her. "What I propose for your support is entirely dependent on the outcome of our liaison. Are the terms of the agreement satisfactory to you?"

Lady Ogden gave a hesitant nod, even as she thought, bleakly, that she was hardly in a position to object to the terms. She could not fathom any point to his lordship's polite query; a strange quirk, perhaps, to satisfy himself of her acquiescence. She cast a guarded glance up at him. "Quite satisfactory, my lord."

"Very good." They walked to the end of the terrace and had turned back again before Lord Ogden broke the uncomfortable silence. There was a decidedly dry note in his lordship's observation. "It is not quite how I envisioned we would renew our acquaintance, Lady Ogden."

Amazed, Lady Ogden was startled into a spurt of strangled laughter. "No, indeed, my lord!" She thought she could almost like him for that mild quip.

Lord Ogden stopped, glancing down at her with a somber gaze. "But this is not what I wished to say. I know you will agree, what passes in private cannot be allowed to affect our public behavior."

Lady Ogden flushed in embarrassment. At the same time, she was appalled at the mere suggestion it could be otherwise. "Oh yes, I do agree," she said emphatically.

She had lived her entire life in the district, where ties ran strong and deep. Theirs was a small neighborhood society. Despite the difficulties of her family's history and the trials of her marriage, she had retained many of her old friendships and acquaintance, though she could no longer count a trusted confidante among their number. A tinge of regret touched her, but she brusquely brushed it aside. A secret such as hers could never be confided. *It is something I will carry to my grave.*

In at least one thing, she could be certain. His lordship's discretion could be relied on. He had left her before they had been discovered together in her bed. Even at his most brutal, in the ground-floor study, he had given proof of his carefulness. Though it had seemed, at the time, to be the monstrous insensitivity of the brute, she had come to realize that Lord Ogden had been entirely correct when he had not allowed her to sit down after – afterwards. Servants were observant. Certainly, if the back of her skirt had been marked by a dampened spot, it would have caused comment.

Her somber reflections inevitably led to the most pertinent point, which was the fear of discovery. Lady Ogden sought reassurance from what should have been the least likely source; she earnestly looked up at her tall companion. "We must exercise utter discretion. No one must ever guess. The servants must not be given any reason to suspect."

Lord Ogden gravely nodded. "This is my feeling also. If you bear a child, there must be no question about the sire. Come, ma'am! You needn't color up! Believe me, it isn't my intent to embarrass you. We must be able to have plain speaking between us."

"Yes, I understand," murmured Lady Ogden, dropping her gaze before his upraised brows and the coolness in his eyes. She marveled at the strange position in which she found herself. Such frank speech as this was unprecedented!

"The proprieties must be observed at all times. We shall always treat one another as polite acquaintances. Since Mrs. Merriweather is also residing in the house and is your chaperone *de facto*, there will be no question of impropriety."

Lady Ogden agreed with the course of conduct he had outlined, and so intent was she on what he said that she had forgotten her earlier discomfiture. She knitted her brows. "The servants. Indeed, I have thought about it. The staff will be quick to notice anything out of the usual."

"Then we must not give ourselves away." The viscount smiled faintly. "There will be no creeping off into the shrubberies. We shall walk together, as we do now, in full sight of the house."

Lady Ogden smiled a little, knowing he had meant it as a small joke. She was willing enough to play to his lead. It was infinitely better than how she had felt a few moments before when he had been in his brown study. "As if I would!"

The viscount and the widow made another sedate turn of the terrace, each occupied with their own thoughts. It startled her when he abruptly asked, "When are your courses due?"

Lady Ogden was utterly confounded. All of her outraged feelings came flooding back. In an agony of embarrassment, she stammered, "That is not something – we should not –" She drew in her breath, pulling her ragged dignity about her. "My lord, such things are never discussed in polite company!"

"We break no code of social etiquette here, Lady Ogden, since we are engaged in convivial society." The viscount's voice was extremely dry, faintly mocking. "I believe we have left the conventions behind. Or have you forgotten?"

She flushed with mortification. "I do not forget it, I assure you," she responded tightly.

He appeared to realize he had trampled her sensibility. "Perhaps I have not expressed myself well. I only wish to know if our uneasy alliance stands a chance of putting a fraud over on the rest of the world."

"You may believe me, when I say there is a short span of time." Lady Ogden's cheeks burned. She could scarcely meet his gaze. Her thoughts were agitated. He was a madman, devoid of normal sensibility.

The viscount persisted. "How long?"

She cast upward a flickering glance, before her gaze sank again. "A-a fortnight, perhaps longer. More than that, I absolutely *refuse* to discuss with you!"

"Ah." The viscount suddenly grinned. If she had lifted her eyes, she would have seen that the whole of his face was lighted up. Amusement laced his voice. "Womanly modesty becomes you, Lady Ogden! You have colored up very prettily."

The deepening mortification was too much for her. She slid her hand free of his arm and turned sharply about. "My aunt awaits me, my lord. I must return indoors!" Lady Ogden felt her boot slip from under her on a patch of gritty ice; thrown off balance, she flung out her hands. Before she could tumble to the flagstones, the viscount caught her up at the waist in the curve of his muscular forearm. His warm strength was startlingly welcome and she clung to his coat sleeve.

"I have you! Are you all right now?"

"Yes, my lord," she said breathlessly. The falter of her lungs was not all due to the near fall. She drew herself out of his steadying embrace. "I shall be more careful, I promise you." She had dropped her muff. He bent to retrieve it and handed it to her.

He was no longer smiling. He had retreated behind his former frosty exterior. "Very good. I shall not see you again until dinner, I believe." The viscount nodded politely and strolled away.

Lady Ogden retraced their earlier steps, frowning as she pondered what little she knew about the gentleman. His lordship had shown yet another unexpected facet: his chivalric care for her safety did not fit with the brute from the terrible event in the ground-floor study, nor did it fit the insistent, lusty bedmate from the night's revels. Ravisher, lover, gentleman. He was incomprehensible.

When Lady Ogden reached the door, she paused, her gloved hand on the latch, and glanced back. The viscount stood at the far reaches of the terrace, his black-gloved hands clasped behind his back. A gust of breeze caught the sides of his open greatcoat, tossing them back. He had lately been a soldier. It was apparent in the way he bore himself, in his air of command and his reserved manner.

"I cannot understand him," she murmured, giving voice to her wondering puzzlement. Opening the door and entering the manor, she went quietly upstairs to her bedchamber, where she slowly put off her black bonnet and pelisse. Lady Ogden went over in her mind the extraordinary conversation with the viscount. Indeed, it seemed other-worldly. She gave a tiny laugh. His lordship had actually asked about her courses! However, in the next instant, an unwelcome train of thought entered into her mind. Servants gossiped amongst themselves about those living above-stairs. As a matter of course, they learned the habits of the persons whom they served in order to perform their duties well, and they became intimately aware of the concerns and the health of their employers. Servants picked up on intimate details, such as when her ladyship's bleeding rags went to the wash.

Lady Ogden caught her breath. She felt the blood drain from her face. "Oh, dear God." The workings of her brain gathered speed. The former viscount was dead. When she began her courses, as she soon must, it would not be anything remarkable. However, it would be something to be remembered if she subsequently came up with child. It would then become very remarkable, indeed, and such titillating gossip would swiftly be broadcast to the entire county.

Lady Ogden was sickened by how incredibly stupid she had been. His seed could already have planted itself, but she would not know unless she missed her courses. If her courses came in – and later, there was a babe – there would be no question of 'legal issue'.

Horrified, she stood stock-still, as her miserable future unveiled itself to her. *"I shall be branded a whore! I shall be driven into the gutters!"*

8

Lady Ogden entered the upper drawing-room, which she and her aunt had appropriated for themselves. It was a cozy room, with faded wallpapering, and narrow, east-facing mullioned windows that generally bathed the drawing-room with morning light, so it was well-suited for the ladies' sedate activities. The upper drawing-room had been a refuge whenever the dissipated viscount and his friends had descended upon Delincourt. Indeed, she reflected, as she turned to close the door behind her, the upper drawing-room had become their gilded cage as the dreary days dragged by until the lord of the manor and his entourage returned to London. *How I detested it. The stifling, shut-in feeling.* The viscount's rare visits to Delincourt Manor usually coincided with his empty pockets; but at times, like the last occasion which had ended with his lordship's untimely death, he had invited his smart London friends down for a long house-party during the shooting season. There was always lavish drinking and restless, sometimes licentious, activities to mark these visits. *And Henry's hatefulness.* She shook herself free of the unpleasant memories and moved away from the door.

The winter morn's light was weak and a couple of branching candelabras had been lit to aid the ladies in seeing their close-work. A merry fire danced in the fireplace, giving off welcome warmth on such a chill day. Her aunt's chair was drawn up close to the hearth and the lady looked up quickly at her entrance.

"There you are, my dear! I was beginning to wonder." Mrs. Merriweather welcomed her niece with a smile, pausing in drawing her threaded needle through her embroidery hoop. "Have you been all this time with the viscount?"

"Yes. As you know, this is my usual hour for exercise. Lord Ogden was kind enough to take a turn with me on the terrace," said Lady Ogden in an off-hand manner. She sat down in her usual chair, which was also situated near the fireplace, and pulled her embroidery stand toward her. Months before, she had embarked on an ambitious project, a set of embroidered seat-covers to replace the shabby ones on the chairs in the dining room, and she was working on the second to last one.

"That was kind of his lordship. But what of his summons to you? What had he to say?"

Lady Ogden concentrated on sorting her silks, covering up her uncertainty of what she should say. *But surely, as much of the truth as I can.* "His lordship wished for his solicitor to discuss a business matter with me."

"Had it to do with an annum?" asked Mrs. Merriweather quickly.

Lady Ogden glanced up, fleetingly, to meet her aunt's hopeful gaze. She had known her aunt would want to know why the viscount had sent for her from the breakfast-room, but to tell her aunt the sordid details behind the summons was completely out of the question. It had not occurred to her ladyship until that instant, but here was another consequence of her folly she had not taken into account. Her mind cringed at the realization. Mrs. Merriweather had lived at Delincourt Manor with her from the beginning and the lady was privy to the particulars of her niece's marriage; how was she to explain a posthumous pregnancy to her aunt? She drew in a ragged breath. *Calm yourself. Do not borrow trouble before its time.* She had chosen her color silk and now, carefully, she threaded the needle. Her fingers barely trembled at all, she was glad to see.

As for the greater world, she acknowledged her saving grace was that a posthumous pregnancy was not out of reason. All the household had known that the late viscount had left his ribald cronies downstairs to their liquid libations and card-playing, with the loudly announced intention to bed his lady wife and had stumbled upstairs to enter her bedchamber. Fortunately for her, his lordship had been too far gone in his cups to perform. She still burned with shame and anger when she recalled that appalling confrontation with her late husband. Her humiliation had been too great for her to confide any but the bare-bones to her aunt. However, it was enough for Mrs. Merriweather to know for a certainty that there was no chance of her ladyship's bearing the late viscount's heir. Putting the troubling reflections out of her mind for the moment, Lady Ogden nodded and replied to her aunt's query. "Yes, indeed! A place at Delincourt and an annum."

"My dear! It is *better* than I hoped!"

Lady Ogden held up a cautioning finger. "If – *if*, aunt! – I am brought to bed of an heir before the end of my mourning period!"

Mrs. Merriweather's expression of eager anticipation clouded. She stared fixedly at her niece. "Oh. I see."

"Precisely!" Lady Ogden gave a faint, ironical smile. "I thought you would."

"Had his lordship anything to say if there was not an heir?" asked Mrs. Merriweather delicately.

Lady Ogden blinked at her aunt. With a tightening of her lips, she shook her head. She wondered at herself for not raising the possibility. However, her excuse must be that her head had been in such a whirl during that mortifying interview with the viscount and Mr. Digsby that she had not thought of that particular circumstance nor questioned its omission. It was a rather glaring omission on his lordship's part, she thought, but perfectly consistent with the base bargain she had struck. Her voice was brittle. "Nothing at all was said, aunt."

Mrs. Merriweather pursed her lips. Her voice was shaded with obvious disappointment. "How shabbily Henry Ogden behaved! It is unfortunate his cousin is cut from the same cloth!"

Lady Ogden gave a short laugh. If her aunt only knew how very like! "You may indeed say so, ma'am!" She drew her needle and the heavy silk through her piecework.

"It is a pity that –" Mrs. Merriweather broke off in some confusion. "Well, well, I do forget what I was about to say! I often do these days."

Lady Ogden raised her eyes and looked across at her aunt's flushing countenance. Rather coldly, she said, "Indeed. I quite failed in my duty."

Clearly flustered, Mrs. Merriweather avoided her niece's gaze. "Well! A year of mourning! Shall we pretend suspense, my dear? I do think we should! Then perhaps we need not be concerned for the future just yet."

"No, indeed, ma'am."

"Perhaps-perhaps his lordship might have a change of heart?"

Lady Ogden merely looked at her aunt and shrugged.

An uneasy hush fell. Mrs. Merriweather was anxious to make amends for her *faux pas* and after several awkward half-casts, which her niece did not pick up, she successfully turned topic. "Have you had any word from Sir Martin? Regarding the viscount's death, I mean?"

Lady Ogden was very willing to follow her aunt's lead. She had become ashamed of her anger, for speaking so harshly to her aunt, and of her deliberate snubs. Her aunt did not deserve her temper; the dear lady had never been anything but supportive of her. She shook her head. "The last letter I had from him dates from more than three months ago, before Henry's accident. The death notice was inserted in the newspapers, as you know. My father never responded to my own letter informing him of Henry's death."

"Sir Martin should have come to pay his respects. No, I shall not allow him even that much forbearance. He should have come for the burial service!" exclaimed Mrs. Merriweather in a burst of righteous anger. "*His son-in-law!* My word, it is insulting! Sir Martin should have been here to lend his support to you!"

Lady Ogden sent an amused glance at her indignant companion. With just a trace of bitterness coloring her voice, she said, "Aunt, you must not agitate so over it. I assure you that I am quite reconciled to my sire's neglect."

"At the very least, he should have sent a note of condolence!" Mrs. Merriweather shook her head. Her ire suddenly deflated to be replaced by perplexed sorrow. "But I suppose it is not to be wondered at, after all. Sir Martin was already so far gone in the bottle before he left us, it's a wonder he was able to legibly sign the rental papers. Never you mind, Charlotte! It must be the heavy drink which makes your father so neglectful."

"That, or the lively fear that I might request asylum of him for you and myself," said Lady Ogden dryly.

Mrs. Merriweather was moved to scorn. "As if we would! My brother-in-law is most likely huddled in some filthy London garret, swilling away his rentals, which is just what we'd discover if we were so pea-witted."

"Just so, ma'am," agreed Lady Ogden with a small laugh. The waywardness of her remaining parent was always a painful subject, but her aunt's tartly-expressed opinion struck her as being bitingly humorous.

"My sister and I each chose improvident men." Mrs. Merriweather heaved a regretful sigh. "Mr. Merriweather, dear soul, tried very hard, but he had the worst luck in investments, so I have remaining only my little pittance." It was a well-worn lament, so Lady Ogden let it pass without comment. In utmost sincerity, Mrs. Merriweather added, "You know that I would set up house with you, Charlotte, if it was possible."

"Yes, and I would have liked nothing better, aunt. But I have no income of substance to add to yours. I had hoped that Henry – well, let us not discuss *that!* – it inflames me too much."

Peace being restored, the ladies worked in companionable silence at their separate needlework pieces, each absorbed in her own private thoughts. Lady Ogden found the close-work to be soothing, but Mrs. Merriweather's amiable face became progressively more troubled. She once stopped sewing altogether, staring down at her hoop in what appeared to be a critical examination of her pattern. She shook her head and began plying her needle again.

The clock struck the quarter hour as a log shifted in the fireplace. At length, Mrs. Merriweather said, "If we must remove from Delincourt Manor, I fear most for your future, my dear Charlotte."

Lady Ogden pushed the needle through the fabric stretched on her embroidery stand and smoothly pulled the silk taut. "Aunt, let us not dwell on such unhappy reflections. I doubt the viscount has any immediate intention to cast us out." Quickly, feeling that her aunt might challenge her confident assertion, and not wishing to get into any questions which could prove impossible for her to pass off with any degree of composure, Lady Ogden hurried to give a legitimate reason for the viscount's forbearance. "Why, Henry has not been gone above a week! Surely, we have the whole of a year before us."

"Oh, yes, yes. Lord Ogden will suffer us for yet awhile. No, Charlotte, hear me out. I don't fear for myself, but you are still so young." Mrs. Merriweather apparently felt an obstruction lodged in her windpipe and cleared her throat. "Unhappily, my dearest, females without support often end as bawds."

Lady Ogden stared over the top of her embroidery stand at her aunt, more than a little startled and taken aback. A little heatedly, she exclaimed, "I haven't the heart of a courtesan!"

"Of course, you haven't." Mrs. Merriweather did not look up from her handiwork. The warmth of the fire seemed to have put heat into her withered cheeks. "However, often it comes down to a choice between one's scruples and survival. For these unfortunate creatures, becoming one man's mistress is infinitely preferable to lifting skirt in a dirty alley!"

Lady Ogden was unable to remove her riveted gaze from her aunt's placid expression. Shocked conjecture whirled in her brain. She took several breaths before she had enough control of herself to speak. "Aunt, are you saying –"

"I'm saying that you must give immediate thought to your future. I will support you, Charlotte, whatever you do. You shall hear no reproaches from me." Mrs. Merriweather had been steadily plying her needle; she stopped suddenly and looked up, pinning her niece with the intensity of her gaze. "*Whatever you do.*"

Lady Ogden felt awash with stupefaction, confusion, shock. *Surely my aunt has not just suggested – but what else can be her meaning?* Actually, Lady Ogden realized, her aunt had said nothing which could not be construed as a well-meant general observation; but she was very sure that it had been an oblique suggestion for her to make a bid at becoming the viscount's mistress. She felt a wild urge to laugh at the exquisite irony, but of course she could not give way to the impulse. "Very well, aunt," she said quietly. "I shall give thought to my future, just as you advise."

Mrs. Merriweather nodded calmly. However, if one had closely observed the good lady, it would have been seen that she was not as sanguine as she seemed; the softened lines of her chin wobbled just a bit.

FAR INTO THE CHILLY afternoon, Lord Ogden rode tirelessly around the estate with his bailiff. The breath frosted on the air, but he did not notice; to one immured to campaigning, in the heat and stifling dust, in the cold and chilling rain, the day was a pleasant one. However, a deep-set frown had settled over the viscount's face, connected to the increasing anger and disgust he felt. He'd had a belly-full of evidence of his cousin's profligacy and gross mismanagement. Once-prosperous holdings sat empty without tenants, and of the occupied croft homes, several were in urgent need of repair. Fencing, fallow fields, roads - all had been left untended for too long. As his gaze roamed over yet another tumbled-down field wall, the restraint which he had held over his temper finally frayed. Lord Ogden swore with terse crudity.

The wooden-faced bailiff had set out being wary of the new master. The man had eventually warmed when he realized that the viscount was genuinely interested in all that he showed him. Lord Ogden's appalled exclamations and demands for enlightenment had cemented the bailiff's good opinion. At hearing his lordship comprehensive swearing, Bartlett felt able to openly express his opinion. "It be a rare mess, milord."

"My cousin must have held the reputation for being the worst landowner in the district!" exclaimed Lord Ogden wrathfully.

The bailiff cleared his throat. "Properly speaking, milord, that would be Sir Martin of the Grange."

Lord Ogden whipped his head around. He remembered the gentleman, all too vividly. "What, is the tipsy old bastard still alive, then?"

As a boy, he had not liked Sir Martin Stockton. A loud, obnoxious man, whose puffy, reddened face had been marked by broken veins. Later, after he had been long enough in the army to gain some experience and insight, Lord Ogden had come to realize that the baronet had exhibited all the physical signs of a choleric and alcoholic disposition.

The bailiff chuckled. "As far as any hereabouts knows, he is, milord. Her ladyship keeps mum, for all that. Sir Martin found himself a gentleman renter and shuffled himself off to Lunnon-town. It must be five years now – aye, it is, for Master Kelton up at the Grange has been there that long. He's a good-enough man, in his way. Proper care he's taken of the Grange, so they tells me."

Lord Ogden frowned. A scrap of memory floated through his mind. That day, the day he'd waited on Sir Martin Stockton to ask the portly baronet's permission to address his daughter, Sir Martin had received him in the library, an untidy room with papers flung down across the desk, a wine bottle and dirty glasses serving as paperweights, a collection of racing forms and old calendars and other detritus scattered around, and cobwebs draping the neglected, dusty books on the shelves. Sir Martin had acquiesced to his request, saying, "I've no objection to your leaving immediately and wedding in Portugal, since I am making off for London." The baronet had added the rider that he would be glad to get the females of his household off his hands, as he had no wish for their company in town. *Strange, I've never recalled that bit before.*

He said absently, "Five years? Is it truly that long since Sir Martin left the neighborhood?"

"Aye, it was. We be coming up on the vicarage soon, milord."

Lord Ogden nodded, still preoccupied. *She must have known she was shortly to lose her home. Why the devil didn't she seize on my offer? Was I so bad a bargain?* Lord Ogden threw off his savage reverie, relegating it to the back of his mind, to the buried past where it should remain. The present, now, was all that mattered. He was in her bed; he meant to make the most of it. At any moment, she might regain her sanity and repudiate his advances. He had made her into his mistress, true, but he had not yet awakened in her a carnal hunger. Then, she would not care whether she bore an heir or not; then, she would be his for as long as he pleased. He did not ask himself on what terms he would keep her.

"Just past this hedge and the milestone, milord, as I'm sure you will recall."

Lord Ogden set aside his pensive reflections. He smiled, genuinely pleased to recognize the old landmarks. For the most part, his had been a happy, untrammeled childhood. He had stored up many good memories, which had become ever more cherished during the harsh years of his soldiering. "Indeed, I do! It will be pleasant to see my old childhood home!"

However, it wasn't pleasant at all. Lord Ogden drew up his mount and looked with astonishment at the vicarage and its overgrown environs. In his day, it had been a handsome, rambling building surrounded by neat outbuildings, a well-tended orchard, and gardens. The place now appeared forlorn and deserted. "But what's this? Whoever stepped into my father's shoes should be taking better care of the old place!"

The bailiff coughed. "But that's just it, milord. His lordship never appointed a new vicar."

Lord Ogden was astounded. He slewed in his saddle to stare at the bailiff, half-suspecting the man to be guilty of an ill-formed joke. "Never appointed a new vicar!"

"The people do feel it keenly, milord," said Bartlett, giving a heavy sigh. "The Rt. Rev. Crawford was a respected man-of-the-cloth. At his passing, it was hoped for just such another good man to come among us. But one never did." The bailiff shook his head, his sad gaze roaming over the empty vicarage. "The people must needs travel to the next parish over for weddings and christenings and the like."

Lord Ogden snapped his brows together. As he stared at the shuttered windows of the vicarage, he tightened his lips. His seething anger was communicated to his horse; even as his mind was occupied in furious retrospection, he mechanically pulled the fidgeting animal under control. He had observed the look of depression in the faces of those of his tenants whom he had met that day. He had thought ill-management was explanation enough for it, but it was obvious that he was wrong.

"This is worse than all the rest." Lord Ogden spoke quietly but in clipped accents, with a great deal of suppressed emotion. A muscle jumped in his jaw. "Though I cannot promptly effect all the changes which must be made, I can at least make a difference here! I think I know just the man."

The viscount swung the head of his mount around. "Come, Bartlett, let us return. I have seen enough on this day!"

9

The late viscount and his friends had always used the dining-room for the setting of their raucous parties; perhaps, as the heir presumptive, Lord Ogden would be much on his dignity and prefer that statelier hall. The ladies had discussed the weighty matter between them and, having nothing to guide them otherwise, it was agreed that the new viscount's coming necessitated a change, no matter how it affected the ease of their own habit. "It's no use to place *our* comfort first, for gentlemen always do just as they like," pointed out Mrs. Merriweather. As a result, dinner at Delincourt had become a formal affair.

Lady Ogden and Mrs. Merriweather had always changed for the evening, of course, but their agreeable custom had been to take their dinner in the more intimate atmosphere of the large front parlor. Lady Ogden had concurred in her aunt's opinion and she instructed that the evening meal was to be henceforth laid in the formal dining room.

Lord Ogden entered the drawing-room, wearing a frown. It did not lift even as he bowed and greeted the ladies. "I trust you are well, Lady Ogden? Mrs. Merriweather?"

The ladies had risen and curtsied, murmuring their assurances of their continued well-being. Upon the sound of the dinner gong, the viscount offered his arm to Lady Ogden, as was proper since she took precedence over her aunt, and escorted her into the dining-room, leaving Mrs. Merriweather to follow.

Lord Ogden and the ladies dined in state in the huge chamber. The click of silver cutlery on plate echoed. Looking about them, Lady Ogden and Mrs. Merriweather were gratified, for it had not looked so well in some time. Signs of the late viscount's dissolute, raucous house-party had been banished. The draperies might be faded, the rugs might be worn, but the dining-room had been thoroughly cleaned, and the wainscoting and floors polished until the room positively gleamed. Several branches of candles shed a dim, golden light. The butler and his two minions waited on the formally-attired trio seated at the table; Lord Ogden sat at the head, as befitted his consequence, Lady Ogden at the foot, and Mrs. Merriweather at the middle. Somerset decanted the wine, oversaw the serving of the meal by the footmen, and carved the meat.

With a long glance passing between them, the two ladies had mutely agreed not to disturb the viscount with too much lively chatter. They were well-versed in dealing with bad-tempered gentlemen. Conversation during the three-course removes was therefore sparse and stilted, made even more limited by distance between the trio at table. The viscount advanced little conversation and that only in response to a direct query.

A large silver epergne graced the table, making it impossible for Lady Ogden to catch more than a few glimpses of the viscount. The dark frown on his lordship's face had deepened. She wondered what could possibly have influenced it.

Lord Ogden, looking about him with a jaundiced eye, decided he did not like the dining-room. It was a long gallery-like room, which he estimated could easily accommodate upwards of thirty guests, and it echoed hollowly with so few at table. He scowled, wondering what advantage the ladies saw in such a barrack.

The dinner seemed interminable to Lady Ogden. She was restless, the sense of it growing until it sat solid upon her. All day, her thoughts had pricked at her, torturing her with lurid imaginations and wild, improbable conjecture. The day was drawing to a close and she felt like the sword of Damocles hung suspended over her head. But she did not need an ominous portent to influence her overwrought nerves. She wanted to pretend that she was mistress of her own destiny; but of course, she was not. She longed to be able to hide herself away.

After the uncomfortable repast, the ladies escaped to the drawing-room, leaving the viscount in solitude to drink the after-dinner port. "It is to be hoped a few glasses will put Lord Ogden into a more congenial frame of mind before he joins us for coffee," remarked Mrs.

Merriweather, arranging the folds of her tasseled Kashmere shawl better about her shoulders. "It's chillier this evening, I think."

"I'd rather his lordship retire altogether," retorted Lady Ogden. She found the backgammon board and began to set it up. "What a perfectly beastly meal! I hope the viscount doesn't wish to take coffee. I would not miss his lordship's company!"

Mrs. Merriweather regretfully concurred. "He does seem to be as prickly as his cousin. White or red, my dear?"

The ladies played a few games, as was their custom, and were just retiring the backgammon board, when the drawing-room door opened. The butler entered, pushing the coffee urn. With a smile, Lady Ogden said, "Ah, Somerset, what perfect timing. Look, aunt, the macaroons which you particularly enjoy."

"Why, so they are! How delightful."

Of a sudden, Lady Ogden heard swift footsteps approaching. The viscount entered the drawing-room, just in time for the serving of coffee. A lowering frown still marked his countenance. Lady Ogden gave a tiny sigh. She had begun to think that his lordship would not join them that evening. In the last twenty-four hours, she had spent quite enough time in his overwhelming company. She needed a respite, a period of calm normality, during which she could persuade herself, if only for that hour in company with her aunt, that all was as conventional as it should be. She had no real illusions, of course. She knew for a certainty that he would come to her bed again.

Observing the viscount's brooding expression, Lady Ogden hoped he would stay for only a few minutes for courtesy's sake. She politely inquired his lordship's preference for coffee.

"I prefer it black, my lady."

"Indeed," murmured Lady Ogden. *As black as your darkling brow. Well, then!* Defensive, resentful – she acknowledged she was all those things that she most despised – she poured the coffee, serving the viscount and her aunt before herself. Then she picked up a thick fashion periodical and opened its pages. Lady Ogden pretended not to see her aunt's amazed expression. She turned a page in the periodical, faking a spurious interest in the latest fashion plates.

After casting a censorious glance at her niece, Mrs. Merriweather inquired politely into how the viscount had spent his day. It was an unfortunate choice of topic. Lord Ogden's frown deepened. His reply was clipped. "I rode around the estate acres with the bailiff, Bartlett."

With determined cheer, Mrs. Merriweather plowed on. "Oh, indeed? A cold day but clear enough for a ride, of course." She turned her head and addressed her niece in a determined tone. "My dear, it's a pity you didn't know of his lordship's plans. You could have ridden out with his lordship, for you know as much as Bartlett and I am persuaded you would have enjoyed the ride. Lady Ogden, my lord, often rides when the weather is good."

Lady Ogden quickly looked up from the pages of the periodical. She cast a glare at her aunt. She had no wish to ride out in the viscount's company, but she could scarcely say so without sounding unpardonably petulant to her aunt. She could well imagine the subsequent scold and the questions she would be subjected to by that lady.

"Then perhaps you will join me horseback one day, Lady Ogden. We shall take a groom with us, of course."

Lady Ogden ignored the viscount's caustic tone. "Of course," she murmured non-committedly.

She was actually curious to hear his lordship's first impressions of what he had seen. "Was your ride with Bartlett instructive, my lord?" She watched the play of anger on his lordship's face. He appeared to be exerting some control over what might have been an otherwise hasty retort.

"I was displeased by what Bartlett showed me, particularly when I visited the vicarage. It was shocking to see the old place so rundown. It was my childhood home, as you know." Lord Ogden's gaze bored into hers. He said, almost accusingly, "I discovered that there has been no vicar here since my father's death three years ago."

"I could do nothing. Henry would not give the living away. He did not want the draw on his pockets, he said," said Lady Ogden quietly. She hesitated. "Did you see the rest of Delincourt's grounds, my lord?"

"I did, indeed! I was appalled. It will take a pretty penny to bring Delincourt back," he said, his brows drawing lower over his aquiline nose. "I must speak to the land steward. What is his name? Why has he not waited upon me?"

The harshness of his lordship's tone left no one in doubt of his displeasure. Lady Ogden exchanged a swift, troubled glance with her aunt as she replied. "Mr. Stockley resides at Briarcrest Cottage, a minor property about a day's ride from Delincourt, from which place he can discharge his responsibility."

Lord Ogden gave a derisive snort. "His responsibility! He will answer *to me* for how he handles his responsibilities! I shall write and have him come here at once."

"Henry never wished to meet or correspond with Mr. Stockley, which is why he is situated at Briarcrest Cottage rather than here at Delincourt. I'm sure it will come as a considerable shock to the poor man when he receives your brusque communiqué," said Lady Ogden dryly.

Mrs. Merriweather shot an astonished glance at the younger woman. She could not imagine what her niece was about to address the viscount in such a fashion! It was the height of folly to make light of a gentleman's ire. She turned her apprehensive gaze onto his lordship. The viscount and Lady Ogden did not notice the older lady's close observation as they gazed a challenge at one other. Lord Ogden's stare was rather hard, while Lady Ogden merely raised her brows.

The viscount suddenly grinned, an exercise which banished his frown and lightened the stern cast of his face. Even his rather hard-held mouth eased. Why, Lady Ogden thought in surprise, he is quite handsome. Of a sudden, a recollection leaped into her mind: Vincent Crawford, in his red-and-gold regimentals, unexpectedly coming upon her in the church. He had stopped abruptly, in a patch of bright sunlight, his magnificence dazzling her. *How brave he looked! I had forgotten.*

The poignant melancholia that caught at her throat startled her.

Unaware of her ladyship's shaken equilibrium, Lord Ogden dipped his head, acknowledging her observation. "Thank you for warning me of Mr. Stockley's delicate sensibility, ma'am! I shall strive to keep it in mind."

His lordship's sarcasm-tinged reply banished her own edgy mood and she chuckled, suddenly feeling more in charity with him. "Not at all. More coffee, my lord?"

"Yes, please." The viscount watched her refill his cup. He leaned forward to accept the saucer from her hands and their fingers brushed in passing. He saw a frisson of awareness quiver in her face, which he ignored; but inwardly, he tasted satisfaction. She was patently aware of the sensual magnetism between them. However, she was as fully sensible as he was himself not to betray it. Her aunt was not to know of what was between them. Lady Ogden turned away her gaze, her expression all cool politeness.

The viscount glanced about him, for the first time taking in the comfortable furnishings and the pleasant proportions of the large parlor. "I do not know, when it is just the three of us, why we dine in that barrack of a hall when we could do so here," he remarked.

Lady Ogden and her aunt looked at one another. Mrs. Merriweather said tentatively, "We were used to be in the habit of taking our dinner here in the front parlor, my lord."

"Then by all means let us revert to custom," said Lord Ogden decisively. "I should prefer it, myself."

"It shall be as you wish, of course," murmured Lady Ogden. "I shall inform Somerset."

Lord Ogden inclined his head. "Thank you." He settled more firmly back into his chair, balancing the cup and saucer. "Lady Ogden, I intend to fill the living at once. I hope you will not take it amiss, but I intend to give it away without further consultation with you. I have a man already in mind, you see."

Lady Ogden was astonished. Casting a glance at her aunt, she could see her own deep surprise mirrored on that lady's face. "My dear sir, it cannot possibly have anything to do with me! You must do just as you think."

The viscount looked straight into her eyes. A queer smile played about his mouth. "Strangely enough, I believe it might affect your comfort here at Delincourt. You will want the new vicar to be someone you will like."

Caught fast by his intent, faintly mocking gaze, Lady Ogden at once realized the significance of his lordship's reference to her comfort. *If I bear 'legal issue', I will be able to remain at Delincourt.* A little color crept into her face. Quietly, she said, "Then I must rely upon your good judgment, my lord, as must we all."

"Who is this man you favor, my lord? Is he perhaps known to us?"

Lady Ogden was grateful for her aunt's interjection. It broke the suspended gaze between herself and the viscount. She had felt an electric shock when their fingers had touched; that was nothing to the voltaic jolt to her pulse when she became entangled in his dark, burning stare. The banked heat at the back of his eyes was unmistakable.

Lord Ogden politely turned to Mrs. Merriweather. "No, ma'am, he is not. But Rev. Major Ledger is an old comrade of mine. When he was badly wounded and was no longer fit for active duty, he decided to take orders. He had always wanted to go into the church, but his situation was such that he deemed it better to make the army his career. I'm glad he did so, for otherwise I would never have met him. He remains one of my closest friends."

"But this is very good news, my lord!" said Mrs. Merriweather with visible approval. "I hope your friend, Rev. Major Ledger, will be amenable to the offer of the living."

"As do I, ma'am." Lord Ogden took a last swallow of his coffee, set aside the cup and saucer on the occasional table which stood close at hand, and rose to his feet. With a bow, he addressed the ladies. "I trust you will excuse me, Lady Ogden, Mrs. Merriweather. I'm eager to repair to my private study and draft my letters tonight."

They murmured their good-nights.

10

When the door had closed behind the viscount, Mrs. Merriweather turned her head and raised her brows. "Well! This is a welcome surprise, indeed!"

"Yes; I do hope this Rev. Major Ledger is worthy of the position," said Lady Ogden somberly. "Our people are in sore need of spiritual and practical guidance. Well, and so are we here at Delincourt! I miss our dear vicar's visits. He was a true friend and I cherished our conversations."

"Yes, indeed." Mrs. Merriweather smiled over at her niece, hopefulness underscoring her expression. "I trust the viscount will become a good friend of ours also."

Lady Ogden mirrored her aunt's smile, but with an ache in her heart; the bonds of her impropriety dictated her silence. Though she believed her aunt had indeed expressed a vague wish that she would attempt to seduce the viscount, she did not believe the good lady actually meant it and, if it came down to it, her aunt would not wish to know any of the sordid details. As for what had actually happened...she did not think there was any explanation she could have made that would not have sent her aunt into strong hysterics.

With a sidelong glance over the rim of her coffee cup, Mrs. Merriweather added, with satisfaction in her placid tone, "I did think it significant, my dear, that Lord Ogden showed some consideration for your feelings."

Lady Ogden shook her head, the disquiet of her spirit deepening with her aunt's complete misjudgment of the situation. She was hard-pressed to preserve her calm. "Aunt, you must not refine too much on it."

"Perhaps I am. But then again, perhaps not." As she set aside her cup and saucer, Mrs. Merriweather directed a sudden reproof at her niece. "I did not like to see your earlier discourtesy toward his lordship. Burying your nose in that periodical! It was not politic of you, dearest."

Lady Ogden was driven to blunt speech. "Do you wish me to sit in his lordship's pocket? Is that what you wish me to do?"

Mrs. Merriweather's withered cheeks reddened as though she had been using the rouge pot. Avoiding her niece's demanding gaze, she fidgeted with the long fringes on one corner of her shawl. "You've mistaken my meaning! I merely wish you to behave with civility."

Lady Ogden saw that her bluntness had discomfited her aunt. With a sigh, she took pity on the elderly lady. It was apparent they would not speak frankly between them of some things. "I shall be as civil as I am able, I promise you."

Mrs. Merriweather looked up, her faded eyes anxious in expression. She was a little perturbed, feeling there was some undercurrent in Lady Ogden's calm response. However, she did not question it but only offered up a tentative observation. "Despite your initial coldness toward him, Lord Ogden smiled at you twice this evening. He seems amiably disposed toward you."

"Does he, aunt? Well, we shall see." Lady Ogden did not think friendship was what his lordship had in mind when he smiled at her; instead, he was probably considering at what hour he could step into her bedchamber. *As often as possible...* Of course, she could not tell her dear aunt of *that*, she thought, afflicted by sudden, inward agitation.

Lady Ogden was desperate to turn a conversation that was beginning to cut too close to things which she could not bear to think on. She picked up the fashion periodical again and flipped the pages, saying "I found a perfectly ravishing walking dress, aunt." She held out the periodical. "What do you think of it?"

Mrs. Merriweather willingly studied the fashion plate. She pursed her lips in consideration. "It is very well, indeed. Of course, you could not possibly wear such a gown until you are out of mourning."

"But I am thinking of my half-mourning. If it was made up in lavender or gray?"

"Oh, unexceptional! The trimming is exquisite."

With relief, Lady Ogden encouraged her aunt in a long, exhaustive conversation about the latest fashions. When the clock struck eleven o'clock, Mrs. Merriweather looked up, startled. "My goodness! We have been so pleasantly occupied, I quite lost track of time."

"Is it late? I had no notion of it," fibbed Lady Ogden. She'd been aware for the past hour of the inexorable move of the clock hands. She simply had not wanted to bring the lateness of the hour to her aunt's notice, nor to point out to the other lady the fact that the viscount had not returned to the drawing-room.

However, once she became aware of the time, Mrs. Merriweather also became cognizant of his lordship's dereliction. "I cannot conceive how the writing of a mere letter or two would take so long," she said, adding charitably, "But then, we do not know what else his lordship might have found of importance which served to keep him from rejoining us."

The viscount's absence had exercised Lady Ogden's own mind to an oppressive degree. Arising out of her imagination, and not for the first time that evening, she had a lurid vision of his lordship in a state of undress, impatiently awaiting her. Of course, it was nonsense, yet her breath hitched. She dared not examine the reason too closely. *A fearful anticipation, much like the horrid fascination one might feel at sight of a wild, predatory beast. No, no, I am too fanciful!* She told herself it simply annoyed her that she should have been thinking about the gentleman at all. Yet, she could not quite ignore the quickened tempo of her pulse.

Thrusting aside the turmoil that afflicted her, Lady Ogden rose from her chair and calmly suggested that she and her aunt retire for the night. Mrs. Merriweather readily acquiesced. Lady Ogden and her companion went upstairs together and paused on the upper landing to take an affectionate leave of one another.

"I will see you tomorrow, my dear."

"Sleep well, aunt." Lady Ogden kissed her aunt's softened cheek before turning and entering her bedchamber. Her dresser was waiting to help her undress and to put her into a thin lawn nightgown.

With a quiet word, Lady Ogden sat down on the vanity bench, so that Mills could begin the nightly ritual of unpinning her hair and brushing it out. At last free to pursue her most private thoughts without interruption, Lady Ogden allowed herself to worry at the knotty problem which had presented itself to her earlier in the day and which had steadily grown to take possession of her mind.

The interview with the solicitor had crystallized the evils of her situation. Any way she looked at it, she was hopelessly trapped. The pulse beat heavily in her throat. Whatever the original circumstances, when the viscount had entered her bedchamber, she had tacitly agreed to a shameful liaison. She could have turned the key in the door which connected the bedchambers; she had not done so. *If only Henry had not been so spiteful.* But there it was: her honor in exchange for the future support of herself and her aunt. As for the viscount – well, she was intelligent enough to comprehend his motive for going against a gentleman's code of honor. His fury had been the clue; the solemn, young military officer had been far more deeply affected by that long-ago rejection than she could ever have imagined. *Fury, resentment – I had no notion.* Recalling the overwhelming sensuality in her bed the previous night, she shivered, for there was lust, too. He wanted her, that was all. So here she was, engaged in amorous congress with a man who despised her and yet was very willing to satiate his passions on her, and set on a course to put a fraud over on the world. She believed she was shrewd enough to see that his lordship was gambling he would not lose the peerage. After all, she had been wedded for five years without issue. She was piqued. Perhaps she would surprise both of them, she thought with a spurt of anger.

The only way to succeed at bearing 'legal issue' was to give herself entirely over to her shameful liaison; the only way to contrive more time, if her courses came on before she bred, was to hide the evidence of her bleeding.

Lady Ogden nibbled at her under lip. *I cannot carry off this desperate venture alone.* Reluctantly, she concluded that her woman would have to be taken into her confidence. She carefully weighed her decision. Mills had been with her before she had wedded the viscount. There were few secrets between a lady and her dresser. Mills had been a witness to the many insults and the indifference to which she had been subjected. The woman knew also how cold and lonely her mistress's bed had been. In any other circumstances, Lady Ogden was certain of her dresser's loyalty. However, she did not know if Mills would be a willing accomplice to a monstrous fraud.

Lady Ogden stared into the mirror, examining the dresser's placid reflection. *I must know! All hinges on it!* She delicately cleared her throat. "Mills, you know how things stood between me and his lordship."

"Yes, my lady." The dresser had finished removing the pins from her mistress's hair. She picked up a brush and began to carefully comb out the long chestnut locks.

"The will-reading came as a shock. His lordship left me an annuity of only one hundred pounds."

The dresser's startled, indignant gaze flew to meet her mistress's eyes in the mirror. "Ma'am! Is that why you were squalling as if the end of the world was come?"

Lady Ogden lifted one shoulder in a small shrug, which her dresser was free to interpret in any way she wished. The query was too upsetting. She tried to set aside the anguish it caused her, but her voice sounded strained in her own ears. "Lord Vincent Ogden looks much like his deceased cousin, does he not?"

The dresser frowned, giving her consideration to it while she worked her fingers and the brush through a snarl. "I don't know, my lady. He's awfully browned. And he's a bigger man."

"But there are similarities in coloring and in the cast of his lordship's face," pointed out Lady Ogden, impatient. "Seeing the two men together, you could not mistake them for other than family."

"Oh yes, there's that."

Lady Ogden twisted her fingers together. Her nerves felt all stretched on end. *I must be careful now, how I lay it out for Mills!* She drew in a breath, letting it out slowly to give herself time to test in her mind the words before she uttered them. She would say only so much, but not enough to condemn her if Mills chose not to throw in her lot with her. All hinged on the woman's reaction. Lady Ogden said in a wooden voice, "I have been informed that if I am delivered of legal issue, I shall receive a widow's stipend."

The dresser's head snapped up; her hands stilled in their task. In the mirror, Lady Ogden doggedly met her dresser's astonished gaze. As she watched, the dresser's eyes gradually widened, then narrowed. For a long, long moment, mistress and dresser stared at one another. The dresser gave a short, sharp nod. "I understand, my lady."

Lady Ogden swiveled around on the bench, anxiously searching her dresser's countenance. "Do you really, Mills? *Can* you accept my intent?"

"It's to his lordship's shame, my lady, not yours."

The dresser's hard tone was peculiarly reassuring. Lady Ogden felt her taut nerves relax. "My courses – no one must know. Will you help me, Mills?"

"Yes, ma'am, I shall do so."

Lady Ogden was unbearably relieved. "Now I may rest easier. Thank you, Mills."

"Let's finish your hair, my lady." When her mistress was finally readied for bed, the dresser said, "Will there be anything else, my lady?"

"No, that will be all." Lady Ogden offered a small smile. With a deep undercurrent of gratitude, which she could not openly express, she added, "Thank you, Mills."

The dresser said a quiet goodnight as she made to quit the bedchamber. On the threshold of the open door, Mills hesitated, looking back at her ladyship. It appeared as though she wanted to say something, but meeting her mistress's steady gaze, she did not. Instead, the dresser shook her head before closing the bedchamber door behind her and going to retire to her own small room.

Lady Ogden settled herself comfortably against the heavy pillows. Sleepless, she watched the play of dense shadows on the wall as the fire burned lower. Mills had warmed the linens with the warming pan but she still felt queerly chilled. *The die has been truly cast.* With the complicity of her dresser, there was no longer any question of turning back. She had committed herself to the wicked, sensual concourse that would shortly take place in her bed.

The viscount came to her that night, and every night thereafter. Her bed became a warm, erotically-rocking boat on a sea of intense ardor. He took her often and thoroughly. He did not allow her to rest. Always, he returned to his own room before the dawn.

When she wakened in the mornings, alone in her bed, she felt as though she was moored to a continual dream of passion, which kept drawing her back down into the murky depths.

It was the daylight hours which seemed unreal to her. The man in the dark, who tangled his limbs with hers, who pushed insistently inside of her body, could not possibly be the same man who sat across the breakfast table from her, who exchanged polite greetings with her and inquired after her aunt's health. It was impossible. A whisper of caution wafted through her mind. *He is not to be trusted.* Yet in some measure, she must indeed trust him. Otherwise, how could she explain the burgeoning pleasure she began to take in his carnal possession. *He ravished me, for pity's sake!*

However, an innate honesty forced her to be fair. The viscount had taken monstrous advantage of her, it was true; but it was not without her consent. It had been a rape, certainly; but she was not without guilt. As for what was now passing between them...she shivered, in mingled revulsion and an unwilling, thrumming sensation low in her belly. Her troubled reflections finally came to an inevitable conclusion. Reluctant though she was to admit it, the viscount was become an agreeable lover. At times, he was even tender with her. She could not hate him, no, nor actually fear him.

She did not understand her own ambivalence.

It was a strange time indeed, and one which Lady Ogden would look back on with a puzzled bemusement. She was living two different lives at once, the one in private so shockingly passionate and the public one so stiltedly correct. It did nothing to help her decide in her own mind whether she dreamed or was awake.

IN LONDON, SOME OF the late viscount's old cronies had met together for a card-party. The small salon was plunged into black shadow, except for the flickering fire and the pools of brilliant yellow light cast by several guttering candelabras, set on and around the card-table. The stained green-baize top was littered with cards and chits, bank-notes and coins. Several wineglasses and uncorked bottles loomed like bizarre sentries over the scattered piles in front of the card-players. The air was close, pungent with burnt candlewax, the stench of sweat, the reek of spilled wine. One gentleman blearily surveyed his companions, sprawled in careless poses in silk-covered chairs set around the card-table. "A miserable lot, forsooth! Not a jest to be had. A pox on us all, I say."

"At least we are alive," retorted another sullenly.

"Poor Ogden. A broken head. A toast, a toast! Raise your glasses, gentlemen, to our departed friend. We miss you, sirruh!"

"Hear! Hear!"

The dour gentleman uttered an unfeeling sentiment. "I miss more our sprints down to Delincourt." He gave a loud crack of laughter. "The good times we had, heh?"

A heavy-featured gentleman, with rather protuberant eyes and a bovine expression, broke into a toothy grin. "Aye! I lifted a servant wench's skirts last time. Lord, how she squirmed! Made me pego stand right up and fire off a fine salvo! She squealed like a stuck pig!"

"Stick her good, did you?" The crude sally was greeted by raucous laughter. In the fireplace, a burning log broke, sending a rash of red sparks and flames shooting upwards. Ruddy light flared, burnishing the howling, grotesquely-shadowed male faces into devil-masks.

Under cover of the wicked hilarity, a foppish gentleman leaned to the side and addressed his nearest companion. "I hear you've gone one better, Sir William. Taken Lord Ogden's place in pricking our dear Mrs. Stonebridge. A luscious, ripened fruit. I envy you, sir!"

Sir William's sardonic smile flickered. "A bit over-ripened, I fear. A bit expensive, too. Shall I pass her on to you, Hadley?"

The gentleman waved a languid, beringed hand. "Not until you are done with her, sir, not until you're done."

Just before dawn, Sir William visited the small house where resided the lady. He rapped the head of his walking cane on the door panel. The sleepy porter let him inside. As though he was master of the house, he climbed the stairs to the lady's boudoir and entered it. There was enough light from the red heart of the dying fire that he could see the curved figure lying in the bed. He threw aside his hat and cane on a cushioned settee and made quick work of freeing his primitive tool. She was asleep but he soon had her awake. There was a short, sharp struggle. "No! Stop! Ah, but you're hurting me."

He paid no attention, but forced in his heavy, swollen arse-opener and buggered her. The rutting noises – strained, choked-off gasps, guttural deep grunts – mingled for a good long while. When he was done, she was weeping. He was breathing rapidly. "Very good, Mrs. Stonebridge. Very good, indeed." He straightened his clothes, picked up his hat and cane, and left as he had entered. It amused him, what had been said about himself taking his friend's place. *Ogden's whore, now mine.* Silent laughter shook him.

Standing outside the house again, the cold dawn air caressed his sweating brow. It cleared some of the alcoholic fumes from his brain. An intriguing thought penetrated his mind. Considering it, he paused on the flagged walkway, the clammy fog eddying around his trouser-clad legs. Then he nodded to himself, well-pleased, and set off, making for his lodgings.

Several hours later, after waking and breakfasting and attending to his attire, Sir William sat back in his chair and stretched out his legs towards the fire, contemplating the thing that had burst upon his brain in the wee hours. He reexamined the notion, now that he was sober. It presented definite possibilities.

*Ogden's whore...*He grimaced; no, she was definitely a lady and if he was any judge, a starched-up one at that, with narrow provincial principles and morals. It would not be easy to seduce the woman; but then, he'd always been one up to a challenge. It was the gaming instinct in him, he supposed.

The only possible hindrance he could see was the unknown factor represented by the heir presumptive. He knew next to nothing about the man. At the burial service, he had barely glanced at the wooden-faced, stiff-rumped upstart who was stepping into the viscountcy, and he had dismissed Major Vincent Crawford for what he obviously was – a soldier, ill-at-ease in taking up his new role. As for the man's frigid manner toward Lady Ogden, and the way that the lady had stared right through him...Sir William snorted. It was plain to be seen that there was no love lost between those two, he thought. He knew nothing of their feud, no doubt one of long standing, and cared less, excepting as it might affect his own ambitions. Lord Vincent Ogden, as he must now be styled, was demonstrably a stolid, patriotic fellow and no doubt adhered to a strict code of honor. Unless the newly elevated Lord Ogden was more intelligent and more devious than Sir William believed him to be, his lordship would not be a great barrier to his own pursuit of Lady Ogden.

It was an outside chance, of course, but he was prepared to put in the effort for a possible and very handsome payout in future. *A seduction, a special license. All done while she is yet in mourning.*

Sir William absently ran his quizzing glass back and forth on its silken ribbon. From what he had seen of the former major at the burial service and from the venomous remarks made in the past by his friend, Lord Henry Ogden, he believed he had a fairly shrewd idea of the new viscount's character. "He'll want to wed, bring up a few brats in his image. He'll tire of housing his despised cousin's widow and her aunt, and he'll want a house free of female rumpus before he brings home a bride," he mused aloud.

As for Lady Ogden, his friend had complained often enough of her ladyship's demands for more than her quarterly pin money. *Household expenses, forsooth!* Sir William believed he knew better than to believe that; the female he had in his keeping now was a rapacious little ladybird. In his estimation, whether ladies or whores, the females all had grasping fingers. Lady Ogden must feel the pinch now, he thought, as well as the awkwardness of remaining on his lordship's charity for her rack-and-room. Sir William smiled slowly to himself. "Perhaps the lady will look favorably on an offer to bring her into a sophisticated society, where she has jewels and clothes to suit her station."

Sir William nodded, satisfied with his conclusions. Now all that was required was careful planning. He rather thought he still knew how to lay siege to a lady, especially one whom he believed to be both naïve and provincial and to be living in uncertainty of her future.

11

Lord Ogden observed mourning for only the proscribed degree. He neither missed nor grieved for his cousin and within weeks he stopped wearing the black armband around his coat sleeve. Mrs. Merriweather also soon put off black ribbons, since she was barely connected by marriage to the late viscount. The lady had said frankly at the outset that it was a good thing, for with her limited income she would not have been able to afford even one full mourning ensemble. "Such a waste it would have been, too, when I disliked his lordship so very much."

Lady Ogden alone was constrained by the proprieties to observe deep mourning, no matter what her feelings on the matter. As her aunt observed, "It is just too bad for you, Charlotte. A whole year in mourning! For a man who treated you with indifference while he was alive and spited you after his death."

"Indeed, aunt, I do feel it. I wish it was possible for me to remove my blacks. However, I did wed Henry and I must mourn him as society dictates."

"It isn't at all fair."

"Never mind. It shan't be forever." Lady Ogden let a faint sigh escape. She felt such a hypocrite to wear mourning. However, she knew very well it would have been shocking to her neighbors, and earned her heavy disapproval, if she had not put on blacks. Propriety dictated also that she was able to receive callers but was barred from attending any social functions or to make any social visits herself. Delincourt Manor existed in a social vacuum. A decent interval would be allowed to elapse by the neighborhood before those residing at the manor would be drawn back into society. Lady Ogden wasn't unhappy about it. For the moment, the enforced retirement from society was a boon. Her private life was too chaotic. There was too much to contemplate. The adaptations she was making in her thoughts and her actions were uneasy ones. Delincourt's quiet, dull routine seemed to ground her riotous emotions and anxieties; she clung to it, much as a shipwrecked survivor might cling to a wooden spar so as not to drown.

Lord Ogden had voiced his wish to her ladyship that all of the management of the household should remain in her capable hands. "I am kept busy with larger affairs. I can see little profit in usurping a role which you are already well able to perform, and so I have informed Somerset," he said with the flicker of a smile.

Lady Ogden was astonished. She was not used to compliment and she felt her cheeks heat. "Thank you, my lord. Shall I refer to you any decisions which must be made concerning the household?"

Lord Ogden waved his hand in dismissal. It appeared the subject was closed. He began to go through the letters and cards that had been brought by the morning post. "I trust you to manage all to admiration, ma'am."

Lady Ogden and her aunt exchanged glances. Mrs. Merriweather raised her brows. Despite having a new master in the house, Somerset and the housekeeper had continued to apply to Lady Ogden for direction. It was nevertheless gratifying that the viscount had endorsed her authority. Lady Ogden smiled and raised her tea cup to her lips. In truth, she was grateful that the viscount was so willing to leave the household in her hands. It was good to have the employment to divert her mind. Indeed, the day-to-day running of Delincourt Manor proved to be her salvation. Her responsibilities were a familiar stability in a world spun out of control and she always attended to them with diligence. With the viscount's stamp of approval, she felt an added zest to see to all the little details necessary to orderly management of the manor house and as she gave her orders to the upper staff.

The household accounts, which were submitted weekly by the housekeeper, were reviewed by her ladyship and she also heard Mrs. Tower's daily report of the activity ongoing in the various work areas of the house, as well as any concerns which the housekeeper had about the female staff. Food and the cooking of it was a major undertaking, requiring much planning on Lady Ogden's part and daily consultation with the cook, since menus were dependent upon what was available in the household stores or what was in season or what was available locally for purchase.

The viscount occasionally took out a gun in the company of the bailiff and he always brought back a brace of gamebirds or a few hares to add variety to the table fare. Lady Ogden was not surprised by his competency. It was to be expected of a gentleman who had spent his boyhood in the country and was thereafter in the army.

She was aware that Lord Ogden was much employed and the running of the estate seemed to have put a permanent bracket between his brows, but there was briskness to his speech and in his stride, so that no one in observing his lordship believed that he found his situation distasteful. On the contrary, his lordship's inexhaustible energy in the pursuit of his duties became a byword at Delincourt and talk of it spread beyond his own gates. Though not much had yet been seen of the viscount in the county, and though it was not yet known to his lordship and the ladies of Delincourt, he was nevertheless the fodder of many conversations.

Mrs. Merriweather's keen interest in the stillroom was to a lesser extent shared by her niece. However, it was accepted by the household that the stillroom was the older lady's domain. Though Lady Ogden did not mind the making of the manor's store of herbal tisanes and delicately scented waters, she could not match Mrs. Merriweather's enthusiasm, and she derived much more enjoyment from her aunt's gentle reports.

Lady Ogden's free hours were whiled away in the ladylike pursuits of taking the air on the terrace or going out for a quick ride, with a groom in attendance – more likely as not in the viscount's company – or the occasional reading of a favorite novel. Most of her time was spent in the amiable company of her aunt, as they sat talking quietly together in the upper drawing-room while their hands were busy with their embroidery or the darning of torn household linens which had been rooted out by the zealous housekeeper.

She was amazed that no one, not even her aunt, who knew her best, realized how unlike herself she felt. The perpetual pendulum swings between icy reserve and passion's demands were a difficult adjustment to make every dawn and dusk. *I could tread the boards.* At the silly notion of herself earning her bread as an actress, she gave a little laugh. *It's not such a stretch, really. I am acting a part each and every day.*

"Pray, what amuses you so?" Mrs. Merriweather glanced up from looking over her silks. She was making a careful choice of a new color.

Lady Ogden shook her head, the shadow of her smile still lingering on her lips. "I only recalled an old joke, aunt. It was nothing great, I assure you." She bent her head again over her handiwork, glad to be able to hide her vagary in her every-day task.

The coffee-urn was brought in. Its appearance was the signal for Lord Ogden and the ladies to put aside whatever it was that they had been engaged in. Lady Ogden laid down the book she had been reading and served the coffee before sitting back in her chair with her own cup. When she recalled the first time that she had served coffee to the newly-arrived viscount, it was with wondering astonishment. She had been defensive and resentful that evening, believing that nothing would suit her better than to hide herself away. While it was true that her life had been unalterably changed, and in many respects, she was still a prey to confusion and alarm at how things stood, she was also experiencing a degree of contentment that was novel. The unhappy, tense atmosphere that had been prevalent at Delincourt when her late husband was in residence had been completely banished.

A pleasant evening routine had been established. After dinner, the ladies withdrew to the drawing-room to leave the viscount to enjoy his port. It was never long before his lordship joined them for conversation and coffee. Lady Ogden and her aunt often played backgammon, as had long been their habit. On occasion, the viscount challenged one or the other to a game. Sometimes, as was true that evening, there was more of a companionable silence, broken now and again by easy remarks, while she read the book, his lordship turned the pages of a newspaper, and her aunt perused the latest fashion magazine.

Lord Ogden stood up and walked over to the hearth. Taking up the poker, he leaned over and prodded a log that had rolled forward, pushing it to the back of the fireplace, sparking and crackling. The task completed, he replaced the poker and straightened again. The corner of his sight was caught by the large painting set above the mantel and he turned full-face toward it. He frowned at the oil portrait of his cousin, the late viscount. It was a fair likeness, he thought. The arrogant look of the eyes and petulant set of the mouth had been perfectly captured. *Henry was always a supercilious bastard.*

Of a sudden, he recalled one of the last days he had been with his father. He had been about to leave for the war, dressed in his proud regimentals, and the hastiness of his departure had torn at him. He had bowed his head, running restless fingers through his thick curls. "I am in despair. I must leave so soon!"

He had felt his father's comforting hand upon his shoulder. "Take heart, my son. Go to her again tomorrow and see if she has made a decision. The lady may yet give you the answer you desire."

He had chanced to look up. Standing at the window, Lord Henry Ogden had been restlessly fiddling with the tassel on the heavy drape. The viscount had turned his head to level a long, unaffectionate glance, and it was then that he saw his cousin's eyes, full of loathing.

Now, from the distance of years, he knew that it must have been in those moments of his own obvious despair that his cousin had formed the decision to wound him in the worst imaginable way, if it could be done, by stealing the lady whom he loved. At the last, he finally understood that his cousin had beheld him with hatred. Anger welled up in him. *Well, by God, I don't have to look at his face!*

Lord Ogden turned around and addressed his cousin-in-law in a clipped, chilly tone. "My lady, I wish for this portrait to be removed from this room. Pray see to it, if you please!"

Lady Ogden was amazed by his lordship's harsh, abrupt command.

"Of course, my lord. I shall leave word with Somerset before I retire. It shall be done on the morrow." She glanced up at the portrait and felt that she understood, at least a little. She thought for a moment. "There is a portrait in the gallery, one of your father and your uncle, posed together as young men. Perhaps you would prefer to set that one in its place?"

Lord Ogden's frowning expression lightened. He regarded her with agreeable surprise. "By God, I recall that portrait! Indeed, it would please me to see it again."

"Then it shall be done," said Lady Ogden, setting down her coffee cup. She wondered that she had not herself thought of removing the portrait. *A melancholy reminder of my past misfortune! It will not break my heart to have it replaced.*

Lord Ogden smiled slightly "Thank you, madam."

Lady Ogden gave a small nod. She watched him, as he returned to his chair and retrieved the newspaper that he had tossed aside, before turning away to her gaze. A backgammon board was set up on the small table between herself and her aunt. "Shall we play, aunt?"

"Yes, of course," murmured Mrs. Merriweather.

Though she and her aunt were engaged in the game, Lady Ogden could still reflect on the differences and yet the odd sameness of her life. She was at all times aware of the viscount. He was a constant in her thoughts; if not always at the forefront of her mind, then at the back of her brain.

The steady, quiet tick of the mantel clock was unobtrusive. Then the clock began to chime, breaking her reverie. Lady Ogden counted the chiming of the hours. Her gaze flew to the viscount's face. He stared back at her. The depths of his dark eyes smoldered. She was beset with an uncontrollable shiver.

The shadows of flickering candles and the glow of firelight played over their glistening, naked bodies. She protested the viscount's insistence. "No, no! I'm not certain. It is strange." But her objection was half-hearted. He wanted to possess her in what she considered to be a taboo fashion. It seemed obscene, animalistic. Yet despite her intellectual rejection, it excited her. He'd positioned her on her hands and knees, with himself kneeling behind her. She had seen horses rutting. The stallion had locked its teeth in the mare's neck to hold her. She wondered if he would do the same. *His teeth closing on the side of my neck* – she could not help but shudder. As she always did with him, she gave way.

Vulnerability made her words sharp. "I feel like a brood mare positioned in the paddock."

He gave a low laugh. "Just so."

And there she was, faced outward from him, her legs parted wide, passively accepting the carnal attentions he was lavishing on her. She was not able to see what he was doing to her, but she could feel it. She wasn't allowed to touch him or kiss him. When she began to speak, he even shushed her. "I will tell you what I'm doing. I will tell you what I'm going to do. Ah, such a pretty twat." The tip of a masculine finger slipped slowly down her feathered slit. She gave a soft gasp but obediently remained silent.

"My prick is hard, so hard. You do that to me." His low-voiced vulgar words made her tremble, while his clever hands played with her heated, melting femininity. "Your quim is hot and wet for me. My prick will dive deep and hard into your warm waters until my head butts the crown of your womb."

Lady Ogden swallowed. Curls of warmth infused her belly. She adored it when he spoke in such crude hyperbole. "Yes, yes, I can almost feel it now."

His voice dropped to a whisper. "Dear Charlotte, I'm going to fuck you soon." He moved his fingers inside of her, finding that shockingly pleasurable spot. She was heaving dry sobs and squirming before he finally shifted into position. The viscount took hold of her naked hips. He held her firmly as he pushed forward and pulled back again.

Lady Ogden cried out with voluptuous delight.

"That's it, my sweet. Tell me how good it feels when I fuck your pretty twat." Her hot sleeve sucked at his cock. He broke out in a fresh sweat. He spread his knees wider and curled his fingers almost cruelly into her rounded flesh. He began slow enough but picked up depth and speed until he energetically worked her; her bottom jiggled with every home-thrust.

She gasped for breath, for he was putting her through an exquisite rogering. She began to become mindless, senseless. She was only a vessel of feeling hurtling toward the celestials. His panting words penetrated the glittering luminance. "I am the master of your delectable body. You will scream for me. You will *beg* for me to release you."

At his guttural utterances, her lips parted in shock. She understood, but it was an effort to pull together her scattered wits. She managed to utter a coherent accusation. "You use me like a whore!"

"Not a whore, my love, but like the good brood mare you are." He mocked her, but he mocked himself more. "And I am your faithful stud! I am but a means to an end."

Stung, she hurled a ragged, choked defiance. *"Yes! Nothing more! A lordly rutting!"*

The cutting words angered him. He reached forward and fisted his hand in the heavy braid of her thick chestnut hair and with it pulled up her head. "You'll learn to take the bit – and like it!" He wrapped the rope of her hair tighter in his fist, as he would a bridle-rein, deeply arching her spine, and held her for a few fierce strokes. But he found he could not finish it thus, not with black temper riding him.

Of a sudden, he freed her. She fell face-first onto the bed, her nether limbs sprawled apart. She lay gasping, her brain suspended, her body a quivering jelly. Then he rolled her over on top of him and thrust up inside of her again. The pulsing of his prick, the rapid rhythm of her own heart, they seemed to be one, and she uttered a low groan.

"Ride me, damn you!" he said savagely.

Craving what only he could do for her, she sat up and settled deeper, pushing down to the root of his shaft. He grunted, jackknifing. She closed her eyes and let her head fall forward. Then she began to move on him, spurred by the insistent, hard hands rocking her hips. It was the most rigorous ride of her life. Together, they took the jumps, soared over the waters, and raced for the glorious finish. In the end, their arms circled tight, holding one another close; in the shudders of release, chained heart-to-heart.

12

The storm-studded, winter days inexorably slipped past and a trickle of visitors began to enliven the slow pace at Delincourt Manor. Lady Ogden and Mrs. Merriweather willingly set aside their piecework and received their old acquaintances with pleasure. The break in the unvarying monotony of their insulated lives was welcome.

All who called had a genteel interest in the new viscount. As the son of the vicar, he had been known in the neighborhood and was recalled by elderly visitors to have been an energetic, wiry lad of cheerful disposition. His lordship was not always available when his neighbors stopped in at Delincourt, which was a disappointment to them. However, Lady Ogden and Mrs. Merriweather were told there had been numerous sightings of his lordship, riding around the countryside, inspecting various parts of the estate and talking to his tenants, which was taken to be a credit in him.

Mr. Kelton, the bluff gentleman from the Grange, made his duty-call at Delincourt, sending his card in to the ladies as was dictated by protocol. It was a happiness to Mr. Kelton that Lord Ogden was also in. He had heard enough gossip and speculation that he was grown curious to meet his lordship. He had not known the viscount as a lad, but he was soon able to form a favorable opinion of his own.

Mr. Kelton stayed the proper half hour, talking with the two ladies and his lordship. Lord Ogden had recognized the style of man at once. The gentleman had obviously made his fortune in trade. Lord Ogden swiftly deduced that Mr. Kelton's wealth, taken together with his innate good manners, had long since made the man acceptable to the social fabric of the neighborhood. The newly-elevated peer and the merchant took an instant liking to one another. Despite their differing backgrounds, each recognized a kindred spirit in the other, as both men were of a forthright nature. Upon the gentleman's leave-taking, Lord Ogden said, "You must come again, sir. I know I speak for Lady Ogden and Mrs. Merriweather as well as for myself."

Mr. Kelton was agreeably surprised to be invited to further his acquaintance. It was an unlooked-for civility on the viscount's part. He expressed his gratification with a deep bow. "I shall do so, my lord."

Lord Ogden gave one of his rare smiles. "I hope you do, sir. I have particularly enjoyed our brief conversation on the new drainage you have put in at the Grange. I am myself much employed with estate business these days, as you might imagine."

"So I have heard, my lord, so I have heard." Mr. Kelton shook hands with his lordship and shortly thereafter rode away from Delincourt Manor. He was very well satisfied with the outcome of his visit.

Sir Edward Thane and his lady were among the fortunate few to immediately establish a footing with the new viscount. The gentleman was a large, rather loose-limbed man, with a shock of thick brown hair that fell over his broad forehead. His wife was good and kind. She had never been a beauty, but she made the most of what she had with an impeccable fashion sense.

Lady Ogden had known Lady Thane all of her life. In their girlhood, they had been the closest of confidantes. That happy state had ended with Lady Ogden's marriage, when she had deliberately distanced herself from the close friendship, being unwilling to articulate anything of her feelings or the details of her unfortunate situation. In her eyes, it would have been a betrayal of the marriage tie, burdensome as it was, and her character could not have borne the pity which Lady Thane would undoubtedly have shown her.

Somerset ushered the Thanes into the drawing-room, where they were received by Lord Ogden and the ladies; bows and curtsies were exchanged all round, accompanied by smiles and courteous greetings. Sir Edward immediately claimed closer acquaintance with the viscount. With a huge smile, he stepped forward, his hand outstretched. "How are you, old fellow? I haven't seen you this age."

Lord Ogden's face lit up; he'd been half-afraid that his elevation might have marred an old friendship, and he gratefully clasped the gentleman's square hand. "Ned! It is good to see you. It's been all of three years! I came back to settle my father's affairs, you will recall. I had wished then that I could have spent more time with you, but I had to get back to the regiment in such a bang."

"Well, you are sold out now. We'll have time to catch up on old times. My word, to think of you becoming a viscount! I should bow and scrape, I suppose!"

"Do not dare or I shall give your head a good clouting!"

"You may try it, *my lord!*"

"*Ned!*" protested Lord Ogden, laughing. "Do not *you* get on your high ropes!"

The three ladies smiled as they listened to the good-natured raillery. It was well-known that Vincent Crawford and Ned Thane had been close boyhood friends and as the two gentlemen fell into easy discourse, it became obvious that the ties between them had weathered time and distance.

Lady Ogden ushered Lady Thane to a comfortable chair close to the warmth of the fire before she seated herself, beside her aunt, on a cushioned settee opposite their visitor. Lady Thane fixed her friendly gaze on Lady Ogden as she loosened and pulled off her gloves. "I'm glad to be able to call on you finally. It has been so disagreeable to be bound by convention. You have naturally been much on my mind, Charlotte." Her shrewd gaze searched the viscountess' face and she seemed to find cause for concern. "I hope you are well?"

"I am well, thank you." Lady Ogden smiled, putting as much reassurance into her expression as she could. She wondered whether her old friend had been able to read anything of her underlying anxiety, that inner turmoil which almost constantly afflicted her, but she thought not. Her own aunt had not noticed anything odd about her, so no doubt it was simply the unbecoming widow's blacks, which made her appear so wan, that had put that anxious glint in Lady Thane's eyes.

"We are glad to see you, Lady Thane," put in Mrs. Merriweather. "It seems such a very long time since we last had the pleasure of your company." She folded her hands in her lap, anticipating what would surely be a pleasant visit, for with the removal of her gloves, Lady Thane had signaled she meant to stay awhile.

"Indeed, it is too true," responded Lady Thane, making a slight bow of acknowledgement.

"I received your kind note, Sarah. I prized your sentiments," said Lady Ogden warmly. "It was of particular comfort to me when you and Sir Edward attended the burial service, for I'm aware that you were not friends with his lordship." The late viscount had made himself repugnant to his nearest neighbors over a property line dispute. There had also been some tension over the disreputable company that the viscount had introduced into the neighborhood, which had raised Sir Edward's ire by trespassing on his lands and indiscriminately shooting his gamebirds.

"Of course! Sir Edward and I would never be in any way backward in our social duty," said Lady Thane with a flickering smile. She included both ladies in her meaningful glance. "You must be aware that we have always counted *you*, Lady Ogden, and you, Mrs. Merriweather, as our dear friends."

Though Lady Ogden's response was couched in polite language, she very much meant what she said, and she hoped that Lady Thane would understand the depth of her feelings. "Thank you, Sarah. You've always been good neighbors to us at Delincourt."

"Very true," agreed Mrs. Merriweather.

The ladies settled in for a comfortable coze that ranged over a great many topics. Lady Ogden was careful to convey the intelligence that Delincourt, and her lot in particular, had much improved since the present viscount had stepped into his cousin's shoes. "We go on much easier now," she concluded.

Mrs. Merriweather snorted. "That is an understatement, my dear!"

Lady Ogden slanted a reproving glance at her aunt, but Lady Thane gave a little laugh. The general consensus of the neighborhood, of which Lady Thane was well-aware, was that Lady Ogden was well rid of her profligate husband. However, Lady Thane was too well-bred to reveal the gossip or to repeat her husband's forthright description of the late viscount.

"A reprobate, a bounder, altogether a bad one," had said Sir Edward Thane with strong disapprobation.

Instead, Lady Thane was quite willing to discuss the improvements which Lord Vincent Ogden seemed to be in the way of putting into place. Of particular interest to her was the news that his lordship had decided to fill the living at the vicarage. "I am glad," she said simply. It went without saying that the neighborhood would certainly benefit from having a new vicar. Marriages, christenings, funerals – the normal fabric of country life would be happily restored.

Across the drawing-room, Sir Edward was saying quietly to Lord Ogden, "I very much disapproved of Henry's way of life. The sort of company which he on occasion brought to the neighborhood! You never saw such dissolute fops in your life, Vincent! And the pranks and hijinks they would get up to! There wasn't a maidservant or village girl safe, not with that lot swaggering around. I'm sorry to say it, for he was your cousin and I knew him all of his life, but Henry was a bad man."

Lord Ogden sighed heavily. He gave a somber nod of agreement. "I am aware of it, Ned. I thought I knew the worst of Henry before I went away, but I've since learned, to my sorrow, that his character was blacker than I suspected. His extravagance, his care-for-nothing attitude, his gambling –" Lord Ogden broke off. "But I shouldn't burden you with my complaints."

"Left you in bad straits, did he?" asked Sir Edward sympathetically.

"I shall be lucky if I can salvage anything out of the estate without beggaring myself," said Lord Ogden baldly.

Sir Edward pursed his lips and shook his head. "That's bad. I'm sorry to hear it."

Chancing to glance across at the gentlemen, Mrs. Merriweather was struck by their change in demeanor. "Why, whatever can have happened? Lord Ogden and Sir Edward look so somber of a sudden!"

"Perhaps they are speaking of the war. It seems that's all any gathering of gentlemen is interested in," said Lady Thane. Smiling, she shook her head. "I confess, I'm wanting to hear about more than politics and troop movements. Have you seen the latest *La Belle Assemblee*? No? My sister-in-law, Augusta, sent it down to me from London. I shall lend it to you."

"That will be most agreeable, Lady Thane," said Mrs. Merriweather eagerly. "I have been wishing to see all the latest fashions."

"Yes, indeed!" Lady Ogden plucked with disparagement at her dull-colored skirt. The deep black bombazine was a heavy and ugly fabric. "It will be pleasant to daydream about wearing something more fashionable than my blacks! So dreary! I cannot conceive of anything worse, unless it was sackcloth and ashes."

The other two ladies chuckled. Mrs. Merriweather patted her niece's arm and said, "Never mind, my dear. The year's mourning will go quickly enough."

"Very true," agreed Lady Thane, still smiling. "And I shall form a dinner party as soon as you have put off your black gloves. There! You have something else to look forward to, Charlotte!"

"I thank you for your kindness, ma'am!" Lady Ogden smiled warmly at her old friend. She introduced a topic that she well knew was dear to her visitor's heart. "I hope your children are well?"

Lady Thane's face softened. She prattled for a little while, dwelling on the many endearing qualities of her small brood, a boy and two daughters, before ending finally, "They are all well and grow strong, my lady."

"I'm glad to hear it." Lady Ogden had listened with genuine interest. She considered Sir Edward and Lady Thane to be among her closest friends and she and her aunt had often enjoyed their hospitality. Of course, it had been some time since Delincourt had reciprocated. She hoped to remedy that before many more months had passed. It would be pleasant to re-establish other ties, she thought, and with that object in mind, she said, "I trust Mr. Thomas Thane and your sister-in-law are in health."

Lady Thane smiled. "They go along splendidly. We are hoping to have them with us for the Christmas holiday. They will undoubtedly wish to call at Delincourt."

"We shall look forward to it." Lady Ogden felt obligated to inquire after all the family, and so she politely asked, "And how is Mrs. Thane's sister-in-law, Mrs. Collings?"

Lady Thane's pleasant expression dimmed. She said in a neutral tone, "My sister-in-law is well. She is fixed in London with Thomas and Augusta until the summer, when she will come down to us for her annual visit in order to escape the heat of town."

Lady Ogden and Mrs. Merriweather murmured suitable responses. They were both aware that Lady Thane was always put to a great deal of trouble by her sister-in-law's visits. Mrs. Collings expected her every comfort to be seen to, but she was not one to express appreciation; she was rarely pleased with any entertainment formed for her pleasure, remarking that country pursuits could not compare to town amusements; she believed herself to be an authority on all things sophisticated and fashionable, which expertise she was only too willing to inflict on poor Lady Thane. In short, she was a very disagreeable guest. However, Mrs. Collings was Mr. Thomas Thane's sister-in-law, his wife being the sister of the late Mr. Collings, and so the lady must be borne with complaisance.

Not many more minutes passed before Sir Edward and Lady Thane took their leave, with promises to return again. They did not say their final farewells before urging Lord Ogden to call upon them soon.

Lord Ogden smiled, inordinately pleased by the open invitation. It was pleasant, indeed, to pick up old friendships, he thought. He felt a burgeoning sense of contentment. "I shall certainly do so."

Some hours later, in the privacy of their own abode, Sir Edward and Lady Thane discussed their visit to Delincourt. Lady Thane reported to her husband what had been said about the possibility of a new man being given the living at the vicarage. Sir Edward approved. "I am glad Vincent is back and has stepped into the title. We must count ourselves fortunate in having a better neighbor."

"Very true. I hope that our ties with Delincourt will be closer, most particularly my own with Lady Ogden. I regretted losing dear Charlotte's friendship, but it was so very difficult when Sir Martin was still in residence, and then there was her unfortunate marriage. That ended it altogether," said Lady Thane. "I have already told her ladyship and Mrs. Merriweather that we will issue an invitation in the near future. A private dinner party, I think, when Lady Ogden has put off her black gloves."

"Very good." Sir Edward was content, as always, to leave all such things as entertaining to his wife's efficient organization. He snorted. "That idiot, Sir Martin Stockton! My father never liked the man and I certainly did not. The man was always in his cups and throwing his weight around. A bully if ever I saw one."

"Yes, and I believe Charlotte suffered for it very much. It was an unhappy situation for many years. I suspect that's really why she accepted Henry Ogden in the end."

"Well, if she hoped to better her fortune, it was a mistaken belief. What a bad man he was! One does not like to speak ill of the dead, but there it is, it cannot be denied. Henry Ogden was a bad neighbor and a bad landowner. However, we now have a new master at Delincourt and I'm heartily glad of it!" said Sir Edward, adding in a reflective tone, "Though I'm not certain that Vincent feels himself to be so very fortunate."

Lady Thane was surprised; to her mind, rising to the peerage was a thing worthy of congratulation. "Whatever do you mean, my love?"

"Why, the man is worn down to the bone. That wastrel, Henry, squandered the estate until there is scarcely anything left of it. Vincent confided the whole to me today. He said that he will be lucky to save Delincourt."

"Perhaps he will lose Delincourt in any event," remarked Lady Thane, thinking and tapping a forefinger against her chin. She was recalling the viscountess' paleness and the dark circles under the lady's eyes. Indeed, she had been shocked at how fragile her ladyship had looked and a conjecture had leaped instantly to her brain.

"Now you speak in riddles, dear ma'am."

"When I saw Charlotte today, how pale she was, it flashed through my brain - there has been gossip, servant's-fare, of course, but in all probability reliable enough. Surely you must have heard it." Lady Thane hesitated, her gaze resting on her husband's puzzled face. "What if Lady Ogden is with child? It's well known, during that last ramshackle house-party that the late viscount visited her bedchamber the night before the accident. It is quite possible that she was gotten with child."

Sir Edward stared. "The devil you say." He frowned for a moment, turning it over in his mind. He shook his head, regretfully. "If it turns out to be so, that *would* put Vincent's nose out of joint; yes, and after he has resigned his commission, too! It would be a bad piece of luck. I should hate to see it, I tell you. A legitimate heir!"

Lady Thane nodded. "Quite so. Perhaps he will wed her and so come into a happy state after all."

"You are of a romantical disposition."

Lady Thane responded to her spouse's fond amusement with a smile. "Am I, dear sir?" Her smiling expression faded. "However, I cannot help feeling it will be a good solution for settling Lord Ogden's uncertain future. Even with an heir, he would at least be master at Delincourt and established in a comfortable position for many years before any such heir came to majority. Hopefully, there would grow to be such bonds of affection that the heir would look upon him as his own father and would make suitable provision for his retirement."

Sir Edward regarded his wife with surprised admiration. "I take it all back. You are prosaic, indeed. Yes, we must hope for such a happy outcome."

THE VISCOUNT YAWNED as he entered his bedchamber and closed the connecting door. The dying firelight behind the grate was just enough to see by. He was already shrugging out of his silk brocaded dressing-gown when he realized that he was not alone. Standing stock-still, he looked across the room and met the shadowed, steady gaze of his valet. "Grimshaw."

The wooden-faced valet said not a word but his silence was eloquent. Lord Ogden sighed. He walked forward as he finished removing the dressing-gown. His naked body, with his thick shaft still proudly elevated, made it obvious to the meanest intelligence what he had been about. He handed the garment to the valet, who took it mechanically. "So, you've caught me out."

The valet burst out in a low, intense voice, "My lord! Do you know what you're doing?"

Lord Ogden shook his head. A brief, wry smile touched his face. "No, I don't. I'm in the devil of a coil, Grimshaw."

"I should say so, sir," said the valet with some severity.

Grimshaw had been in his lordship's company. They had been together a long time, often in very dangerous circumstances, and they held one another in mutual respect. When he had offered the position of valet to him, Grimshaw had not hesitated to accept. Lord Ogden did not want his man to believe him to be a libertine, merely taking a fleeting obscene pleasure. He said quietly, "I intend to wed her."

Grimshaw appeared astounded. But his expression shifted almost at once into sharp, frowning reflection. "I see, my lord."

"I may rely upon your discretion, of course."

The valet looked affronted. "Of course, my lord."

"Good man." Lord Ogden climbed into the bed. He drew up the bedcovers and settled with a sigh against the cool pillows. He closed his eyes and went to sleep.

13

Lord Ogden's time was fairly consumed by the myriad responsibilities he had inherited with his elevation, yet he made it his consistent practice to interact with his widowed cousin-in-law. In the early mornings, before breakfast, instead of diving at once into the urgent affairs of the estate, the viscount had formed the agreeable habit of walking with Lady Ogden on the long terrace. When the weather was good, there was the occasional ride, chaperoned by a groom. He enjoyed these short outings as much for the company of the lady as for the fresh air.

He wanted – no, he corrected himself, he needed to build up a cordial footing with her. The pleasures of bed-sport sated his physical craving for her – he did not think he had ever felt better in his whole life – but he found it was not enough. The dark, fleeting hours, spending his passion in her lissome body, were unspeakably satisfying. Yet he wanted more. He thirsted for more. It was imperative to him to understand her. However, there the matter had remained. Even during the private morning strolls, their conversation did not stray from civil, polite exchanges, the kind which might be expected to pass between members of a household that were loosely connected by familial bonds.

However, their interrupted history and his unanswered questions had become a constant irritant to his mind. He had to know what had happened, those long years past. He said, suddenly, "You chose my cousin over me."

Lady Ogden was startled by the abrupt introduction of the tacitly avoided subject. She said, with unthinking frankness, "But, of course I did!" Where her gloved fingers rested, she felt the tensing of the muscular forearm beneath his coat sleeve. She looked up quickly, anxiously. At sight of his gathering frown, she intuited the thing behind his dour expression. Defensive, and despising herself for it, she asked, "Why should you hold it against me? You know how my family was situated – how I was situated! – and Henry professed love for me."

"Did he love you?" She was caught by surprise; the careful guard she had constructed in her mind cracked. The viscount watched her with his half-hooded, sharp eyes. His falcon's gaze had the power to unnerve her. Yet, pondering his query, she was for once immune. Finally, she shrugged. "I believed so." Searing, wounded memory brought with it a sorrow that burned her throat. "If it is of any moment, Henry swiftly came to despise me."

Lady Ogden thrust away the unpleasant memories. *It is done. It is in the past.* She was dealing with another man. She glanced up at her escort, and her face suddenly twisted in the travesty of a smile. "Perhaps he learned to despise me even before I lost the two babes."

There was a subtle shift in his lordship's set expression. She made a sharp, repudiating gesture and turned her face aside. Her ripening womb had twice poured the life out in cramped rushes of blood. She had keenly felt the losses, believing that children might have eased her unhappiness and made her life more fulfilling. The viscount's tepid regret had been shallow and of short duration. She still recalled, with piercing heartache, how her lord had said, with a shrug, "I'm in no hurry to set up a nursery, in any event." He'd flicked her tear-stained cheek with a negligent finger and observed, "It seems I made a bad bargain." Inwardly cringing, she wondered why she had blurted out such a personal thing.

She had wakened with a painful throbbing behind her temples; it could be her only excuse for being so weak. It horrified her that she had exposed one of her innermost secrets. She was ever mindful that she could scarce afford to trust his lordship. It was certainly no intent of hers to cultivate his pity. The tattered shreds of her dignity wouldn't permit it. Melancholy welled up inside of her. *If he is even capable of sympathy! He showed me none when I beggared myself to him.* Lady Ogden did not make the mistake again of looking up at her tall companion. She had no wish to see whatever was in his expression – pity, resentment, or a peculiar mingling of those emotions.

"I had to make a choice!" She paused in front of the terrace wall, perforce drawing the viscount to a standstill as well. The dull headache was growing in intensity and battered at her, crushing her defenses, and resignation arose. Whatever the consequences, perhaps she did owe him some explanation.

Lady Ogden grasped the edge of the balustrade. The cold from the stone seeped through her kid gloves, numbing her fingers. "Accepting your offer meant following the drum, not knowing from one day to the next if I was to be made a penniless widow. I also doubted that your pay would be sufficient to support a wife and an aunt-in-law." She dared a fleeting glance upwards at his lordship's tight-lipped profile. "Henry's position in the world was different. He offered a security which I could ill-afford to turn down. He offered a home for me *and* for my aunt."

"I see." Lord Ogden turned his head to her. "You have said nothing of your heart, madam."

She dropped her eyes to avoiding the demand in his unblinking gaze. "I-I held Henry in proper affection, of course."

Lord Ogden was amazed. The obvious lie angered him. He wanted the unsavory fact out in the open, acknowledged between them. He bit out what he knew to be true. "You mean, he held a title and an estate. *That* was the sum of your affection!"

"Yes!" Lady Ogden was equally blunt. She frowned up at him. At sight of his contemptuous expression, her carriage stiffened, and she said defensively, "I am not the first to wed for such reasons. I did what I felt was most prudent!"

A flash of white-hot fury burned him. It was irrational of him, he knew. Indeed, it was beneath him, for he was fully cognizant of the social code which strongly dictated making an alignment to best advantage. Lord Ogden knew what she had said was a reality. People of their class habitually formed such marriages. Nevertheless, it galled his soul. He uttered what else he knew to be true, what still had the power to embitter him. "Your damnable pride, Charlotte, still blinds you. Henry never loved you. He only wanted you because I did."

She was stung by his injustice. "That's *not* true!" she cried. "How dare you! This is spite, indeed! He told me that he loved me!"

The viscount pulled himself under rigid control. After a moment, in a colorless voice, he said, "Forgive me, ma'am. It has grown brisk, has it not? Let us go back inside."

Lady Ogden did not object. That morning, she had wakened feeling out of sorts. The lamentable conversation, ending with the viscount's astonishing, wounding assertion, had served to exacerbate her distress. By now – and she felt certain it was entirely due to her companion's horrid verbal attack – her headache was turned vicious. "I have the headache."

The viscount shot a glance at her. He said nothing, but his lips thinned. It was obvious to her that her abrupt, apropos declaration was suspect. She did not care.

Lord Ogden led the way back inside, where a footman relieved them of their outer garments, and then his lordship escorted Lady Ogden on into the breakfast-room. After politely greeting Mrs. Merriweather and seating her ladyship, he went to sit down at his own place. Already seated at the table, Mrs. Merriweather returned the viscount's greeting with her usual good spirits. She was happily unaware of their quarrel. She did, however, note that her niece seemed paler than usual.

The butler and a footman served plates laden from the buffet of cooked eggs, slices of cold ham, and toast. After making certain that the teapot was well within the ladies' reach and that his lordship had his usual tankard of ale, Somerset and his minion quietly exited.

Mrs. Merriweather carried the bulk of the conversation. It was a sore trial to Lady Ogden to respond appropriately to her aunt's cheerful chatter. The viscount withdrew behind a frosty exterior, his brows lowered in a dark line. He barely uttered a word more than the obvious civilities. When he was finished, he tossed his napkin beside his plate. He excused himself at once, saying that he intended to go for a ride. Without another word, he exited the breakfast-room.

"Well! Lord Ogden is not very sociable this morning," observed Mrs. Merriweather, pouring herself another cup of tea. "Perhaps exercising his poor horse will put his lordship into a better frame of mind."

Lady Ogden's pounding head had been joined by a nagging ache low in her back. With sudden, blinding clarity, she realized the physical symptoms were all too familiar. Lady Ogden felt oddly like weeping. *It's all been for naught.* She set aside her napkin and rose from the table. "Aunt, I must attend to a few things. Pray excuse me."

Mrs. Merriweather looked surprised, but she only nodded. "Of course, my dear."

Lady Ogden left the breakfast-room. She paused in the hall to issue a quiet order to a footman. Then she went upstairs to her bedchamber and tugged on the bell-pull for her dresser. It seemed an age, but in reality, must have been only a few minutes before Mills came into the room.

"You have ordered a bath, my lady?"

"Yes, Mills." Lady Ogden let the dresser help her out of her clothing and into a dressing gown. She said nothing until the menservants had been in to fill the brass bath and had taken away the empty water cans. When she was private again with her loyal woman, she said, "Mills, I feel unwell."

The dresser looked sharply at her ladyship's pallid face. She nodded with decision. "You'll take a luncheon tray later in your room, my lady."

"I cannot! I must go down when the bell rings." Lady Ogden smoothed her hair with trembling fingers. "His lordship will note my absence. I must behave just as always."

"A little coddling will not be remarked, my lady."

Lady Ogden felt the prickle of tears. *I have not bred.* She was torn by equal measures of relief and regret; her guilt over the secret affair paled beside her failure to be got with child. The diabolical conundrum made for heartsick anguish. *It's all been for nothing, nothing!* But her even tone did not betray her shocking unhappiness. "My bleeding rags, Mills."

"I'll take care of them, never fear. Now step into your bath, ma'am. Soak a bit and see if you don't feel better."

Lady Ogden allowed herself to be persuaded. As the warmth of the heated water eased the unpleasant cramp in her lower back, relief made her sigh. The next instant, she was fretting aloud. "I feel so tired! So stupid and weak!"

"Your courses will soon be done, ma'am."

Lady Ogden dozed off in the warm water. She roused when her dresser came back to get her out of the bath. Mills dressed her mistress in a fresh nightgown and helped her into bed, gently smoothing the covers over her. Mills had run a warming pan between the sheets and the warmth was luxurious.

Lady Ogden reminded herself the first day or two were always the worst. She would be better presently, she promised herself. Then she would go about her usual routine. The melancholy realization hit her. *I will have to tell him.* She didn't want to think about that, so she didn't. She turned her head into the pillow and slept.

FOR A LONG TIME, LORD Ogden rode over the park and through the stand of woods beyond. He had acquired a rational explanation at last, distasteful as it was. Aside from keenly-felt hurt and his long-lingering disappointment, despite his deep resentment, and the bitterness of his cousin's betrayal in going behind his back to secure her hand, he thought he could understand what she had done. His recent recollections during his ride with Bartlett had already begun to direct his thoughts into a new, untried channel. He hadn't wanted to accept the modification in his perception, but here was confirmation. Sir Martin had been all impatience to quit the county and had not greatly cared what would become of his daughter and his sister-in-law. *I had to make a choice.* She had known she was losing her home. She had not only her own position to consider, but also the well-being of a beloved aunt.

Set against all that, he had indeed been a bad bargain.

He reluctantly conceded the rationality of the point she had made. He could not easily have supported two women on his meager officer's pay and she'd had the wit to guess it. So, when his cousin Henry – damn his soul! – had hurried up to the Grange after hearing of his own rebuttal, she'd been given more to consider than a diligent search of her affections. She had accepted Henry as much for her aunt's sake as she had for herself.

Lord Ogden recalled her ladyship's upturned, lovely face. She had been wary and there had been trepidation in her green eyes. He had wanted to reassure her, but he could not. Instead, he had lashed out at her. His intellect could accept what had happened, but he found it was otherwise with the deepest-buried of his emotions. The bitterness would not entirely, nor so quickly, be laid to rest. He had held onto it for too long.

He sighed, weary to the bone.

14

U pon Lord Ogden's return, Somerset informed him that a letter had come in the post, directed to his lordship from the land steward. "I have placed the letter on your desk, my lord."

"Thank you, Somerset." Still in his riding dress, the viscount strode immediately into the ground-floor study. Tossing aside his hat, gloves and crop, he picked up the missive, broke open the seal, and unfolded the sheet. In reply to his own letter, Mr. Stockley had humbly responded that he would wait on his lordship as soon as he was able to conclude his present business, which had taken him farther afield than Briarcrest Cottage. Afterwards, depending upon the weather and the condition of the roads, he would set out at once for Delincourt Manor.

Lord Ogden checked the date of the letter. "Three days ago!" He tossed the letter down onto his desk. He was frustrated by the delay in meeting the land steward. He wanted to be put into possession of all the facts of his inheritance. The solicitor's records had been meticulous about the affairs of Delincourt Manor but lacked certain pertinent details about a few other, smaller properties. He had been informed of the generalities, but what those properties were worth or what shape they were in, he had no notion. Surely, he could expect an up-to-date report from the land steward. He hoped that what Mr. Stockley had to say would make a difference in Delincourt's fortunes.

The viscount walked over to the tall window and twitched back the heavy curtain hanging. With a preoccupied frown, he looked out, taking idle note that the lowering sky was a portent of more rain. The gloom fit his somber frame of mind. Lord Ogden stared out at the winter-blasted, dead gardens. "Henry, what the devil were you thinking?" he muttered. His troubled reflection was mirrored in the glass pane. "Your profligacy has left everything in the deuce of a mess! One could almost suspect you of deliberately reducing the estate, but that's nonsense. You had a wife and the prospect of an heir."

Night and day, he had been grappling with measures to bring the crumbling property back into shape. *If it is even possible.* The enormity of the task weighed down on him. It was not just the outlying lands. All around him was evidence of deterioration. The overgrown grounds and the wild, tangled gardens; the manor house itself with its leaking roof, smoke-blackened ceilings, and shabby, worn furnishings. He balled a fist and smashed it down on the wide windowsill. "I was not bred to an estate. I am a soldier. I'm making a mull of it!"

He allowed his anger a bit more rein but quick enough, along with a wearied sigh, he gave it up. The self-castigation was unfair and as a reasonable man, he knew it. "Damn it all! I'm muddling through the best I can with the rampant neglect at Delincourt. I must trust that this man Stockley was able to do better with the rest."

As always, whenever he deliberated about Delincourt Manor, he spent considerable thought on the lady of the house. The two were intrinsically bound together in his mind. It was inevitable that he should dwell on the discord between himself and Lady Ogden earlier that morning.

Two facts stood out to him. The first, she had not loved Henry when she had wed him. Then, was it possible that she had once felt something for *him*? She had never said so, never even hinted at it, at least not since that incoherent entreaty of hers when he had originally offered for her hand. She'd begged him to give her time to search her heart. Surely, that had meant something.

The second, she had lost two babes. He believed she had not meant to tell him that. The shadowed pain in her expressive, green eyes and her instant withdrawal had informed him of that much. His sympathy had been quickened. As much as it had been unwanted by her ladyship, it was nevertheless real and enduring. Given her past history, birthing a live heir must seem almost an unlikelihood to her. Of course, he felt sympathy, he thought. Yet there was an exultant, grim satisfaction in him, too. She was braving what must be her very real fear of losing another child, if one could even be conceived. After the rocky beginning, when he'd taken her like a camp whore, she'd had the courage to continue their liaison. *A devil's bargain, in truth, yet she is bold enough to accept the risk. While I willingly hazard my soul!*

He could not read the future. He did not know what the end of it all would be. There was too much at stake, too many unknowns. "I've never been a gamester. Yet I have risked it all on a single throw," he muttered. Made restless by his uneasy speculations, he dropped the curtain and abruptly turned on his booted heel. Striding over to pick up hat, gloves and crop, he left the ground-floor study.

Lord Ogden went upstairs to change out of his riding clothes. His valet was waiting with fresh linens and the proper attire for a gentleman at home. The cravat at his throat was neatly tied, his waistcoat was buttoned up over a clean shirt, and his biscuit-colored pantaloons were smoothed into another pair of gleaming boots. He preferred Scott's looser military cut, so he did not have to be thrust into a stylish, too-tightly cut garment by a muscular valet. However, he allowed Grimshaw to ease the frock coat over his shoulders and smooth its lines. At his lordship's murmured thanks, Grimshaw bowed. The valet took away the mud-splattered coat, breeches and boots for cleaning.

With a resigned sigh, the viscount returned downstairs to put in a few hours on the estate papers. It seemed to him that he no sooner had finished with one, then another had spawned three more in its place.

When the luncheon bell rang, he went into the front parlor, where he supposed that Lady Ogden and Mrs. Merriweather would already be waiting. However, he saw that only Mrs. Merriweather was present. He bowed and after an exchange of civilities, he asked, "Where is Lady Ogden? Is she not to join us also, Mrs. Merriweather?"

"I shall inquire, my lord." Mrs. Merriweather signaled a footman and murmured a few words to the manservant. The footman bowed and exited. Mrs. Merriweather turned to the viscount to engage him in polite conversation. "Did you enjoy your ride, my lord?"

Lord Ogden gave a nod. "It was most enjoyable. I stopped at Thane Hall on my way back."

"Indeed! How did you find Sir Edward and Lady Thane? I trust they are well? And their children? Such a promising family!"

"Quite well," said Lord Ogden, impatient with the exchange of inanities. His stubborn mind was puzzling over Lady Ogden's unexplained absence. Word was shortly brought downstairs by the returned footman that her ladyship had wakened with a putrid throat, which had grown worse since she had taken her usual morning exercise in the chill air. Instead of joining the viscount and her aunt downstairs for luncheon, her ladyship was having a tray in her bedchamber. Lord Ogden contracted his brows in a swift frown. "Lady Ogden said nothing of this to me this morning."

"Depend upon it, my niece simply did not wish to concern you, my lord," said Mrs. Merriweather in her usual placid manner. "Let us think no more about it."

"As you say, ma'am."

Though Lord Ogden maintained a civil conversation with Mrs. Merriweather and partook of the light meal with good appetite, he was abstracted. He couldn't shake a gathering unease. It had first leapt to his mind that Lady Ogden, so affronted by what he had said to her, had taken to her bedchamber in a fit of petulant anger. He had swiftly dismissed that as it did not fit what he knew of her strong character. He did not believe she would run shy, but rather, was far more likely to bring him to book for his transgression. He was forced to conclude that her ladyship was actually feeling ill.

Lord Ogden frowned again. He could not recall his cousin-in-law ever to be sickly, even as a young girl. On the contrary, Lady Ogden's spirit and physical energy were an integral part of her. He could not for long contain his gathering concern. He said abruptly, "Mrs. Merriweather, should we not send for the physician?"

Mrs. Merriweather's own anxious reflections had led her to a prosaic conclusion. She was thrown into dismay by his lordship's suggestion. The elderly lady hastily touched her napkin to her lips and set it down beside her plate. Mrs. Merriweather gave a polite, distancing smile. "I shall go up to my niece, my lord. I shall certainly let you know whether her condition warrants a visit by Dr. Manning."

"Of course, ma'am." Lord Ogden nodded, forced to acknowledge Mrs. Merriweather's right to form any decision regarding her niece. Convention prohibited him from saying more. In the eyes of the world, the connection between himself and his cousin-in-law was of the slightest. It would surprise Mrs. Merriweather very much if he was to behave otherwise. Indeed, it could well set up just such suspicions as he least wanted. *She is my mistress, yet I can do nothing.*

Lord Ogden rose to his feet and bowed as the elderly lady passed out of the room.

At once, Mrs. Merriweather hurried upstairs. After a knock, she entered Lady Ogden's private sitting room. As she closed the paneled door behind her, Mrs. Merriweather turned to look at her niece. She held an open novel in her hands. She was attired in a frilly morning wrapper, her hair covered by a cap. She reclined on the settee, propped up against a pillow, and had a large shawl thrown across her legs. Lady Ogden met her aunt's concerned regard with slightly raised brows.

Mrs. Merriweather walked across the worn carpet. "Well, my dear, you present the very picture of the invalid! All you lack is a hartshorn bottle to hold to your nose."

Lady Ogden laughed. She placed a thin blue satin ribbon to save her place in the book and closed it, before stretching out her hand to her aunt. "I am glad you have come, ma'am! I was feeling such self-pity, you can't imagine! I'm so bored with my own company."

"I see you are reading one of Miss Austen's volumes." Mrs. Merriweather remarked. She caught hold of her niece's hand and bent to kiss a pale cheek. She straightened and closely studied her niece's wan face. "You've gotten your courses, haven't you?"

"Yes, but I asked Mills not to advertise it," said Lady Ogden on a sigh. "I feel so stupid and very unlike myself."

Mrs. Merriweather sat down on the chair opposite the settee. "Yes, of course you do. My dear, a putrid throat?"

Lady Ogden gave a shrug. "It's better than the truth."

"His lordship was asking about you. He is quite concerned. He wants to send for Dr. Manning."

"Good God," said Lady Ogden blankly. "Whatever is the man about to take such a serious tack! Please hedge him off, aunt. Everyone contracts a cold now and then!"

"Very well. We shall simply deepen the fiction. I shall ask Mrs. Tower to prepare a saline draught." Mrs. Merriweather thought for a moment. She pursed her lips. "Perhaps a mustard pack, too."

"Oh, heavens! Don't you dare order a mustard pack! Lord Ogden will be convinced I've taken bronchitis to the lungs," she exclaimed, horrified. "He'll send for Dr. Manning straightaway!"

Mrs. Merriweather laughed. "I was only teasing you, dear child. Pray don't be anxious, Charlotte. I believe I can manage the delicacy of the situation without embarrassment to you. Indeed, I think it very wise of you to disguise the nature of your malady." Her niece's gaze darkened and she hurried on. "I haven't forgotten that we agreed to pretend to suspense as long as we could. We want to remain at Delincourt for as long as possible, don't we? As long as there appears to be the possibility of an heir, his lordship will not turn us out, will he? So for now, you have a putrid throat, which will keep you abed for a few days. Who knows what malady will afflict you next month?"

Lady Ogden winced. "Aunt."

Mrs. Merriweather's cheerful scheming cut her to the quick. For the sake of a roof over their heads, even her dear, kind aunt was willing to perpetrate fraud, though it was on a far smaller scale. The lady knew nothing of the depths of her own depravity.

"You think me conniving, no doubt," said Mrs. Merriweather, shrugging. "But bless every day of your mourning, Charlotte! A full year! Perhaps by the end of it, something will occur to brighten the future."

"As you say, aunt." Lady Ogden's voice was colorless. *I do not know how to make it right. How shall I bear it?*

"You look pale and tired, my dear." Mrs. Merriweather's smile was full of sympathy. She rose to her feet. "I shall let you rest, Charlotte. I assure you that you may rely upon me."

"Thank you, aunt."

———— ⟨๑⟩ ————

LORD OGDEN EXITED THE front parlor and hesitated. The thought of shutting himself up again in the ground-floor study to labor over ledgers and legal documents was repugnant. *The labors of Hercules, forsooth!* He paused in the entrance hall to order the footman to carry a message to the stables. "I will want my horse again in a quarter hour. Send word to Bartlett that he is to meet me."

"Aye, milord."

Lord Ogden bounded up the stairs and entered his apartment, calling for his man to attend him. A quarter hour later, the viscount returned downstairs, attired in a greatcoat which was buttoned over a riding coat and breeches, and left the manor house to make for the stables.

Lord Ogden spent the remainder of the day out-of-doors with his bailiff, inspecting the progress which was being made on repairs to two of the crofters' homes and listening to the details about some other urgent matters which the bailiff brought to his lordship's attention. When he returned to the manor, it lacked but a half hour before the dinner hour. He left his horse at the stable in the ostler's care and strode up to the manor and in through a side entrance. He went swiftly upstairs. Though he had been immersed in estate business, at the back of his mind there had been a nagging concern. He shed his riding clothes and took a quick splash in the washbasin, toweling himself dry. As he dressed again, he inquired of his valet after Lady Ogden's well-being.

"Her ladyship's dresser has reported that Lady Ogden seems to be recuperating well after a nap and a regimen of mild tea and soup," said Grimshaw.

Lord Ogden grunted, thinking it over, while he finished buttoning a silk-and-twill waistcoat over his starched white shirt. The valet held out a well-cut brown coat at the ready for him to put on. Lord Ogden slipped his arms into the coat sleeves and allowed the valet to adjust the well-tailored garment over his shoulders. He smoothed the ends of the brown sleeves, so that the white tips of his shirt cuffs appeared evenly from beneath them. The viscount would never have been taken for one of the dandy set, but his appearance always reflected a certain neatness. "And Mrs. Merriweather? She is not anxious?"

"Mrs. Merriweather does not appear anxious, but goes about with her usual placidity, my lord. The household is comfortable that the mistress will soon be fully recovered."

"Good. I'm glad to hear it."

When his lordship went downstairs to the drawing-room, the only lady present was Mrs. Merriweather and he escorted her in to dinner. As he seated her, the viscount politely inquired of her health. "I trust the capricious weather we have been having has not troubled you?"

Mrs. Merriweather was pleasantly surprised by his lordship's unlooked-for solicitude. "I go on very well, my lord."

Before going to his own place, Lord Ogden glanced at the viscountess' empty chair. *Of course, I care for her well-being. It would seem odd if I did not.* A casual query was in order. "And your niece, Mrs. Merriweather? How is her ladyship?"

"I believe it's only a mild cold, my lord." The lady smiled up at him with not an ounce of guile in her faded blue eyes. "Believe me, I would be the first to send for our good doctor if I thought it to be more."

Lord Ogden received the lady's reassuring report with a slight bow and moved away to take his own seat. He was relieved and it was only natural that he should be. He did not understand the depth of the feeling, however. It disconcerted him and caused him to respond with studied indifference. "A cold, you say? I trust you are right and it's nothing more. I don't like to think of her ladyship suffering." He picked up the starched linen napkin and snapped it open, laying the white square across his thigh.

Mrs. Merriweather temporized. "My niece is merely a trifle under the weather, my lord. I've had a saline draught taken up to her. She is resting well now."

"Very well. Thank you, Mrs. Merriweather."

Over the first course, consisting of soup, a few assorted entrees and the fish, it occurred to Lord Ogden that there would be no bed-sport that night. It was disappointing, of course, but the lady must have her rest. He did not wish to make himself more of a villain than she already thought him. He would be a brute, indeed, to force himself into her bed when she was ill. He foresaw a long night ahead, perhaps several nights to come, and mocked himself. *It will be character-building, sirruh.*

15

It stormed overnight. The thunder and cloudbursts continued long into the morning. The blackened sky made the day so dark that at an early hour all the candles in the house were lit. Late in the dismal afternoon, Lady Ogden finally left her apartment and went downstairs. She had put on her best daydress and smoothed her hair under the black widow's cap. She might not have looked her best, as pale as she was, but at least her appearance was neat. She inquired of a footman and was told she would find his lordship in the billiards room.

Lady Ogden heard the clack of the balls even before she opened the door. She stepped inside, closing the door behind her so that she could be private with the viscount. She was nervous about the interview. She was anxious that she conducted herself well and dispatched it with proper dignity.

Lord Ogden was bent over the billiards table. She thought she knew better than to distract a gentleman in the middle of his shot and she waited for his lordship's notice, folding her hands at her slim waist.

Lord Ogden straightened from his position, stick in hand. He had taken off his coat and was in his waistcoat and shirt sleeves. Neither was struck by the impropriety. His state of *dishabille* must have rendered their interview awkward, were it not that they were already involved. He bowed slightly to her and she curtsied. His steady gaze seemed to bore straight into her in search of her secrets. "You were not at luncheon or at dinner yesterday, and I do not think you were downstairs earlier today."

"No, my lord."

"I was informed that you have been ill. I hope you are better?"

Lady Ogden hesitated. She did not know how to say it to him, but she must. He could not come to her bedchamber that night nor for the remainder of that week. An explanation had to be given. "My lord." She swallowed convulsively and was appalled to hear herself just blurt it out in the worst fashion possible. "My lord, my courses have begun."

"So, you have not bred."

The flat statement was so akin to what her late husband had once said – *"It seems I made a bad bargain."* – that she flinched. It was her failure, that was what he meant. She looked down quickly at her folded hands. Her lips trembled. Perhaps it was her fault, perhaps she was not much of a woman. At any rate, she thought with misery, she could not remain standing there in his formidable presence. *I shall not endure his contemptuous regard.*

Once more, pride came to her rescue. Lady Ogden lifted her head high. She said in a credibly normal but cold voice, "Pray excuse me, my lord. I must speak to the housekeeper." She whirled around, jerked open the door, and swept from the billiards room, closing the paneled door sharply behind her.

Lord Ogden stood staring at the shut door, astounded. He wasn't certain what had just happened. Chagrin washed through him. The woman had no business getting that wretched look on her face. She hadn't bred. It was obviously a disappointment for her, but surely, she must realize the possibility still remained. He could still get her with child. "What the devil did she mean by flouncing out of here like that?"

He was uneasily aware that he should have said something more, perhaps something a little more tactful; but what it might have been, he had no notion. Women were odd creatures, he reflected. One never knew exactly what to say. It was obvious, too, that they were particularly prickly during their courses.

"I did not handle that well," he muttered, still frowning at the door. He was aware of a curious let-down. He had been glad to see her. The inevitable tightening of his body whenever he saw her come into a room had not been a surprise. Of course, he had been in hopes of returning to her bed. It struck him, with mild astonishment, that he also missed her presence at table and their easy conversations. Perhaps he should have told her so. The glimmer of insight grew into certainty. He had bungled royally. He wasn't sure how to correct it.

With a shrug, he decided to put the matter out of his mind as an insolvable poser. He bent over the green-baize billiards table and lined up his shot. A couple of pocketed balls later, when he was lining up for another shot, it finally dawned on him that he wouldn't be slipping into her warm bed for a number of nights to come.

The badly-hit ball smacked too hard against the side of the table and bounced over the edge. "Oh, bloody hell."

Lady Ogden hurried away from the billiards room. Her lips were folded tight. She was angry and hurt, but knew it for her own fault that she had done so badly in the brief exchange with his lordship. She had planned a dignified explanation. Instead, she had blurted out what shouldn't have been uttered at all to any gentleman and earned the bruising observation. She had not even gotten out all that she had set out to say. *Idiot, idiot.*

Lady Ogden lifted the hem of her skirt out of the way of her feet and ran up the carpeted stairs, her destination her private sitting room. She had told the viscount the truth, but not in its entirety. Mrs. Tower had indeed requested a consultation with her, but she had set the time for their meeting on the half hour.

She wished now that she had not agreed to see the housekeeper. The short, painful interview with the viscount had greatly upset her. However, she could not very well put off her meeting with the housekeeper on that score. It would not do to give rise to servants' gossip, as she had done once before by going all to pieces. She was known to have sought out his lordship on this occasion as well. There must not be any indication, by her words or her actions, to indicate that she was agitated by her conversation with the viscount.

Lady Ogden entered the sitting room and firmly shut the door behind her. She did not immediately move away, however. With her fingertips still touching the panels behind her, she bowed her head. Hot tears pricked at her lids. The viscount's callous words had ripped at her, laying open and exposing an old wound. She felt as though she had been eviscerated. In a low, trembling voice, she exclaimed, "Abominable, wretched man!"

A firm knock on the door shocked her system. Lady Ogden started like a hare and her heart skipped. At once, she was certain that his lordship had followed her. In the next instant, her rational mind told her that was ridiculous. Her heart was still foolishly pounding. It must only be the housekeeper, come early because she had been observed returning upstairs. *But what if it was not? Whoever it is, I won't be found in such an unsettled state!* She swiftly moved away from the door and rushed across the room, her black skirt flaring around her ankles. She seated herself on the settee near the warmth of the hearth fire. Lady Ogden took the time, with trembling fingers, to adjust the folds of her black shawl in an elegant drape over her shoulders. She took a deep breath and composed herself. "Enter."

It was the housekeeper who came into the sitting room. After firmly closing the door, the woman trod heavily over the carpet. She curtsied, surprisingly graceful for one of her bulk. "Thank you for seeing me, my lady."

Lady Ogden gestured at the chair positioned opposite her. "Pray sit down, Mrs. Tower. What may I do for you?"

Mrs. Tower perched herself on the front half of the chair cushion and folded her pudgy hands in her ample lap. "Well, it's about one of the under-maids, my lady. She's confessed to me that she's with child." The housekeeper paused meaningfully. "It happened when his lordship – Lord Henry, I should say – was down with his friends from Lunnon-town that last time."

"I see." Lady Ogden compressed her lips. It had been a riotous house-party, lasting for days. The late viscount and his drinking cronies had practically raised the roof with their raucous hilarity. Drinking and gaming and outrageous bets had been their ruling passions. Their revelries could be heard throughout the manor. She and her aunt had not made an appearance at the convivial party.

Instead, Lady Ogden and Mrs. Merriweather had retreated to the upper drawing-room, where they had spent the slow, dull hours in hushed conversation and needlework. Vulgar company was not to their taste. Almost a week passed, when they scarcely dared to show their faces outside the pleasant room, all to avoid any unpleasant discourtesy.

Toward the last – she perfectly recalled the incident, for it was after the frantic fright of that night – there had been her encounter with Sir William Talley. His insolent, slow perusal of her person had been singularly unnerving. She had never forgotten her impression of an unholy interest. Barely hours later, she was stationed at the viscount's bedside, waiting for her husband to die.

Lady Ogden shook free of her morbid recollections. She never thought of that time if she could help it. Her voice was sharper than she intended. "Mrs. Tower, I gave strict orders to you and to Somerset. The maids were warned to go about their duties in pairs, and then only when the gentlemen were below-stairs or out-of-doors."

"Yes, my lady. But Mary had forgot something. She turned back, you see. And so did the gentleman. He came up on her all unawares."

"Poor girl." Lady Ogden felt genuine empathy. *The crude deed, it's so swiftly done!* A singularly unpleasant possibility arose to her mind which made her feel nauseous. "Was it – Mrs. Tower, you must be completely honest with me! – was it my late lord?"

Mrs. Tower's round eyes opened very wide. Shocked, appalled, the housekeeper hurried to reassure her mistress. "No, *no*, my lady! I swear it wasn't!"

"I'm glad," she said simply. The relief she felt was immeasurable. She did not think she could have borne it if it had been her husband who had forcibly got the maid with his by-blow. *Henry could be such a bastard at times.* On a visceral level, the very idea that some other woman might carry the late viscount's child sickened her to the depths of her soul. Despite her troubled marriage, she had still been his lordship's wife and it had been her station in life to bear a child of their union. She had been despondent and sorrowed by her sad inability to fulfill her duty.

"What do you wish to do, my lady?"

"Do?" Lady Ogden blinked back to the present. "What do you mean?"

"Why, I wished to know if you was wanting me to turn the girl off, ma'am"

Lady Ogden was at once repelled. *Cast the poor girl out?* Destitute and with a bastard child, the maidservant's harsh fate would be sealed.

It was ironic, she thought grimly, that she had chosen ruination to *save* herself from abject poverty. "This girl – Mary, is that right? – is she good in her position? Does she have any relations?"

"Aye, my lady. Mary is good at her work. As for relations, I believe she has a married sister in the next county over."

Lady Ogden nodded, her thoughts evolving. She said slowly, "Then we shall send her to her sister. After the birthing, Mary will decide if she wishes to return to her position here. I will not simply turn her off without a character. I can see you are surprised, Mrs. Tower."

"It's not what I expected, I own."

Lady Ogden allowed herself a smile, though she felt not the slightest amusement. "We must take care of our own, Mrs. Tower."

"Aye, my lady." The housekeeper appeared impressed. She nodded her understanding. "I shall attend to the matter, just as you have said."

"You may go, Mrs. Tower."

After Mrs. Tower had left her, Lady Ogden sat for several minutes staring into the fire. The housekeeper's visit had stirred up things she wished she could forget.

Lady Ogden shuddered, haunted by past horror. The details of that last awful night were etched into her brain. *Mills had just left me.* She had been settling for bed when the door of her bedchamber had burst open. The late viscount had staggered in and thrust shut the door again. He had advanced on her. Loud, drunken, he had demanded his husbandly rights. He had violently backhanded her. She had worn the livid bruise on her face for weeks.

Lady Ogden tightly closed her eyes. *I can still feel him, clawing at me. The sodden brute.* But her husband the viscount hadn't been able to perform. Repeatedly, he'd attempted to mount, bellowing out his frustrated curses, roughly bruising her body...she shuddered.

"Enough, enough!" She beat the heels of her hands together. "I will not continue to sit here, shackled by the ugly memories."

For several months, particularly when she had the blue megrims, she had enjoyed the contentment she derived from working on her embroidered set of chair coverings for the dining room. It was an ambitious project. The intricate work was just the thing she needed to soothe her agitated spirits.

Lady Ogden fled her private quarters and made for the upper drawing-room. She was unsurprised to find her aunt was already ensconced in the pleasant room. Candlelight and a glowing fire welcomed her. Mrs. Merriweather's greeting was characteristically cheerful. "Oh, you are up from your couch. Come, my dear! We'll enjoy a delightful coze."

"I'd like that," said Lady Ogden, smiling fondly at her aunt.

The heavy blowing rain beat against the mullioned windows. The howl of wind was a primal discordant sound without. Several candelabras and wall sconces had been lit to provide illumination against the dimness of the afternoon. Lady Ogden settled comfortably near the warmth of the fire. She drew the needle in and out, listening with only half an ear to the gentle patter of her aunt's conversation. Lady Thane had sent over the latest *La Belle Assemblee* as she had promised and Mrs. Merriweather was voluble about the newest fashion plates.

Lady Ogden found her work did not wholly absorb her as it usually did. She could not shake out of her thoughts the under-maid's unfortunate predicament. It had sharply pointed up the deficiencies of her own situation. She had entered into a sensual bargain, a dishonorable means to win future security for herself and her elderly aunt, and she had nothing to show for her shamelessness. Her courses had come, just like clockwork.

So, you have not bred.

The viscount's hurtful words rang in her mind. She could not forget them, nor could she ignore the persistent question that kept popping up in her reflections. She let out a small, dispirited sigh. She had endured a fruitless five years of marriage. She had lost two babes and had never quickened again. Even if she did conceive out of her convivial society with the viscount, she wasn't at all certain that she could carry a child to term.

Her husband the viscount had not often coupled with her. He had never displayed a passion for her. Perhaps if her lord had spent more time at Delincourt...she shook her head. She knew she was trying to delude herself. *The last time he came to my bed* – she couldn't repress a shudder. *I'm glad, glad, he was impotent!* The horror of it still wielded power over her.

It was little wonder, when the new viscount had first voiced his shocking suggestion, that she had accused him of being as hateful as his cousin. She hadn't experienced much good at a man's hands. *Then my witless acquiescence, his immediate cocking. It's an astonishment that I am adjusted so well!* Unlike the late viscount, his lordship had demonstrated a robust carnal appetite where she was concerned. The lustful congress in her darkened bedchamber was proof that he thoroughly enjoyed their illicit liaison and his seed had been copiously spent. It would not be from any inadequacy on the viscount's part if her courses were not arrested.

Lady Ogden's unhappy brain circled around again – was she barren or was she not – and she murmured in despair. "How can I really know?"

"Did you say something, dearest?"

Lady Ogden looked up quickly. She was horrified by her indiscretion. "Why, nothing, aunt." She had been startled into jerking too hard on her thread and knotted the silk. She bent close over her work, hiding her face. Her fingers were trembling, but she managed to unsnarl the strand. The erratic tempo of her heart shortened her breath. She was appalled at herself. She had been so deep in melancholy reflection she had forgotten she wasn't alone.

"But I heard you quite plainly. What don't you know, Charlotte?"

Lady Ogden lifted her head and stared over at her aunt, who was waiting for her reply. *This is what comes of speaking one's thoughts aloud!* She lowered her eyes to hide her panic and began unsteadily plying her needle again. Her disordered mind floundered in a vast blank landscape. Scrambling for something to divert her aunt from the dangerous query, she began to rattle away in a disoriented, hasty manner. "Mrs. Tower came to see me. One of the under-maids is breeding. The girl was got with child. Remember when Henry and his friends were last at Delincourt? Oh, of course you do! I asked Mrs. Tower, but she assured me that it wasn't Henry who –"

Mrs. Merriweather clucked in distress. "Oh, my dear child. You mustn't fret yourself. *Of course*, it wasn't Lord Ogden!"

At her aunt's exclamation, Lady Ogden rapidly passed through mental review exactly what she had said. She flushed. "Yes, well, I had to make a decision, whether or not to turn the girl off without a character." She lifted her shoulders in a brief, telling shrug. "I couldn't do it, aunt. I couldn't turn her off. Not when I know for myself the sort of desperation this poor girl must be feeling."

Mrs. Merriweather stared at her niece in consternation. Societal rules were firmly established when it came to such unpleasant matters. "But whatever are you thinking? There is no question about what should be done," she exclaimed. "We can't have the girl *remaining here!*"

"She is to go to a married sister. When her confinement is done, and if she chooses to do so, she will return to Delincourt." As Lady Ogden repeated what she had said to the housekeeper, she became more certain of the soundness of her judgment. *At least in this matter,* she thought with acerbic self-mockery. "We must look after our own at Delincourt."

Mrs. Merriweather was struck by her niece's explanation. She said slowly, "Your compassion in the handling of a difficult situation might be unorthodox, but there is much to agree with in it." Mrs. Merriweather nodded. "Very well! It sounds a wise decision. But what are you going to say to his lordship?"

Lady Ogden hadn't considered that. Her aunt had raised a valid question. She deliberated for a moment, wondering whether she dared to go further. She decided she did have courage enough. She flashed a sparkling smile at her aunt. "Lord Ogden left the management of Delincourt Manor in my hands. I shall not tell his lordship anything about it."

Mrs. Merriweather was dismayed. "My dear! But Lord Ogden is master here. You are surely aware that you must advise him of the situation! You cannot set yourself up against the viscount."

Lady Ogden raised her chin. "Mrs. Tower is in charge of the female staff and she answers to me. The viscount put his stamp of approval on my management of the household. As I say, we shall not bother his lordship."

"Oh, my dear, are you certain that's wise?"

"This is women's business, aunt," said Lady Ogden, amazed at herself. Like her aunt, she had been trained from her earliest days to defer to the male head of her world. First, it had been her father, then her husband. She was dependent on the viscount. In all good conscious, she should indeed inform Lord Ogden of the under-maid's deplorable condition. However, she believed it was likely his lordship would take the usual action of their class when faced with the transgressions of their servants, which would be to terminate the wretched girl's employment and give the order for her immediate removal from the manor-house. Lady Ogden found she disliked very much that her decision would, in all likelihood, be summarily overturned. "No, I shall not inform Lord Ogden."

Mrs. Merriweather shook her head. However, she had seen that stubborn expression before. She gave way, not wanting to continue an argument, perceiving as she did that it might be exhaustive. It was easier to cede to her niece's judgement, so she shrugged philosophically and returned to her needlework. "Just as you like, my dear."

In the companionable silence that followed, Lady Ogden realized her happy accident; she had managed to divert her aunt's uncomfortable query. She breathed in a sigh of relief. The near-slip made her more aware of her surroundings and her subsequent reflections were not so deep that she forgot caution again.

*If I am barren...*She gave that pensive consideration. She could well be engaged in a futile endeavor. Not for the first time, she wondered why the viscount was willing to enter into a scheme that went counter to his own fortunes. Again, she brushed it aside. He was a man with a virile man's strong sexual appetites. That was reason enough. She was an easy conquest; she had fallen into his hands like a ripened fruit. With five empty years as hedge to his bet, he was willing to gamble that she would not produce an heir, all for the sake of regular bed sport. It was as simple as that.

If I am barren, what then? It did not bear contemplation. She would have become his lordship's carnal plaything without even the sop of justification that it was for procreation.

She did not know much of such matters, but it seemed to her that a mistress was always vulnerable to the caprices of her protector. *Vincent will surely tire of me. Henry certainly did.* Her husband the viscount had become quickly disenchanted with the wedded state. They had ended by living almost entirely separate lives. He was mostly situated in London, where he had lodgings, while she remained at Delincourt Manor. It had not made her unhappy. Instead, she had only felt relief that they lived apart, making more bearable the mistake she had made in her marriage.

The apprehension that was a constant specter, hovering at the back of her brain, flicked her like a whip. She could well be committing a far worse mistake. She steeled herself. *But I have to be certain! This is the path upon which I have set my feet. I have to go on! I must still have the viscount in my bed.* She knew she should hate with every fiber of her being the necessity.

Lady Ogden's feelings were ambivalent. She had learned to take breathless pleasure in the viscount's lovemaking. He was by turns tender and demanding, drawing forth her sighs and moans in the tumbled shadows of her bed. He was a sorcerer, working his magic on her quivering, shattering body. Yet she must not ever forget that their shocking liaison was solely for the conception of an heir. And to that end, she had bartered her body to him for his pleasure. *I am nothing more to him than his mistress, a convenience, one day to be discarded and forgotten.* For some inexplicable reason, she felt a dull pain flare beneath her breastbone.

Lady Ogden ignored the queer ache as she pursued her reasoning. She would not know if the viscount had gotten her with child until the following month. If her courses returned...The sliver of time that was her opportunity to change her precarious future was inexorably closing. *Either I shall be carrying his seed or it will be the poorhouse for my aunt and me. And I shall be forever his discarded whore.*

Lady Ogden had spoken up on behalf of the maidservant, but she was unhappily aware that there was no one who would champion her.

The clock struck the hour. Surprised, Lady Ogden glanced up at the clock face and began to put away her stitchery. The time had flown by while she was sunk in somber reverie. "Shall we go change for dinner, dear ma'am?"

"Of course. I shall meet you downstairs, Charlotte."

Lord Ogden was surprised when his cousin-in-law came into the drawing-room. He looked sharply at her. There was a pinched look about her face. He didn't know whether it was because she was feeling unwell or if her faintly dyspeptic expression was due to the clumsy way he had received her news that she had gotten her courses. He rather suspected it was the latter. He did not know how he was to retrieve his position in her good graces, and it was important to him on more than the physical level. Before he could think of anything worth saying to the purpose, Mrs. Merriweather entered the room and the opportunity was lost. Silently, he offered his arm to escort her ladyship in to dinner, and just as silently, she accepted.

The three-course remove was a testament to the cook's competency. However, two of the parties partaking of the dishes barely noticed what they were eating. Lady Ogden's appetite was indifferent. She did not attempt to break the subdued atmosphere that pervaded the dining-room, barely smiling at her aunt's desultory attempts at making civil conversation. The viscount wore a deep frown, obviously preoccupied with some weighty matter. She was very much aware that not once, since he had escorted her in to the table, had the viscount glanced in her direction.

Not that she wished him to do so, of course. However, if he had, it would have given her keen satisfaction to give him the cold shoulder. He had hurt her with his insensitive, flat statement. Letting the viscount know of her hidden anger would have been a balm of sorts to her lacerated emotions. *I might need him to bed me but I will not tolerate his disrespect,* she thought resentfully.

Shortly thereafter, she and her aunt rose from the table to leave Lord Ogden alone with his after-dinner port, retreating to the drawing-room.

"Why, Charlotte, such a drooping mouth and you are pale. Are you feeling out of sorts, my dear?"

"I have the headache a little" said Lady Ogden. Strangely, she felt sudden tears pricking at her eyes. Appalled by her lachrymose emotion, she said, "Forgive me, aunt. I will retire early to bed."

Mrs. Merriweather made no attempt to detain her. She would have liked a round or two of backgammon, but she satisfied herself instead with a few games of solitaire. When she was bored with that, she picked up the fashion periodical that Lady Thane had so kindly sent over.

Somerset eventually brought in the coffee urn. Mrs. Merriweather served herself and waited for Lord Ogden to put in an appearance but he did not join her. "A breach of courtesy, but I am willing to overlook it," she murmured to herself. She had a shrewd notion that his lordship was also feeling out of sorts, but for the life of her, she had not a clue why. "It's all very odd."

16

Lord Ogden entered the breakfast-room. At a swift glance, he saw only Mrs. Merriweather sitting at the table. A crease formed between his brows. Lady Ogden's absence hinted that she was indisposed again. He realized that his intention to engage Lady Ogden in civil conversation and request that she take a turn with him on the terrace had to be set aside. He had wanted an opportunity to smooth over his mismanagement of her news. It frustrated him that he could not talk with her.

His lordship brusquely nodded to Mrs. Merriweather and inquired of her health. The elderly lady responded with her usual cheerfulness. "And what of your niece, ma'am?"

"I understand the putrid throat is still making her feel under the weather, my lord."

"Indeed." The viscount heard the lady's response with skepticism. He thought it likely that Lady Ogden had confided to her aunt the truth. She was not suffering from a putrid throat at all, but from her womanly complaint. As a gentleman, however, he could never broach such a topic to the lady's aunt. He said only, "I trust Lady Ogden is swift to recover, Mrs. Merriweather."

The elderly lady offered firm reassurance. "Indeed, my lord. I'm sure she *will* soon be fully recovered."

Lord Ogden nodded. At Mrs. Merriweather's request, he politely passed over the marmalade. He was not feeling sociable. He had spent a restless night. He was not used to retiring to his own bed. It had cost him not to open the connecting door between the two bedchambers. When he had envisioned the desirable woman on the other side, curled warm in her bed, his shaft had throbbed with need. His frustration had been great. He had finally taken his pleasure with his own hand, only then being able to seek slumber.

After breakfast, Lord Ogden took a short, clipping ride across the acres of park, clods of mud thrown up by his mount's speeding hooves. The fresh air and exercise did him good. His dour mood lightened. *So I will not slip into her bed for a few nights. What is that?* When he returned, he was gratified to be informed by Somerset that the land steward had arrived by way of his own gig. The message served to restore his humor. "Excellent!"

Lord Ogden went to change out of his mud-splattered riding dress and in short order returned downstairs. He addressed the butler as he passed into the ground-floor study. "Somerset, I will be closeted all morning. Pray see that I am not disturbed."

"Very good, my lord."

Lord Ogden waited for Mr. Stockley to be brought to the ground-floor study. A few minutes later, the man entered. He carried by the handle a large and obviously heavy leather bag. The viscount observed that the land steward was a small man, his manner of dress countrified. "Mr. Stockley, I'm glad you have come."

Mr. Stockley bowed, his expression impassive. "My lord." The land steward did not expect much to come out of his meeting with the new peer. His experiences with the former viscount had left him with the gloomy impression that the nobility were capricious care-for-nothings, who wanted to be told nothing except what they could wring out of their encumbered estates. Without much optimism, Mr. Stockley opened the cumbersome leather bag to withdraw from it numerous documents, ledgers and a mass of other papers. Within minutes of meeting his new employer, he was already revising his expectations. The gentleman who had stepped into his cousin's shoes was decisive, his intellect engaged, his questions incisive. A cautious hope began to bloom in Mr. Stockley's spare chest.

The viscount and his land steward plunged into the business at hand and they kept at it all the morning. Lord Ogden was swift to appreciate Mr. Stockley's acumen, which his cousin obviously had not bothered to avail himself. For his part, Mr. Stockley was astonished by the energy which his lordship brought to the task at hand and the clipping pace he set over the process. The viscount asked for such detail that Mr. Stockley genuinely had to think over some of his answers. It was borne in upon him that his lordship was actually interested, which was a novel experience for the land steward.

At length, Lord Ogden pulled on the bell-rope to request that a luncheon be brought to the ground-floor study. Somerset and a footman carried in two heavily-laden trays, containing a cold collation of meats, cheeses, bread and fruit, along with wine. Mr. Stockley's eyes brightened. He had risen at an ungodly hour of the morning, sparing time only for a strong cup of coffee and stale roll before setting out for Delincourt Manor. He was very glad to see the plain meal, in particular the bottles of wine. He was famished and his throat was parched from speaking.

Lord Ogden himself barely broke for the mid-day meal. He was too keen to hear what the land steward had to tell him, and he was determined to absorb and understand everything in the shortest time possible. He took up a stance before the mantel, where he set down a wineglass and a laden plate. With a sandwich in one hand and a sheet of closely-written parchment in the other, he questioned the land steward on the document's contents. "You say that this record has to do with a property line dispute. Was it satisfactorily resolved?"

Mr. Stockley hastily swallowed a mouthful of cold beef. Clearing his throat, he said, "Aye, my lord, to each of your questions."

"At least something is satisfactory," said Lord Ogden caustically, giving another glance down at the parchment.

Mr. Stockley gave a perfunctory smile. He was uncertain yet how to take the new viscount. However, his lordship did not seem inclined to rail at him in blame for the dismal reports that he was obliged to make.

The hours passed, day eventually giving way to dusk, and the viscount ordered a footman to light the candles in several candelabras, so that he and the steward could continue to work long into the evening. Another cold collation and more wine constituted supper. At last, Lord Ogden decided to bring the day's work to a close. "We shall meet here again in the morning, Stockley."

"Aye, my lord."

For another two days, Lord Ogden spent most of his waking hours closeted with the land steward, breaking only for meals or for short rides for the exercise. He took Mr. Stockley with him on one such ride. By the time they returned to the manor, the land steward was much impressed and encouraged by what he had been shown of the improvements which his lordship had already begun to initiate.

Lord Ogden seemed indefatigable. Mr. Stockley's stores of energy were beginning to flag, and he had begun to seriously wonder whether he was going to ignobly fall over from exhaustion, before his lordship at last called a cessation to their labors.

"We have spent many long hours at this, indeed. We have covered a lot of ground." Lord Ogden wryly smiled. "I know you must be as wearied as I am, Stockley. So, let us part for what remains of this afternoon. Over the next few days, I shall read over the notes and think about all you have told me. Then I shall call on you again."

"Just as you wish, my lord," said Mr. Stockley, relieved to have a respite at last. "I shall drive back to Briarcrest Cottage, my lord, and I will hold myself ready against such time as you require my return."

"No, stay on here at Delincourt until I have need of you," said Lord Ogden firmly. "I want you close to hand. There are immediate decisions that must be made."

Mr. Stockley hid his surprise. "Very good, my lord." He bowed and effaced himself from the room.

When the land steward closed the door, Lord Ogden leaned his head back against the top of the tall-backed chair. A dull headache hammered at his temples, as it had done for several hours. His brain was seething with all of the information that had been fed into it and he ran in review some of the most worrisome points. His tired reflections turned more and more black. He'd hoped – but his cousin Henry had systematically gutted the lot. Now that the full facts about Delincourt Manor and the minor holdings had been laid before him, he was bitterly certain that what he had inherited was more a burden than a blessing. The entire estate was encumbered in one way or another; it was going to be a terrible draw upon his purse-strings. He'd already been forced to settle his cousin's outstanding gambling debts and most of the tradesmen's bills. The sums had been substantial.

Lord Ogden wearily glanced down at the stack of reports and accounting ledgers laying atop the desk. Mr. Stockley had carefully gone over every figure and every document with him. There had been little of good to impart. Most of the damage had been done at Delincourt, but the rents from the minor properties were not much better. "It was through no fault of Stockley's," he murmured, rubbing at his temples. The land steward had not been advanced funds or given permission to address the problems arising out of neglect. The viscount had seen for himself the crying need for the outgo of capital for repairs to the tenants' homes, for fencing and roads. He could well imagine what state the other properties were in.

At Delincourt, he had at least begun repairs on the worst of the inhabited cottages, endeavoring to give the tenants snugger dwellings to weather what remained of the harsh winter. He knew for himself what wretchedness the cold could bring, the aching of a man's bones, the misery of chilblains on hands and feet. He'd been bivouacked in the poorest of conditions on several occasions. The viscount snorted. *The horses here are better housed!* He had been surprised, then sardonic, when he had first inspected the stables. His cousin had not stinted when it came to the welfare of his precious horses and his custom-built carriages.

The manor house itself was drafty and needed attention. Dry rot had settled into some of the rooms where leaks in the roof had done damage. Sections of roofing obviously had to be replaced, but how much of it could be salvaged was not yet known. He would have to hire an architect, as well as skilled workmen.

Most disastrous of all, Mr. Stockley had informed him that most of the unentailed properties were newly tied up in outstanding mortgages. That had come as a crushing blow. He already knew he had not inherited a large, prosperous estate, but he'd clung to the hope that there were income-producing properties somewhere. If he was not to see the estate eventually cut up into pieces, with only Delincourt Manor and its demesne left, he must sink a large portion of his personal fortune into retiring those mortgages.

He wondered wearily whether it was worth the struggle, as struggle it surely would be. Every day he felt the lack in himself because he had not been bred to be a landowner. He was ignorant of most of what had best be done. For the thousandth time, Lord Ogden felt himself overwhelmed by insecurity and dread, a combination of emotions which he hadn't experienced since his subaltern days in the army on the eve of his first battle. It was a mentality alien to him. He had never seen his path less clear, not even when blinded by the acrid, lung-stinging smoke of the battlefield.

While it was true that his prize money had made him a wealthy man and most of his personal fortune was now invested in 'Change and was bringing in a tidy sum in interest, his income was not infinite. Redeeming all of the mortgages and making all of the necessary improvements to the estate would cost him dear. *Perhaps too much.* The viscount pressed the pads of his fingers against his tired eyes. "Damn you, Henry, you bloody stupid bastard!"

Lord Ogden jerked up from the chair and rounded the overladen desk. Striding to the nearest window, he stared out. He clasped his hands behind his back, his unhappy thoughts running rife. He would have to retrench, wherever he was able, as quickly as possible. He'd already sold off most of Henry's race horses at a loss. The rest of the expensive horseflesh would have to go, along with the custom-built racing curricles and one of the two phaetons. It was a pity. He'd hoped to be able to hold off until the hunting season to get a better price for the hunters. He sighed, dispirited. "I'll have Digsby handle the sales in London, as he did before."

He'd keep a couple of riding hacks and hunters, Lady Ogden's riding mare, a decent team to draw the phaeton and the old coach, and a horse for the gig. He'd have to study what other options might be available to him.

Mr. Stockley had diffidently expressed the opinion that some of the smaller properties ought to be sold. He'd have to look into that. Perhaps he should make a tour with Stockley of the places in question. The vision of a beautiful face came into his mind's eye. *But I cannot be gone from Delincourt just now.*

With determination, he brought his mind back to the issue before him. Economizing was all well and good, of course, but he also had to invest in his holdings to bring the estate back where it would begin to pay for itself again. Empty croft houses needed to be occupied by diligent tenants. Fallow fields needed to be plowed and put into prosperous service again. It would be a lengthy, careful process which would take years.

He saw what a fine line he had to tread. He had to keep wisdom close, listen to his advisors, and carefully weigh the benefits and disadvantages of every decision. He could not afford to make many false steps. In the end, if he was unlucky, he might find himself staring at ruin. *If I cannot persuade her to have me...*

"I could spend every groat, then lose it all if she is brought to bed of a boy!" Not once did it cross his mind to cheat on the hellish bargain he had made – his seed in exchange for her charms. There were ways to spend outside her body or French sleeves, after all, but he was no hardened libertine to thus use her. Pensively, he wondered what he would do, if he was so unwise as to sink all he had into the estate and ended as penniless as he had been when he first joined the regiment, all because he could not bring his cousin-in-law to the altar.

Lord Ogden gave a short bark of laughter. The answer was plain. "I'd buy another commission in the army." He was a soldier, trained for nothing else. He tried to persuade himself that if the worst happened – if he lost Delincourt and everything else he most desired – he could win back his fortune in the lengthy, ongoing war. The army had been forced to retreat for winter bivouac, but he was certain Wellesley meant to strike up deep into the heart of Spain. The viscount's reflections were grim. It would be by no means a short or an easy campaign. However, if he returned to the military during that campaign, it was entirely possible for him to win a larger fortune in prize money than before.

"If I survived the war, of course, God willing." No man knew when his time might come. He had never brooded on that and would not now. No doubt in the end his prize-purse would be large enough. He could begin again elsewhere. But it wasn't what he wanted. He stared out the window at the grounds and the wooded park beyond. "I want

Delincourt." He had spent most of his boyhood on these lands. It was his home as no other place could be. He wanted a loving, submissive wife and he wanted to be the proud progenitor of a growing family.

His bleak gaze was caught by a whip of movement below and he sharpened his gaze. The afternoon was drawing on and winter days were short. The hour's deepening shadows concealed much; but he recognized the flutter of a drab pelisse. Dressed warmly against the cold, Lady Ogden was walking in the dead gardens. Lord Ogden twitched his brows together. The lady no longer took exercise on the terrace in the mornings, as had become their pleasant habit, and one which he still observed. Instead, she took the air late in the day, when it could be reasonably supposed that he would be at his desk, deep at work on estate business. For all practical purposes, with Stockley's arrival, he had been in hibernation. Driven by his desire to grasp and understand the elements of his inheritance, he had taken most meals in company with the land steward.

For days, he had seen little of either of the ladies, except for a few minutes over the evening coffee in the drawing-room. On those occasions, Lady Ogden had been chilly in her manner. Indeed, she'd rebuffed most of his efforts to engage her in civil conversation.

Lord Ogden's frown deepened as he watched her ladyship's dawdling progress. His experience with the fairer sex tended more to bed-sport. When it came to the winsome creatures' minds, he admitted he was somewhat at a loss. However, he was certain the lady was avoiding private speech with him. Not since that day in the billiards' room had they exchanged anything more than shallow civilities. He still recalled the wretched look on her face when he had stated the obvious. The change in her exercise routine suddenly struck him as significant. He had assumed it had to do with her courses because she always seemed better later in the day. Now he wondered and he came to a most logical conclusion.

Obviously, she had not yet forgiven him.

"Damn it." He hadn't got her with child yet – that was still his entrée to her favors. He desired her. He admitted it. He craved her like a dying man wanted to slake his thirst. *Returning to her bed...* his loins tightened. He fervently hoped it would be soon.

He had told himself that he was taking revenge against his cousin – and against her for choosing his cousin over him – by mounting her as his mistress. He had long since recognized the delusion for what it was. For her sake, however it ended between them, he wanted her to birth a healthy, live child so that the largest of the annuities would become hers.

"Oh, bloody hell, L2,000 per annum," he muttered, appalled. He tightened his lips as he realized what the draw of such a large annuity would mean to the already heavily-encumbered estate. Yet of all the things he could possibly do to retrench, he could never draw back from that agreement. It was a point of honor to him. He'd sacrificed his personal honor - *my ghastly conduct in this very room!* - in the scorching affair. The weight of it had become a constant chafing against his conscience. *I can bear no more. I cannot. I will not.* Whatever the means he was forced to take to save Delincourt, he was determined he would not deprive her ladyship of one farthing of what had been promised. He had already demanded so much from her.

The black frown deepened over the proud bridge of his nose. His smoldering, intent gaze followed the figure of the woman slowly walking the frozen grounds. Grim, he muttered, "I will demand more. I must if I am to succeed."

THE DARK TENOR OF THE viscount's ruminations were not carried by some ominous spectre to disturb Lady Ogden, but her own thoughts were not easy. Her breath puffed white on the air and her gloved fingers were cold even inside her fur muff. Biting wind harried the hems of her skirts, circling ghostly fingers round her ankles. It was all very well to take a turn in the winter-blasted gardens, but the exercise didn't serve to distract her from somber reflection. Her inchoate fears and insecurities couldn't be escaped. *I must have him still...but am I barren? This affair...this wicked alliance...the uncertainty is insufferable!* She knew her mind was all of a jumble, disordered. It would have been a relief to have been able to communicate something of her anxiety. Her aunt was her only possible confidante. However, Mrs. Merriweather had made it abundantly clear that though she might have hinted at a hypothetical seduction of the viscount, the lady did not really want to discuss the actual possibility. Lady Ogden was certain her aunt would disown her if she were to reveal the reality of her carnal liaison.

However, being unable to confide in her aunt had placed her in an awkward situation. Over the past few days, Mrs. Merriweather had more than once remarked that her niece was acting distant toward Delincourt's lord. Just an hour earlier, in the stillroom, Mrs. Merriweather had gently chided her. "Your manner is unbecoming, Charlotte. You are too chilly. Pray recall that our dependence is all upon his lordship's generosity."

"I do recall it, aunt," she replied sharply. "I'm never allowed to forget it."

There was a short silence. "I hope that is not a rebuke directed at my head," said Mrs. Merriweather in hurt accents.

"No, no, aunt." Lady Ogden at once regretted her outburst. She managed to bring up a credible smile. "I'm just out of sorts. I will be better presently."

"Well! I *certainly* hope so. Gentlemen respond so much better to honey, my dear Charlotte!"

Lady Ogden had bitten back a hasty retort and left the stillroom. She had gone straight upstairs and rung for her dresser. Once Mills had outfitted her for the cold, she had fled from the gloom-ridden house out to the lifeless gardens. Lady Ogden cast a glance up at the imposing façade of the manor, wishing that she had never come to it. *Everything, everything is gone wrong.*

"I want to leave this place, if only for an hour!!" It would be lovely to be able to enjoy a different society, but she was still restricted by convention from making social calls on her neighbors. She wished fervently she could set the question of her problematic future behind her. With the viscount and her aunt as her sole companions, and being unable to be open with either one, it was becoming insupportable. The atmosphere was stultifying, adding to her restlessness. *I shall go mad. I must get out.*

A good, long ride would surely answer the purpose, but her mare hadn't been worked for days. No doubt a hard gallop would be needed to shake the fidgets out of the mare. A spirited, jarring ride was out of the question. She felt unequal to such a physical contest. There was another way to get away from Delincourt, she realized. *A drive in the gig!* If she was to add a shopping visit to the village, she could actually be gone for hours. Her spirit leapt at the welcome thought.

An outing to the village quickly took on an irresistible appeal. Once the inspiration had entered her mind, she wasted no time. She returned indoors with a spring to her step that had not been there before. After she had put off her outer garments, she descended the narrow back stairs to the kitchen to consult with the cook.

Half an hour later, Lady Ogden swept into the upper drawing-room, holding in her hand a small, closely-written sheet of paper. All of her earlier irritation with her aunt had vanished. "Aunt, I have a list from Cook and I'm driving the gig into the village. Would you like to go with me? The weather has remained constant."

"Yes, indeed! What an excellent suggestion. An airing will do me good," declared Mrs. Merriweather at once. She neatly folded up her work and put it into her workbasket. "A bit of shopping sounds like just the thing to raise one's spirits. Such a dreary afternoon! It has been so gray and cold! If you would not mind it, I should like to stop in at the milliner's and look at ribbons for retrimming my oldest bonnet. You will recall, I tacked black ribands onto it for mourning. Well! It's time to refurbish it with a bit of color!"

"I haven't the least objection. I'm always happy to while away time at the milliner's shop. Since Lord Ogden advanced me the new quarter's pin money, I'm plump enough in the pocket to indulge some of my fancies." With gathering cheerfulness, Lady Ogden led the way out of the upper drawing-room and walked with her aunt down the hall. "I've already sent word for the gig to be brought round. As soon as we have put on our bonnets and pelisses, we can be off."

Mrs. Merriweather nodded. Her mind was busy. She pursed her lips. "Perhaps we should look at muslins, too. The weeks are passing so swiftly. I think we should purchase some lengths to make up for your half-mourning. Some black pin-stripes would be nice, I think."

Surprised, Lady Ogden looked at her aunt. "Do you think so? I was not anticipating it to be necessary so soon. We are only just entering into February."

"Oh, yes, indeed." Mrs. Merriweather paused outside the door of her bedchamber. "You forget, Charlotte, it will take time to cut out the pattern pieces, sew them up and trim the garments. That elegant walking dress you showed me from the fashion plates, for instance, will require many hours of fine embroidering."

"I do see your point, dear ma'am." Lady Ogden's spirits rose even higher. It was just the sort of project she would most enjoy. She gave a happy laugh. "I have finished the last of the dining-room chair covers, so I'm eager to turn my fingers to something else. It will be so pleasant to refurbish my ugly, shabby wardrobe!"

"Just so, my dear Charlotte. I'm persuaded it *must* lift the gloom from your brow. You've been frowning so much of late."

"It will be a happy day, indeed, when I can throw away my blacks!"

17

Lord Ogden frowned out at the pelting rain. He was in a foul mood. He turned away from the window and glowered at the massive mahogany desk. It seemed to him to be hunkered down like some great beast, waiting to pounce upon him. That morning, he had pushed himself to go through more of the paperwork, but his inability to concentrate had finally driven him to his futile window-gazing. He had kept the land steward kicking his heels at Delincourt for the remainder of the week while he came to some decisions. There were other things he should settle, but he found that his mind was too fatigued to grapple with the intricacies.

"Stockley must wait," He had no wish to bend his tired mind anymore to the unending estate business. "I shall send him back to Briarcrest. He can at least make a beginning with the directives I've already given him."

Of course, it was inevitable that Lady Ogden should come into his thought, and once his brain fastened on the fascinating woman, he couldn't shake her free from his mind. *Six days.* Since her ladyship's courses had begun, it had been six days. Lord Ogden had counted every day and night. He had only a dim notion of how long a woman's courses lasted, but he'd watched her closely. He'd taken note when Lady Ogden began to come downstairs to the breakfast table again, how her languid air gave way to her usual energetic mannerisms. Most tellingly, she was taking the air almost daily once more.

Three days previous, she and Mrs. Merriweather had driven the gig on an afternoon's outing to the village. They had returned with all sorts of interesting parcels, wrapped in brown paper and string, most of which had obviously been destined for the kitchen, which a footman had carried away. However, there had still been several packages that they had carried upstairs, chattering cheerfully to one another of dress patterns and ribbons and trimmings. He had been glad to observe Lady Ogden in such good spirits. Her cheeks had been rosy from the outing. She had glowed with health and seemed completely recovered from her ailment.

Six days. Not by a flicker of her ladyship's lashes or by a whispered word did she signal him to return to her bed.

He considered that unpalatable fact, brooding over it. When she had told him of her courses, his lack of tact had wounded her. He had tumbled to that at the time. *She is herself again. The paleness is gone from her face.* Since she hadn't bid him to come to her bedchamber, he decided that she must still be angry with him. He felt that her ladyship was carrying a grudge too far.

"She holds onto her hurt like a shield," he muttered. "I must attempt to make amends."

The decision made, he didn't spare any more thought on his course of action

Lord Ogden quitted the ground-floor study. With outward calm, he made his way upstairs and went along the hall to the ladies' upper drawing-room, where he had never been invited. When he opened the door and entered, he spared the room a fleeting glance, gathering a rapid impression of a pleasantly-situated room, with light coming in from the east-facing windows and cozy warmth radiating from the crackling fire in the fireplace.

Lady Ogden and Mrs. Merriweather looked across the expanse of the room at him, with very similar surprised expressions, holding threaded needles poised in their fingers above their handiwork. They sat at a wide table, upon which was scattered a profusion of cloth pieces, scissors, pin cushions, pattern papers and open fashion periodicals.

The viscount felt he had stumbled into foreign territory. Some of his natural confidence deserted him. It was not unlike reconnoitering the enemy's ground. However, he told himself that one's social training could always be trusted to carry one forward. He'd get over the rough ground as fast as he could. Lord Ogden therefore smiled and bowed. "Forgive my intrusion, ladies. I hope I find you both well?"

"We are well, my lord," replied Lady Ogden, wondering at his lordship's sudden appearance. She couldn't imagine what could possibly have persuaded the viscount to invade their inner sanctum. It was awkward at best. She warily regarded him. She had not forgotten his blunt and painful statement to her. Surely, there must be some ulterior purpose behind his lordship's extraordinary visit.

Lord Ogden at once made his intention clear. "Lady Ogden, I know your habit of regular exercise. Since it is raining today, which makes it impossible for you to walk much outside, pray take a turn with me in the gallery."

Lady Ogden inclined her head, but she drew in the corners of her mouth. Her response was civil enough. "You are too good, my lord, but I'm quite comfortable where I am."

"Oh, go on, dearest! You've been fidgeting so for the past quarter hour! You are beginning to agitate *me*, and I am of the most placid of natures," said Mrs. Merriweather quickly.

Lady Ogden was amazed and indignant. She threw a disgusted glance at her aunt. It was a blatant falsehood. *Agitate, indeed!* She had not thought it possible that her aunt would resort to such unsubtle tactics, but here was an underhanded, obvious attempt to throw her together with the viscount. Good manners would not allow her to refuse. "Very well, aunt." She slipped her needle into her work before she rose to her feet. She inclined her head. "Thank you, my lord. The exercise will be welcome."

Lord Ogden offered his arm. She lifted her hand, but she barely touched her fingers to his forearm. She made certain her expression betrayed nothing, but her reluctance to accompany him was patent.

The viscount inclined his head to the other lady. "Do you care to join us, Mrs. Merriweather?"

"Oh, dear me, no!" Mrs. Merriweather shook her head. She said, with a deprecating chuckle, "It's kind of you to ask, Lord Ogden. But I'm not as spry as I used to be and would keep a dawdling pace. No, no, you and my niece will do very well without me, my lord."

Lady Ogden fumed over her aunt's cheery dismissal. At one stroke, Mrs. Merriweather had unwittingly undercut the agreement for discretion between herself and the viscount. While they saw one another on a daily basis, it was for short periods of time, always under the eyes of Mrs. Merriweather and the servants. Outside her bedchamber, she and Lord Ogden were circumspect. They did not keep company without Mrs. Merriweather's presence, their conversation was all polite civility, and they did not touch one another, unless it sprang out of protocol, as it did in this instance when she had accepted his lordship's escort. Besides all that, she didn't *want* to be in company with the viscount. She didn't want to be civil. She detested him. *Why had he come?*

Though she had concluded she must continue in their illicit liaison, she had not yet forgiven him for his hurtful *faux pas*. Nor had she formed a way to preserve her dignity while indicating to his lordship that she was willing for their convivial society to resume. *I'm no courtesan. I haven't any wiles.*

So, she erected her defenses and deplored the viscount's latest transgression. He had invaded their sanctum. In addition, his lordship's invitation to walk with him in the gallery, away from the rest of the household, broke every rule they had set down. For the last, however, even reluctant as she was to give his lordship any credit, she could not quite persuade herself that he was to be held at fault. He *had* invited her aunt to come along. It was of no consequence, however. *I really have no inclination for polite conversation, or indeed, any other kind, with his lordship.* With that stubborn conviction, she maintained what she hoped was a dignified silence. Unfortunately, she imagined she heard her aunt's voice in her head, saying that she was being pettish.

By now, they had walked through the passages to enter the gallery. It was a long room, on one side a row of curtained windows, interspersed with marble busts and statuary, and on the other, a wall mounted with numerous oil portraits of Delincourt ancestors. There was a massive fireplace at the far end, but no fire had been laid and the gallery had a decided chill. Lady Ogden withdrew her fingers from the viscount's forearm and with both hands pulled her large black shawl more closely over her shoulders.

Lord Ogden put his hands behind his back in an easy clasp, pacing along beside her. He waited until they had walked half-way down the long gallery before he spoke. With a glance down at her calm countenance, he said, "I'm glad Mrs. Merriweather did not accompany us. I wished to have a private word with you. Several days ago, I spoke brusquely to you. I wounded your feelings. I am sorry for it."

"Indeed, my lord? I don't know what you mean," she replied. She did not look up at him but stared straight ahead. She was surprised. She had not expected an apology. Such had never come her way before, not from her father nor from her late, unlamented husband. She didn't know what to make of it. It required an adjustment in her thinking, in her assumptions about relationships.

The viscount tried again. "I was naturally disappointed by your news. I did not express myself well. Forgive me, my lady."

Against her wishes, Lady Ogden was shaken. The viscount's obvious sincerity sliced through her defenses. Perhaps the anger she had borne against him was unreasonable. He could not have known what effect his blunt statement would have on her. She bent her head forward to avoid his penetrating gaze. She was not ready yet to acknowledge she had been even a little in the wrong.

Beside her, Lord Ogden sighed. "Please, Charlotte. Of necessity, there must always be frankness between us. Tell me, what was it about my words that so upset you? I wish to make amends."

Lady Ogden lifted her head. "It is just that –" She took a breath that hurt her constricted lungs. The confession would be painful, as she had known it would be. "When I lost the last babe, Henry said that he had made a bad bargain. He blamed me, you see."

The viscount thought he did. He inwardly cursed his blunt tongue. No wonder his reaction to her announcement had abraded her sensibility. "I'm sorry for it, indeed. My words were not meant to wound you, my lady."

"Indeed, you must not concern yourself, my lord," she responded in a stilted fashion. She was unused to such kind treatment and it threw her off-balance. She felt an ache in the region of her heart. Instinctively, she threw up the walls of her defenses again, and she snapped, "It's entirely my fault. I should be used to your ungentlemanly, boorish behavior."

Lord Ogden stopped stock-still to stare at her, astonished and stung. "My dear ma'am! We may have begun very ill, indeed. But I am persuaded that we have gone on better, have we not?"

Coldness swept through her. *He still thinks only in terms of what he can take of me!* She bitterly regretted the weakness that had led her to confide in him. All of her angst returned and she withdrew behind an icy exterior. She dipped a formal curtsy. "We have reached the end of the gallery. Thank you for your escort, my lord. I wanted a word with the housekeeper. I can easily reach Mrs. Tower's sitting room from this door." She opened the side door and shut it behind her, disappearing from his lordship's sight.

Lord Ogden was flummoxed. She'd acted as though he had not offered her an apology at all. *Boorish, ungentlemanly!* He was forced to concede there was some accuracy to her charges, but the admission didn't deflate his annoyance. Nor did it have any beneficial effect on the aching fullness that had gathered in his loins. He had been enduring for days a near-permanent state of semi-erection. Walking beside her, breathing in her distinctive feminine scent and the lavender water she bathed in, catching tantalizing glimpses of the swell of her bosoms, had been a pleasurable assault on his libido.

"Why does she have to consult with the housekeeper so bloody much?" he asked himself irritably. He swung around and strode quickly back down the length of the gallery, his bootsteps ringing on the worn plank floor. He had no more time to waste on the contrary woman. He had accounts to look over.

"I always have accounts to go over," he ground out, disgruntled. He would return downstairs to the ground-floor study and set about wrestling the figures into balance. While he did so, he thought savagely, he'd pretend each of the long columns was her lovely, white throat and he was throttling her into submission.

His fury abruptly collapsed on itself. *No, no, I wish to clasp her face between my hands, push up her chin with my thumbs, and kiss her into insensibility!* His angry yearning and her compliant reception of his attentions seemed all wrapped up together, somehow involving a great deal of stroking and murmuring. It was too much. His imagination was fired. All of a sudden, he was rock-hard. With an explosive imprecation, Lord Ogden made an abrupt detour to his private apartments.

After leaving the gallery, Lady Ogden threw herself into all of the household minutiae that she could find, all to avoid his lordship, and it evolved into a long busy afternoon. She went over the household accounts with Mrs. Tower, the menus with Cook, and accomplished sundry other such housewifely responsibilities. She also ran her aunt to ground in the stillroom, where that lady had retreated, and discussed with her aunt her most recent projects. It was a favorite hobby of Mrs. Merriweather's to make simple cosmetics and scented soaps. Though she wasn't a proficient like her aunt, Lady Ogden shared the lady's enjoyment in the making of rose- and lavender-water.

Though she had planned to spend much of her time in the upper drawing-room at work on the making of a new morning dress, done up in a lavender and black pin-stripe muslin, she did not return to her sewing. Lord Ogden had invaded once; he could do so again. She rather resented having the original plan of her day overset. Nevertheless, she ended with a feeling of satisfaction over what turned out to be a productive day.

By tea time, she was feeling a pleasant tiredness. Lady Ogden decided to recoup her energies in her sitting room for an hour or so. She wanted to pick up where she had left off in what was becoming one of her favorite novels, Miss Austen's *Sense and Sensibility,* which had only come out the November past. On her way back upstairs, she paused to tell a footman to relay the message that she wanted a tea tray in her sitting room. "Please inform my aunt that I shall be resting after tea."

"Aye, milady."

When Lord Ogden strolled into the drawing-room, he saw that Mrs. Merriweather was already seated behind the tea urn, preparing to pour. He made a civil bow. "Mrs. Merriweather, it's pleasing to find myself in your company again. I trust your day has gone well?"

The elderly lady smiled. "Very well, my lord. Shall you take tea?"

"I will, thank you." The viscount seated himself and glanced once or twice toward the drawing-room door. It remained closed. He became irritated but he hid it from Mrs. Merriweather as she served tea to him. "Thank you, ma'am." The lady offered a plate with a selection of biscuits, which he politely declined. He lifted his cup to his lips, sipped the brew, and set the cup down again with measured precision. "I trust Lady Ogden will be joining us for tea?"

He had not seen her ladyship since the inadequate, dissatisfying conversation in the gallery. However, he had heard through channels that Lady Ogden was dispatching her duties with characteristic efficiency. He was glad that her energy was back in evidence. In light of that, however, it was odd she was not present for tea. He came to the disgruntled conclusion that she wished to avoid his company.

"My niece sent word down to me that she is taking tea in her sitting room. She intends to rest afterwards." Mrs. Merriweather eyed the viscount with deep speculation. She wondered what had transpired between him and her niece while taking exercise in the gallery. Mrs. Merriweather considered herself to be an optimist. She hoped whatever it was would prove to be in her niece's best interests.

Lord Ogden frowned. He studied Mrs. Merriweather's countenance. There wasn't a jot of disquiet in that lady's amiable expression that he could see. "Is Lady Ogden not feeling well?"

"Oh, I shouldn't worry, my lord." Mrs. Merriweather deliberated over a choice between two biscuits. "These putrid throats, you know. One does feel a bit low afterwards."

"Of course, ma'am." Lord Ogden's voice was polite, but he didn't believe it. He was easily able to put another construction on her ladyship's absence. *She's taken a pet.* She certainly had not accepted his olive branch earlier that morning! Rather than socialize with him over the tea, she had chosen to shut herself up in her private apartment. She was acting as though they had quarreled and they had not. He was frustrated by her behavior. *What ails the woman?*

Lord Ogden slowly drank every drop of the tea in his cup. He bent a polite ear to Mrs. Merriweather's chatter, replying only when necessary, which was not often since the lady could run on quite happily on her own. He was therefore free to pursue his own speculative thoughts. His cousin-in-law was angry with him. She had escaped from his company as quickly as possible, but before doing so, she had made certain he would take her point that she would have none of him. All very well, but he could not bring himself to believe Lady Ogden had given up on securing the large annuity she would be entitled to for being brought to bed of an heir. By his calculations, there was still a narrow window of time for him to get her with child. He had been servicing himself by his own hand. It was an easy thing to picture her beautiful, ripe body and to cum, but it was not the same. His prick demanded release of a better kind. His heavy balls ached from need. *Too many days since I've screwed her sweet quim.* It was a state of affairs which could not be tolerated. He needed a good rogering. She had willingly entered into their bargain. *By heaven, I will not take meekly to the breaking of it!*

"So, have you had any word, my lord?"

Lord Ogden stared, uncomprehending, at Mrs. Merriweather. He realized from the lady's inquiring expression that she was waiting for his reply. Quickly, he ran through his mind what he vaguely recalled he had last heard her say. "Oh, Rev. Major Ledger! I have indeed had a letter from him, ma'am. He informs me that we shall have the pleasure of his company before the end of the month."

"What excellent news! We shall be most happy to welcome the gentleman to Delincourt, especially if he is anything like our dear Rev. Crawford. *He* was a such good friend to us!"

"It's kind of you to say so, ma'am." Lord Ogden was pleased to hear the lady's good opinion of his late father. Rather more attentively, he inquired into Mrs. Merriweather's plans for what remained of the afternoon. The lady prattled on about her projects in the stillroom, and as he listened, Lord Ogden began to realize that Mrs. Merriweather's work would most likely keep her occupied for some time. His attention sharpened and he put several questions to Mrs. Merriweather, who was very gratified by his lordship's interest. Then tea was over and he civilly parted ways from the amiable lady. Without a backward glance, Mrs. Merriweather bustled away to tend to her own business in the stillroom.

Lord Ogden did not hesitate. He seized on the opportunity that was so fortuitously granted to him. Mrs. Merriweather would be occupied at the other end of the manor. It was late in the day and the servants were going about their remaining chores downstairs. The wing where Lady Ogden's private sitting room was situated would be near deserted.

He had attempted to mend the rift between them. She would have none of it. Her ladyship was still holding him at arm's length. The viscount intended to put an end to that. He might not be the most flowery of fellows in conversation, but he did know how to pleasure a woman. He was confident that he could overcome any reluctance on the lady's part to willingly participate.

He swiftly trod up the stairs, rounded the turn to the upper landing, and leaped up the remaining flight to enter the hallway. He was already in anticipation of having the lady to himself. *My God, my prick is eager!* Behind his fall, the building pressure was nearly unbearable. There would be no leisurely undressing or making use of a soft bed, but that was of little moment.

He'd take a flyer.

18

Lady Ogden poured another cup of tea from the china pot and sweetened it with a small lump of sugar. Lifting the cup to her lips, she sipped in contentment. It was peaceful. The clock on the mantel ticked. Behind the latticed metal screen, the fire quietly crackled. She settled back, lifting the novel up, and became absorbed again in Miss Austen's work. She felt she now had more insight into the two sisters' characters than when she had first read the story. *I exhibit Elinor's cool, outward appearance, but I have experienced Marianne's passionate nature.* She set aside the tea cup and turned another page.

On a knock, the door to her sitting room was opened. Lady Ogden glanced up, setting a finger to mark her place on the book page. She supposed a servant had come to take away the tea tray, but it was not. It was the viscount.

When she met the banked heat in his dark eyes, she caught her breath. She didn't know why her heart lurched, *trepidation...anticipation,* and she didn't she want to explore it. *I am not in the least like Marianne, plunging with reckless abandon into passion! Of course, I'm not!* Being reduced to scolding herself angered her. She said coldly, "I did not wish to be disturbed."

Lord Ogden shut the door behind him. Without taking his gaze from hers, he deliberately turned the heavy key. At the distinct click, she widened her eyes before narrowing them again. She was conflicted, a prey to speculation and indecision.

The viscount bowed. "I'm sorry to disturb you, my lady. But I shall not allow you to hide away from my company."

"I'm not *hiding away*, my lord! I merely wished for my own company this afternoon." She gestured with her hand at the open book on her lap.

149

"You have forgotten the urgency behind our *tête-à-têtes*."

Lady Ogden blinked, then blushed rosily. She was furious with herself for that self-betraying fluctuation of color. It was infamous of him to refer to their private dealings. Yet on another level, she was glad; *she* had not been able to broach the matter. She responded frostily, "I have forgotten nothing."

She hated that her heart was uncomfortably thumping. She certainly had not forgotten the hurt he had dealt her, nor his callous evaluation of their relationship. As for what else she recalled...of a sudden, her cheeks scorched. *I must not – no, I will not think of such things!* She closed the book with a snap. She *was not* like the passionate Marianne, she repeated to herself. "I do not believe it constrains us to sit in one another's pockets."

"You are wrong, my lady. That is precisely what it means." His lordship gestured at the upholstered settee situated across from her wingchair. "May I join you?"

"You may not!"

He ignored her sharpness and sat down anyway. He sprawled at his ease, one knee bent and his boot planted flat, his other leg stretched out, his heel on the floor. Anticipation tightened his taut middle, beat heavily in his veins. "I believe we must come to a better understanding, my lady. Time runs short. You would do well to avail yourself of my singular...services."

"You are despicable," she breathed, even as tiny goose-bumps rose up on her arms. His words resonated powerfully inside of her; a quiver blossomed low in her belly. *No, I am merely annoyed,* or so she told herself. He was bent on pricking at her sensibilities and undermining her composure. Uneasily, she recalled the suggestive grate of the key turning in the lock. She inhaled sharply, at once certain. *The look in his eyes...it is not for conversation he has come!*

The viscount shrugged. "I care little what you think of me, my dear."

Struck on the quick, she exclaimed, "That is quite obvious!"

"Perhaps I should tell you that I do not mind performing the services of a seed-ox."

Lady Ogden hastily got to her feet. She was breathing rather faster than normal. With a few crude words, he'd conjured up robust carnalities and sweet intimacies. A pleasurable thrill fluttered through her nerve-endings. "You are insulting, my lord."

"On the contrary. I make compliment where it is due." The viscount smiled up at her. His falcon eyes glittered in his sun-browned face. "Come here, my sweet puss. Straddle my lap."

"I will not!"

"I think you will." Lord Ogden's mirthless smile twisted. "Tell me now! Tell me that you do not want me! And you don't want me to get you with an heir!"

They stared at one another, his demanding gaze challenging, hers defiant; but in the end, it was her gaze that dropped first. Without a word, she set aside the volume on the occasional table and moved toward him. Her pulse ran a swift, pattering rhythm. She vowed she wouldn't let him see how much he affected her. She haughtily looked down at his sprawled, wide-parted legs, and said shortly, "I have no experience of this."

He held out his hand, a polite gesture which set her teeth on edge. "Allow me to help you into the saddle, my lady."

She flushed scarlet, but she merely pressed her lips together and took his hand. He guided her down onto his lap until she straddled him, her legs bent at the knees alongside his muscular thighs and resting on the settee cushions, her skirt and petticoat bunched up around her hips. Vulnerable, exposed in more ways than one, she asked sarcastically, "I trust you are comfortable, my lord?"

He reached between them, his fingers brushing her belly, branding her with the slight touch. He unbuttoned the fall of his pantaloons and freed his thickened member from confinement; it sprang forth, hard and upright. "I will be more comfortable presently, I daresay."

She could not help casting a downward glance. Her eyes widened. His large, swollen shaft jutted up from the opening in his nether garment. The turgid, ridged flesh pulsed slightly in time to his heartbeat. The broad head was nearly purple in color; milky fluid beaded at the pouted slit. She had never seen him in the light of day. The sight was shocking – but unspeakably arousing.

Lord Ogden's ears caught from her a swift, in-drawn breath. Relief and carnal expectancy coursed through him. He felt her legs tense alongside his thighs. His eager prick jerked in reaction. *I am burning for her, as she will burn for me.*

The viscount guided one of her half-reluctant hands to his waiting flesh. He curled her slim, warm fingers around his prick. "We shall learn better how to please each other. This is how it is done." Clasping her hand beneath his, he showed her the rhythm he preferred. He half-closed his eyes. The feel of the tight circle of her fingers, slowly pumping his shaft, was exquisite. His breath quickened. "Just so, Charlotte," he murmured huskily. "That's very well done."

She made another breathless hiccough, realizing it only when she felt the soft air escape from between her lips. Resistance crumbled. The flexing of her hand, the feel of his thick, velvet erection sliding between her fingers, stirred in her a liquid heat, pooling deep beneath her pelvis.

He put a calloused hand behind her neck and gently pulled her head down to meet his lips. His breath was warm, his taste was the clean bitter of dark tea. His kiss was bold and possessive. She opened her mouth, greedy for more, and his hot tongue slid along hers. She sank into the sensual delight, barely aware of her brain's incoherent alarm. *I am undone, undone!* When he reached beneath her, sliding his fingers lightly over the lips of her intimate entrance, she reacted with a light shudder, as he must have known she would.

The viscount lightly worked her warm, furry quim with his fingers and palm. He knew well what pleasured her. It wasn't long. She was breathing more rapidly. Her moisture wetted his hand. The pearl at her gate swelled. The head of his prick was weeping. Much longer, and he would spend in her hand. Driven by urgency, he reached under the dark folds of her daydress and grasped her hips, rocking her forward against him. "Guide your pretty twat onto me, Charlotte," he commanded hoarsely.

"Oh, yes, *yes.*" She was gone too far. She wanted him inside her. She got to her knees and used her hands to position his thick organ. She shuddered when his cap breached her slick, heated opening. She bore down onto his hard shaft, taking him in, feeling him stretch her, filling her. Her whole being quivered with sensation.

Lord Ogden growled as his taut, strained prick slid home into the dark, constrictive sleeve of her core. He avidly watched her face. Her eyes fluttered shut; her lips parted; her head dipped forward in a weighted nod. Her hands fell onto his shoulders, her fingers tightening through the fabric of his coat. *She wants it, too, by God!*

Lust torched him. He could hold no longer. Curving his hands around the sides of her firm, bare buttocks, he pulled her more firmly into place. His hot prick flexed inside of her and she uttered a sibilant moan. "You like to ride, do you not, Charlotte?"

He lifted and lowered her in slow rhythm, his cock moving in and out of her juicy quim with a moist, sucking sound. He said gutturally, "Tell me, love. Tell me how much you like to ride." Her eyes suddenly opened, her green stare a blaze of resentment. He mockingly smiled up into her flushed, indignant face. *"Do you not?"*

"Very well! If you must hear it, I do!"

"We shall canter just a little longer." The viscount gripped her flanks tighter. With all the fabric bunched between them, he could not see their joining, but he could feel every tight slide of his full prick, the retreat and approach, again and again. *Fuck, fuck, fuck, fuck, fuck.* It was like measured hoofbeats – it was the heavy drum of his heart.

The hands gripping tight the globes of her arse mastered her, directed her, set her rocking in his heated saddle. She gave in to the deliberate rhythm. The delicious sensation began to consume her. Slowly, slowly she was spinning out onto a hot, churning sea; waves gathered, swelled, receded, only to gather and crest – she was buffeted again and again. *I am lost, lost!* Somewhere, from down deep in her throat, she gave a low mewl.

Through a narrowed gaze, he watched the intensity in her flushed face, reveling in her ripening passion. Her eyes were closed tight, her lashes feathered against her delicately-tinted skin. She was biting her lips to crimson. Soon, there was a tell-tale hitch in her breath. A slight quake rippled through her tiniest, most intimate muscles, squeezing his sensitized cock. *She was ready at last,* he exulted.

"Now for the gallop!" He thrust hard upwards, burying himself. She cried out in hoarse delight. He bucked, impaling her, burying himself to the hilt, over and over, every time he brought her down onto his strong shaft. She was making sounds, little whispery, breathy sounds, that spurred him on.

Lord Ogden shut his eyes, awash with intense pleasure. His breath came fast and hard in his chest. The friction of his powerful prick, sliding against the hot resistance of her walls – the rogering was an elemental, burning forge. He thrust again, more powerfully, canting his shaft at a different angle.

"Vincent, *yes!*" She was almost sobbing. She sunk her fingers into his shoulders. "Do that, do that!" She twisted in his arms, tossing her head.

He snapped open his eyes to a fetching sight. Under the confining gauze of her fichu, her lush breasts spilled over the top edge of her daydress, indecorously bouncing. He huffed a short groan. "Such pretty little apples! I should like to bite that white flesh, to suck on those rosy nubbins!"

"You-you shouldn't say that," she gasped. Exhilarated delirium was swiftly pushing her to the cliff's edge. But it was his words that fired the sensuous vision in her fevered brain. She made a mindless shimmy, side to side, setting her breasts to gamboling in their lacy cage.

He gave a low laugh. "It excites you, doesn't it? Then I shall tell you more." In rhythm with the rapid tempo, he spoke to her roughly, deliberately titillating her. "I *enjoy* fucking your tight little body. Your twat is hot and tight!" He thrust again, to graze the place that made her so wild, and was rewarded by an ecstatic squeal. Gritting his teeth, he panted, "I'll split you in half with my lusty cock! I'll roger you to the bollocks! My seed will spew like thick bull-mettle!"

His low-uttered, coarse words filled her eager ears. Her thrilled brain was made drunk by his vulgar expressions. She became more and more aroused as his shocking monologue continued. *Quim...bull...fuck...*

She moaned low in her throat. The rising crescendo of her pleasure could not be long endured. His ridged, thick-veined shaft rubbed fiercely against the little quivering nubbin, his flint striking sparks at her tinderbox. "There! Ah, there!" He obeyed, thrusting upwards at an exquisite angle. She shivered, she shivered. A champagne froth bubbled through her brain. Fire enveloped her flesh. The whole of her skin flushed hot beneath her clothing. Her breath sawed as she began to beg. She dug her nails like claws into the shoulders of his coat. *"Vincent, do not stop!"*

His grating reply rasped in her ears. "Have no fear! I shall screw you soundly!"

Reaching the heights came seconds later. She threw back her head and her spine arched. His tight fingers flexed almost cruelly on her hips, holding her tight in place. His flanks surged upward and he stiffened beneath her, digging his heels into the floor. They shuddered together in *la petit mort*. She collapsed forward against him. His muscular arms came up around her. Swift-beating hearts echoed one another. Heavy, shortened breathing marked the silence. At length, she stirred, and he helped her to dismount and stand.

Shaken, Lady Ogden shook out the folds of her black skirt and petticoat. Her heartbeat was still tumultuous. A fine sheen of moisture glazed her skin. She mechanically adjusted her bosoms back into their proper place beneath the modest round bodice of her merino daydress. His spent warm seed seeped from her still-thrumming, feminine core. Her tumbling thoughts seemed like so much flotsam. *I shall...I shall need...*

In concert with her faltering thought, his lordship pulled a fine linen handkerchief from his coat pocket and wiped white beads of spume and glistening moisture from his virile shaft, before tucking himself away and buttoning up his fall. Again, the sight of his physicality in light of day was a shock to her. She watched in dazed bemusement as he leisurely got to his feet. He turned and walked toward the door.

The viscount reached out to turn the heavy key. With the click in the lock, he remarked, "A delightful tiff, my dear." He opened the door and strolled out of her private sitting room, closing the door behind him.

Lady Ogden snatched up a cushion and threw it at the oak panels of the door. "Insufferable man!" The quiver of a smile edged her lips.

The viscount had made his point. The carnal exercise had left her feeling marvelously well. On a delicious shudder, she folded her arms around herself. *I had forgotten! How hot, and velvety, and impossibly hard!*

Flushing, she realized the glow left behind by her sensual satiation made her yearn for more. She wanted the thrilling experience again. She wanted to be possessed, to be made to squirm and shudder, until she broke into a thousand pieces.

I want him to speak coarse words that make me burn.

Lady Ogden put her hands to her hot cheeks. "What madness is this? What possesses me? He has some power, some hold, over me. I cannot be such a fool!"

Yet it seemed she was just such a fool.

When the viscount entered her bedchamber that night, she lifted her arms to him. It was a sweet surrender which he savored to the fullest.

19

The butler brought the post, stacked on a silver salver, into the breakfast-room. He placed it on the table beside the viscount's elbow. "Thank you, Somerset."

Lord Ogden flipped through the mail. A few duns – he'd send those to Digsby – a letter from the solicitor himself, and a few others he did not recognize but which he thought might be condolences from neighbors and acquaintances. He plucked one from the rest. "Lady Ogden, you have a letter." He stretched over the table to hand it to her.

"Indeed?" Lady Ogden did not receive much correspondence, excepting from neighbors or the rare piece from her sire. She took the missive, glancing curiously at the direction but as it meant nothing to her, she assumed it must be from her father, Sir Martin Stockton, writing from his new address. Breaking the wax seal, she unfolded the crackling sheet, and saw that the letter was written in an unknown hand. Her gaze swept to the signature, and she said blankly, "Why, it is from Sir William."

"Sir William! How very odd, to be sure." Mrs. Merriweather at once set down her marmalade-and-toast, looking over at her niece. "What does it say, dearest?"

Lady Ogden had by this time acquainted herself with the contents of the short note and she handed it to her aunt. "Read it for yourself, ma'am."

"Sir William?" inquired Lord Ogden, raising a dark brow. "Is this someone whose name I should know?"

"Sir William Talley. He was one of Henry's bosom-bows," said Lady Ogden briefly. "He has sent his condolences."

"Very proper," commented Lord Ogden. He was unheeded by the two ladies, whose mutual astonishment was open. The viscount felt a stir of interest and watched their faces.

"Extraordinary!" pronounced Mrs. Merriweather, giving the note back to her niece. "Quite unexceptional, however."

"Isn't it," agreed Lady Ogden, slowly refolding the letter.

Lord Ogden noted the perturbation in her ladyship's expression. "I take it, then, that you did not expect to hear from this gentleman."

Lady Ogden shook her head, her brows puckering in a frown as she looked down at the unexpected communique. She recollected with perfect clarity the awkward, mortifying encounter with Sir Willian that morn in the upper hallway. He had fairly stripped her with his bold, knowing gaze; she had detested the gentleman's overt salaciousness, and for an instant, she had even known a spark of fear. Yet he alone, of all Henry's friends, had offered a few kind words to her after the burial service before leaving for London. *And now this, weeks later, a note from his hand.* Her puzzlement was echoed by her aunt.

"One does not know what to make of it," said Mrs. Merriweather with a baffled shake of her head.

"Sir William is not the sort one would expect to extend his condolences upon the death of a friend?" queried Lord Ogden.

Lady Ogden and her aunt exchanged a quick glance, which spoke volumes between them. Catching the byplay, Lord Ogden wondered just what was going through their minds. His curiosity was not satisfied by Lady Ogden's murmured reply. "Henry's friends were not given much to the social courtesies."

Mrs. Merriweather snorted at her niece's restrained remark. "Ramshackle care-for-nobodies!"

"I see." Lord Ogden thought he did, too. Taken with what he had already known about his cousin's character and what he had since learned, it came as no surprise to him that the late viscount had surrounded himself with the same sort of wastrels as Henry had been himself. He was unfortunately reminded that there was work awaiting his attention. He'd delay it as long as conscience would allow, though. On the thought, he smiled at the viscountess. "Lady Ogden, we've not taken our usual exercise yet this morning. The day bids to be fair. Would you care to take a turn on the terrace?"

Her ladyship's gaze waivered. She fiddled with the laces at the front of her gown. "I think not, my lord."

Lord Ogden inclined his head. He returned to sorting through the mail. Shortly thereafter, he excused himself to the ladies and repaired to the ground-floor study, where he closeted himself for several hours.

Lord Ogden was sick to death of staring at columns of figures and forcing himself to read through lengthy legal documents. As for the necessary correspondence that was required, it had become a heavy burden. He got up out of the chair and stretched mightily until his bones popped. "A good, hard ride would suit me." He entertained the notion of asking the viscountess to join him, but she had already turned down a walk on the terrace when he had suggested it at breakfast. She had given no explanation and he had asked for none. He had a shrewd notion that her feelings were in conflict over what had occurred the day before. *The lady's pride is sorely tried.* The corners of his stern mouth turned upward. The delectable flyer in her sitting room had been followed last night by her eager welcome of him to her warm bed. His loins stirred in remembrance. He had enjoyed her submission to his insatiable desire.

Lord Ogden thought he would have the bailiff go with him on an inspection. *No, not a ride with Bartlett.* He stood irresolute for a moment, before he formed the decision to return a courtesy call to his neighbor at the Grange. He had neglected his social duties for too long, he reflected. "I would be surprised if the gossips have not already labeled me an inhospitable hermit."

He was glad he had at already returned a call to Thane Hall. His old friend and the lady of the house had been all affability. It was good to establish amiable relationships with his nearest neighbors. He would not be backward in doing the same with Mr. Kelton. He went to the door and called a footman to him, ordering the man to carry a message to the stables to have his horse brought around. Over his shoulder, and already making his way upstairs to change into riding clothes, he added, "I shall be down in a quarter hour."

"Aye, my lord."

Lord Ogden enjoyed the ride. For once, it was for the sheer physical exhilaration. He was not accompanied by the bailiff or the land steward. He was not on his way to inspect the progress being made on some project or other. His brain was not consumed with profit and loss or weighing options for the wisest improvements. He was simply out riding the countryside without any object but to call upon a neighbor. The prominent crease between his brows eased.

When Lord Ogden arrived at the Grange, the butler opened wide the door and without hesitation ushered the viscount into the drawing-room before going away with his lordship's card. It was only a few moments before Mr. Kelton entered and came forward to shake the viscount's hand. "My lord! This is a welcome surprise! But come into the library directly. There is a warm fire and I shall offer you a good glass of sherry." While he was speaking, he led the way out of the drawing-room, across the shallow circle of the entrance hall, and into a well-appointed library.

Lord Ogden looked around. While doing so, he drew off his riding gloves, placed them inside his hat and set the beaver upside down on a small table, together with his crop. He had been curious to see the Grange. On his ride up the graveled drive to the front door, he had been impressed what a happy difference had been made in the grounds since his last visit some five years before. Now he observed, since the day he had waited upon Sir Martin Stockton, that the inner sanctum had also undergone a welcome transformation. The dirty, chaotic clutter he recalled had disappeared and the books on the shelves were well-dusted and organized. Daylight streamed through the clean panes of the double windows. The candles of a candelabra sitting upon the desk were lit, shedding a paler light. "A pleasant room, Kelton."

"Oh, aye. It is where I attend to my accounting, which is why you have discovered me still inside this salubrious morning."

"It's good of you to see me, then."

"Not at all, my lord." Mr. Kelton gestured toward the wingback chairs sitting in front of the fireplace. A well-fed fire burned behind the iron grate. "Pray be seated. I'm glad you have come to call upon me." As Lord Ogden chose a chair and sat down, Mr. Kelton moved to a credenza where a decanter and glasses stood on a tray and poured a measure of sherry into two glasses. He walked back to hand one of the glasses to his visitor. "This was in my last order from the vintner. Give me your opinion, my lord."

Lord Ogden admired the pale, straw-colored sherry in the glass before he tasted it. He was surprised by the quality; it was light, delicate, and tangy on his palate. Mr. Kelton obviously did not believe in stinting on the cost of stocking his wine cellar. "Very nice indeed!"

His host was obviously gratified. Mr. Kelton sat down in the wingback opposite, sipping from his glass and content to wait upon his lordship. For a few minutes, Lord Ogden simply relaxed, tasting the dry sherry with appreciation more than once. "Kelton, I understood from our previous conversation you have been renting the Grange for a few years. How do you find it?"

"I have, my lord, for five years now. It's a tolerable place, very much more tolerable than it was when I found it," said Mr. Kelton with a hearty chuckle. "When I first set eyes on the house, I desired to live here, no matter that it was very neglected."

"My bailiff, Bartlett, told me that you have a good reputation for managing the land."

"Indeed?" Mr. Kelton blew out his cheeks, pleased. "I thank him for his kind opinion, my lord. It's true, I have diligently undertaken to repair the damage resulting from a bad landlord. I've plowed more of my blunt into the Grange than I should, since it is not my own property but rented from Sir Martin Stockton. Are you acquainted with the gentleman, my lord?"

"I knew him when I was a boy. My cousin-in-law, Lady Ogden, is the baronet's daughter and her aunt, Mrs. Merriweather, is the gentleman's sister-in-law."

Mr. Kelton's blunt features turned ruddy. "I beg your pardon, I'm sure, my lord. I would not have spoken so disparaging-like if I had known. I have no wish to offend."

Lord Ogden laughed. "You haven't offended me, sir! Indeed, I recall that I heartily disliked Sir Martin. He was not a prepossessing gentleman and he proved to be an embarrassment to his family, so you have no need to apologize. I like frank opinions."

Mr. Kelton's face relaxed. "I'm glad to hear it, Lord Ogden, for I like blunt speech myself. I shall say only one thing more. I wish very much that Sir Martin would see his way clear to sell the Grange to me, but he has refused me many times."

"Perhaps Sir Martin will eventually change his mind," suggested Lord Ogden. He raised his glass to his lips and swallowed some more of the excellent sherry.

Mr. Kelton shook his head. "I doubt I shall see such a happy outcome. When I last saw the gentleman, this past fortnight, I was shocked at how unwell he appeared. I should be saddened, indeed, to part with the place if Sir Martin should meet his maker. Sir Martin's heir, whoever he may be, might well want the place for himself."

Lord Ogden lowered the wineglass. He was surprised and showed it. "You have seen Sir Martin so recently, Mr. Kelton?"

"Aye, it was just above a week ago. Sir Martin comes up rarely from London, but there have been times when he wishes to have the rent paid to him a little early. Otherwise, the matter is handled through a solicitor in town, which I own I do prefer." Mr. Kelton eyed the viscount's thoughtful expression. "Has he not called at Delincourt, my lord?"

"No, he has not," said Lord Ogden slowly. His inevitable reflections he kept to himself, but his host was not at all stupid.

Mr. Kelton pursed his lips. He shook his head. "His daughter so recently widowed, too! Forgive me, my lord, but I disapprove of such a lack of respect."

Lord Ogden returned an indifferent answer and passed on to a question about the new drainage at the Grange. A lively discussion evolved, during which Mr. Kelton retrieved the bottle of sherry and refilled the two wineglasses. Despite their disparity in rank, the viscount and Mr. Kelton found that they had much in common. They were each attempting to bring back prosperity to ill-managed lands. Lord Ogden was not above soliciting his neighbor's advice on a matter or two and Mr. Kelton was pleased to discover that his lordship wasn't at all high in the instep. He thought perhaps it stemmed from Lord Ogden not having been bred up as one of the peerage, but rather, had been an officer in the army and was familiar with dealing with his fellow men.

When later it was learned by his neighbors that the viscount had called at the Grange, Mr. Kelton was asked for his impressions of the new viscount. He replied that his lordship was as long-headed as he was affable. "A good, sound man. I liked him," he stated unequivocally.

The gentlemen got along famously and they talked until Lord Ogden chanced to glance up at the mantel clock. He realized he had been sitting with his host for more than an hour. He exclaimed, set aside his glass, and got to his feet. "I have taken up too much of your morning, sir! I shall take my leave now, but we must certainly talk again." He retrieved his hat, gloves and crop.

Mr. Kelton had also gotten to his feet. "You are welcome here at the Grange at any time, my lord."

"Just as you are at Delincourt, sir." Lord Ogden held out his hand. Mr. Kelton shook it, much gratified by his lordship's civility. "Thank you, Kelton. Good day to you."

Mr. Kelton walked out with his lordship, calling for the viscount's horse to be brought round. He stood on the porch, talking casually with Lord Ogden, while his lordship placed his beaver on his head and pulled on his leather riding gloves. The groom led up the viscount's horse. Lord Ogden went down the flagstone steps and mounted his gelding. He touched his crop to the brim of his beaver and set heel to the sides of his mount, his last sight being that of a friendly wave from his neighbor.

Lord Ogden left the Grange at an easy pace. He had enjoyed his conversation with Kelton, he reflected, and he had formed a good opinion of him. The man was intelligent and well-versed in land management. If he had been privy to his neighbor's good opinion of him, however, Lord Ogden would have been grimly amused. He did not feel particularly shrewd when it came to dealing with a landed estate. He was not bred to it, he reflected somberly, for the hundredth time. He had been the son of a clergyman and he was a seasoned soldier.

Lord Ogden keenly felt his own inadequacies. He was educating himself as quickly as he could but he was aware of his own ignorance. The bailiff was an able man and seemed to approve so far of the orders he had been given, but Bartlett was not the sort of man who took initiative and, indeed, was not placed in a position to do so.

He spurred his horse to a ground-eating cantor, his mind worrying at the nagging problem. *It's all very well to pump a man such as Kelton. A good enough fellow, but I must have someone at hand to advise me.* He had already made a push toward that end.

When the lengthy discussions with the land steward had drawn to a close, Lord Ogden had put forward the suggestion that the man take up permanent residence at Delincourt Manor. "I shall not disguise from you, Stockley, that I shall feel better able to manage all of this business with you close by to advise me," he had said with his rare smile.

"I am honored by your confidence in me, my lord," said Mr. Stockley gravely and bowed his acquiescence. The invitation was a balm to the land steward's oft-lacerated sensibilities at the hands of his former master. "I shall remove from Briarcrest Cottage at the earliest opportunity, my lord."

"Good. I look forward to our closer association, Stockley."

As the viscount rode back to Delincourt, he wondered how long it would be before Stockley was back. There were matters that could not be put off much longer, such as finding an architect to inspect the roof of the manor and oversee repair. He had written Digsby about the matter and was in hopes of having one hired soon. Though he was perfectly capable of rendering decisions, it would be comforting to know whether or not they were the soundest, in Stockley's opinion. Also, with the land steward finally in residence, he could shuffle off much of the burden of the paperwork which still had to be waded through and the massive amount of correspondence. He would elevate Stockley to be his factotum, he decided. The land steward had already been handling the day-to-day business concerning the minor holdings to the best of his ability under a very limited scope. Of a certainty, once he took up residence, Stockley would take on many similar such responsibilities concerning Delincourt, so it was not such a stretch to add the correspondence which related to the estate to the man's duties.

"It will be an advantage to have such a shrewd assistant in close proximity," mused Lord Ogden, looking between his horse's twitching ears. For the first time, he entertained a cautious hope. *Digsby. Stockley. Bartlett. A good company of advisors.* Perhaps he would be able to make something out of his cousin's mess, after all.

He frowned then, recalling what he had heard at the Grange. *Sir Martin had been in the neighborhood.* He wondered whether Lady Ogden was aware of it, but he did not believe so. Otherwise, surely either she or her aunt would have dropped some remark. He was annoyed on her ladyship's behalf. He had not seen the baronet at the burial service, he realized; now it had come out that the gentleman had been at the Grange, only a short distance from Delincourt. Sir Martin should have come to pay a long-overdue courtesy-call. His son-in-law was dead, his daughter recently widowed. It was a solecism of no mean order.

Lord Ogden shrugged his shoulders as if to throw off something distasteful. "Sir Martin's neglect of his responsibilities is all of a piece. The Grange is in better hands now."

He decided he would say nothing to Lady Ogden about her father's recent appearance in the neighborhood; better to spare her the hurt.

20

The succession of windy, drenched dawns left Lady Ogden with the dismal feeling of being penned up. She longed to escape every day outdoors, with or without Lord Ogden's companionship, even if it was for only a sedate walk on the back terrace. Whenever the weather permitted, she and the viscount often rode together with a groom in attendance. As the weeks passed, the two riders began to dispense with the servant, having agreed that their relationship as cousins-in-law had come to be well enough established in the neighborhood. They could forego the groom without raising eyebrows or engendering undue gossip.

The winter was giving way to spring when Lady Ogden finally missed her courses. Her relief was sharp. She had half-believed herself barren. However, she kept silent because of the vivid, painful recollections of the miscarriages. Her fickle womb had twice rejected the precious life nestled within it. She was hesitant to inform the viscount until she was very sure that she had a chance to carry to term.

Lady Ogden decided if the time came that she needed a private word with the viscount, it would be best during one of their unattended rides when there would be no chance of other ears overhearing them.

Lady Ogden missed her courses for the second time. She began to feel hopeful. On a sunny March morning, when a flurry of snow had already melted and the cold ground was wet and muddy under the churning hooves of their horses, she chose her moment. They had ridden the long way around the lake and dismounted at the ruined octagonal folly in the park to tether and rest the horses. In mutual accord, they stepped up into the abandoned folly to shelter out of the cutting wind.

Lady Ogden quietly told her news to the viscount. He stared at her for a long moment. "Are you certain?"

"My courses are never late, my lord." She was startled when he flattened a palm against her belly. She could feel the warmth through her clothing. Even after all of the liberties he had taken with her body, she felt the flush of embarrassment heating her cheeks.

When he spoke, his voice was low-timbered. "You please me, Charlotte."

She did not move, her breath going shallow. She didn't know what to expect of him. He confused her. "If it is a boy, then..." Her voice trailed off awkwardly.

He finished for her. "Then the boy will become my cousin's heir. He will inherit the title."

Lady Ogden curiously regarded him. She did not have the key to the workings of his mind. She never had. Three months into their torrid union and he was still an enigma to her. "Don't you resent it? Not acquiring the peerage, I mean."

His dark gaze was unreadable. He gave a twisted smile. "Why should I feel resentment? I'm comfortably enough placed. My prize money made that possible."

"If it is a girl, you will have the title...everything." She could not keep the biting edge out of her voice. Their bargain would be done. No longer would it be necessary to have him in her bed; it would be a natural end to their secret affair. She wondered what would become of her then. An annuity, a permanent home, all lost. *There will be more than that lost,* her mind whispered.

The viscount did not appear to notice how sharply she spoke. His tone was measured. "If it is a girl, it is still my get off of you."

Lady Ogden flushed. She wasn't sure she liked his phrasing. It struck her as being peculiarly vulgar. He could be unexpectedly crude at times. He had not been bred up that way, she thought. She supposed it came from being so many years in the army. "My child *will not* be illegitimate, my lord!"

"Ah no, true enough. The little bastard will be considered my cousin's legal heir, whether boy or girl."

Perplexed, she gazed into his dark, falcon-sharp eyes. His inscrutable, stern-lipped expression told her nothing. He had thrown her off-balance.

She didn't know what he meant by it in addressing her in such a way. "My lord! You must not say –"

Her remonstration was only half-formed. She caught her breath. His wiry fingers had begun to trace lazy circles over her stomach. Butterflies fluttered beneath her navel. She grasped his wrist. "Vincent, I am *breeding*."

He gave a low laugh. "Charlotte, I never said I would stop fucking you."

Her face flamed. She stepped back, evading his caress. "Your language is objectionable, my lord!"

"Is it? I've said that and worse and you didn't object at all, my love."

It was true and she knew it. She liked it when he used obscenities and murmured vulgarities to her in the throes of their passion. But that certainly didn't mean she would admit to it or tolerate it outside the bedchamber. The strange duality of her life struck her anew.

"Take off your clothes, Charlotte."

"What?" She stared at him, aghast. The bold heat in his eyes assured her that he was serious. She looked around at the cold, dirty interior of the ruined folly. Piles of debris had blown into the corners. The arched openings in the covered octagon overlooked the dense woods and the ice-rimmed lakeshore. *"Here?"*

"Right here." He tapped the end of his riding crop against the side of his top boot. He watched as indecision flashed across her face. He raised a dark brow. "Here, Charlotte."

Lady Ogden recognized the implacable set of his mouth. She tossed her hat and crop aside. "Very well!" she snapped. She knew how he was when in this mood. She tugged the white stock from her throat and dropped it. She didn't linger over the buttons or parting the layers of fabric which she wore; but anxiety had flooded her. She bit her lip. *No one will see or know.* She pushed her long habit and petticoat down, down over her hips and her legs, before she straightened and pulled the short-waisted linen shirt up and over her head. The cold struck her bared skin. "There! Have I satisfied your reprehensible voyeurism, my lord?"

"Voyeurism, is it? Your drawers."

With an irritated exclamation, she lifted the knee-length chemise and untied the waist tapes of the open drawers. She bent to angle the two cotton tubes down over her gartered stockings and her half-boots, finally stepping out of the entire pile of clothing.

Lady Ogden stood before the viscount wearing only the thin chemise on her upper body with a short corset cinched over it. She stared at him in defiance. The corset laced up the back. Unless he wanted to do the honors, she was done with her stripping. She was certainly not going to suggest he assist her. The harsh cold had already chilled her skin and she began to shiver, the tiny hairs standing up on her bare arms above the casing of her leather riding gloves. She folded her arms under her bosom; her breasts plumped up. Beneath the embroidered, gauzy edging of her chemise, her pert pink nipples pebbled.

The viscount's dark eyes narrowed, their depths smoldering like burning coals. He lightly drew the tip of the riding crop across her peaked nipples. "You already look aroused."

"I'm not. I'm cold," she retorted.

He laughed as he unbuttoned the large mother-of-pearl buttons that closed his long greatcoat. "Don't be concerned, love. I'll warm you soon enough." He sat down on the wide, wooden bench that circled the interior of the folly and set aside his hat and crop. He gestured at his lap, where the tell-tale bulge behind his buttoned flap was unmistakable.

Lady Ogden's gaze was naturally riveted by it. She tried to look away, but she couldn't.

"Come here."

She slowly walked over and began to straddle his legs.

"No, no. I want you like this." Lord Ogden eased her over onto her stomach so that she lay across his muscular thighs. Her head and arms dangled down over one side of him, her stocking-covered calves hung over the other side, with her booted toes barely grazing the stone floor. Her bottom was upended over his lap. He pulled the chemise up to the small of her back, exposing her bare bum to the cold. For a moment, he merely looked down at her pale rounds. He started to breathe more harshly. *My God, but she's beautiful.*

"Vincent?" She was uneasy. The position was unfamiliar. She couldn't imagine how they were going to do the business. Against her side, from behind the flap of his breeches, she could feel the press of his thickening erection.

"I'm going to play with you a little while, Charlotte."

His voice sounded peculiarly guttural to her. She felt his gloved hands caress her chilled buttocks. The glide of the fine leather against her bare skin was pleasing. After a moment, she relaxed and closed her eyes. Her middle was warm enough. As he moved his gloved hands over her, caressing her, she felt the blood rising under her skin, the warmth making the cold retreat.

The viscount kneaded and squeezed her pale round globes with his hands, enjoying the firmness of the feminine flesh. *She is so beautiful. I will never have enough of her.* Slowly, he traced the line of her delicate spine up and down, plucking lightly at the laces of her short corset. He murmured, "Spread your legs for me, Charlotte."

When she complied, he began to lightly rub the slit of her twat with a leather-encased finger. He felt the tremor which went through her. He grinned in delight at her responsiveness. The leather had to feel rough on her most delicate flesh, but it had pleasured her. *What else might arouse her, I wonder.*

In the military, he had become inured to the every-day reality of discipline. It was necessary to keep order in the ranks and to keep troops responsive to command. He stared down at his leather-cased hands sliding over the pale slopes of her perfect arse. *A bit of discipline isn't a bad notion.* He breathed a little faster. *If it is handled well.*

Lord Ogden rested his forearm over her narrow shoulder blades. He raised high the other arm and brought his gloved hand down across a plump buttock. She yelped in surprise, her upper body jerking beneath the restraint of his forearm.

"Vincent! What are you doing?"

He did not reply but smacked her again, more smartly. The imprint of his gloved palm pinked her skin. He regarded it approvingly.

"*That hurt!* Let me up! Let me up, I say!"

She struggled to rise from the position in which he had placed her. Her slim, corseted figure wriggled and her bare bottom pitched this way and that. The fair vision set him aflame; arousal flared the base of his nostrils.

Lord Ogden smiled. *Ah, Charlotte! Catch your breath, dear love. We're not done.* He methodically spanked her until her bum was crimson. Through it all, she screamed and cursed and pleaded. He turned a deaf ear. She wriggled and writhed to get free, but he easily held her down for his pleasure. And it was a pleasure. Her buttocks bore his mark of possession. Every twist of her supple, lithe body incited his passion. Behind the flap of his breeches, the swollen head of his prick leaked. He was breathing deeply, harshly, in anticipation.

Lord Ogden laid his palm gently against her reddened flesh and she flinched under the touch of his glove. He caressed her abused skin, moving his hand soothingly over and over the quivering curves which bore the exquisite testimony of his attention.

Lady Ogden caught her breath on a sob. Her bum felt on fire and the intimate depression between her legs throbbed in tandem with her heart. Her whole being seemed centered at her melting core. She was breathing too rapidly. The blood had rushed to her head; she felt dizzy. "Vincent, Vincent, I pray you! No more!"

"You are doing fine, Charlotte," he crooned. He moved his gloved fingers back to her quim and gently rubbed between the swollen pillows guarding her hidden portal. The leather turned dark with damp. He began to stroke in and out with two stiffened, curved digits. "I will see you satisfied, my dear."

She sobbed again, but he knew it was no longer from the smarting sting of his spanking. Without his prompting, she parted her stocking-covered legs wider to grant him greater access to her intimate secrets. He did not give her the satisfaction she so openly desired but kept his two fingers moving shallowly. Under his slow, deliberate stimulation, her reddened bum began tensing in a different way than it had only minutes before.

She clutched the edge of the bench in one hand, wrapped her other gloved hand around the back of his tall stiff boot. The rapid, rushing pound of her heart almost deafened her with the roar in her ears. She felt the subtle quivering in all of her heightened nerve-endings. It was almost upon her, that tidal wave which she strained toward. She could barely speak; her voice sounded ragged, breathy. "Vincent, speak filthy to me! Please, please."

"I'm going to mount you. I'll tup you hard, my white ewe."

She moaned at the potent words. "Yes, yes, tell me!" Above her, his voice thickened. "My thick prick will split open your flanks. I'll pound your tender mutton with my prick. Your hot juices will gush down upon my tool." She whimpered in response, beginning to tremble from head to toe. She could feel the rising rush of her blood.

The viscount pushed deep, twisted his stiff fingers, and felt her womb clench. A little faster, he stroked into her dark, secret place. His hand was clumsier in the glove but with his thumb he found her swollen nubbin. He pressed and flicked it. He was rewarded by her small, strangled shriek. He gritted out, "Pitch for me, Charlotte, my beautiful one." She reacted to his command – writhing under his lewdly-working hand – and her stiffened stays scraped against his breech-covered thighs. In the throes of her carnal agony, she shrieked high and clear.

He did not wait any longer for his own pleasure. He ripped the buttons open on the flap of his riding breeches. The length of his thick-veined prick eagerly sprang forth. He clasped her by the waist and swung her up onto his lap, leaning her back into his chest. "Take the saddle, puss."

He opened her legs with his knees until she straddled the wide spread of his thighs. She sobbed something incoherent. He shifted her upper body forward to fit the white-beaded cap of his purpled cock to her soft-pelted lips. His broad, moist head easily breached her swollen slit and he urgently pulled her onto the impaling girth. Reveling in the snug sensation, he grunted, *"Ah! There you are, my beauty!"*

His strong shaft sank swift into her heated pith. She cried out again, tossing her head back against his shoulder. Her body jerked and shook in her all-consuming ecstasy. The constriction of her tight glove, squeezing his rigidity, was such exquisite pleasure that it almost popped the top off his head. Groaning low in his chest, he measured his harsh breaths, holding himself still inside of her until her frenzy had rippled away. It was sheer torture. His deep-buried, swollen cock throbbed with pain. Gutturally, he ordered, "Place your hands on my thighs, my love."

Her ears were ringing. She could barely take in his command. Breathless, still trembling in her whole body, she did as he bade her. He slid his arms under hers, angling his forearms across her front. She felt gloved fingers firmly cup a sensitized breast. He squeezed lightly and she hissed. The other leather-covered hand slid around her middle and gripped the curve of her waist. The sides of his greatcoat fell forward to drape over her bare flanks.

"Now we will see how warm it becomes." The cup of his fingers tightened on her breast. She felt him take a firmer grasp of the side of her middle. He moved her, tipping her forward toward his knees and back again. Slowly, his engorged prick pulled in and out. She was frantic for the delicious sensations. She pushed her hands down against the hard musculature of his bunched thighs, pressed her naked legs for leverage against the outside of his clothed thighs. *Ah yes, yes!* Her elevated bum placed his penetrations at an exquisite angle. His fullness rasped her clit with every thrust. She was soon shuddering again in a rising spiral of blinding, white-laced sensuality. She was deafened by the loud, hard pound of her heart. Her rapid breathing hastened faster. She never wanted it to end! *But it must end! It must! It must!*

His glistening, lusty prick was sliding, again and again, beneath the wide-spread apple of her quivering arse. His palm prints were livid against her pale skin. The viscount was riveted at the sight. "Oh, Charlotte! Your cheeks are so pretty and rosy from my discipline."

A strong tremor ran the length of her delicate spine. She groaned. "Vincent, Vincent." His rhythmic plundering of her hot, moist depths set her off. She suddenly bucked in his arms. The turbulence of her rising pleasure provided a pleasing resistance to the thrust of his heavy prick. Squeezing his shaft, he felt the tiny flutterings begin to ripple outward again.

"Oh God, Vincent!"

He knew she was taking wing. He closed his gloved fingers hard on her soft breast, giving the budded nipple a twist. She reared up her head.

She cried out, and was gone, her body breaking from its bounds, caught up in a strong paroxysm. She jerked against him as though in a violent fit. He held on through the writhing of her body, the snap of her hips. He gasped...the throbbing contractions of her quim on his prick...his eyes squeezed shut.

She abruptly collapsed, the sag of her weight heavy in his banded arms. He grunted, tightly supporting her limp torso. His pulsating, pained prick was buried in her fiery heat. His heart thundered. He thought he'd die or go mad. He'd almost crested. *Finish it! Finish!* He lifted her and brought her down, driving himself deep. His agonized thrust bumped the knob of her womb. His seed exploded from his body into hers. The forceful rush bowed him over. He enfolded her in the strained arc of his shuddering body. *"Oh, God! My only love!"*

Lord Ogden gasped in and out, breathing raggedly. Sweat dripped into his eyes. He was satiated to the outer limits of his being, but his pleasure was quite destroyed. Dread tightened his guts. He brought her limp body up to rest against his chest, so he could look down into her flushed face. Her head lolled back against his shoulder and he blew out his breath with sharp relief.

He'd betrayed his most closely-guarded secret. Fortunately, she had not heard him. She was senseless.

21

L ady Ogden floated back to herself. Something pressed into her shoulder; her fingers found the hard, round object and grasped it. *A button...large...a man's coat button.* Disorientation receded – her addled senses sharpened, bringing a kaleidoscope of impressions. She was cradled against the viscount's chest, circled by the strength of his arms. His musky scent and warmth enveloped her. She sat in his lap, partially wrapped in his greatcoat. The folds of the heavy garment draped her legs. The familiar stickiness of their joining streaked her inner thighs. Her buttocks felt strangely tender. Memory burst in her brain. *Vincent...the things he did!* The rush of emotions was confusing: outrage, shame, and a peculiar, shivering eroticism.

"Welcome back, my dear."

The viscount's breath ruffled her hair. She stiffened in his warm embrace. *"Let me go!"* Her voice was breathy, not at all imperious as she had intended. She felt the wall of the viscount's chest move as he gave a low laugh.

"I am yours to command." Lord Ogden opened his arms. She awkwardly scooted off of his lap, stumbling and catching herself with one hand on his shoulder, before she got her balance. He leaned back against the wooden bench, stretching his arms on either side along its back. He tilted his head, a smile riding his lips. She knew he was enjoying the sight of her scantily-clothed body. "A titillating mix, that. Corset and chemise, paired with riding gloves, stockings and half-boots. It's peculiarly arousing." She darted an angry glance at him. He laughed quietly.

Lady Ogden hurried over to the pile of her abandoned clothing lying on the floor and scrambled into the cold garments. She burned with embarrassment. Her fingers trembled, making her clumsy as she tied tapes and buttoned buttons. She was all too aware of her audience. The viscount watched her with a faint, lascivious smile on his bronzed face. At last, breathlessly, she exclaimed, "Stop it! At least turn your eyes away!"

Lord Ogden shrugged and rose from the bench, picking up his riding crop. He clapped his beaver hat onto his head. "Why, my love? I'm enjoying the peep show. But I must object! It's going in the wrong direction!"

"You will have your fun," she uttered tersely.

"You'll disrobe for me tonight, in just that way, and leave on the things you wore during this charming interlude."

"Charming?" Lady Ogden gasped in outrage, despite a familiar, pleasurable thrill. She was heated by recollection of the feelings he had elicited. However, the inordinate wantonness of her own body alarmed her. Her loss of control had been complete. It left her uneasy. Defying her feelings, she focused on the indignity she had suffered. She clenched the length of her crop between her gloved fists. "You beat me!"

He stepped close, his amusement open as he looked down into her indignant face. "I chastised you," he corrected. He ran a caressing gloved hand along her flank.

"You are a brute!" she exclaimed, flushing hotly. She remembered all too clearly how her quivering, lusty flesh had responded to the humiliation inflicted by his labor. Fresh mortification filled her. *It seems there are no bounds to what he can do with me. There is some strange perversion in my nature!*

"You did not dislike it."

With revulsion, she repudiated what he had said. "I detested it!"

Lord Ogden whipped his crop up against the back of the skirt of her riding habit. It was not a harsh blow. It did not even penetrate through the layer of heavy wool, yet she jumped. She fastened a shocked gaze on his uncompromising features. "Pray do not lie to me, Charlotte!"

His fierce, heated stare couldn't be borne. She was forced to avert her eyes. The acknowledgement he demanded was dragged out of her. "Very well! It was-was enjoyable, damn you!" she said, her low voice vibrating with suppressed emotion.

Lord Ogden nodded in stern-lipped satisfaction. "We understand one another in this, at least. We are well-suited in amorous congress. Come, I will help you mount. It is time to return to Delincourt. I have my bailiff coming to see me."

As though they were out for a sedate stroll, Lord Ogden tucked her hand inside the crook of his arm and drew her with him out of the octagonal folly and down the steps. She could no longer contain her silence about what had happened. She was too troubled by it. Lady Ogden gestured back at the abandoned folly. "Vincent, what...what precisely *happened* to me?"

"I believe you fainted from carnal ecstasy."

Lady Ogden's lips parted. She was amazed. She did not know such things could happen. As the viscount walked her over the barren ground to the tethered horses, she glanced sideways up at his calm profile. *After what we did, how can he be so unfeeling, so unmoved – while I am shaken to the very depths of my being!* Driven by the need to penetrate his cool imperturbability, she said cuttingly, "Perhaps he is not *your* bailiff, but rather, my son's instead."

Lord Ogden tossed her up into the saddle. With one gloved hand resting on her booted foot in the stirrup, he looked up at her. He said gravely, "Perhaps it is as you say. But for now, my word is law."

With a low, incoherent exclamation, she shortened her reins and kicked her mount. The horse jumped forward and quickly found its stride. As she bent over the mare's flying brown mane, Lady Ogden raged inside. *His word was law! Damn him, damn him, damn him!*

Lord Ogden, once the lowly military officer Major Vincent Crawford, had settled in with incredible naturalness to the exalted position he had attained. Perhaps it was the habit of command in him. He had swiftly gained the respect of the household staff and the tenants. He had only to utter a request for it to be done. He managed everything with seeming ease.

She didn't exclude herself. The viscount held sway over her, too. *Especially my body.* Every time he demanded anything of her – *everything* he demanded of her! – she gave willingly to him, because she had learned the pleasures of carnality from him. She had become submissive to his governance.

The pounding of hooves behind her broke through her raging thoughts. A blur of movement, an outthrust arm. Then a strong, gloved hand was bearing down on the bridle of her horse. The viscount forced her mount to an ever-slower pace before he brought them both to a standstill. Under his sun-burnished skin, his features were unnaturally pallid, a phenomenon that scarcely penetrated her fury. "Unhand my bridle! What do you mean by it, my lord?"

He narrowed his eyes at her. Temper crackled in his voice. "You are reckless, madam! I shall not have you endangering yourself and the babe with this abandoned pace!"

"Pooh! Nonsense! I'm an excellent rider."

"Yes, when you are not in a flame!"

"Well, if I am angered, it is your doing!"

Lord Ogden spoke through gritted teeth. "Perhaps I should have done better to slap *my crop* against your backside, my lady!"

Lady Ogden sucked in her breath. She was trembling, but her pride kept her spine ramrod-straight. "I will not answer to rough handling, my lord, I promise you!"

The viscount's expression changed, his anger visibly draining away. "I don't wish to handle you roughly! I think only of your welfare! You confided in me of your losses." His bronzed face faltered into a smile. "Charlotte, my dearest Charlotte, will you not have a care for the babe?"

She was shaken. The sudden tenderness of his appeal undid her. She did not want him to know it, however. She gave a stiff nod. "Very well, my lord. I shall be more circumspect on horseback."

"Promise me, if I am not with you, that you will ride with a groom."

It was not an unreasonable request, not when she was breeding. A fall from her horse could have dire consequences. "I promise you."

He reached out and squeezed her forearm. It was a testament to her over-stretched nerves that even such a brief touch burned through the cloth to her flesh. "It's all I ask, ma'am. Now let us turn for home."

She drew in her breath and let it out on a long sigh. All of her fury had evaporated. Meekly, she rode beside him. *Oh, yes, he manages me quite well!*

It occurred to her ladyship again to question what possible motive Lord Ogden could have in conspiring to commit fraud, a motive so compelling that he would be willing to risk losing a landed estate. On the face of it, the viscount had nothing to gain and everything to lose. *But he has a mistress conveniently at hand, a mistress who is completely at his command.* One, moreover, which he did not have to pacify with baubles or jewelry. She had come cheaply, she thought sadly. She had required only room and board and the teasing promise of an annuity. Her cynicism was such that she believed the viscount was not unusual in taking his pleasure where he found it. Many gentlemen would seize upon such an easy arrangement for amorous congress, while lending little thought to the future. After all, a gentleman could always walk away, without detriment either to his personal consequence or his social standing. It was otherwise with a woman. It was always the woman who bore the consequences and the stigma of a lost reputation.

I am with child.

She was at once both elated and petrified.

22

Upon entering the manor house, the butler informed his lordship that his friend, Rev. Major Ledger, had just moments before arrived. Lord Ogden exclaimed and threw aside hat and crop onto a side table in the entrance hall, and stripped off his gloves, tossing them beside the rest. He strode swiftly toward the drawing-room. Lady Ogden followed close behind, the tail of her habit caught up over her elbow. She was very curious to see the man whose arrival had put such an open expression of delight on his lordship's face.

When the viscount crossed the threshold into the drawing-room, he called out, "My word! Arthur!" The newly-arrived gentleman broke off his polite conversation with Mrs. Merriweather and dragged himself to his feet from the chair. He took a halting step forward to meet the viscount.

"My dear fellow!" exclaimed Lord Ogden, advancing with his hand outstretched. "I am glad to see you!"

"As glad as I am to see you." Rev. Major Ledger was grinning, equally delighted to see his old comrade. He tightly grasped the viscount's hand but it was not enough. The men laughed and embraced, pounding one another's backs. Rev. Major Ledger stepped back to keenly survey his friend from head to toe. "You're looking fit, Vincent. You've been out riding, I see. And with a lovely lady, too!"

Lord Ogden made rapid introductions. "My cousin-in-law, Lady Ogden – Rev. Major Ledger. You've already met Mrs. Merriweather, I take it."

"I've had that pleasure, yes." Rev. Major Ledger took Lady Ogden's offered hand and bowed over her gloved fingers. "Lady Ogden, it is an honor."

"Thank you, Rev. Major Ledger. It is for me, as well. My aunt and I have heard something about you from Lord Ogden. I hope you will like it here at Delincourt," replied Lady Ogden graciously.

"I'm sure I shall," said Rev. Major Ledger, smiling down at her ladyship.

The gentleman had such a friendly gaze that it was easy to return his smile. She felt an instant liking for him. Still smiling, Lady Ogden said, "I must go up and change, sir. We shall meet again later."

"I shall accompany you upstairs, Charlotte. Lord Ogden and Rev. Major Ledger must have much to talk about," said Mrs. Merriweather. She turned to address their guest. "Rev. Major Ledger, you shall do us the honor of dining with us, of course."

"Of course." Rev. Major Ledger readily agreed. He bowed. "It was very good to meet you, Lady Ogden, Mrs. Merriweather."

As the ladies exited, Lord Ogden overheard Mrs. Merriweather say in an aside, "You have a parcel bearing Sir William's direction, my dear. I had Somerset put it in the upper drawing-room."

"Oh, lord. Thank you, aunt. I shall open it directly I have changed."

Lord Ogden spared a second for irritation. *A parcel now from this impudent fellow, Sir William Talley.* No doubt about it, there had been curiosity in the light tone of Lady Ogden's casual response. He liked none of it. He thrust the whole matter out of his mind and clapped his friend on the shoulder. "Come! Let us go up to my private study. We will be comfortable there."

Rev. Major Ledger gestured toward his host's riding apparel. "Why don't I change instead? I've been shut up in a rocking carriage all day. I'd rather sling my leg over a good hack and shake out some of the stiffness."

"Capital! Meet me down at the stables. Your baggage has already been taken up? Good." They had walked out of the drawing-room and into the entrance hall. Lord Ogden motioned the butler forward. "Somerset can have someone show you up to your bedchamber. Did you bring your man?"

"Yes, Totten is still with me."

Lord Ogden nodded. "Meet me at the stables, then, whenever you are ready." He watched his old comrade ascend the stairs behind a footman. He was still smiling. Behind his expression of amiability, however, he was abstracted. She was thinking of another man, so soon after the extraordinary passage between them. He puzzled over the alien feeling in his chest. Astonished, he realized it was jealousy. *One might almost call it a feeling of being cuckolded.* It was an unpalatable revelation. He turned on his heel. Picking up his hat, riding gloves, and crop, he strode outside to make his way to the stables.

After freshening up, Lady Ogden changed into a dark daydress. It was not proper mourning but instead a deep brown, but it would do with her black shawl arranged over her shoulders. Her dresser brushed out her windblown hair and rearranged it in a knot, leaving soft curls at her temples and her nape. "There you are, my lady."

"Thank you, Mills."

Lady Ogden rejoined her aunt in the upstairs drawing-room. "Where is it, aunt?"

"There, my dear." Mrs. Merriweather pointed at the worn work table. Lady Ogden went over to pick up the small, flat parcel. She turned it over in her hands, surprised at the bulk of it. "I wonder what it could possibly be?"

"I confess, I'm just as curious," said Mrs. Merriweather. "*Do* open it!"

Using a small pair of scissors, Lady Ogden cut the string tied around the parcel and unwrapped the brown paper, discovering a note from Sir William Talley together with a gilt-edged chapbook of psalms. She was astonished. "Look, aunt! What do you make of this? It's a collection of the psalms."

Mrs. Merriweather's countenance was shaded by a slight frown. "An unexceptional gift, of course, but why should Sir William send a gift at all? My dear, do you suppose – but it is so nonsensical! Do you think Sir William is *courting* you?"

Lady Ogden chuckled at her aunt's absurd flight of fancy. Carrying the chapbook with her, she walked over to her usual chair and sat down. "I'm very certain he is not! What have I to offer any gentleman? I'm a widow of no means."

"There's that, of course." Mrs. Merriweather pulled a dainty handkerchief from beneath her cuff and dabbed at her nose before tucking it away again. She sat down in the chair opposite her niece. "This weather! It makes my nose itch. What was I going to say? Oh, yes! I don't understand it, then. There is no cause for such a gesture. After all, you are mere acquaintances and barely even that."

"No, you are quite right, it is odd. I had not supposed any of Henry's friends to be so kind. It's a pleasant surprise," said Lady Ogden. She gently paged through the chapbook while turning over the question troubling her mind. "I suppose I must write a note of thanks. It would only be civil."

"Yes, so it would," agreed Mrs. Merriweather, but hesitantly. She cast a suspicious glance at the chapbook in her niece's hands.

Lady Ogden believed she could guess her aunt's thoughts. She closed the small chapbook and set it aside on an occasional table standing beside her chair. "Rest assured, aunt, I shall not say anything which will encourage the gentleman. I do not forget that he made up one of Henry's obnoxious set."

"Exactly! One of those intemperate louts who invaded our home and cut up our peace!" Mrs. Merriweather's heated indignation was pulled up short when she saw Lady Ogden's wince. "Forgive me, dear. I couldn't help but recall the discomfort which we endured. You especially, cooped up in here for *days*, unable even to take your walks or exercise your horse, for fear of crossing the path of one of those-those *rips!* And you need not look so shocked at my language, miss! Nor laugh at me, either!"

Lady Ogden banished her smile and made her mouth prim. "I wouldn't dare laugh at you, ma'am. Your prodigious frowns frighten me so!"

Mrs. Merriweather eyed her disrespectful niece and chose to take the high road, ignoring that piece of errant nonsense. "*However*, I daresay you are right to want to express your appreciation for the chapbook, though I'm certain Sir William hadn't a notion that it would really suit you and it's simply a happy accident on his part!"

Lady Ogden inwardly agreed with her aunt's assessment. "I don't see the harm in responding to Sir William's note, aunt."

Mrs. Merriweather heaved a sigh. "Nor I, Charlotte, not really. Perhaps the gentleman is turning over a new leaf?"

Lady Ogden laughed. "Perhaps, dear ma'am, but I shan't hold my breath."

Later in the afternoon, when she returned to her sitting room, she carried the chapbook to her private desk. She laid it down, her hand resting on top of the slim volume. Her expression was thoughtful. In a moment, she gave a little shrug. She penned a short word of thanks, put it into the penny-post, and forgot about it.

The two gentlemen spent the afternoon on horseback, their easy conversation roaming through past reminiscences, to what each had been doing since they had last seen one another, and to discussing various points of interest on the lands. At length, Rev. Major Ledger observed, "You're a lucky man, Vincent. It's a fair estate, even though it is, as you say, crying out for better management. I like the country hereabouts."

"Yes, it is beautiful country. I hope you will come to like it as much as I do myself."

Rev. Major Ledger grinned over at his companion. "Why, as to that, I'm certain of it! You've shown me none but fair prospects – not a French line in sight! There is no one shooting at us!"

Lord Ogden laughed. "There is that!"

When the riders reached the place that was naturally of the most interest to Rev. Major Ledger, they pulled up their horses, and Lord Ogden pointed with his riding crop at the mellow-stoned front of the edifice. "Here is the vicarage, Arthur. It has been empty and shut up since my father's death three years ago, so I've been told. As you can see, the place requires some care given to it."

Lord Ogden spurred his mount and slowly rode round the outskirts of the property, making occasional comments and observations to his companion. Rev. Major Ledger's thoughtful gaze roamed over the sprawling three-story house, the deserted outbuildings, and the overgrown garden and lawns. At length, they had made the circle and reined in again at the front of the vicarage. The viscount waved a gloved hand at the building. "Well, what do you make of it? Will it do?"

Rev. Major Ledger nodded. He was well satisfied with what he had seen. "It's a fair property. With some work, I daresay it will be quite charming. A good place to settle, I believe, and perhaps one to bring a wife to and establish a family. It's a large enough place, anyway."

Lord Ogden slewed in the saddle. He grinned over at his friend. "Oho! Do you have a fair lady in mind? Would I know her?"

"Oh no, I think of no one lady over any other. However, a man must make his plans."

"Come, let's go in." They dismounted, tethered the horses, and walked up the overgrown gray flagstones to the front door. Lord Ogden took a key out of his pocket and inserted it into the lock. He opened the door and pushed it wide. As he entered into the gloomy interior, he said, "Allow me to show you around. What a dark place it is with all the drapes shut!" He heard Rev. Major's halting step echoing on the wooden plank floor behind him.

Lord Ogden dragged back the heavy curtains so that sunlight streaked in through the dirty windows, and he turned to critically survey the room. "That's better! I daresay we'll have to open all of the drapes as we go room to room or otherwise find ourselves stumbling over a warped floorboard or a piece of furniture. I haven't been in here myself since I returned, so I warn you, we may see dry rot and all sorts of disrepair."

However, the vicarage was discovered to be in remarkably good shape, considering that the property had been shut-up for so long. The stuffy air was stale and dust motes danced on the beams of sunlight, but the furniture had been properly covered in Holland covers so the pieces had all been protected.

"I doubt anything has been changed here since I was a boy. You'll probably want to be rid of some of this," said Lord Ogden, eyeing the shrouded furniture with a critical gaze. "Bring in those things more tolerable to your taste and that will make the place more comfortable to you."

Rev. Major Ledger expressed himself to be very happy with the house. "Time enough to be thinking about making any changes."

They emerged from the building to find the lengthening shadows advancing across the ground. Lord Ogden threw a quick glance at the clouded sky. "We should start back. It will be getting dark soon."

Lord Ogden mounted his horse. He waited while Rev. Major Ledger also mounted, which was rather more awkwardly accomplished due to the gentleman's bad leg. The viscount knew better than to offer his aid. Rev. Major Ledger was fiercely independent. Rejoicing that he had not lost his leg altogether, he had rejected the prognosis that he would never walk again and proven the physicians wrong. He had eventually thrown aside the leg brace and crutches. Though he had been left with an observable limp, the only physical activity still denied to him was foot racing.

Lord Ogden gathered his reins and nudged his mount into a brisk canter. "I'm glad you're here, Arthur."

"No more than I am to be here. Clerking for a bureaucrat at Horse Guards was damned tedious, as you know."

"Yes, so I gathered from your correspondence."

"I was beginning to despair of ever securing a decent living. Then your most welcome letter came."

Lord Ogden glanced across at his friend. "I immediately thought of you. I couldn't envision a better man to fill the living."

"Thank you, my lord." Rev. Major Ledger mockingly bowed from over his mount's withers. As he straightened, the laughter faded from his face. "I mean it, Vincent, from the bottom of my heart."

"I know that neither of us will ever regret it," said Lord Ogden with equal solemnity. Neither man voiced it, but they were moved by deep emotion. It was a moment which they would both always recall with vivid clarity.

The riders returned to Delincourt in time to dress for dinner. They went downstairs again to join the ladies in the drawing-room for conversation. Shortly, Somerset came in to announce dinner was served. Lord Ogden escorted his cousin-in-law into the front parlor, while Rev. Major Ledge gallantly performed the same service for Mrs. Merriweather. It was a convivial meal with much interesting conversation, mainly due to Rev. Major Ledger's easy discourse and his way of drawing everyone in. The viscount was relaxed and ready laughter sprang to his lips several times. Lady Ogden was amazed by the transformation wrought by the presence of his lordship's friend. She thought she had rarely spent a more enjoyable evening.

At length, it became time for the ladies to retreat and leave the viscount and Rev. Major Ledger to the enjoyment of their after-dinner wine. Lady Ogden rose gracefully from her seat at the table. With a smile, she said, "Pray do not feel obligated to join us for coffee. I know my aunt will agree. We have no wish to interrupt your reunion."

"Indeed, I do agree," said Mrs. Merriweather, taking her cue and also rising to her feet. "You must have many reminiscences to share."

Lord Ogden smiled and thanked the ladies. He was grateful for their courtesy and tact. After the ladies left them, Lord Ogden and Rev. Major Ledger did not linger over the dining table, as was the usual custom. Instead, Lord Ogden requested that the after-dinner wine be taken upstairs to his private study, where they subsequently retreated. While the two friends partook of the heavy port, their talk was desultory, moving freely between conversation and companionable silences. There was no awkwardness, no search for something to say. It was enough to be in company with one another.

Lord Ogden stared into the flickering fire. He was vastly content. He did not know when he had enjoyed a day or an evening more. It was idyllic to relax from all of his cares in the company of an old and trusted friend.

Another comfortable silence had fallen, interrupted once by a falling log. It was broken at last by Rev. Major Ledger. "You've tupped her."

At his friend's succinct statement, Lord Ogden felt his heart lurch. He held himself still through the rush of shock and dismay. Turning his head, he kept his face expressionless, showing nothing of his inner disquiet. He did not immediately reply. Rather, he studied his companion. His old comrade-at-arms sat at ease in the wingchair, his long legs outstretched toward the fire. There was a knowing expression in the man's clear, world-weary eyes. In that moment, Lord Ogden knew his first instinct to pretend misunderstanding or to utter a denial was not possible.

Rev. Major Arthur Ledger had been his closest comrade to hell and back during the war in Portugal until the wound that had forced that gentleman home. The bloody cauldron of their shared experiences in many ways bound them closer than brothers. Their brains had become so closely attuned to one another's private thoughts that, even had he wanted, Lord Ogden could never lie to his friend. "Damnation," he said quietly. "I was not aware we had betrayed ourselves."

"There was nothing to remark in the conventional manners which you and Lady Ogden have adopted," his friend assured him. "It's a trick of expression, possibly an informality of gesture. I cannot tell you. But it was obvious to me."

"I trust it is not universally obvious," said Lord Ogden acidly.

"Only to me, I think. Mayhap because I am newly come into your company." Rev. Major Ledger shrugged. "Or perhaps it is because I know you so well. But what the devil do you mean by it, Vincent?"

"Once her ladyship's mourning is over, I intend to wed her," said Lord Ogden evenly. "Our present liaison was not initiated by her wish, but by mine."

"My very dear fellow! Of course, I wish you all the best." Rev. Major Ledger's steady gaze was sympathetic. He would not condemn but his reservations were strong. He pursed his lips in a thoughtful manner. "You are running a terrible risk, man."

"I do know it, Arthur."

"What if you get her with child?"

Lord Ogden swirled the port in his glass. In a deliberate, significant manner, he said coolly, "If it is born early enough, within her period of mourning, the child will be declared my cousin's heir."

Rev. Major Ledger's gray eyes widened. He sucked in an amazed breath, only to blow it out again. Shaking his head, he said, "I must admit, *that* did not occur to me."

Lord Ogden was faintly smiling as he regarded his companion. "Do you still wish to have the living, even knowing the full depravity of your patron?"

"Of course, I want the living! There is no question of that!" retorted Rev. Major Ledger. "I do quail, however, at thought of the coming years of our association! The qualms of conscience I will surely suffer at your hands!"

Lord Ogden laughed, throwing up a hand in a fencer's gesture of acknowledgment. "*Touché*!"

Rev. Major Ledger eyed him in speculation. "As I recall, you were never one to give indiscriminate chase after the ladies."

Lord Ogden protested. "I was not a monk! I enjoyed a few liaisons." He scowled with mock-fierceness. "I suppose now that you are to be the vicar, I must expect such impertinent observations."

"I also have a vague recollection of a confidence once told me in the dark of a French prison camp...what was it now? Oh, yes, something about a lost love. One who shattered your heart. A chestnut-haired lass from your own district."

Lord Ogden felt uncomfortable heat rising to his cheekbones. "Quiet, Arthur!" He took his friend's empty wineglass and refilled it before he thrust it back into Rev. Major Ledger's hand. "I supposed you to be in a dying stupor!"

"Dying men may not speak, but sometimes, they do hear things they should not," said Rev. Major Ledger, his eyes crinkling at the corners as he quietly laughed. He raised the glass in a toast. "But truly, I drink to your good success."

Lord Ogden raised his glass, too. "To success." However, he privately thought it would be miraculous indeed if he succeeded in storming the lady's obstinate heart. She had finally accepted – and even welcomed – his lovemaking, but all else she resisted.

Rev. Major Ledger tossed back what remained of his port and set down the wineglass. He yawned and stretched. "I feel half at sea. It's all this jogging about, I expect. As jolly as all this has been, I'm for bed. I'm knackered."

"Very well, old fellow. I will see you in the morning." Lord Ogden walked with Rev. Major Ledger out of the study. With a handshake, they parted in the hallway. Neither mentioned what had been said about the viscount's revelations. It was not necessary. It was mutually understood the conversation would remain solely between them. Rev. Major Ledger walked away with his limping step.

Lord Ogden went into his bedchamber, where he found his valet tidying the room. He could see the newly cleaned riding clothes neatly bestowed in the wardrobe. The man was a wonder, he thought. He had come in from the day's riding bespattered with mud. "You shouldn't have waited up, Grimshaw. I could have done for myself."

"I would be failing in my duty, my lord."

The valet helped the viscount off with his coat and carefully eased off his top boots. Lord Ogden unbuttoned his waistcoat and shrugged out of it, handing it to his valet. He shucked his shirt and knitted pantaloons. The valet picked up the discarded clothing and the boots. Lord Ogden was aware that his manservant would polish the boots before going to bed. "I shall put out the candle, Grimshaw."

"Very good, my lord."

After the valet left, closing the door softly behind him, Lord Ogden turned his thoughtful gaze to the door connecting his bedchamber to that of her ladyship. He recalled the toast to his success he had shared earlier. *In all of our association, she has never once breathed a syllable to me from a lover's heart.* For once, when his thoughts rested on Lady Ogden, his uppermost feeling was not desire; instead, he felt a curious mix of melancholia and disappointment. *She is safe enough from me tonight.* Licking wet a finger and thumb, he extinguished the candle flame and got into the bed.

23

Rev Major Ledger stayed a fortnight before he announced it was time to take his leave. His decision was regretted not only by Lord Ogden but also by the ladies. Lady Ogden and Mrs. Merriweather had learned to like the gentleman very well and they deplored his imminent departure. Rev. Major Ledger himself was reluctant to leave Delincourt, but it was necessary for him to return to London, where he still had obligations and social engagements. He was hopeful that it would not be long before he could return to Delincourt for good.

Lord Ogden accompanied his friend outside to the waiting carriage. A light drizzle was falling. Droplets dampened the shoulders of their coats but neither man paid heed to the wet; after the extremes in the Peninsular, such mild weather changes seemed insignificant.

Before reaching the open carriage door, Rev. Major Ledger turned to briefly grip his lordship's hand. "I shall take care of that spot of business for you while I am in town."

Lord Ogden nodded. "Thank you, Arthur."

Rev. Major Ledger was smiling, but his gray eyes were somber and it was reflected in his voice. "I don't know how long it will take me. If it was solely up to me, I would not leave at all. But I must return to London in order to resign my office, as you know, and to wind up my affairs there. I shall return as soon as possible."

Lord Ogden smiled back at him. "Make it soon, indeed. The sooner the better, my friend."

Rev. Major Ledger laughed. "Yes, the sooner the better!" With his quick, halting step he crossed the remaining distance to the carriage and swung himself up into it.

Lord Ogden put up the iron step and shut the door. He signaled the driver. Raising a hand, he called out, "*Au revoir!*"

Within hours of Rev. Major Ledger's departure, Mrs. Merriweather was struck down by an all-too-familiar seasonal malady. When Lady Ogden entered her aunt's chamber, she found the good lady laid up in her bed. A lace-and-muslin cap was tied on her head and she was attired in a voluminous nightgown, with the pillows plumped up behind her and the coverlets tucked up almost to her plump chin, despite the heat from the roaring fire that had been built up in the fireplace. Mrs. Merriweather catalogued her several ills to her attentive niece: her head pounded abominably, her eyes watered, and her nose was stuffy. She sighed in a piteous fashion, adding nasally, "My body is racked by aches, too. I am sure I must be dying!"

Lady Ogden addressed the sufferer in a soft tone. "You must try to rest, dear ma'am. Here is the tisane which Mrs. Tower specially brewed for you. Do drink a little, it always makes you feel better."

Mrs. Merriweather obediently sipped down some of the draught from the small glass that her niece held to her lips. With a turn of her head, she rejected another swallow. "Enough, Charlotte, I pray! I want only to be left alone in my suffering!" She burst into ragged sobs. "Oh, I'm so miserable!"

Lady Ogden crooned soothingly to her aunt, and by dint of patience and gentle bullying, she was finally able to get Mrs. Merriweather to take the rest of the tisane.

During the several minutes of melodrama, Mrs. Merriweather's dresser busied herself adjusting her mistress's pillows to a more comfortable angle. At Lady Ogden's signal, the woman retreated from the bedside toward the door along with her ladyship. In a lowered voice, Lady Ogden addressed the dresser. "You will know better than anyone what to do, Waters. Pray send word if you should need me."

"Of course, my lady."

When Lady Ogden finally left her aunt's bedchamber, she felt drained. Her aunt's histrionics had worn her down. Mrs. Merriweather was very unlike her usual placid self. The first several hours of Mrs. Merriweather's seasonal bout with illness were always the worst, since that lady refused to acknowledge how badly she felt until the symptoms could no longer be ignored. By then, it took a regimen of saline draughts, herbal tisanes and prolonged bedrest before Mrs. Merriweather would begin to recover her spirits or her customary well-being. Mrs. Merriweather's dresser had been with her for a long time. Lady Ogden was confident that Waters knew just how to nurse the elderly lady back to health. However, it always fell to her lot to override Mrs. Merriweather's initial protests that she was not ill and to persuade her aunt to finally take to her bed and allow herself to be doctored. It was a farce played out at around the same time nearly every year. The household was always aware when Mrs. Merriweather, who was generally of a cheerful, stout constitution, was cast down into such doleful, sickly straits.

Lady Ogden slowly made her way downstairs to the drawing-room, where she was glad to find a substantial tea being set out by the butler. She briefly exchanged greetings with the viscount, who had been awaiting her appearance.

"How is your aunt?"

"Thank you for inquiring, my lord. My aunt is better. She is resting now."

"Very good. I'm glad to hear it."

Lady Ogden sank down in a wingback chair that was angled to the warmth of the fire. She cast a smile at the butler, who had personally taken it upon himself to prepare her tea. "Ah, Somerset! This is just what I need – a good, strong cup of tea and some of Cook's little tartlets."

"So I supposed, my lady." With a bow, Somerset handed a cup in saucer to her ladyship. The butler placed a plate with a selection of meat tartlets, cheeses, and fruit on top of an occasional table, within easy reach of her ladyship's chair. Somerset also poured for the viscount and bowed at his lordship's brief word of thanks.

Lady Ogden took a sip from the cup. There was plenty of milk and sugar in the hot tea and she sighed blissfully. "Perfect. Thank you, Somerset." The butler bowed again and left the drawing-room, quietly closing the door behind him.

Lord Ogden had observed the short passage from his place standing before the fireplace. Of course, he had heard of Mrs. Merriweather's illness but he had not realized for some hours that Lady Ogden would supervise her aunt's sickroom. He did not like to see how care-worn her ladyship appeared. With the butler's exit and the subsequent privacy which it afforded, he set aside his own cup and saucer on the mantel and turned full-face toward her ladyship. The viscount frowned down at her, his sharpened gaze considering her almost-haggard appearance. "You are too pale. Are you quite well?"

"Oh, yes. I am merely feeling a trifle weary. It is always so when I care for my aunt. I must bully her a little, you see," said Lady Ogden, ending on a small laugh. She sipped some more tea. She did not think it necessary to say that she was more tired than she cared to admit. She set the cup back into the saucer, and added, "But I do not begrudge the effort. She is very dear to me."

"Is it wise for you to nurse your aunt yourself?" he asked in a low voice. "I'm thinking of your own health."

His lordship's narrowed gaze was intent on her. Lady Ogden blushed but she met his eyes with a steady look. She knew very well what he meant when he spoke of her well-being. "I don't believe I will take ill, my lord. It is a malady which comes upon my aunt each spring with the severe changes in our weather. Though my aunt genuinely suffers a great deal, she has never communicated her affliction to anyone else. She will be better once the weather settles and it is dryer."

"I trust that is true, for I don't like Mrs. Merriweather to suffer. But I believe I shall send for the doctor anyway. He shall have a look at you, too, while he is here." The viscount smiled apologetically at her. "It isn't that I don't accept your judgement, my dear, believe me. I merely wish to alleviate my own natural concern."

"If you say so, my lord." At any other time, Lady Ogden might have rejected his lordship's high-handedness, but in all truth, she was very weary. It did not seem worth the effort to exert her independence over what was, after all, such a small thing. His lordship was simply being considerate of her and her aunt. Oddly enough, once the viscount had been made aware that she was with child, his way with her had altered. He was more considerate of her feelings and her creature comforts. In bed-sport, she felt he had also changed. Oh, there was still intensity, but it seemed to her that their lovemaking had deepened in some inexplicable way. The new tenderness of his coupling with her moved her on a subliminal level which the most vigorous rogering had never done. Oftentimes, they spent as much time in languorous kissing as they did in the actual act. She knew she was in danger of falling in love with him, all over again. It was becoming a source of despair to her. *I am still naught but his mistress.*

Lady Ogden felt her lips quiver. She lifted the cup again and drank. The sweetened tea began to have its reviving effect, helping her to dispel her maudlin sentimentality. She resolutely turned from her unhappy reflections back to her aunt's sufferings. "Perhaps it's not such a bad idea for Dr. Manning to see my aunt. His opinion must weigh with her even more than my own."

"Now I am considerably alarmed, ma'am." She looked inquiringly at him, and Lord Ogden added, dryly, "You have not made much token protest to my suggestion."

Lady Ogden laughed up at the viscount. "No, for the reasonableness of it is clear even to me, my lord!"

"So, you will allow Dr. Manning to examine you, as well?"

Lady Ogden made the slightest gesture with one hand. "I'm too tired to argue, my lord."

Lord Ogden's dark brows creased. He reached out to tug on the bell-pull. "I shall send a man at once." Her ladyship's admission bothered him. He wondered whether her weariness was due more to the stress of nursing her aunt or to her interesting condition. Her body was beginning to show signs of her ripening. He did not mind her rounding belly or the heavier fullness of her breasts. It was proof of his virility. He gloried in the sensuality of their amorous congress, which she was flatteringly eager to engage in. However, it concerned him that there were an increasing number of days when she seemed to tire more easily. More than once of late, he'd entered her bedchamber only to find her already asleep. Sliding into her bed and drawing her curved warmth into his arms, it had added a piquant pleasure to rouse her to wakefulness by teasing her somnolent body. He'd even taken her while she slept. She had stirred restlessly, shifting her firm round bum against the cradle of his hips as he slipped his full prick in and out of her quim. She'd been wet and hot and she'd moaned, never fully awakening. She'd even shuddered to a gentle completion. His own consummation had been extremely satisfying.

Lord Ogden tore himself from his salacious remembrances. It was scarcely the moment to entertain such arousing contemplations. His member had stirred, but he ignored the awakening twitch. He reflected that it seemed that he was always thinking of spending himself. It would strike him at the oddest times.

The door opened and a footman entered the drawing-room. Lord Ogden briefly relayed his order. "Send for Dr. Manning. That will be all."

"Aye, milord."

As the door shut again, Lord Ogden turned his full attention once more on the lady. She was nibbling on a meat tartlet and he thought it was a good thing that she was taking some sustenance. The viscountess' face had thinned. She had always been a slender woman and, excepting the new plumpness of breasts and belly, he thought the contours of her figure had grown slighter to an alarming degree. The obvious weight-loss worried him, but he said nothing of that. She would not thank him. He pointed out the obvious. "Dr. Manning will realize that you are breeding."

"Yes, but it will come as no surprise to our household," she calmly replied. "Mills has informed me that ever since I kept to my bedchamber during my courses, there have been whispers of speculation. Then I had the true morning sickness for several weeks before I spoke to you. Chamber pots tell tales, my lord! When I give her leave, Mills will discreetly confirm the rumors."

He nodded. "Very good. I'm glad to hear it."

Lady Ogden lowered her eyes. She passed a slow finger back and forth over the rim of her tea cup. "I must soon inform my aunt of the news. I don't wish her to hear of it through servants' gossip."

Lord Ogden heard the tremor in her voice. Her words and the pensive way she stroked the edge of the teacup illustrated a strong undercurrent of feeling. He tried to discover the root of her disquiet. "Will Mrs. Merriweather not take your announcement well?"

Lady Ogden gave a flickering smile. She did not directly reply to his question. "I believe it's for the best to inform her. The intelligence will inevitably become known outside of Delincourt."

"Yes, of course." Lord Ogden deliberated for a moment. He could pursue it, but she had sidestepped his query. Instead, he reached into his coat pocket and withdrew a folded letter. "I have received correspondence from my sister, Amarys. Do you recall her?"

"Indeed, I recall Amarys very well! She was a few years younger than myself, so we were not bosom-bows, but I do remember she was a lovely girl."

The viscount held out the letter to her. Lady Ogden set aside the cup and saucer. With an inquiring glance, she took the neatly folded square from his hand. She turned it over and saw that the wax seal was already broken. She hesitated before venturing further. She looked up again. "My lord, are you certain you wish me to see your private correspondence?"

Lord Ogden gestured at the missive. "I invite you to read it, ma'am. The gist is this. Amarys is also a widow. She was wed to a captain of the line, a Captain Dalton, before he was killed at Ciudad Rodrigo. She has since been residing with one of my married sisters, but she writes that she has been feeling nostalgic for our home country. She wishes to come to Delincourt for a visit."

Lady Ogden unfolded the letter and swiftly perused the closely penned lines. It was just as his lordship had said, though the lady had not written anything half as concise. She smoothed the crinkled sheet, saying as she did so, "I will be glad to see her again."

"Then you do not mind if she comes? It will not be an inconvenience to you?"

Lady Ogden looked up at the viscount in considerable surprise. She wondered what it could possibly have to do with her since he was the master at Delincourt Manor. His lordship could issue an invitation to anyone he chose. The viscount was deferring to her almost as though she was in truth Delincourt's lawful mistress. Perhaps he simply wished to ascertain whether having his sister would be an inconvenience to the household, she thought, which of course was absurd. Her aunt would soon be as well as ever and there were plenty of spare bedrooms at the manor. All that was needed was to issue the appropriate orders to the housekeeper. "Of course not! It will be no inconvenience at all."

"Good. I did not wish to put an undue burden upon you." The viscount nodded, with a meaningful glance to indicate her figure. "In light of your thriving state."

Lady Ogden felt a sudden tide of heat sweep her cheeks. It had not occurred to her that her condition could possibly be behind his inquiry. She had not given that point a thought. She shook her head, believing it was but another display of his lordship's recent solicitous consideration for her, which was a confusing phenomenon. Of a certainty, she did not know *what* to think about her relationship with his lordship. She was bowled out by what the viscount said next.

"I overheard Mrs. Merriweather say that you had received another correspondence from your friend, Sir William Talley."

His lordship's gaze rested on her face. There seemed only lazy idleness in his casual observation, but she was not deceived. There was possessiveness in his dark, falcon-sharp eyes and she was struck with an astounding realization. *He will not allow another to take his place, even in my own mind. I am to be his, only his. I see it in the heat of his eyes.* Her heart thudded painfully in her breast. She felt pulled and twisted into shapes that coiled and turned again upon themselves. She was his mistress. She was afraid that he was beginning to bind her emotions. She was dependent upon him for the roof over her head and the clothes on her back. In every way, he was master of her fate.

Intuition made her perceptive. *He is jealous.* She was astonished, and suddenly made afraid. She could not afford to rouse the ire which she knew resided within him. *Only see what came of it the last time!* She thought it would be especially absurd to come to points over a member of her late husband's intimate circle.

"Sir William was Henry's friend," she corrected. "I'm barely acquainted with the gentleman."

"And yet the gentleman sends you gifts and writes you letters."

When she said nothing, he asked in a neutral voice, "Did you take a liking to Sir William when he visited here?"

He watched as Lady Ogden's expression went curiously blank. Her shrug was eloquent of nothing. "Sir William was one of Henry's friends," she repeated. There was nothing to be read in her expression and nothing in her non-committal voice. He did not know what to make of it.

Assuming an indifference that he was far from feeling, he turned to pick up the fire tool and nudged the log further back in the fireplace. A shower of sparks crackled out of the flames and rose up the chimney. *Damn his eyes,* he thought savagely. Against his will, he said over his shoulder, "You may invite any of your acquaintances to Delincourt that you wish. I have no objection."

There was a short silence. "That is most generous of you, my lord."

The viscount set aside the fire tool with careful deliberation. Then he looked over at her. "It is your home, too, Charlotte. I hope it will remain so."

The look in his eyes left Lady Ogden in no doubt of his meaning. A bit flustered, she glanced down at the letter again and pretended to be making a quick attempt to ascertain its full contents. "When might we expect Mrs. Dalton, my lord?"

Lord Ogden allowed her to change the subject. The tack was obviously meant to close an uncomfortable conversation. "She wants to come next month."

Lady Ogden looked up with a smile. "Wonderful! My aunt and I will be glad of her company."

"Then I shall write to her immediately."

Still smiling, Lady Ogden refolded the letter and offered it back to him. "I must tell my aunt. She will be so pleased."

"Will Mrs. Merriweather be equally pleased to learn of your breeding?"

Lady Ogden's smile vanished. Suddenly, she found it difficult to breathe. He had put into words what she did not want to address. Lady Ogden bent her head, avoiding his lordship's keen gaze. She twisted the fringe of her shawl between her fingers. "I cannot say, my lord. In truth, I fear what she might say."

Lord Ogden shook his head, a cleft forming between his brows. "With what I know of Mrs. Merriweather's amiable character, I cannot believe she would be so mean-spirited, yet this is what you imply."

Lady Ogden looked up quickly. She could not allow his lordship to misjudge her aunt so badly. With considerable restraint, she said, "My lord, Mrs. Merriweather was fully in my confidence. My aunt is aware that there was no chance –" She made a mute gesture at her waistline.

The matter was explained. Lord Ogden frowned. He had not considered that anyone but himself and the viscountess would ever come to know the truth behind the child's birth. His closest friend had discerned it, for which he blamed himself. *Arthur and his sharp eyes...his infallible understanding of his fellow creatures. I should have been more on my guard.* Rev. Major Ledger had refrained from condemning his morals once he'd owned up, but he recalled that he'd experienced an instinctive, defensive impulse to deny the truth. Of course, Lady Ogden would feel some anxiety over the reaction of her beloved aunt. It was only natural. He did not know what could be done about it. He clasped his hands behind his back. "In short, Mrs. Merriweather will instantly conclude that you and I have been dallying in amorous congress."

"An affair, yes." Lady Ogden brain was running riot. She could all too easily imagine what her aunt would think. Perhaps Mrs. Merriweather *had* once obliquely hinted encouragement for her niece to engage with the viscount in such a shocking, illicit relationship. But that, she thought unhappily, was far removed from what her aunt could actually have wanted. She couldn't imagine that her aunt would possibly accept it. The bitter pill of regret lodged in her heart. "A most reprehensible liaison."

Lord Ogden's bearing stiffened. Behind the rigid line of his back, his clasped hands tightened. *Reprehensible.* That was her feeling for him, for what they had fashioned between them. It angered him. *Of a certainty, it began ill but it is something else now. She welcomes me to her bed.* His mind whispered treason...*Of her own will?* He felt the lash of his conscience, which but further angered him. *Reprehensible!* He regarded her ladyship in simmering silence for a moment or two. Then he fulminated, speaking in a clipped, awful manner and with heavy sarcasm. "Is your aunt's good opinion so elevated, ma'am? Does not the prospect of a large annuity outweigh any ill regard? Will not Mrs. Merriweather forgive your moral depravity once you have explained that it was done for her security as well as your own?"

Lady Ogden's cheeks stained. In a low voice, she said, "You cut deep, my lord. I have become your mistress. Is it to be marveled at that I have regrets?"

"I am cruel. You must forgive me." His lordship's voice was utterly cold.

Lady Ogden felt tears spring to her eyes. "Yes, you are cruel." She swallowed against the thickening in her throat. She rose to her feet and curtsied. "Pray excuse me, my lord. I will go inform Mrs. Tower now that we shall be expecting Mrs. Dalton as a guest."

Lord Ogden made an abbreviated bow as she left the drawing-room.

24

When Lady Ogden left the housekeeper, it was to be informed by the butler that Dr. Manning had arrived and was examining Mrs. Merriweather. Afterwards, he would be entirely at her ladyship's disposal. She saw the viscount's sweeping hand in the message, but simply thanked Somerset and went upstairs to her bedchamber to await her own turn with the physician. She pulled the bell which would summon her dresser to come to her room and help her partially undress.

The local physician took a genuine interest in his patients and it was with a good deal of satisfaction that he finished his examination of Lady Ogden. He sat down to talk to her of sensible diet and exercise, finally ending, "I am very glad for you, my lady. It's a pity that his late lordship - well, well, it seems to me that you are right on schedule. Your health appears to be excellent. I will call upon you again in a month to see how you are progressing. How will that be?"

Lady Ogden nodded. She knew that the physician had assumed the late viscount was the father of her child and she was inordinately relieved. It had been an unacknowledged worry at the back of her mind that the medical man's expertise would expose her lie. A release of tension caused her quick smile. "Of course, Dr. Manning. But how did you find my aunt?"

"Ah, we both know how it is with Mrs. Merriweather! I have prescribed a draught for her aches. She shall rest easier. My prescription and Mrs. Tower's tisanes ought to do the trick. Give it a week or two and her symptoms shall pass off." The physician got to his feet and bowed. "I must be off, my lady. Pray do not hesitate to send word should you have need of me before I am due to come again."

"Thank you, Dr. Manning." Lady Ogden waited until the physician exited and the door was safely shut behind him before she addressed her dresser. "Mills, help make me tidy. I must go to my aunt."

"Yes, my lady."

As she had observed earlier to the viscount, there were already rumors in progress. It was probably only Rev. Major Ledger's earlier presence in the house and her aunt's illness that had kept the inevitable servants' gossip from reaching Mrs. Merriweather's ears. After the physician's visit to herself, she thought with a sigh, there was no question of keeping the news of her condition from her aunt any longer. Mrs. Merriweather's dresser might at that very moment be dropping the interesting tidbit to her mistress.

Lady Ogden knocked on Mrs. Merriweather's bedchamber door, and when she went in, she found her aunt awake and in surprisingly good spirits. Mrs. Merriweather addressed her in a cheerful manner which was quite in contrast to her previous pathetic tone. "My dear! Our dear, good Dr. Manning has quite raised my spirits! I am not dying after all!"

"I should hope not!" Lady Ogden advanced and bent to kiss her aunt's cheek. She sat down on the bed and smiled with affection at the lady. "You are looking much better, dear ma'am. Can you stand my visit or do you wish me to go away?"

Mrs. Merriweather reached out and caught her hand. "No, stay with me. Waters, your flitting from here to there has quite put me on the fidgets! Pray leave us. I shall not need you again for some little while, for I intend to nap."

"Very good, ma'am." The dresser left the bedchamber and shut the door.

Lady Ogden's heart began to beat heavily in her breast. She had half-hoped that she could postpone the inevitable conversation for at least a little while longer, in hopes of shoring up her wavering resolution. Now that the time for confession had come, her courage nearly deserted her. She was unsure how to begin. *I am such a coward.* She shut her eyes, for just a moment. When she opened them again, she said starkly, "Aunt, I am breeding."

Mrs. Merriweather stared fixedly at her, not uttering a word. Her hand was still in her aunt's grasp and she felt the old fingers tighten convulsively. Her aunt's silence, the blank look in her eyes – Lady Ogden's heart sank. She could not bear her aunt's frozen expression. She interpreted it as condemnation. Her eyes suddenly flooded with tears and she hastily turned her head away. With her free hand, she covered her eyes. "I have disappointed you, aunt! I'm so sorry!"

"Oh, my dear, *dear* child!" There was an insistent tug on her fingers. "Dear Charlotte, no, no! You have not disappointed me! Indeed, you haven't!"

Shame-faced, Lady Ogden reluctantly turned back around. She could barely force herself to meet her aunt's distressed gaze. "I bargained my virtue, ma'am! All for a decent living. You must despise me!"

"I hinted and encouraged and positively *pushed* you into it! If there is any blame, it is mine. Oh, Charlotte!" Mrs. Merriweather's face crumpled. "I thought if you could bring yourself to it – if you could love him again – Oh, surely, it would not be such a *wicked* thing, after all!"

As Lady Ogden watched, astonished, two fat tears rolled down her aunt's quivering face. "My dear ma'am! No, you mustn't blame yourself. It's my fault entirely. I must be – *I am!* – depraved. That is the true explanation."

So it went for several minutes, each lady heaping condemnation upon herself and exonerating the other, until Lady Ogden realized how ridiculous they must sound and she began to laugh. Her laughter was tinged with more than a hint of hysteria, but nevertheless, it served to break the cycle of recrimination. Mrs. Merriweather gave a short, broken titter.

"Oh, aunt!" Lady Ogden threw herself into Mrs. Merriweather's arms. She and her aunt clung to one another, mixing tears and hiccoughing on their watery chuckles. At last, Lady Ogden straightened, drawing away out of her aunt's embrace. Mrs. Merriweather settled back against her pillows again. Sniffing still, the older woman took out a scrap of handkerchief from her wristband and dried her eyes. "Well, my dear, enough of that! What is to be done?"

Lady Ogden shook her head. She wiped her fingers across her damp lashes. A tremor in her voice, she said, "I don't know! I can only wait upon events."

Mrs. Merriweather took hold of one of her niece's hands again and patted it in a comforting manner. In a hopeful voice, she said, "You mustn't fret, Charlotte. Whatever happens, it will be all right. You will see."

"Yes, we shall see." Lady Ogden was subdued, her spirits further sinking. Short minutes later, she left her aunt's bedchamber, saying that she was needed downstairs in the kitchen to consult with the cook over the week's menus. However, what swam uppermost in her mind was the ugly rift that had so swiftly sprung up between her and the viscount. Her natural apprehension concerning her aunt's reaction had been taken in such bad part by his lordship. She could not understand it. Surely, the viscount must have recognized the validity of her apprehension. Her brows knit. Then again, Lord Ogden had seemed often enough to willfully misinterpret what she said to him. It was as though he had no inkling of the workings of her mind.

On the turn of the stairs, Lady Ogden ran into the viscount. She gave a little jump of fright. "Oh!" His lordship's sudden appearance, just when she was thinking so deeply about him, shook her equilibrium. As it always had, her pride came to her rescue. "My lord," she said in a chilly voice. She bent her head in a stiff nod and started to walk past him.

He detained her by the simple expedient of catching her elbow. "Lady Ogden, I was just coming to find you. Pray, let us go into the upper drawing-room, for there is something I wish to say to you in private."

"Very well." Lady Ogden allowed herself to be escorted back up the flight of stairs she had just come down. She was ushered into the upper drawing-room and the viscount shut the door. She turned around and eyed him with some hostility and trepidation. "What is this about, my lord?"

"I wished to apologize, ma'am. I was curt and insulting. I cast a slur against Mrs. Merriweather's integrity and yours. It was badly done."

Lady Ogden was utterly taken aback. She could not imagine what had motivated him to ask her pardon. He had thrown her off-balance again. After a moment, regaining some sense of dignity, she gave a nod. "I thank you, my lord. It is good of you to say so."

Clasping his hands behind his back, he walked forward. He stopped only a few steps short of her. His dark gaze searched her face. "I spoke with Dr. Manning before he left. I'm glad to hear that you are doing well, ma'am. I was concerned for your health."

She replied with all the calm at her command. She felt oddly like weeping. He had completely overset her again with his unexpected solicitude. It seemed it was to be a day for being rocked this way and that, not knowing what to think or feel from moment to moment. "Pray do not be concerned, my lord. I am perfectly well."

He nodded gravely. "Very good." He stepped to the side, making way for her. She walked toward the door. Once she had turned the brass knob, she hesitated and looked back. Silently, he gestured for her to proceed him from the room. Lady Ogden inclined her head, opened the door, and fled.

Mrs. Merriweather eventually felt well enough to quit her sickroom. The lady bounced back to her characteristic cheerful self, but she treated his lordship with a new reserve. She was civil, she was polite, but she was distant, whereas before she had readily introduced conversation between them. She regarded the viscount doubtfully, as though unsure what to make of him. Lord Ogden felt that her thoughts could practically be read on her face. *It seems I've become a hostile force, and she must reconnoiter her position.*

He waited for the lady's irresolution to abate. However, Mrs. Merriweather began to avoid his lordship's company. Whenever possible, she left a room when he entered and if she could not do that, then she studiously avoided engaging in discourse, whether over the dinner table or at evening coffee. The stilted conversations were becoming increasingly awkward, leading to a sharpening tension whenever the viscount and the two ladies were together. In addition, Lord Ogden was fairly certain that Mrs. Merriweather's extraordinary behavior was becoming noticed by the servants.

The viscount's temper was exacerbated. But he was ruefully aware that the uncomfortable atmosphere was a direct result of actions he had initiated, so he held back from voicing his natural annoyance. As for Lady Ogden, her unhappiness was obvious; he read it in the strain of her expression and the stiffness in her carriage. He knew the situation could not be allowed to continue.

It was not many evenings before Lord Ogden decided that he would have to clear the air. "Mrs. Merriweather, I would like to sit down with you privately. Pray, will you join me in the study?"

"Certainly, my lord." With great dignity, Mrs. Merriweather rose and went toward the door. Lord Ogden opened it and made a polite gesture for the lady to precede him from the drawing-room. As he exited, he glanced back. Lady Ogden looked anxious and her gaze followed them from the drawing-room.

Lord Ogden opened the door to the ground-floor study and entered, turning to wait for the lady. When she had entered, he shut the door. Mrs. Merriweather regarded him with apprehension on her face. Lord Ogden walked past her. As he sat down behind the large mahogany desk, he heard the rustle of the lady's skirts as she followed him across the room. He looked up and gestured to one of the wingback chairs in front of the desk.

"Pray be seated, Mrs. Merriweather." The chair creaked faintly as the elderly lady sat down. Lord Ogden saw that her faded, blue eyes were regarding him with deep wariness. He did not ever recall seeing that watchful look before. Mrs. Merriweather was not much given to somber expressions.

Lord Ogden steeled himself for the necessary but difficult conversation with the lady. He knew he was not a subtle man and so he did not attempt to soften his blunt admission with pretty words. "I will be frank with you, Mrs. Merriweather. Lady Ogden and I are engaged in an illicit affair. However, I don't wish you to think Lady Ogden is in any respect a wanton."

"That I know, my lord."

The viscount found he could not continue under Mrs. Merriweather's distressed gaze. It was harder than any conversation he had ever undertaken, up to and including informing someone of a relative's battle-death. Lord Ogden got up, deserted his place, and walked toward one of the windows. Before reaching the window, he swung around, putting his back to it. He did not know it, but the way he stood – with his hands clasped behind him and with the candlelight flickering over his harsh features – filled the elderly lady with nervous dread. Without roundabout, Lord Ogden harshly stated, "A bargain was made between us. It was not respectable. I am very sure Lady Ogden had second thoughts. I did not."

Mrs. Merriweather believed she was having heart palpitations. Her eyes darted everywhere, trying to avoid his lordship's stern countenance. She wanted to be somewhere else, anywhere else – *such unpleasant flutterings*! – but then, her overwhelming concern for her niece emboldened her. She gathered up all of her courage and looked up to meet the viscount's forbidding expression. Mrs. Merriweather came straight to the point. "My lord, do you care at all for my niece?"

The viscount did not immediately reply. His face was inscrutable. At length, he said, "If you will recall, I offered my hand to your niece once. I cared for her then. I care for her now, though perhaps in a different fashion than I did in my callow youth. I wish her to be happy. I mean to see her future made secure. I believe that must satisfy you, ma'am."

For several seconds, Mrs. Merriweather stared at the viscount. He was made unaccountably disconcerted by her unwavering gaze. The murky blue eyes had become surprisingly sharp. She did not say anything for some minutes, but she appeared to be thinking very hard. Then she nodded, slowly. "Very well, my lord. I understand."

Mrs. Merriweather got up and shook out the folds in her skirt. She turned away from the viscount, and without a backward glance, she exited the room.

Lord Ogden let the tension drop from his shoulders. *Extraordinary business. Glad it's done.* He hoped the short conversation had done some good in mending the fences between himself and the elderly lady. He had grown to be fond of her and he would regret losing her good favor. Lord Ogden decided to wait a few minutes before he followed Mrs. Merriweather, believing that Lady Ogden would be anxious to know what had passed between himself and her aunt, and the ladies must be allowed an opportunity to confer between themselves. After what he judged to be a long-enough interval, he returned to the drawing-room. Lady Ogden was smiling; she gave the slightest nod when she saw him. He read what he interpreted to be gratitude in her warm glance. As for Mrs. Merriweather, the elderly dame greeted the viscount with all of her former friendliness.

None of them ever spoke of it again.

Mrs. Merriweather reverted to her usual placid manner. From that hour, Lady Ogden was able to be more open with her aunt and there came to be altogether an easier atmosphere, evident even that same evening. Lord Ogden and her ladyship did not feel constrained by Mrs. Merriweather's presence any longer. Without being conscious of it, the viscount and Lady Ogden adopted a relaxed, informal manner. Over coffee, Lady Ogden carelessly addressed his lordship by his Christian name, an intimacy reserved to wedded couples. Almost at once, she realized her mistake. Her gaze flew to meet the rueful amusement in the viscount's eyes. She and Lord Ogden looked over at Mrs. Merriweather. When that lady did not appear shocked, they relaxed alike in their mutual relief. Perhaps her aunt had not heard, she thought.

However, Mrs. Merriweather had indeed heard and she uttered a mild reproof. "You must be more careful, Charlotte. It's all right with me, but you mustn't let your guard down too much. What if we were sitting with one of our neighbors who had come to call? Discretion must continue to be observed by you and by his lordship. Such careless address will persuade any hearers of your being engaged to each other."

The color fluctuated in Lady Ogden's cheeks.

The viscount acknowledged the lady's observation with a bow. "You are right to reprimand us, Mrs. Merriweather," said Lord Ogden gravely, even though a faint smile curled his lips.

"And I do think Somerset or Mrs. Tower would have an apoplexy were they to stumble upon the pair of you *lurking* together in a doorway, so don't do it," said Mrs. Merriweather tartly.

"Aunt!" Lady Ogden turned scarlet, but the viscount was shaken by what she considered to be reprehensible laughter.

25

Somerset brought in the post. As Lord Ogden glanced through the mail, he saw that there was again something from Sir William Talley. "You have a communique, ma'am." Lord Ogden reached over the plates and crockery on the laden breakfast table and handed the thin packet to her ladyship. Lady Ogden did not open the piece of mail but set it aside, obviously intending to open it when she was in private.

Under his lowered brows, Lord Ogden observed her ladyship with some disapprobation. He was aware of the continued correspondence, of course. He had even admired the small chapbook when it had been shown to him. His speculation about what lay behind Sir William's gilt-edged token had coalesced into an unwelcome conclusion – the gentleman was making up to his cousin-in-law. The only thing he was uncertain about was what her ladyship thought about it. He did not like it that she no longer opened the gentleman's correspondence in front of her aunt and himself.

He suspected it bespoke an attachment that had not been there before.

Lord Ogden tightened his lips and turned his attention to his own mail. He found a letter directed in a familiar, firm hand. He opened it at once and scanned the brief lines. Rev. Major Ledger had written to inform his lordship that he expected to return to Delincourt at the end of the week. He was pleased. "Very good!"

The viscount looked up and at once informed Lady Ogden and Mrs. Merriweather of the letter's contents. He was expecting to hear exclamations of pleasure at the news. Instead, the ladies chorused in obvious dismay. "So soon!" "Oh, dear, that is unfortunate!"

Lord Ogden regarded his table companions with astonishment. "But I thought you were looking forward to having Rev. Major Ledger back with us!"

The viscount's thunderstruck expression made it plain that an explanation was required, and Lady Ogden said, "Indeed, we are! But we decided between us only yesterday afternoon that the vicarage must be put into some kind of order. A week will leave us very little time to accomplish our goal."

Mrs. Merriweather nodded. "We will be showing a poor welcome to Rev. Major Ledger otherwise."

Lord Ogden obviously thought their concern was nonsensical and unwarranted. He was quick to assure them that they were in error. "Rev. Major Ledger is an old campaigner, like myself, and will not care all that much. Believe me, Arthur is impervious to the lack of creature comforts."

Smiling at his lordship's ignorance, Lady Ogden shook her head. "You must allow us this, my lord. We will fret ourselves to flinders if we are not given our way! We have a duty to make the vicarage as tolerable as possible."

"Quite so! It is a point of pride, my lord," put in Mrs. Merriweather.

The viscount threw up a hand in surrender, laughter in his face. "Very well! Have it as you will! I'm certain Arthur will be very grateful for a clean-swept floor and a vase of flowers."

"Why, what a very odd notion you have of our enterprise, my lord," exclaimed Mrs. Merriweather. "There's a great deal more to be done than arrange a few flowers! That is to say, if the garden was in bloom, which it isn't."

"Indeed, there is much to do! The Holland covers must be removed and the drapes opened and the carpets beaten," said Lady Ogden, ticking off each task on her fingers. "An inventory needs to be done of the crockery and the linen closet. Aunt, I suspect we shall find a number of the linens and sheets have been damaged by mice, so there will be darning and mending."

"Very true, dear. Then there is the polishing and sweeping and arranging the furniture to the best effect," said Mrs. Merriweather. She shook her head but a small smile began to light her face. "Oh, dear me, it is quite a formidable undertaking."

With a laughing glance at the viscount, whose expression was incredulous, Lady Ogden said, "I assure you, my lord, we shall be very busy."

Lord Ogden shook his head. He was thoroughly amused. "I see that you will be, my lady. But Mrs. Merriweather! You have not been out of your bed so very long. Are you well enough to take on such a formidable project?"

"Surely you jest, my lord! I am well enough! This is just the sort of thing I most enjoy. What glad tidings! I shall go along to inform Mrs. Tower of Rev. Major Ledger's expected return and consult with her." The elderly lady pushed back her chair and got to her feet. Her speech and manner were brisk. "We must begin this very day if we are to get done by the end of the week! We shall take some of the staff with us. Perhaps we should hire a couple of girls from the village. Dear me! So much to think about! Pray excuse me, my lord."

Lord Ogden politely stood up. "Of course, ma'am." Mrs. Merriweather, humming tunelessly, hurried out of the room. Sitting back down, he said, "A company of maids must be deployed, all armed with their brooms and brushes, along with the footman to lift and carry."

Lady Ogden chuckled. "You mock, my lord, but it *will* be quite an undertaking, especially since everything must be done in such a rush. Rev. Major Ledger will need to employ a household staff, too. Has he written to you of his wishes?"

"No, he has not. I doubt such details have even entered his head, for it did not occur to me," said Lord Ogden ruefully. "But of course, he must have a housekeeper, a groom, and a cook."

"At the very least," agreed Lady Ogden. "He'll need an all-round maid and a gardener, as well. If you do not think Rev. Major Ledger would object, I could set about making inquiries. Somerset and Mrs. Tower might know of some respectable persons in the county who would be suitable candidates for Rev. Major Ledger's household."

"Arthur will have no notion how to set about the business. I know he would be grateful to you. It will not be an imposition on you?"

"Of course not. I shall be happy to help out in such a way."

Lord Ogden inclined his head, acknowledging her assurance. With a grin, he observed, "Mrs. Merriweather has made a remarkable recovery."

"Indeed, the milder weather we are enjoying has worked its miracle."

"I was thinking it was housewifely zeal that has cured her."

Lady Ogden laughed. "Just so!"

They were alone in the breakfast-room. Without conscious awareness, they had adapted an informal manner between themselves. Apropos of nothing, Lady Ogden remarked, "I have given Mills leave to inform the household staff that I am *enceinte*." She regarded his lordship with a question in her gaze.

Lord Ogden nodded. "It's time." That was all the reply he gave, but she was reassured. Sometimes they were in perfect alignment in their thinking. Nothing more was said on the subject. Instead, smiling, he suggested, "Come riding with me. Let Mrs. Merriweather have her fun. She obviously enjoys the bustle of organization."

Lady Ogden gave a laugh. She was very ready to oblige him. "Yes, I mustn't steal her thunder. Very well, my lord! Give me a quarter hour to change into my habit and I shall meet you."

"Good."

Such singular rapprochement had spilled over in their other activities. When Lady Ogden had again started to regularly exercise her horse, they had formed the agreeable habit of riding together almost daily. She could never recall how it had come about, but it was agreed between them enough time had elapsed since the viscount's arrival at Delincourt that their riding out together would not cause undue gossip. More often than not, they dispensed with a groom, with the tacit understanding that their conversation was able to roam freer without the presence of a servant. Such outings were filled with a slow deepening of companionship.

Lady Ogden was helped by her dresser into her old dark brown riding habit. It was furbished with black ribbons, as was everything else in her wardrobe. Meager funds had made impossible the ordering of an entire wardrobe of mourning and hiring a tailor to make a new habit in black had been completely out of the question. She was heartily glad of it. *I look such a fright in black.* A new riding habit was a major expense and the garment would have years of use before it would go to the rag basket. She had no desire to wear black beyond what mourning dictated. When it came time to replace her habit, she wanted one done up in the latest color and style. "I'm glad you have let out the seams, Mills. It was becoming tight."

"Well, ma'am, you cannot expect otherwise. Before much longer, you will have to give up your riding altogether."

"Shall I, indeed! Aside from the possibility of splitting my seams, I don't see that at all." Lady Ogden was loath to give up what she felt were halcyon hours, all too fleeting ones at that. She up on her mare and the viscount mounted on his gelding, they had spent many pleasant hours riding over the damp countryside. She met her dresser's disapproving expression and pursed lips reflected in the mirror and laughed. "Pray do not look so dour, Mills. I shall quit when I must. Then I shall take to driving about in the gig. Will that better suit your notions of propriety?"

"Indeed, it will, my lady!"

Lady Ogden enjoyed her outing with the viscount. The heavy air was damp and chilly, but the breeze generated by being on horseback chased it away. His lordship suggested that they ride over to the vicarage. She agreed and they made their way there. Reining in their mounts, they surveyed the shuttered vicarage house and the surrounding outbuildings.

"It was a happy place to spend one's childhood," remarked Lord Ogden, surveying the mellow walls of the stone buildings. "I'm glad that it will be put to good use again."

"Let us go in," said Lady Ogden suddenly. She was curious to see the inside of the place where he had lived as a boy. She could not recall ever having visited the vicarage, but then, she would have been too young to accompany her mother on social calls. After her mother became ill, of course, there had been only a restricted kind of social interaction all during her girlhood. She had thirsted for friendships and she had treasured each and every invitation to visit one of the other respectable families in the neighborhood. She had always recalled the Rt. Rev. Crawford's faithful visits to her mother at the Grange, rare highlights standing out from a somewhat bleak upbringing.

"Very well." The viscount dismounted and tied his reins to an iron post. Then he turned to aid his companion to get down from her mare. His hands were firm about her waist as he helped her descend to the ground. There was no awkwardness attending their close proximity to one another. Anyone seeing them would have taken them for a wedded couple.

Lady Ogden picked up the tail of her riding habit and slung it over her elbow, carrying her crop in her gloved hand. Lord Ogden escorted her up the path. He still had the key and opened the door. "After you, ma'am. You shall see at once what a task you and Mrs. Merriweather have set yourselves."

Curious, Lady Ogden walked from room to room. "I see that you and Rev. Major Ledger have dragged open some of the drapes. It's better than I expected. Dusty, of course, but that shall soon be remedied." She began pulling Holland covers from off some of the furniture. "Oh, the pieces are old but most are still in good condition. I think we shall be able to salvage the majority of them for Rev. Major Ledger's use."

"I have told Arthur that he must change anything that is not to his taste," said Lord Ogden, critically surveying the revealed contents of the room. "You are right, everything is out of fashion. My father did not attempt to refurbish after the death of my mother."

"But it's still a comfortable place. The rooms are all in good proportion. I wonder if the chimneys smoke?"

"They probably do! I don't doubt several bird's-nests have been built inside of them. I should have thought of that myself. Smoking chimneys will be all too reminiscent of our soldiering days and I shouldn't wish to subject Arthur to that!" said Lord Ogden with a grimace. "I shall have some men over to clean them out and repair any damage that might be found."

Lady Ogden chuckled. "You see, my lord, you are as keen as my aunt and myself to make the most of the vicarage for Rev. Major Ledger."

"Of course, I do! I don't want Arthur to turn tail and run back to London," retorted Lord Ogden. "Come, let us be gone. We must get back before Mrs. Merriweather's army sets out, for I can see that I must add a few tasks to the good lady's list!"

Emerging from the vicarage, they walked companionably to where they had tethered the horses. His lordship offered his laced hands for her to step into and he threw her up into the sidesaddle. She landed light as a feather and arranged her riding skirt to modestly cover her legs, while he mounted his own steed. The two riders gathered their reins and turned their horses for home. Their conversation was all about the vicarage and Rev. Major Ledger's return. After reaching Delincourt, Lady Ogden and the viscount walked up from the stables to the manor house. They entered the back of the edifice through the servants' entrance and went their separate ways.

Lady Ogden changed out of her riding clothes and with her dresser's help donned a black merino daydress. She placed the black shawl over her shoulders and arranged its dark folds to her satisfaction. "Thank you, Mills." The dresser nodded, folding the mud-splashed riding habit over her arm and bearing the heavy garment away to be sponged clean.

Lady Ogden went into her private sitting room. She had carried her one piece of mail upstairs before the morning's outing. Now with a small penknife from her desk, Lady Ogden slit the wax seal on the thin packet she'd received from Sir William Talley. When she pulled forth the contents, she said, "Oh my, whatever is the man's object?" The gentleman's latest offering was pianoforte sheet music and it was not just any piece, but a love ballad. On the instant, she decided that she would tell only her aunt about it. She would say nothing of it to the viscount.

When she had shown the chapbook to his lordship, he had examined it and remarked that it was indeed a fine copy of the psalms. Lord Ogden had not said so, but she had formed the impression that his lordship disapproved of Sir William's little present, however unexceptional it was.

Lady Ogden rather thought his lordship would behave even stiffer over Sir William's newest offering. She suspected he might even say something that she would find objectionable. She wasn't keen on being thrown on the defensive or made to feel in some way at fault, especially over a favor that she cared nothing about.

However, she did not escape recrimination, after all. Mrs. Merriweather was very ready to express her disapproval. "My dear Charlotte, I begin to suspect in good earnest that Sir William is of the mind to court you. Yes, yes, you pooh-pooh the notion as too fantastic! But this makes two gifts!"

"I can count, aunt."

Ignoring her niece's dry observation, Mrs. Merriweather held up two fingers. "Two gifts from a gentleman who is barely an acquaintance and this one is more intimate than the last. A lover's ballad, indeed! If Sir William was some sort of relation, there would be no question of impropriety, but as it is, I cannot like it."

"I do agree with you, dear ma'am. Except for your flight of fancy that Sir William is making up to me," said Lady Ogden. She shook her head at her aunt's chuff of annoyance. "No, I cannot believe that, and even if it was so, I'm of no mind to give my hand and my heart away. Poor Sir William will simply have to look elsewhere!"

At her niece's light tone, Mrs. Merriweather could not help chuckling. "Poor Sir William, indeed! Charlotte, do be serious. What are you going to do about acknowledging this newest offering?"

"I haven't decided. Perhaps I shall seek his lordship's advice," said Lady Ogden with flippancy.

Mrs. Merriweather regarded her with something akin to horror. "You will not! He was positively *frosty* over the chapbook!"

Lady Ogden laughed and agreed she would not. "His lordship holds himself on as high a form as you do, aunt. I suspect his sense of propriety will be as affronted as yours. I shall not mention it to him at all."

However, his lordship missed very little and she should have known the receipt of the thin parcel would occasion remark. At evening coffee, the viscount said, "I noticed the mail you received this morning was from Sir William Talley, my lady."

Lady Ogden exchanged glances with her aunt, hers half-accusatory, but that lady shook her head in denial. Lady Ogden turned her head and, in a cool voice, said, "Why, yes, I did. It was in the way of a small favor, I suppose."

"The gentleman is all politeness. What was it, may I ask?"

More than a little taken aback by his lordship's blunt curiosity, Lady Ogden gazed at him for a long moment before she replied. "Sir William sent me some sheet music."

"Ah; I did not know you played."

"Not well, I fear. I was never a great one to practice, which I now regret."

Lord Ogden took some satisfaction in hearing it. The London gentleman was not so well-enough acquainted with her ladyship to have known that particular fact about her. It quite lightened his humor. Whatever her ladyship's private reflections, he was determined to wean her brain away from thoughts of Sir William Talley. However, what he had in mind would have to wait; outside the confines of Lady Ogden's bedchamber, the bounds of propriety were never strained beyond what was considered proper behavior.

With a faint, teasing smile, he said, "Sir William appears to harbor hopes that his gift will inspire you to better practice. I must admit, I do believe practice is essential to elevate the ordinary act and bring it to an artful height." He was amused when her ladyship's green eyes widened.

"More coffee?" asked Lady Ogden pointedly, putting a period to the conversation. She wasn't quite certain what to make of his lordship's oblique remark, though she could hazard a guess, she thought indignantly. *And my aunt sitting right here, too!*

"Yes, thank you," he said meekly.

She was not fooled by his lordship's bland affability, not for a moment. He was inwardly laughing at her, at some jest of his own. At once, Lady Ogden became fixed in her determination to learn the pianoforte piece. She knew the viscount had meant to put her out of countenance, just a little; to punish him, she decided to ignore the reprehensible gentleman for the remainder of the evening. *That will serve the viscount his just desserts!* "Aunt, what do you say to another backgammon contest?"

"I am very willing, my dear."

Lord Ogden wasn't at all perturbed by what he rightly perceived to be her ladyship's snub. He settled into a wingback chair to read a lengthy, interesting treatise on agriculture.

When the mantel clock struck ten o'clock, Lord Ogden glanced up at it. He turned his gaze to the lovely lady whose bed he would shortly be occupying, and he smiled. He enjoyed practice of the carnal sort, he admitted to himself. *It is indeed elevating.*

26

Upon Rev. Major Ledger's return, he professed himself very well-satisfied with the vicarage. Walking from room to room in company with Lord Ogden, he expressed delight at how well the interior of the place appeared and highly praised the efforts of the ladies. Lord Ogden felt pride in Lady Ogden and Mrs. Merriweather for their success in cleaning up the old vicarage and making it habitable. He had hoped that the sprawling house would meet with Rev. Major Ledger's approval and was glad that it did. He wanted his old friend to be happy in the living.

Sunlight streamed into every room through newly-cleaned window panes, glistening on the dark wood of polished furniture. "It's almost a different place altogether," marveled Rev. Major Ledger. In one of the east-facing bedrooms, he sat down on the side of the bed, bouncing a little to test the thick mattress. He smoothed a reverent hand over the bedcoverings, murmuring, "Pillows and clean linens and a plump mattress. A comfortable bed, indeed."

"Never mind the bed, dear fellow," said Lord Ogden with a grin. He was glad to have been able to supply such a luxurious item as the new mattress. It had cost a pretty penny to have it shipped by cart from London to the vicarage, but he did not begrudge the expense. "For my money, the bowls of dried flowers and bits of sticks in every room are the nicest touch It's just what we old campaigners most appreciated after a hard skirmish. Potpourri, forsooth!"

Rev. Major Ledger laughed. "Just so! I want for nothing. Pray express my thanks to her ladyship and Mrs. Merriweather."

"You may do so yourself when you come to dine tonight."

Rev. Major Ledger got up from the bed and bowed. "I accept the invitation with alacrity. Otherwise, I will have to lay a snare and hope to catch a hare for my supper tonight."

Lord Ogden laughed. "Lady Ogden is looking out for staff for you, so it will not ever come to that. I believe she has already settled on a housekeeper. The woman will be sent to interview with you."

"Good Lord, I know nothing of such matters! I'd rather her ladyship handled all the details for me. I will trust in Lady Ogden's judgement," said Rev. Major Ledger, alarmed. "The mere thought of having to arrange for domestics makes my knees knock."

"Chicken-heart!" said Lord Ogden with a grin. "But I told her ladyship how it would be. I'll wager she will soon have a full staff for you. However, you must come to Delincourt to dine every day until you are settled."

"You have overwhelmed me with kindness. I feel truly welcomed."

The viscount warmly smiled at the man whose friendship he valued most in the world. He clapped him on the shoulder. "Of course, you will always be welcome! I would not like to think of you, presiding alone at your own table, when you can sit down with us."

"That will be agreeable, indeed. I will be the richer for the company." Rev. Major Ledger reached inside his coat and drew out a folded parchment. "I had wanted to give this to you earlier, except with all the flurry over my arrival and the ladies being present, I thought it best to wait until we were alone."

Lord Ogden took the legal document and slid it carefully inside his own coat pocket. He felt a leap of his spirit as he did so. He hoped the day would not be too far away when he might use it. "Thank you for obtaining it for me, Arthur. I will put it safely away."

Rev. Major Ledger regarded him with curiosity. "When do you think you will make use of it?"

Lord Ogden shrugged. "I hardly know."

For several weeks, Lady Ogden had been working on two new gowns. She was very well-pleased with the results of her needlework. She had done the gowns in half-mourning, heeding her aunt's advice to make an early start in changing over her wardrobe. One gown was a walking dress made up in a lavender-and-black pinstripe jaconet muslin, with delicate embroidery running up the front and across the bodice; the other was a daydress in a dove-gray figured muslin, with a ruff of triple lace, and long full sleeves tied in three places with ribbon. Comparing her creations against the fashion plates she had used for her inspiration, she said complacently, "I am quite set up in my own esteem, aunt. Perhaps I should set up as a modish dressmaker."

"Very likely!" retorted Mrs. Merriweather. She was not as notable a needlewoman as her niece, but she had finely hemmed a lovely square of gray cambric muslin for a new shawl and was placing tiny stitches of elaborate embroidery in the corners. She held up the square, spreading it aloft between her two hands, and looked critically at her handiwork. "It's not a paisley or a Kashmere, and of course you couldn't wear such strong colors yet, in any event." Mrs. Merriweather cast a disparaging look at her niece's shawl. "But at least, this is an improvement over what you have on now. You shall soon be able to put away that awful black thing, which makes you look positively hagged and very like an old crow."

"It's lovely! Just what I most need!" Lady Ogden reached over and fondly hugged her aunt. "Thank you, dear ma'am!" The mantel clock struck the hour and she looked up at it in surprise. "Why, how the time has flown! We will be hearing the dinner bell soon." She pushed back her chair and stood up, shaking out the deep creases in her black bombazine skirt. "Well, aunt! Another day in our cozy den is at an end."

"Indeed, and it's such a relief that we may leave it with light hearts. Do you recall, dearest, what it was like before? When we suffered the affliction of the late viscount's guests? Every day, I wished passionately that his lordship and his horrid friends would return to London!"

Lady Ogden was astonished. "Why ever are you thinking about that?"

"I don't know, it just struck me. So odd!" Mrs. Merriweather shook her head. Her expression was pensive. With a quick glance, she added, "It is perhaps wicked of me to say it, my dear, since you are *widowed*, but I don't regret how things have turned out."

Lady Ogden gave a low laugh, well able to appreciate what her aunt was saying. His lordship's rare visits to Delincourt Manor usually coincided with his empty pockets, but at times he had simply invited his smart London friends down for a long, debauched house-party. The dissipations had been no different on the last occasion, except that it had culminated in the viscount's ghastly, lingering end and her deathbed vigil. "No more than I do, dear ma'am! However, since the viscount was always eager to return to his haunts in London, we had only to endure a little while each time."

"It was worse for you, my dear. I know how much you dreaded those visits. You were miserable. There was no escape, was there? You could not get away, even to take the exercise which you were used to," said Mrs. Merriweather with a sympathetic smile. As she rolled up her needlework and put it away, she cast another glance at her niece. "We were cooped up here in a gilded cage, as it were."

"Indeed, ma'am." Lady Ogden shrugged. "It was a small price to pay to avoid disagreeable situations." It was better to feel akin to a wretched prisoner, reflected Lady Ogden bitterly, rather than come face-to-face with a drunken gentleman staggering along the passage. She had experienced one such unhappy encounter on a previous visit when Lord Henry Ogden and his friends had descended like locusts upon them. It had been unnerving, and faintly alarming, to be the object of such fawning, intoxicated civilities, and she had been of no mind to repeat the unpleasant experience. As for her anxious concern for the maids, she had tried to avoid any dire consequences by issuing orders that the servant women were to work together in pairs. Lady Ogden thinned her lips. It had not sufficed, as she had lately been made aware of by her housekeeper.

As for my horrid encounter with Sir William, that awful dawn...

Putting it out of her mind, Lady Ogden slipped her arm around her aunt's ample waist and opened the drawing-room door. Only half-joking, she remarked, "At least we were never importuned in getting to our bedchambers, aunt."

"No, indeed!" Mrs. Merriweather grimaced. "Those dreadful creatures seemingly popped up out of the woodwork when one least expected them! I nearly shrieked once from the shock. My heart positively *leaped*! It was a happy notion of yours to station a footman on the landing, close by the upper drawing-room. I found it a comfort."

"That was my object, dear aunt. Now, let us have no more melancholy reminiscences, I pray you! We've just got time to change for dinner." The ladies exchanged a fond embrace before separating to enter their bedchambers where their dressers already awaited them.

The dinner held in the front parlor that evening was a pleasant and extended affair. Rev. Major Ledger's company was a welcome addition, Lady Ogden thought. The gentleman made of himself an agreeable guest by his pleasant manners and his willingness to be pleased. He praised the soup and the several entrees, removed by poultry, beef and mutton, along with several vegetables and the sweet savories.

"I've had only bachelor fare while living in London. This is a rare pleasure, believe me!"

"But surely, you must have had invitations to dine," said Mrs. Merriweather, wondering at it.

Rev. Major Ledger waved away his former social repasts as inconsequential. "Ah, but never was any such dinner invitation seasoned so well by my company!"

Lord Ogden cracked a grin. "Flatterer! Offering Spanish coin!"

Rev. Major Ledger laid his hand over his heart and managed to look wounded, even though his gray eyes were alight with laughter. "My lord! I must protest! You wound my sensibilities."

The viscount snorted and it was Rev. Major Ledger's turn to laugh.

The gentleman enlivened the overall conversation and kept Lady Ogden and her aunt in a ripple of amusement. He even made an amusing account of his eagerness to accept his lordship's invitation to dinner. "Otherwise, I was faced with the necessity of snaring my dinner and I did not wish to be taken up for poaching." The gentleman's droll humor roused general laughter.

"Ah, but we old campaigners were all poachers," said Lord Ogden with a flickering smile. He was sitting back, relaxed, in his chair, with his head turned in his friend's direction. "A scrawny chicken in the pot was to be savored."

"Indeed, it was! And a rare treat, too! But here, let us toast to better days." Rev. Major Ledger raised his glass, followed immediately by the rest of the company. "A toast to the future! May every day's pot be full to the brim of viands and savory to the tongue!"

"Here, here!" exclaimed Lord Ogden, laughing. His lordship's keen amusement was echoed by Lady Ogden and Mrs. Merriweather, who had expected a solemn speech and were taken pleasantly by surprise by the merry declaration. Lady Ogden reflected that the resulting conviviality was as uplifting as might have been any statement of elevated sentiment.

The ladies eventually withdrew, once the covers were removed, and left the gentlemen to enjoy their after-dinner wine. Lady Ogden and Mrs. Merriweather retired to the drawing-room to play at backgammon, as was their usual custom in the evenings. When Lord Ogden and Rev. Major Ledger joined them in the drawing-room, the gentlemen exchanged a few civilities with the ladies, but it was not long before they sat down at a small table to play a few hands of piquet. Their lively discourse was interspersed freely with bursts of laughter.

When Somerset rolled in the coffee-urn, the separate parts of the party came together again. As Lady Ogden poured for the company, Rev. Major Ledger asked her and Mrs. Merriweather if they enjoyed playing whist. They assured him that they did and a larger table was cleared for the four-handed game. During the play, following her thoughts, Lady Ogden remarked, "We must have a supper at Delincourt to introduce you to the neighborhood, Rev. Maj. Ledger."

"A capital idea," declared Lord Ogden. He grinned at his old comrade-in-arms. "We must tout you off, Arthur, and publicize you as a being of great worth! That will set you up properly as the new vicar."

"Good Lord!"

"Well, so we should! Everyone should be made aware that you are, indeed, a worthy man," said Mrs. Merriweather, without lifting her eyes from looking over the cards in her hand. "Otherwise, why would anyone come to listen to your sermons?"

Lord Ogden and Rev. Major Ledger looked at one another, their gazes locked, sharing a mutual enjoyment of the lady's unique perspective. Gravely, Lord Ogden said, "Very true, ma'am. Why would anyone wish to sit through one of Arthur's pontifications otherwise?"

"That's very good, Vincent," murmured Rev. Major Ledger appreciatively.

"Well, no one will wish to come until the church is cleaned and some repairs have been made," said Lady Ogden matter-of-factly. "It has been quite neglected and I'm very sure there must be bats."

Mrs. Merriweather looked up at that, horrified. "My dear! You are quite right!" The lady turned to Rev. Major Ledger, distress creasing her face. "My dear sir, you will not be able to take the pulpit this Sunday, or indeed, the next sabbath! Oh, I am quite distracted now!" She plucked willy-nilly from her hand and made her discard.

When Lord Ogden saw the discard made by his partner, he said dryly, "So it seems, madam."

Lady Ogden also looked at her aunt's discard and she was sorry that she had raised the topic during the card game. "Calm yourself, aunt. I shall send out notes to our neighbors to explain our need. I'm certain we shall have all the help we need for the task."

"That's a capital notion, ma'am," said Rev. Major Ledger with a quick, warm smile. "Such a gathering will be a unifying one for the parish and make my work much easier, for I shall meet everyone before my first sermon."

"It's settled, then," said Lord Ogden, very well pleased. He was glad that his old comrade-in-arms was settling into Delincourt's circle and had been so well-accepted by the ladies of the household. He could foresee only good coming out of his appointment of Rev. Major Leger to the living.

It was late when Rev. Major Ledger finally declared he must tear himself away from such good company. A full moon was up, so he was confident enough of seeing his way back to the vicarage on horseback. The beast was lent to him by Lord Ogden, who told him to keep the horse for as long as he wished.

"I shall acquire my own mounts and a gig, too, as soon as possible," promised Rev. Major Ledger. "The only thing is, I don't wish to make the trip back to London so soon only to buy a couple of hacks and a second-hand carriage."

Lord Ogden had a happy thought. "I'm forced to sell off the majority of my cousin's mounts and carriage horses. His curricles and phaetons, too. You must come and look at them and take your pick from the lot. I will give you a good price, better than you could find at Tattersall's or a carriage-maker."

"Vincent, you are too good," protested Rev. Major Ledger.

"Nonsense! You will be helping me, too, for I shan't get full price when I send them up to London. I must put them up on the auction block, you see," said Lord Ogden.

"As bad as that, old fellow?" asked Rev. Major Ledger quietly.

Lord Ogden gave a twisted smile. "Worse, Arthur. If I can't turn the thing around, I shall have to sink most of my funds from 'Change into the place. My cousin Henry left the devil of a mess."

"What of her ladyship?"

Lord Ogden was slow to respond. Even to his closest friend, he was unable to articulate his insecurities, or reveal the nagging fear that he would not succeed in his fixed goal. He shrugged fatalistically. "She'll be taken care of, one way or another. I shall see to that." Perhaps he revealed more than he was aware, at least to the man who knew him best.

Rev. Major Ledger's expression altered. His voice deepened. "My dear Vincent!"

Lord Ogden flushed under his friend's ready sympathy. "Never mind! I must take it as it comes. Away with you, Arthur. I will undoubtedly see you on the morrow."

LADY OGDEN STRETCHED languidly. She felt the wonderous throbbing in her well-dissipated body. The viscount had just left her, but she could still feel the imprint of him, taste his skin, smell his musky scent. It was barely past dawn. She could see the faintest lightening between the drapes where the edges were not quite pulled together. The meanderings of her mind were tranquil. A new understanding seemed to have been established between herself and his lordship. He did not demand to be in her bed, but rather, he sought her acquiescence. He was also grown considerate of her well-being.

A smile hovered on her lips. He was a considerate lover, too. He made certain she was tremendously pleasured before he left her. It was astonishing how energized and amorous she was feeling, she sleepily ruminated. Her desire for having him moving deeply inside of her, filling her ears with guttural indelicacies, his body laying tightly bound in her arms, had intensified. *I am a strumpet,* she decided, and where once she would have felt a scorching self-reproach, she now felt only amusement. She had not noticed the exact moment when her self-recrimination had faded, but she knew it had gone. She was in an odd frame of mind these days. She marveled at the strangeness of it. She found she was able to contemplate a future which for some unfathomable reason did not appear so ominous or daunting. For the first time, she felt the stirrings of hope. *It's only the babe, that is why I am content.*

Lady Ogden turned over on her pillow and closed her eyes, drifting away again. When it was time, her dresser would come in to waken her and make her ready for the new day.

27

Since she had been widowed, Lady Ogden paid her first social visit and it was to the vicarage. Underneath her merino pelisse, she wore her new walking dress, pressed by her dresser only an hour before, and thought herself to be very fine indeed. She was a competent whip and drove herself in the gig. A large covered basket was sitting on the leather seat beside her.

Rev. Major Ledger had heard the approaching sound of the wheels and the clopping of the horse's hooves and came down the flagstone path to meet her. He hailed her with a welcoming smile. "Lady Ogden! It's a pleasure to see you. I trust you are well?"

She returned his greeting with a smile. "Very well, sir." She snubbed the reins and he put up a hand to help her climb down from the gig. When she had reached the ground, she said, "I have brought some things for your larder."

"Ah! What a fine thought, my lady. It is most welcome." Rev. Major Ledger carried the basket and escorted her inside the vicarage. "I shall give this into my housekeeper's care and request her to put on a kettle. An estimable woman! Mrs. Tompkins anticipates my every want."

"She is a cousin of my own good housekeeper, Mrs. Tower."

"Well, that explains it! While we are waiting for our tea, pray do me the honor of walking with me about my back garden. I've had a man in to begin clearing it. You must tell me what you think."

"I'll be glad to see what progress you have made," said Lady Ogden with genuine interest. She had an excuse for her visit, which was to bring the basket of dainties for the vicarage's larder, but she also had an ulterior motive. However, it could wait a little while. She and her aunt had spent many industrious hours inside the vicarage, so she had a natural curiosity about everything about the place. She was willing to spend time seeing the vicarage surrounds.

Rev. Major Ledger left her in the front parlor for a few minutes before he returned, remarking, "Mrs. Tompkins appreciates the pickled onions and jams. As for the roast tied up in brown paper – well! She assures me that it will do very well for my dinner. I've heartily agreed with her."

"I suspected Mrs. Tompkins had not yet had opportunity to visit the village butcher," said Lady Ogden.

"You were right, ma'am. You are kindness itself to have thought of it." Rev. Major Ledger ushered his guest out of the parlor and they walked through the vicarage to the back door. He opened it and they emerged outside.

The weather had warmed and brought out the bees, the gentle buzz presaging the beginnings of the summer months. The garden had grown up wild and tangled, sprawling out of its formal beds over the years, but from somewhere there wafted the delicate aroma of antique roses.

Lady Ogden sedately walked with her host on the paths that had been cleared, her hand curved inside the crook of his arm. She made allowance for his halting step, matching her gait to his pace. For a time, Rev. Major Ledger pointed out particular areas where the weeds and encroaching bushes had been rooted out and told her of the plans he had made for new plantings to bring the garden back to its former glory.

She had no need to subtly guide the conversation, as she had anticipated she might. Eventually, inevitably, the bent of their talk turned to the gentleman who was such a large part of their lives. It seemed natural to pose her question. "Have you known his lordship for a long time?"

Rev. Major Ledger laughed. "His lordship! How strange and grand that sounds. He shall always be plain Vincent Crawford to me. Yes, we have known one another for years. We have been the best of comrade-in-arms. Indeed, we have become brothers." He glanced at her curiously. "And you, my lady? Were you not previously acquainted?"

"Yes, my family and the Crawfords were neighbors of sorts. I dimly recall when it was that the boy was sent away to school," said Lady

Ogden. "He did not return except for holidays and by then my mother had become ill and we had become somewhat reclusive from society."

Rev. Major Ledger's expression was thoughtful, as he murmured, "So, you did not know Vincent at all well."

She shook her head. "Our paths did not cross until he came back home again from university for the short time before he went into the army."

"Ah, that's when I met him, in the army. A devil of a fellow."

Lady Ogden had a burning curiosity to know more about what had formed the viscount's character and if anyone could tell her anything to the purpose, it was her host. "What was your Vincent Crawford like then?"

"Why, he's always been the best of fellows. Whatever the cost to himself, he will do anything he must to attain a goal."

"You describe a man of extraordinary character," said Lady Ogden with a sidelong smile.

"He *is* an extraordinary man. I owe my life to him." Rev. Major Ledger gestured with his hand down at his halting leg. "We were taken up by the French. I was wounded – I think bleeding to death. Vincent made a tourniquet and bound up my wound. One night, we daringly made our escape from the prison camp. When I could not walk any further, even with his aid, he picked me up and carried me on his back. He was staggering like a drunk when he found an English patrol. Of course, I knew nothing of that until later, for I had long since swooned."

"Extraordinary, indeed!" Lady Ogden was affected by the gentleman's account – *Vincent carried him on his back, for miles!* – but of course she could not show it. Even though she was in awe of such remarkable heroism, she told herself, she must maintain a façade of only civil interest. Anything more would be to raise speculation that she harbored greater feelings than she should. *And perhaps I do.*

Rev. Major Ledger had a reminiscent smile. "Vincent has the heart of a lion."

Lady Ogden rather thought the viscount had the look of a fierce bird of prey, and the raptorial instincts of one; but she did not say so. With a teasing smile, she asked, "What of you, Rev. Major Ledger? Are you also a lion-heart?"

She was surprised when Rev. Major Ledger considered her light question with unexpected seriousness, furrowing his brows "No, I am no lion. I'm more of an eagle." He glanced down at her with a self-deprecating grin. "I'm fierce enough, but from my dizzy heights I can see the folly of it all."

Lady Ogden laughed. They walked for a while in companionable silence before Rev. Major Ledger remarked, "Vincent survived the Forlorn Hope at Badajoz, you know. Just as I did."

She gave him an inquiring glance. "The forlorn hope?"

Rev. Major Ledger rallied her. "My dear lady! That was the storming of the breach! Volunteers all! None of us really expected to live."

"I'm sure I read at the time that our army outnumbered the French." Lady Ogden did not reveal that she had kept up with the war through the newspapers. She had always read the military dispatches, scanning the recommendations and wounded lists for any mention of Vincent Crawford's name. It had been her close-guarded secret, kept even from her aunt, and a thing which she would never have dared to tell to her husband. She had soon enough come to know of her lord's excessive dislike for his heroic military cousin.

Rev. Major Ledger nodded. "Indeed, we did outnumber the enemy, but that had little to do with storming the breach. Hundreds of British troops were killed and maimed by the fury of the respective assaults, during which we saw our comrades and brothers slaughtered before our very eyes. Our gallant fellows had to climb the mountain of our dead and dying to cut through to the curtain wall. Vincent was one of the first to survive to the top."

Lady Ogden shot an astonished glance up at her companion. She stuttered a little because she had not expected such an encompassing, frank reply. "I cannot even imagine such a slaughter. It-it must have been terrible, indeed."

Rev. Major Ledger's gray eyes suddenly turned to winter ice. In harsh accents, he responded, "We lost 2,000 men in less than two hours. Bodies piled high, blood running like rivers in the ditches and trenches – I shall never forget it!"

Lady Ogden exclaimed in horror. She saw Rev. Major Ledger swiftly look down at her face and knew that he had noted her appalled expression. He flushed, obviously embarrassed that he had overset her. She still had her gloved fingers on his forearm and he brought his opposite hand over to gently squeeze them. Contrition coloring his voice, he said, "Forgive me! I was caught up in my memories. I should not have related so much detail. It's not a suitable topic for a lady."

Lady Ogden shook her head, acknowledging his apology with a brief smile. "As I recall from the reports, the losses were staggering."

Rev. Major Ledger nodded. "We lost 4,800 troops that day," he said somberly. "The French should have surrendered the fortress as soon as a practicable breach was made. It would have saved so many lives if they had done so, not just those of our soldiers but of the poor civilians inside the city."

"What do you mean?" asked Lady Ogden quickly.

The gentleman uttered a short, clipped laugh. "I'm a garrulous fool! I've already said too much. I should say no more."

"No, do tell me! I want to understand." Lady Ogden saw how he hesitated. "Please, sir. It will give me a better insight into his lordship's character." It struck her how her insistence must appear to him. She wondered at her indiscretion. She hoped that hers seemed to be only the ordinary curiosity one might have in a close acquaintance, but she very much doubted it. Surprisingly, Rev. Major Ledger did not question her, either by word or by expression. Whatever he might have thought, she was not to be put to the blush by the new vicar.

"Very well." Rev. Major Ledger did not immediately respond to her appeal. For some moments, it appeared that he would not oblige her after all. As they walked, Lady Ogden glanced up at her tall companion. An abstracted frown had overtaken his handsome face and she realized that Rev. Major Ledger's thoughts had turned inward.

Finally, slowly, he said, "I do not believe I have ever seen such fury. The extreme losses, the abandonment by the French of the rules of war – our army went mad. The city was sacked. Pillage, rape, murder – all were committed." Rev. Major Ledger's clear eyes were the dark silver of a turbulent ocean. His finely-molded lips thinned. "The officers could not control their men, and in some cases, were killed themselves by those under their command."

"How horrible!" Lady Ogden anxiously searched the gentleman's grim expression. "You and Lord Ogden were there? You saw this?"

"I saved Vincent from being bayoneted by a British regular," said Rev. Major Ledger coolly. He gave a bleak smile when she exclaimed in astonishment. "We were among those who tried to stop the carnage. It was seventy-two hours before order was restored. I do not excuse what happened, but I do understand it. The losses were too great. The army knew that many, many lives would not have been sacrificed if the French had surrendered earlier. It maddened them beyond bearing."

She was silenced. She had been given far more than she had anticipated when she insisted upon having her curiosity satisfied. Somehow, hearing the gentleman's brief descriptions, it brought home to her the brutalities of war that no amount of reading military dispatches and wounded lists in the newspapers had ever conveyed. The glorious romanticism she had harbored, along with everyone she knew, had been an enormous distortion of the truth. She could finally understand something of the viscount's ruthlessness, his drive and his energy. It had taken such qualities to survive a terribleness that was alien to her.

With some relief, Rev. Major Ledger saw that his housekeeper was standing at the back door. He had begun to feel a stab of conscience at revealing so much unpleasant detail to a lady and had wondered how to adroitly extract himself. "Ah, there is good Mrs. Tompkins, waving to us. She must have our tea ready. Shall we go in, my lady?"

"Yes, of course," said Lady Ogden quietly.

When it came time for her to take leave of her host, Lady Ogden thanked Rev. Major Ledger for his hospitality and commended his housekeeper's way with a plum cake.

Rev. Major Ledger flushed with open pleasure. "I shall be sure to tell Mrs. Tompkins of your kind words." He walked with her ladyship outside to the gig and handed her up into it. When she was seated and shook free the reins, he rested a hand for a moment on the seat rail and looked up at her with a flickering smile. "Thank you for coming, my lady. I have enjoyed your visit. How strange it is! I have never in my life had a place to hold household. I feel such immense satisfaction at being able to offer hospitality to a visitor!"

Lady Ogden laughed and gathered up the reins. "Good-bye, sir!" The new vicar stepped back from the carriage and waved as she drove away.

Lady Ogden's smile faded as her mind turned over what Rev. Major Ledger had related to her. She had been given much to ponder, particularly about the magnificent character which Rev. Major Ledger had painted of Lord Ogden. The two men's shared history was such that she must accept Rev. Major Ledger's perceptions to be true. Of a certainty, it did something to further shape her own evolving understanding of the viscount.

28

As Lady Ogden had hoped, the open invitation for the church restoration garnered enormous support from the neighborhood. The evening before the appointed date, seated in front of the fire in the drawing-room, Lord Ogden remarked that he expected that Delincourt Manor would provide the bulk of the labor. "The responsibility for the living is Delincourt's, after all. And my cousin was not popular with our neighbors. That must color things."

"I believe you take a pessimistic view, my lord," said Lady Ogden, smiling. She was confident that his lordship was wrong. "I have received nothing but enthusiastic assurances of support."

Mrs. Merriweather was swift to add her voice. "Indeed, I think your lordship will be agreeably surprised."

Lord Ogden smiled at them. "I must bow to your superior knowledge of our neighbors. Let us hope you are right."

As the chilly day dawned, and the numerous occupied carriages and other equipages arrived at the church, Lady Ogden chuckled softly to herself when she overheard his lordship express delighted surprise. She knew many who came saw it as an opportunity to meet the newly-appointed vicar. Nevertheless, it was a worthy cause that had drawn all together. After a lengthy discussion about the major repairs needed to the church and its environs, which had suffered much from weather damage and neglect, the convention split into groups to accomplish several different tasks. Rev. Major Ledger shouldered his share of the labor, as did many others. Sir Edward Thane and Mr. Kelton had brought several laborers. It seemed to Lady Ogden that the viscount was everywhere, pitching in a hand wherever he could, and it was his lordship who directed workmen from Delincourt in the necessary repairs of the church roof. He had learned much from the architect who had set in motion the roof repairs at Delincourt.

All of the ladies brought quantities of wine and ale, baskets of foodstuffs, polishing cloths and beeswax and brooms, and a gaggle of women servants to help with cleaning the church interior and bringing it to its former glory. There was a great amount of good-natured talk and gossip, which Lady Ogden and Mrs. Merriweather thoroughly enjoyed. At one point, Mrs. Merriweather addressed her niece in an aside. "I am taking such delight in this!"

"So am I, aunt. It's the largest social gathering on Delincourt lands I can ever recall," said Lady Ogden, her smile reflecting the gladness in her heart. For a long time, she had been humiliated that Delincourt had not been able to offer the hospitality that it should have to neighbors. The fault had been in the late viscount's lack of interest. When in residence, he'd preferred a far different society than the country one. In addition, his stinginess to her in housekeeping monies had made it difficult, if not impossible, to entertain on any scale.

At the end of a long day, the church's interior shone. Several broken roof slates had been replaced and the bats eradicated. The soaring, stained glass windows were clean and the exterior walls had been rid of clinging vines. Around the quaint edifice, trees had been trimmed of dead branches; the cemetery stones had been cleared of overgrown weeds, and the grounds had been cleared of debris. Most importantly, Lady Ogden reflected, the viscount and Rev. Major Ledger had been fully introduced to all the neighborhood. She was tired but satisfied that her object had been attained.

Rev. Major Ledger thanked all who had come to volunteer their help and announced that he would take the pulpit on Sunday next. The crowd responded with an enthusiastic huzzah before they departed in a flurry of carriages and on horseback, their servants following in cumbersome carts and wagons.

Lord Ogden was grinning. He clapped his hand onto his friend's shoulder. "Well, Arthur, you have made a fine start! Everyone has received you very well."

"Indeed, I'm overwhelmed with the number of invitations I have received," said Rev. Major Ledger, flushed with gratification. "I never expected such an outpouring of welcome."

"You'll be flitting like a regular beau now on your social circuit," said the viscount with a laugh as he placed his boot in the stirrup and swung up to mount his horse.

Mrs. Merriweather had already made her adieus and was seated in the carriage. "I hope you will not neglect us at Delincourt," said Lady Ogden, smiling at the vicar before taking her leave.

"As if I would," retorted Rev. Major Ledger, handing her up into the carriage. Lady Ogden sat down beside her aunt and the vicar put up the iron step and shut the door. The driver gave the office to the team and the carriage jerked forward. Lord Ogden rode ahead on horseback, leading the way back to the manor house.

On Sunday, Lady Ogden was happy to see that the gleaming, burnished church pews were filled by neighbors and villagers to a flattering degree. She nodded to the Thanes as she went by and entered the Delincourt family pew, followed by Mrs. Merriweather and the viscount. Rev. Major Ledger gave his first sermon to an attentive congregation and afterwards was rewarded with several compliments from those attending the service. The neighborhood was very well pleased with their new vicar and Lord Ogden came in for his share of accolades for bringing such a personable gentleman into the living.

Lady Ogden was at last able to put off black gloves. Lady Thane was as good as her word and she set about organizing a small, select dinner party. It was to be an unexceptional affair, meant to signal Lady Ogden's return to society, but it would also serve to bring the viscount and the new vicar together again with some of their nearest neighbors. The invitation to Thane Hall was received and accepted with alacrity by those fortunate enough to receive it. At Delincourt, Lady Ogden and Mrs. Merriweather gave such exclamations of pleasure over the invitation that the viscount good-naturedly laughed at them. When the designated evening arrived and the party from Delincourt set out, Lord Ogden rode escort beside the equipage. Rev. Major Ledger had also chosen to ride and he joined the party. The ladies ensconced in the coach were filled with high anticipation.

"*Such* a long time since we accepted an invitation," exclaimed Mrs. Merriweather, obviously looking forward with unalloyed pleasure to the evening's entertainment.

"Indeed, it has been a long time. I only wish I had a better evening gown to wear than this old one. It's quite two years old and sadly out of fashion," said Lady Ogden. She had refurbished the crepe gown with a new satin slip underneath and it looked well enough, but she was insecure about her appearance. She tugged for a third time at the square neck of her gown. "Mills had to let out the bosom, too, and the décolletage is much too low."

"You look very well, my dear," said Mrs. Merriweather, smiling fondly at her. "Besides, the gentlemen appreciate low décolletages."

"But I'm still in mourning! I shouldn't be flaunting my charms!"

"You're a young widow, Charlotte, not a corpse." Mrs. Merriweather reached out and patted her niece's arm in reassurance. "I do realize how nervous you are, but recall we shall meet with none but old friends. Aren't you the least bit excited to be getting out for an evening?"

"Oh, yes! Yes, I am," said Lady Ogden on a soft laugh. "You cannot imagine how much, aunt." She felt as though the lock had been released on the cage of her life. No matter how her nerves betrayed her, she was grateful for the chance to resume some semblance of a social life. She had been buried at Delincourt Manor, her marriage to her unlamented lord always a constraint, whether to entertaining at Delincourt Manor or in accepting the few invitations which she and her aunt had received. She glanced out the window and caught a glimpse of the viscount astride his mount riding beside the carriage. The future was uncertain but it must be better than what she had already experienced. *How strange! That it rests upon that man, a man from out of my past.*

At their destination, outer garments were given to the footmen, the butler announced them, and they were received with warm greetings by their hosts. Others had already arrived and there was a good measure of conversation in the drawing-room before dinner was announced. As was proper, Sir Edward bowed to the highest-ranking lady present. "My lady, pray do me the honor."

Lady Ogden inclined her head, feeling a wonderful glow. She could not recall when she had last enjoyed a social gathering with gentlemen present. She laid her fingers on his lifted forearm. "Thank you, Sir Edward."

Sir Edward escorted Lady Ogden in to the dining room. Lord Ogden extended his arm to his hostess, which Lady Thane accepted with a gracious nod, and the rest of the company followed in pairs. The party was a relaxed one, where everyone knew one another and were at ease in their conversation and shared a universal pleasure in their company.

After dinner, when the gentlemen had rejoined the ladies in the drawing-room, the entertainment for the evening consisted of charades and musical selections performed by a few of the ladies. Lady Ogden sang and accompanied herself on the pianoforte. Performing in company was not a norm for her, but she had decided she was among friends who would not be overly critical. Her fingers were a little rusty, but she was pleased to account herself well enough that her performance earned a smattering of applause.

The viscount strolled over to the pianoforte as she was putting away the sheet music. He looked down at her, a raised brow quizzing her. "I was given the impression that you did not play, my lady."

"I have practiced a little, my lord."

"I did not recognize the selection. It's a new piece, is it not? The music which Sir William selected for you, my dear?"

Lady Ogden replied with a touch of defiance. "Just so, my lord."

Lord Ogden nodded, while his lips curled. "You have a good singing voice and played it well. I believe the gentleman would have been flattered by your performance."

Casting a glance toward her aunt and Rev. Major Ledger, who stood close by engaged in genial conversation with some others of the company, she frowned a warning at his lordship. Though no one seemed to be paying the least attention to her and the viscount, Lady Ogden nevertheless lowered her voice. "Pray do not trifle with me, Vincent."

His lordship's dark gaze betrayed some strong emotion, gone in a flash. "I think the selection a very pretty piece. A lover's ballad, forsooth! You must perform it again. Though...I think not for Sir William."

Lady Ogden uttered a low exclamation, believing his caveat was a deliberate provocation. As if she would ever play the ballad for any one gentleman, she thought indignantly. She would never telegraph her feelings, nor tease, in so outrageous a fashion. "What nonsense! Really, you are being ridiculous!"

The viscount bowed in what she took to be mockery. He extended his forearm toward her. All politeness, he suggested, "Let us join the others, ma'am. The coffee urn will shortly be brought in and you will wish to speak to our hostess."

Lady Ogden stood up from the pianoforte bench. She cut a glance up at his lordship's bland expression. He had ruffled her composure with his crack about Sir William and the sheet music. A little sharply, she replied, "Of course, my lord. I am very willing."

"You soon will be," murmured Lord Ogden.

Lady Ogden felt warmth pinkening her face. With those few whispered wicked words, he had shaken her. Moreover, she knew that he had meant to put her to the blush. *Damn him!* Hoping that the yellow glow of the candlelight served to disguise her flushed cheeks, she pasted on a smile and with the viscount sedately walked over to join her aunt and the rest of the company.

However, Lady Thane was a keen observer and she saw the blush on her friend's face. She suspected Lord Ogden must have paid some pretty compliment to her ladyship about her performance, but she didn't inquire of Lady Ogden. She kept her hopeful conjectures to herself until later that night, when she was private with her husband.

"I do not believe she is indifferent to the viscount," said Lady Thane. "His lordship has a great deal of natural charm, when he allows himself to display it. No, I don't believe Charlotte is immune to Lord Ogden at all."

"We must trust that Vincent reciprocates," said Sir Edward, covering a broad yawn with his hand.

"Oh, if he decides on it, Lord Ogden will have to woo her. There is no doubt about that! Charlotte is prickly and proud," said Lady Thane, before she sighed and shook her head. "I so hope Charlotte has the wit to make the most of her opportunity. After all, she is still at Delincourt and that must be to her advantage."

"Vincent's to be caught in parson's trap, do you mean?" Sir Edward chuckled at his wife's affronted expression.

"I would not put it in those terms," said Lady Thane with dignity.

Sir Edward caught up her hand and lifted it to his lips to kiss her fingers in apology. "A wedding between Vincent and her ladyship, performed by Rev. Major Ledger! That would be something, indeed. Certainly, it would be a neat wrap-up."

"His lordship could become stepfather to Delincourt's heir. He'd act as regent of the boy's inheritance, of course," said Lady Thane, already musing on other possibilities.

Sir Edward yawned again. "It makes little difference to me. I just wish to keep Vincent close as my neighbor and my friend."

"Whatever his fortunes, he will always be a friend to you, dearest."

"Yes, Vincent is a good fellow, whether he is heir or regent." Sir Edward frowned, some realizations belatedly touched off by his wife's observations. "What of your earlier suspicions, my dear? About her ladyship, I mean. Do you think she is – you know."

Sir Edward made a gesture at his own lady's waistline. Lady Thane had no difficulty in divining what he meant. She looked thoughtful. "I'm not certain, mind you. Nothing has ever been hinted at by her ladyship. However, I have borne three children and I can fairly say that her figure has changed. This evening, I saw it when she turned and her dress pulled a little with the movement. I strongly suspect her ladyship is with child."

"Poor Vincent! If you are right, he must be in the devil of a stew. He must be unable to think of anything else!"

He mounted her from behind, pushing his heavy cock into her quivering quim. Bit by bit, his hard, velvety shaft stretched her tight and full. She groaned, long and low. The final seating of his thickened member made her throb with want. He put his warm hand on the small of her back, a familiar weight. "Steady now, my love. My prick weeps for you. Feel it slide deep between your warm furry lips...yes, I can tell that you do!" With reined-in control, he slowly advanced and retreated, pushed and pulled. With the pleasure of his measured spearing, the drawn-out, exquisite friction built a fierce fire, spreading from low in her belly.

"Ah, such a delectable round bum. My palm itches. I cannot resist."

"No, Vincent, don't," she uttered. Yet she bit her lip in ragged, excited suspense.

"Quiet, now. One. Two. Three." He smacked his free hand lightly against one globe of her arse each time he retreated; then he pressed forward again, his thickened girth pervading her narrow vessel, the pressure of the heated advance palpable.

Lady Ogden moaned, caught by a strong shudder. *I do not know how I am to bear it!* He had already set her simmering before he mounted her, before he spanked her. The tingle was a fine counter-point to her rising turmoil. Her roiling, molten center was gathering force, swiftly overtaking her, overwhelming her reason.

"One side is so nicely flushed. The other so pale. I'm going to spank you again, Charlotte. Three strokes. While I screw the depths of your prim sleeve." He switched hands on her back and suited actions to words. *One, two, three.* The sound was loud in her ears, the sting a titillating shock to her nerves. He suddenly thrust with greater force, rocking her forward for a fiery beat.

"I take such delight in tupping you."

She gasped on quick, jerky breaths. Her heartbeat came fast. His deliberate, curbed pace was maddening to her. She pushed back against him, meeting him stroke for slow stroke, becoming desperate to spur him on. His shaft felt white-hot, branding her from the inside out.

He slipped a square, hard hand under her rounded belly, the toughened skin of his palm grazing her. She felt it slip lower, brushing over her intimate silky curls. Then his clever calloused fingers delved into her plumped moistness. A strangled noise exited her throat.

"The pearl at your gate is a hard, little bead."

Reacting to what he was doing with his fingertips, her breath hitched. Her heart raced faster. Moisture sprang out on her skin. She dug her fingers into the bed linens to steady herself.

"Tell me how much you like it."

"I do, I do!" She was aching, throbbing. She was surely dying.

"Give the bull a squirm – *there's my sweet!* Such a good, sweet, tight little quim."

She whimpered. She could hear her own dry sobs, his harsher breathing.

"Yes, there you are! That's it, milk me – *ah!* – I'm fair to bursting with mettle! Come, meet my lusty cock in a faster dance! It's eager to finish our business!"

She arched up her bum into the hollow of his lean belly, straining to possess every powerful, heavy thrust. The salacious, sucking sounds of their joining, the give-and-take of their rapid stroking, became more than she could bear. She threw up her head, shrieking. "*Vincent!*"

"*That's it, love! Shatter for me!*"

29

A fortnight later, a carriage drew up to the manor and a fashionable young woman was set down. Attired in a pelisse of drab over a light-yellow poplin carriage dress, she was of a neat figure but stood a shade too tall for fashionable tastes. A feather-trimmed velvet hat crowned her head and from beneath the brim peeped blonde curls. She tilted her head back to appreciatively assess the front of the imposing manor house. A smile blossomed on her countenance. "Here at last!" she exclaimed and trod up the front steps.

The front door had already been opened and the porter and a footman emerged, going down to the carriage to retrieve the luggage. The young lady was accompanied by her maid, a sharp-faced creature who immediately began to oversee the unloading of her mistress's belongings, while the lady herself stepped inside. In the main entrance hall, the butler bowed to her. "Welcome to Delincourt, Mrs. Dalton. May I say it's a pleasure to see you again."

The pleasant-faced lady drew off her kid gloves. Her eyes sparkled. "Thank you, Somerset. It has been an age since I was at Delincourt. It's good to be back. Is my brother in?"

Behind her, the porter and footman were bringing in her luggage. The butler ordered the manservants to carry it up to the bedchamber which had been prepared in anticipation of Mrs. Dalton's arrival before he replied to her query. "Indeed so, ma'am. His lordship is at luncheon. Lady Ogden and Mrs. Merriweather are also present. I shall inform them of your arrival."

Mrs. Dalton threw up her hand. "No, no, do not interrupt them! I should like to freshen up a bit."

However, the sounds of arrival had already been heard. The door to the breakfast-room opened and through it strode Lord Ogden. "Amarys!"

Mrs. Dalton turned swiftly. "Vincent, my dearest brother!" They embraced, laughing and exclaiming a bit over one another's appearance.

"You're all grown! A lovely lady!"

"Why, how browned you are! But you look very well, indeed!"

Lady Ogden and Mrs. Merriweather had also come into the entrance hall. They stood to one side, smiling, and watched the happy reunion. Finally, Lord Ogden drew his sister forward. "Lady Ogden, Mrs. Merriweather, allow me to introduce my sister, Mrs. Amarys Dalton."

The ladies all dipped in courteous acknowledgment, murmuring greetings. Then with a friendly smile, Lady Ogden stepped forward and held out her hand. "It's not necessary, my lord. I recall Mrs. Dalton very well, I assure you."

"Why, I would know you anywhere." Mrs. Dalton warmly shook her ladyship's hand. She twinkled down at her hostess, over whom she could claim a couple of inches. "I was with my eldest sister during her confinement. Otherwise, we would have attended your wedding to our cousin, Henry. How do you do, Lady Ogden?"

"Very well, I assure you." Lady Ogden half-turned with a polite gesture of her hand. "Perhaps you will also recall my aunt?"

"Of course! Mrs. Merriweather, what a delight to see you again," said Mrs. Dalton, moving forward to greet the elderly lady with a ready smile and a handshake.

"Likewise, Mrs. Dalton."

Mrs. Dalton gave a peal of laughter. Her eyes gleamed with amusement. "Oh, if you are both to stand upon such ceremony with me, I shall not feel myself truly welcome. Pray call me Amarys, do!"

"I shall certainly do so, if I may be Charlotte to you," said Lady Ogden at once. She was thoroughly charmed by the lady's warm manner and thought there was still much of the friendly young girl she recalled in the present Mrs. Dalton. "You must need refreshment. Pray come into the breakfast-room. We have been at luncheon. Somerset will bring in a new pot of tea directly."

"Actually, I should like to refurbish my appearance a bit first," said Mrs. Dalton, wrinkling her nose and gesturing down at her pelisse. "I must look the most dreadful fright! I'm quite rumpled from the journey and I spilled tea on myself at the last stop. After wearing this hat all day, I fear my hair will be sadly crushed, too."

"Of course! I shall take you upstairs to your room," said Lady Ogden. "I should have realized that you would wish to have a few minutes to yourself. But as soon as you are ready, you must join us."

The two ladies went upstairs with Mrs. Dalton's maid silently following them at a respectful distance. Lady Ogden's remark could be clearly heard by those left below. "You must be tired from your journey."

"Oh, no," came the cheerful reply. "I am never tired. I'm disgustingly healthy, you see."

Lord Ogden watched them ascend, a lingering smile on his face. Standing beside the viscount, Mrs. Merriweather commented, "Your sister will undoubtedly enliven our company, my lord. She is quite lovely."

"Yes, I believe you're right, Mrs. Merriweather." Lord Ogden turned his head to look down at the elderly lady, his smile broadening. "I'm very glad she has come."

Lord Ogden realized, with an unexpected degree of pleasure, that his sister was to be readily accepted by the other ladies. Within a matter of days, Mrs. Dalton was genuinely felt to be a welcome addition to the household by everyone. The lady was of a happy disposition and willing to be agreeable. The viscount's sister quickly established her place within the household and settled into Delincourt as though she had always been there.

Lord Ogden was glad to have a close member of his family residing with him. Though he had written to all of his family about his change in fortune and received their felicitations in return, he had not visited with his two sisters and brothers-in-law for many years. Since returning to England, he had been caught up with the affairs of the estate and, of course, his torrid affair with Lady Ogden. He had not realized how much he had missed the familial ties. He rather thought that he would like to strengthen them once he felt himself to be in a position to do so. However, he reflected, much depended upon Lady Ogden, her confinement, and the final denouement of their liaison.

Lady Ogden and Mrs. Merriweather very soon came to enjoy Mrs. Dalton's lively company. Somewhat to her surprise, Lady Ogden discovered a friend in the lady. Perhaps it was not so odd as she supposed. They were of comparable age, they had a shared childhood background in the county, and both were young widows. The only real difference between them was that Mrs. Dalton had never been with child and she was openly interested in Lady Ogden's journey to motherhood.

"I will soon have a new little cousin! I think I shall like to play with the baby," she said cheerfully. "I shall help you make a lovely christening robe, Charlotte. My needlework is quite neat, I promise you."

Lady Ogden laughed. "I assure you, your help will be most welcome. My aunt has been telling me that I must refurbish the rest of my wardrobe, too. We have begun to make up a couple of new patterns. I'm now able to wear half-mourning, so I shall be able to add a bit of color."

Mrs. Dalton's face lit up. "Why, how wonderful! I like nothing better than sewing up a new pattern! We shall have such fun!"

On the day of Mrs. Dalton's arrival, Rev. Major Ledger was not at Delincourt. He was the last to meet her and he did not do so for some days due to some trifling business of his own which had taken him up to London. Lord Ogden had sent a note to the vicarage to apprise his old friend of his sister's arrival. Upon his return from his journey, Rev. Major Ledger sent a very proper note of apology and promised to come to Delincourt the following evening.

Lady Ogden and Mrs. Merriweather were as one in their agreement that Mrs. Dalton was a pleasant companion. Despite the handicap of her height, she was also quite lovely. Rev. Major Ledger was certainly aware of it. The first instant he saw her and her lively countenance turned toward him, her fine eyes regarding him with interest, he appeared stunned. When he was introduced to the lady, he seemed to have to shake himself loose of a paralysis before he made his bow and uttered the formal greetings. From that moment on, he quietly followed her with his eyes and when his gaze rested upon her expressive face, there was a perceptible glow in the depths of his gray eyes.

Mrs. Dalton appeared completely oblivious of the gentleman's patent admiration. However, she was not as unaware as she pretended. She liked very well the Rev. Major's gray eyes and the high cheekbones that gave distinction to his lean features. The sensuous mold of his lips was intriguing, while the look in his gray eyes when his gaze rested upon her gave her a fluttery feeling. The amusement which never seemed far from him was certainly an admirable trait. However, Mrs. Dalton was in no mind to venture on a flirtation. She had once wed in a whirlwind of romance and lived to regret it. She wasn't about to make the same mistake again.

Lady Ogden derived much of this from bits and pieces of her new friend's conversation. It was not long before Mrs. Dalton also confided the particulars of her marital experiences. "We were separated almost the entire time of our marriage. He left me in England, not deeming it fit that I should follow the drum."

"That must have been difficult for you," observed Lady Ogden. They were taking the air on the terrace and she looked out over the park rather than directly at her companion. She did not wish to embarrass her new friend by too plain a curiosity.

Mrs. Dalton nodded. "It was most painful. I longed to be with him. We had been betrothed only three months before we wed and we thought ourselves to be madly in love. Our correspondence was always full of affection." She slid a glance sideways at her companion. "Then two things occurred. I heard through roundabout channels, from acquaintances and friends who knew us both, that my husband had set up a mistress in Portugal. As for myself, I realized gradually, silly little chit that I was, that I had been in love with the *romance* of it all – not the gallant captain himself."

Lady Ogden was taken aback. She cast a quick glance at her companion. She didn't know what to say. "Oh. I see."

"You surely despise me now that I have confessed to such a foolish thing."

Lady Ogden had been enough in Mrs. Dalton's company to think well of the lady. Always quick to sense slight and innuendo, she believed there was nothing like that in Mrs. Dalton's nature. She therefore thought such frankness deserved equal honesty. "Not at all. My folly is worse. I must despise myself the more, for you merely mistook your heart. I married for the sake of the marriage-bond, solely for the security it offered to myself and my aunt."

Mrs. Dalton was wide-eyed. "Did you not bear affection for my cousin, then?"

Lady Ogden gave a low laugh, mocking herself. "I thought I did. I persuaded myself that I did. It seemed to me that surely I must, when Henry said that he loved me."

Mrs. Dalton blinked a few times, digesting what she had been told in all its nuances. "You sound as though you do not believe that he did, after all. Love you, I mean."

"No, he did not." Lady Ogden gave a swift, humorless smile. "Believe me, the disillusionment came swiftly. I realized my mistake within a few short months."

Mrs. Dalton lowered her gaze to the flagstones as together they slowly trod further along the terrace. After a minute, she remarked, "Mrs. Merriweather let drop, in her inconsequential way, that my brother was once your suitor."

"Yes," said Lady Ogden shortly. "And that must of necessity be all that I shall say about that."

Mrs. Dalton quickly raised her gaze. Her expression was one of surprise, which was shaded almost at once by compassion. "My dear!"

Lady Ogden was sorry for the sharpness of her tone. She smiled apologetically. "Forgive me, I did not mean to snap. It's merely that my recollections of that time are not my fondest."

"I am persuaded I may guess the rest," said Mrs. Dalton composedly. "Henry was envious of my brother's wooing of you, so he thrust himself upon your notice."

Lady Ogden stopped short and stared at her companion, amazed. "What?"

Mrs. Dalton crowed a laugh. "I see I've hit on it!"

"You have hit on it exactly," agreed Lady Ogden, recovering from her astonishment. "But how ever did you surmise it?"

The ladies resumed their stroll, arm in arm. Mrs. Dalton leaned close so that their shoulders nearly touched. "You must understand how it was, Charlotte. There was always a competition existing between them, not with my brother but on Henry's side. He was always jealous of Vincent."

"But why? I don't understand. Henry was heir to the title and Delincourt. It seems it would have been the other way around."

Mrs. Dalton shook her head. "Our uncle was uncommonly attached to Vincent from his earliest childhood, which was always an irritation to Henry. My uncle's favor animated a spiteful jealousy in my cousin. Henry's intemperate character was such that he could never set it aside."

"That explains much," said Lady Ogden slowly. "I had often wondered why Henry regarded Vincent Crawford, his heir presumptive, with such rancor." She remembered the day Lord Ogden had told her that his cousin had only offered for her because *he* had wanted her. She felt sickened as she realized how true his assertion had been. Henry Ogden had never loved her. *Fool, fool!* "I cannot believe how stupid I was not to have seen it before."

Mrs. Dalton cast an amused, sideways glance at her. "Why should you have? You were not intimate with our family. Unless Henry was honest enough with himself and had the fortitude to express it to you, I cannot conceive how you could have known. Vincent certainly never broadcasted it."

"Your brother once said something of the sort, which I rejected at the time." Lady Ogden shook her head at her own blindness. She had been duped by Henry Ogden's lie, and willing to be so because it had seemed an answer to her prayer. She and her aunt had been in desperate straits and needed a place to go. She had chosen to listen to her head rather than her heart. "I did not wish to believe it, I suppose. One wishes only to believe the best of one's husband."

Mrs. Dalton smiled at her. "It seems we share more in common than either of us realized, Charlotte. We have each been singularly foolish in our romantic follies."

"Of a surety, I can say that my own folly was the worst of the two," said Lady Ogden wryly.

Mrs. Dalton laughed. "Oh, I don't think so. I was as blind in my way as you were in yours, dearest Charlotte."

Lady Ogden was silent. Her conversation with Rev. Major Ledge, and now Mrs. Dalton's newer revelations about the viscount, had confirmed what she had begun to form in her own mind. The gentleman was far more complex than she had ever imagined. She had once believed his lordship was a mere mirror-image of her husband the late viscount, that he was simply a caricature dressed in a larger frame. She had not seen past the rough violation of her person or the subsequent lasciviousness performed in her bed. She had not seen anything of the real man, and she was ashamed. *He is so far above Henry. It's little wonder Henry despised him.* She did not like to think about what it said about her and her own too-ready assumptions.

30

Lord Ogden read in the Times, with great interest and perhaps a touch of nostalgic envy, that on June 21st, the army under Wellesley had won a major victory over the French at the Battle of Vittoria. He reported the news to his three breakfast companions. "We'll soon be pushing the French out of Spain," he predicted, refolding the newspaper. The butler brought in the mail stacked on a silver salver and placed it at his lordship's elbow. "Thank you, Somerset."

Lord Ogden flipped through the pieces of mail, pausing when he saw a letter for the viscountess. It was addressed in a hand which had become all-too-familiar to him. He handed the sealed square across the table to her. "A letter for you, ma'am."

Lady Ogden glanced at the inscription on the front. She did not open the letter but slipped it into the inner pocket of her skirt. "Thank you, my lord," she said quietly.

"Who writes to you, dear?" asked Mrs. Merriweather with mild curiosity.

"An acquaintance, ma'am" replied Lady Ogden briefly. She met her aunt's inquiring gaze, which deepened with sudden understanding. She saw her aunt's sudden frown. Hoping to deflect any further queries that might be launched by her aunt, and which might prove to be embarrassing in her present company, Lady Ogden hastily turned to the lady seated beside her. "Amarys, I'm thinking of cutting a new pattern for a daydress this morning."

"Oh, I'd be delighted to help you," said Mrs. Dalton cheerfully. "The last one turned out so well. Don't you think so, brother? Lady Ogden appears quite fine in it."

Lady Ogden cast down her eyes. She did not know where to look. On the one side, her aunt would put to her awkward queries about her correspondence. On the other, her friend had just put her to the blush. All of her conversation had been effectively squelched.

If Mrs. Dalton had hoped to elicit a compliment for the viscountess out of her brother, she was disappointed.

Lord Ogden was only half-listening and he replied with a grunt. *An acquaintance!* He barely repressed a snort. She had received another missive from that encroaching bastard, Sir William Talley. She no longer opened the gentleman's correspondence before him. Instead, she took the letters up with her to her private sitting room. Lord Ogden imagined her ladyship reading the newest billet, perhaps with a smile on her face, and then putting it carefully away in a jewel box or other such place for treasured items. He slowly clenched his fist on top of the folded newspaper.

"What is it, my lord? What does the news mean?"

Lord Ogden looked blankly at Mrs. Merriweather's anxious face. Then he glanced around the table at Lady Ogden and his sister, who were also regarding him with fixed expressions. They had responded to his tension, he realized. He relaxed his fingers and drew the marmalade bowl toward him. He dipped the tiny spoon into the sweet concoction and dropped a dollop onto his toasted bread. "It means there will be coming a long, hard campaign. Many of my friends and comrades will be in the thick of it."

He shrugged. "I fear for them." He realized it was true. Of a sudden, he felt restless, disquieted. He tossed down the tiny spoon, making it clink against the rim of the marmalade bowl.

"And it would be easier for you if you were with them. It's understandable, my lord," said Lady Ogden quietly.

The viscount looked sharply at her and she calmly met his eyes. He smiled across at her. "Exactly so, ma'am." It was a shock to him that she had discerned his half-formed thoughts before even he had. As for his previous irritation, he would say nothing of that. It was beneath him to reveal that he was jealous of a man whom he had never met. Such feelings were irrational. Instead, he would endeavor to wean her ladyship's own thoughts away from her persistent correspondent, Sir William Talley. "But come! Let us not dwell on such things. It's a fair day. Will you ride with me this morning, Lady Ogden?"

"Of course, my lord." Lady Ogden's earlier embarrassment had disappeared. His lordship had far greater things to think about than her fine new daydress, she thought. She was disappointed, though, that he had not seemed to notice how well the dove-gray color became her.

Lord Ogden turned to his sister. "Would you like to join us, Amarys?"

"Oh, I think not, dear brother," retorted Mrs. Dalton. "You are such intrepid riders! I've no wish to go careering over the countryside as soon as I have breakfasted! Perhaps later Mrs. Merriweather and I shall take an airing in the gig." She turned a friendly smile on the elderly lady. "What do you say, ma'am?"

"A gentle airing is just the thing," agreed Mrs. Merriweather, looking pleased by the suggestion.

Lady Ogden smiled at her companions and put aside her napkin. "I will go upstairs directly to change into my habit, my lord. Amarys, will you mind it if we put aside our project until my return?"

"Of course not. I will be pleasantly employed until then, I assure you. I have a little embroidery to finish on the christening cap."

A half hour later, Lord Ogden gave her ladyship a boost into the saddle. Swinging astride his own mount, he waited until she had arranged her heavy riding skirt to her satisfaction and gathered her reins. Lord Ogden gathered his own reins between gloved fingers. "We'll shake the fidgets out of the horses, shall we?" He set spur to his mount and Lady Ogden followed suit. They set out on their ride at a brisk gait until reaching the open park where they galloped the horses.

Several minutes later, they reined in to a more leisurely pace. Lady Ogden glanced over at her companion. His lordship appeared relaxed, swaying easily in the saddle with the gelding's smooth motion. The earlier ill-humor seemed to have lifted from his brow. The conversation at breakfast was still fresh in her mind and she asked curiously, "Did you like the soldiering life?"

Lord Ogden frowned as he considered his reply. "I don't know how best to phrase my answer. There was much to like about it – in the camaraderie, in the exercise of mind and body, and also the relative freedom of such a life. Of course, one inevitably makes interesting observations about a country which is different from one's own, too." The viscount glanced over at her. "As for battle with the enemy, I performed my duty. I think I'm just a man who was once a soldier." His smile came suddenly, like sun breaking through cloud. "I was certainly better fitted for it than Arthur, whose higher sensibilities suffered more than my own. I was always the more ruthless."

Lady Ogden's memory winged to her recent conversation with the viscount's former comrade-in-arms. "Rev. Major Ledger says both of you survived a forlorn hope." She hesitated a beat. "He also explained to me something of the siege of Badajoz."

"Fiends seize him! What maggot got into his brain?" exclaimed Lord Ogden with disapproval. "He has no business sullying a lady's ears with such things."

Lady Ogden ignored the interjection. "What happened to the city – it was a horrible, horrible thing."

"Indeed, it was." Lord Ogden did not say anything for some minutes, his brows knitted. Finally, as though he could not help himself, as though the recollection had to be aired, he said curtly, "The storming of a fortress is not the same as a battle where men expect casualties to occur. When a practicable breach is made, rules of war dictate surrender. Instead, there was an unnecessary slaughter, which perhaps not unnaturally led to heightened emotions."

"But to sack the city! Surely something could have been done to prevent it!"

Lord Ogden shook his head. "No, nothing." His stern features turned bleak. "The infuriated soldiery resembled a pack of hell hounds vomited up from the infernal regions than what they were but twelve short hours previously – a well-organized, brave, disciplined and obedient British Army, and burning only with impatience for what is called glory."

"It is shocking!"

"Of course, every finer feeling must revolt!" exclaimed Lord Ogden in clipped accents. His strong emotion was transferred to his mount. The gelding uneasily shifted under him but he scarcely noticed, instinctively managing the horse. "However, I cannot condemn these men for feeling some degree of bitterness. I begrudged them none of their feelings of anger and desire for revenge."

Lady Ogden was horrified by his lordship's opinion. She had not thought him to be so callous or unfeeling. "Surely you do not condone their actions!"

"Certainly not! Such savagery must swiftly be put down, by whatever means necessary – by sword, pistol, flogging, even hanging," said Lord Ogden grimly. "But once the soldiery had broken into the alehouses, there was no arresting the pillage of the city."

Lady Ogden faced front again, looking over her horse's twitching ears. The argument of the effects of drunkenness on an enraged mob was unanswerable. Inevitable reflections kept her silent for a long moment, before she murmured, "I know something of what excessive drink does to a man."

The viscount threw a glance at her profile. She had been easily silenced. His childhood recollections, and more recently from what Mr. Kelton had related to him, persuaded him that she was making a reference to her sire. Perhaps she also spoke of his cousin. He wondered about that, almost at once concluding that he had the right of it. He had learned much about his cousin's life since his return. The late viscount had reputedly often been deep in his cups. *Henry's excesses were considerable. She has had her bad opinions shaped not by prejudice but by experience.*

Of a sudden, he recalled when he had first seen her at the burial service. There had been a yellowing bruise on her pale cheek. He had noted it at the time, but now it came clear to him what it might have meant. "At the burial service, your cheek was bruised."

He had not phrased a question, but nonetheless she answered it as such in a low wooden voice. "No, it was not the first time he struck me."

"Damn his eyes!" he said with suppressed fury.

He thought grimly that she'd had a great deal to bear from his cousin. Then *he* had come along and perpetuated the bad experiences. The strength of his self-revulsion inwardly shook him. The darkened train of his thoughts was so far removed that her next remark disconcerted him.

"Rev. Major Ledger said you have the heart of a lion."

Lord Ogden was completely taken aback. Then he laughed. "Does he, indeed!" He shrugged off his friend's generous assessment, which he knew was kindly meant. "Perhaps he is right. But I was never one of the death-and-glory boys. I attempted to keep those under my command together and from as much harm as possible. At times, it required making gut-wrenching, hard decisions. *That* was evidence of the lion's roar, if you like!"

Lady Ogden did not reveal her fancy that to her, with his tanned, sharp-cut visage and piercing falcon-eyes, he resembled a magnificent fierce bird. Instead, with a smile, she said, "Rev. Major Ledger likens himself to the mighty eagle, which sees everything but is above it all."

Lord Ogden cracked another laugh and his face lit up. She thought when he laughed in such a way, with the shuttered alert appearance wiped from his face, he looked at his most attractive. "That's very good! Just like Arthur, indeed. He is one of the most far-sighted, wisest fellows I know."

They had ridden around the lake and come upon a wild glen, situated between the gardens and the lake and bounded on one side by the woods, a perfect setting for the ruined folly. Even in its dilapidated state, the octagonal building was still attractive. They drew rein to regard the abandoned, forlorn-looking edifice.

Lady Ogden's heart quickened. She vividly recalled what had taken place within the folly. She tossed a quick glance at her companion. Lord Ogden's gaze was pensive, while a faint smile curled his firm lips. Lady Ogden hurriedly turned her eyes away from him. She scarce dared to breathe, wondering whether he would bring up what they had done in the folly. *If he wishes it again...*a rash of heat prickled over her flesh.

"So much was simply let go to rack and ruin," remarked Lord Ogden. His grave voice brought her gaze back to him. He shook his head. "Henry was such a foolish man. He had everything a man could wish for, but he squandered it all." Suddenly, he turned a startlingly intense gaze on her, meeting and holding her eyes. With deliberation, he repeated himself. "He had everything and he squandered it all."

Lady Ogden lowered her eyes, a heated scorch in her cheeks. "That is very prettily said, my lord." She looked up again and smiled. "Thank you, Vincent." He nodded, and almost as one, they put their mounts back into motion and rode on.

The conversation about his soldiering experiences, along with what he had read that very morning in the newspapers, turned Lord Ogden's thoughts to a preoccupation about the war. He felt the restlessness rise up inside of him again, a bunching tension pulling between his shoulders. More than once, he started to utter an observation, before biting it back. The company was not one in which he could readily speak what was in his mind.

When he and Lady Ogden returned to Delincourt and stepped the horses around behind the manor house to the stables, Lord Ogden said, "I will not come in with you, my lady. I believe I shall ride on to the vicarage. I have not seen it since Arthur has taken it in hand."

Lady Ogden dismounted from her mare with a groom's assistance. She looked up at the viscount. He was still mounted and held the reins in a firm grip that kept the gelding at a stand. Some minutes before trotting into the stable yard, she had become aware that the viscount's thoughts had turned inward, bringing a crease to his brows. She did not ask what was chafing at him. His lordship's desire to seek out his good friend was none of her business. She said only, "Then you must go. The improvements which Rev. Major Ledger has made are remarkable."

Lord Ogden raised the tip of his crop to the brim of his beaver hat in farewell and touched spur to his mount. The gelding was still relatively fresh and settled into its paces. It was not a far distance to the vicarage and within a short space of time, Lord Ogden dismounted and tied his horse at the gate. He trod up the flag stone path to knock on the front door. Welcomed inside by the housekeeper, he was ushered into the study where his old comrade-in-arms was at work on his accounting ledger. "I've come when you are busy, I see."

"Ah, Vincent!" Rev. Major Ledger threw down his pen. He rose from his chair and limped forward to greet him. The two gentlemen clasped hands. "A pleasant surprise. Will you join me in a glass of claret?"

"I will and gladly."

"Then come into the parlor. We will be more comfortable there." Rev. Major Ledger led the way into the other room and waved the viscount toward a wingback chair sitting in front of the quietly crackling fire on the hearth. "Make yourself comfortable. I will get the claret." After retrieving the bottle and glasses, the vicar sat down in a wingchair opposite, an occasional table between them, and poured out a measure of the deep red wine for each of them.

Lord Ogden accepted the wine glass but he did not lift it to his lips; instead, he slowly swirled the drink around in the glass in an absent manner. He said abruptly, "Have you seen the *Gazette* this morning? The article about Wellesley?"

Rev. Major Ledger tasted the claret in his glass. Then in a quiet voice he responded. "Yes, I have. It brought to my mind many somber reflections."

"It did the same for me." Lord Ogden tossed back a small amount of the claret, before he admitted aloud what he had been thinking. "It's not that I *want* to be in the fight, but I can scarcely bear *not* to be in it, if that makes a bit of sense."

Rev. Major Ledger lazily smiled at him from across the small table. "My lord, can it be that you miss the trumpet call? Such an old war-horse!"

Lord Ogden scowled back with false ferocity. "Beware how you mock me, vicar. I can slash your generous income to a pittance!"

Rev. Major Ledger laughed. However, he quickly sobered to eye his friend with curiosity. "But seriously, Vincent, *do* you miss it at all?"

Lord Ogden shrugged his shoulders. He turned his glass around and around between his browned fingers, watching the light refract in the red depths of the claret. "Fighting for king and country – perhaps I do, in some part of me. But I shall never miss the killing or the extremity of anguish I felt at the rude passing of a comrade-in-arms."

The two gentlemen were silent for several moments, each recalling the names and faces which they would never encounter again on their side of heaven. Lord Ogden lifted up his wine glass. His dark eyes glittered with an unfamiliar wetness, even as a smile twisted his face. "A toast, Arthur! Let us toast Wellesley and our fine fellows. May they make an end to it!"

"Hear, hear." Rev. Major Ledger raised his own glass. "May God keep their gallant souls."

31

In early July, with the end of the London Season, most of the nobility and gentry fled the heat of the metropolis and returned to their country seats. The local society around Delincourt Manor increased in numbers with several personages. The widow Collings had lately returned to Thane Hall from a lengthy sojourn in London. The lady heard much from her in-laws, Sir Edward and Lady Thane, about the new viscount. It annoyed her very much to receive such particulars secondhand. She was therefore anxious to call at Delincourt Manor and did so with all possible speed.

When the lady's card was brought in to the drawing-room, Mrs. Merriweather made a *moue* of distaste. Mrs. Collings had never been a favorite. The ladies of Delincourt were of the opinion that the widow's preference for London society was a boon to the whole countryside. However, Lady Ogden and Mrs. Merriweather had long ago become resigned that whenever Mrs. Collings was in residence at Thane Hall and chose to call upon them as their neighbor, they were obligated to extend courtesy to the lady.

As though it was tainted, Lady Ogden held the lady's card between thumb and forefinger by one corner. She looked hopefully at the butler but knowing better because there had been only one card brought in. "Has Lady Thane accompanied Mrs. Collings?"

"Regretfully, no, my lady."

Lady Ogden sighed. She dropped the card on an occasional table before she walked over and sat down on the settee beside her aunt. She smiled at her aunt's resigned expression; her own sentiments were fully appreciated. "Well, we are in for it, aunt."

Mrs. Merriweather shook her head. "It's really too bad that dear Lady Thane did not come."

Lady Ogden addressed the butler. "Somerset, bring tea without delay. We shall hurry the lady's visit as best we can."

The butler permitted himself a small smile. "Yes, my lady." He went away. A few minutes later, he opened the door again to announce the visitor. "Mrs. Collings."

The widow entered with a cordial smile on her lips. "Lady Ogden! Mrs. Merriweather! I am delighted to find you at home this afternoon and receiving callers!" She made sweeping gestures with her hands, flinging one out and pressing the other to her spare bosom, to emphasize her delight.

Lady Ogden had always thought the lady to be theatrical in her manner and watched her approach with a critical gaze. Reluctantly, she acknowledged to herself that Mrs. Collings did dress well. The lady was modishly attired in a carriage dress with ruffs of triple lace, a spencer buttoned over it. The fashionable cottage bonnet perched on her head filled Lady Ogden with envy.

Lady Ogden and Mrs. Merriweather rose to their feet to exchange curtsies with their visitor. Lady Ogden said civilly, "Mrs. Collings, you are welcome. Please be seated." She and her aunt sank back down in their former places on the settee. Mrs. Collings sat down in a chair opposite them and began to pull at the fingertips of her kid gloves, the removal of which was a sign that she meant to remain for a long visit. Lady Ogden exchanged a speaking glance with her aunt.

"Pray do not think I am behind in my civilities. I do assure you, I came to call upon you, Lady Ogden – and you, dear Mrs. Merriweather! – as soon as I was able. I have just come down from London, you know."

"It's good of you to come, Mrs. Collings," said Lady Ogden with a polite smile pinned to her lips, feeling the perfect hypocrite. "I hope you are well?"

"As well as can be expected. I'm certain you will recall that my constitution has always been delicate," said Mrs. Collings as she finished removing her gloves and laying them neatly in her lap. "I suffer from the occasional nervous upset, but I do not complain."

"One hopes not," murmured Lady Ogden. The familiar irritation that the lady always engendered in her was beginning to stir. She must have shown it in some small, telltale way because her aunt cleared her throat.

With a glance at her niece, Mrs. Merriweather hurriedly struck in. "How are you situated at Thane Hall? I suppose Sir Edward and Lady Thane are glad to have you back for your annual visit."

"Oh, tolerably, tolerably. I begin to suffer from *ennui* already, however. Such provincial entertainment! Really, my sister-in-law could go on very much better if she would only heed my advice a little. I am an arbitrator of taste, after all," said Mrs. Collings, ending with a simpering smirk.

Lady Ogden didn't like for her friend to be so belittled. She could not let it pass and defended Lady Thane. "We are all provincials, Mrs. Collings. It is the country, after all."

Mrs. Collings gave a tinkling laugh, her ripple of amusement sounding brittle. She playfully shook her forefinger at her hostess. "You are in a funning humor, indeed! I do hope that Lord Ogden is also in to visitors? I should like very much to be introduced to his lordship. I should like to proffer a greeting."

The lady's query was on the surface civil enough, but she sounded a little too bright, too inquisitive. Rather than express honest regret for the lady's bad luck, Lady Ogden's instinctive response was one of cool, dismissive civility "I fear not, ma'am. I believe his lordship is out with the bailiff and will not be back for some hours."

Mrs. Collings was put out at having her ambition thwarted and exclaimed at boring length about it. "I am excessively disappointed! I so wished to have a sight of Lord Ogden. I have heard ever so much about his lordship! How much I wish the viscount was in to visitors. It is so vexing, I must say."

The sound of the door creaking open interrupted the lady's plaintive monologue and Lady Ogden was able to break from her attitude of courteous attention. She turned her head with a sense of relief. "Ah, here is our tea. Somerset, you may set the tray here. We shall not need anything else, thank you. I will serve. Mrs. Collings, will you join us?"

Mrs. Collings accepted the tepid invitation to take tea. Her self-absorbed character was such that the lack of enthusiasm in which the overture was uttered was taken as a completely proper courtesy. "I was sorry to miss Lord Henry Ogden's funeral. I did see the notice in the *Gazette*, however, and pointed it out to my dear sister-in-law. You are acquainted with Augusta and my brother-in-law, Mr. Thomas Thane; but of course, you see little of them, being buried here in the country. I have been staying with them in town, you know. How are you, dear Lady Ogden? The recent bereavement must weigh heavy on your spirits."

"I'm well, Mrs. Collings. It is good of you to inquire." Lady Ogden poured out the tea. "Do you take sugar, ma'am?"

"Oh, you tease me, Lady Ogden! You must remember! One lump, if you please." Mrs. Collings leaned forward to accept the cup of tea and saucer from her hostess. "I have come to condole with you, Lady Ogden. Such a sad trial to you! The viscount was so young and handsome. It is a tragic loss. You are such a young widow." The lady's bird-bright, speculative gaze raked her hostess's figure. Her eyes sharpened and up went her thin brows. "Forgive me, dear Lady Ogden, but how pale you are! Are you sure you are well?"

"I am very well, ma'am," said Lady Ogden firmly. She didn't like the avid spike of interest in her caller's expression. She wondered what winged thought had inspired it and decided that she probably wouldn't like the answer. She knew the lady for an inveterate gossip and with her wagging tongue, mere speculations became half-baked truths.

Mrs. Collings sniffed, looking her hostess up and down again. "Black doesn't become you, more's the pity. You will miss the late viscount very much, I daresay."

Lady Ogden was wearing the awful gown made up in bombazine crape and she resolved then and there to put off her blacks entirely. She had two lovely half-mourning gowns, one in a dove-gray and another in a lilac and black stripe, and a third just finished that she had not yet worn. She was put out that she was not attired in one of the new dresses rather than the black mourning gown.

As for what else Mrs. Collings had said, she discounted the sincerity of it. She inclined her head in acknowledgement, but she couldn't help a faint smile at the widow's expression of condolence. It was known to the neighborhood that the late viscount had enjoyed the liveliest doings of town life, making rare visits, so her visitor's spurious sympathy was very much a polite nothing. She said dryly, "Just so, Mrs. Collings."

Beside her, she felt her aunt's shifting on the settee. She glanced out of the corner of her eye and saw that her aunt had summoned up her pleasantest smile. Mrs. Merriweather said, "We manage not to think of it overmuch, Mrs. Collings."

"Of course! Of course! But I do feel for you, my dear ladies," sighed Mrs. Collings, shaking her head. She wore a small cottage bonnet of fawn-colored crape, trimmed and tied under the chin with ribands of the same color. It was set far back on her head to display a lace cap. "You are so awkwardly situated, are you not?"

"My aunt and I go on quite well, I assure you," said Lady Ogden with determined politeness. She had liked the bonnet on first sight, but now as she eyed the fashionable headgear, she decided the color made the lady's face look sallow. She knew she was being petty and she didn't care. Her growing annoyance with all of Mrs. Collings' little digs and pointed comments was becoming a trial to her temper.

"Indeed, we do," agreed Mrs. Merriweather, presenting a united front with her niece. "Delincourt has long been our home. It is a pleasant place."

Balked, Mrs. Collings irritably clinked her cup down onto the saucer she held. She tried a different tack. "I have heard that Sir Martin did not attend the funeral services. Surely, Sir Martin has called to condole with you over his son-in-law's death? I feel certain it must be so. You've had a recent visit from Sir Martin, of course?"

"No, I have not." Lady Ogden knew well that if her father had called at Delincourt, it would have been common knowledge in the neighborhood and Mrs. Collings would already have heard of it, so the lady's questioning was an impertinence. She began to seethe under her calm exterior. *What a beetle mind she has, scuttling here and there!* "Sir Martin is still in London."

Mrs. Collings nodded. "Indeed, I do recall that now! Such a pity that Sir Martin had to break household and rent out his encumbered estate.

That was quite four – no, it was five years ago, was it not? The same year you were wed to the viscount, I believe." The lady's sharp eyes watched her hostess's face. Her smile was all syrup. "Wasn't it that same year the Rt. Rev. Crawford enjoyed a short visit from his son, who was on leave before rejoining his regiment when the war broke out on the Peninsular? He must have made a dashing figure! He *must* have called on you at the time. He was a neighbor, after all. Such an *eventful* year!"

Lady Ogden held herself in hand, only lifting a brow, but inside she was incensed. *Insufferable woman! Out for any gossip she can pry out!* Much as she wanted to deal the woman a strong set-down, she could not indulge herself in such indecorous behavior. It would cap Mrs. Collings' vile fishing expedition with success. With a determined smile, Lady Ogden picked up the teapot. "More tea, ma'am?"

"Please, and one lump." Mrs. Collings looked back and forth between the ladies. "What are your plans now, Lady Ogden, dear Mrs. Merriweather?"

Lady Ogden exchanged a glance with her aunt as she refreshed their visitor's tea cup. "At present, we are fixed here at Delincourt."

"Really! Why, that is most wonderful." The lady raised her thin brows in exaggerated surprise. Her eyes held an avid gleam. "His lordship must be an amiable man. For how long will you be situated at Delincourt, if I may ask?"

"For an indefinite period," said Lady Ogden with finality.

"You must be thankful, indeed, for his lordship's generosity."

Lady Ogden felt a gathering chill in her expression.

Tossing a perceptive glance at her niece's face, Mrs. Merriweather hurriedly interposed. "Mrs. Collings, how did you find the shops in London?"

It was an admirable cast. Besides gossiping about her acquaintances, Mrs. Collings liked nothing better than to talk about her fashionable purchases. The topic was thoroughly explored, with Mrs. Merriweather diligently encouraging Mrs. Colling's running discourse. Lady Ogden contributed little but monosyllabic utterances and busied herself with plying the teapot and offering the biscuit plate. However, not even fashion could hold off Mrs. Collings for long from her penchant for gossip. She turned a determined smile on her hostess. "My friends know all about the late viscount, of course. Situated as you are, it is thought strange by some of my acquaintances that you are still here at Delincourt Manor."

Lady Ogden felt a surge of anger and knew she was skating close to losing her temper. "In what way is it strange, Mrs. Collings?"

"You've said you are *fixed* here at Delincourt – *indefinitely*." There was something sly in the way the lady uttered the words.

Lady Ogden just stared at Mrs. Collings for a long moment. Then she gave a cool, disdainful smile. She was determined there would be nothing forthcoming from her to fuel gossip. "Yes; what of it?"

Mrs. Collings threw out her hands. "Why, surely you must see, Lady Ogden! His lordship's benevolence could be misconstrued."

With difficulty, Lady Ogden held her tongue in check. She looked at her aunt. She had taken Mrs. Collings' declaration in bad part, but she was already angry. She wanted to know what her aunt thought about it. She saw that Mrs. Merriweather was staring at the lady with considerable astonishment.

"What nonsense! My niece is in mourning. Nothing, *nothing*, could be more natural than that she should continue here!"

Mrs. Collings' gaze dropped unmistakably to Lady Ogden's waistline. She raised her eyes again to her hostess' face with a meaningful smile. "Well, naturally, extenuating circumstances must be taken into account."

Lady Ogden immediately understood the insolent insinuation. She barely heard her aunt suck in an appalled breath as she pinned her visitor with a steely gaze. "You've stated you are familiar with the late viscount's set."

Suddenly looking uncomfortable, Mrs. Collings fiddled with her gloves. "I would not say *familiar*, for we were not of the same circles, but we were on bowing terms and in society one does hear things."

"Then you will know already that the late viscount and his friends were here, at Delincourt, some weeks prior to his death," said Lady Ogden coldly.

Mrs. Collings gave a careful nod. "Indeed, that is true."

Lady Ogden spoke out of effervescent fury, every cutting word tipped with ice. "Then surely, Mrs. Collins, my reputation is safe! Surely, my aunt Merriweather's chaperonage is sufficient to repel any such outrageous speculations as you seem to suggest. Surely, these whispers are but the overblown malice of the foolish!"

Lady Ogden paused to gauge the effect of her words. The widow appeared discomposed and was eyeing her as though she had come face-to-face with a wild, unpredictable beast. Mrs. Collings' succor came from an unexpected direction.

"We do appreciate your kindness, Mrs. Collings! It must pain your sensibilities to bring us such vulgar chatter. But you were quite right to do so," stated Mrs. Merriweather with a determined smile. "Lady Ogden is grateful, indeed, to be forewarned of such horrid gossip."

Mrs. Collings was disconcerted. She looked uncertainly at Mrs. Merriweather's pleasant features. There was nothing to be read in the elderly lady's face but civility. "Why-why, yes, of course." Almost visibly gathering her dignity about her, and with a quick glance at her hostess's set expression, she stiffly added, "I merely wished to be of service to you, Lady Ogden."

Lady Ogden inclined her head. She rose from the settee, saying dismissively, "Thank you for calling on us, Mrs. Collings. Your concern for our welfare is duly noted, but I assure you, quite unnecessary. Pray do not let us keep you any longer! You must have other social calls to make!"

Mrs. Collings gawped at her ladyship, apparently rendered speechless by such highhandedness. She glanced at Mrs. Merriweather for support, but that lady merely looked back at her. With no alternative offered her, the widow at last got up and took her leave, her kid gloves clenched in one hand. High gudgeon marked her expression and her farewell was coldly civil. "Thank you for tea, Lady Ogden."

As Mrs. Collings moved toward the door, it opened, and Mrs. Dalton entered. With a bright, inquiring glance, Mrs. Dalton said, "Pardon me, Charlotte. I did not know you were entertaining."

Mrs. Collings at once perceived that the intruder was no country dowdy. On the contrary, the fashionableness of the lady's daydress filled her with envy. She had thought herself to be dressed in the height of fashion, but the lady eclipsed her. The lady was younger and prettier than she was, too. Mrs. Collings detested the lady on sight, envying her all but her superior inches, which she pettishly decided made her appear something of a long-Meg. Mrs. Collings raked Mrs. Dalton with a chilly glance, which very much astonished the lady, before she turned with raised brows to her ladyship.

Lady Ogden felt forced to make the introduction. She would have spared her friend the noxious acquaintance if she could, but she could not. For good or ill, Mrs. Collings was situated in the neighborhood and the two ladies would inevitably meet. "Amarys, this is Sir Edward and Lady Thane's sister-in-law, Mrs. Collings. Perhaps you will recall hearing of her? Mrs. Collings is down from London for the summer, staying at Thane Hall. Mrs. Collings, Mrs. Dalton is Lord Ogden's sister." The two ladies exchanged curtsies. Lady Ogden cynically watched as, upon learning Mrs. Dalton's identity, Mrs. Collings' ill-humored expression underwent transformation.

With her friendly smile, Mrs. Dalton said, "Mrs. Collings, how do you do. I seem to recall that Sir Edward had sisters-in-law, but I have never met any of your family before. I was already gone up to a private seminary before Sir Edward's brother was wed to Miss Augusta Collings. You were married to *her* brother, I believe."

"Indeed, that's so! I wed Mr. Percival Collings before my sister-in-law, Augusta, came out," said Mrs. Collings, all cordiality, her face wreathed in an ingratiating smile. "Well! Lord Ogden's sister! It's a pleasure, I'm sure! I know we will be wondrous great friends. How I should have liked to speak with his lordship, but I am not so fortunate today. Perhaps another time."

Lady Ogden ignored Mrs. Collings' expectant glance. She thought she knew what the lady was playing at and she gave no encouragement to Mrs. Collings to linger. *Detestable woman! The creature will not shame me into a false civility!* She had as good as dismissed her caller. She stood by her decision. "Give my regards to Lady Thane, ma'am."

After a moment, during which her narrow face tightened, Mrs. Collings returned her gaze to the viscount's sister. "I must be off or otherwise I would sit down directly, so we might get to know one another, dear Mrs. Dalton." She could not quash her rancor and she tittered an artificial laugh. "I'm certain that her ladyship values your presence just as she ought. It's so pleasant to have another lady to add to one's consequence."

Lady Ogden decided she had taken enough. Good breeding could endure only so much. She uttered an arctic set-down. "Quite true. We shan't suffer from the slings of gossip *now*. Mrs. Dalton has a very good reputation." It was a master stroke. All of the lady's volubility was crushed. Looking rather pinch-faced, Mrs. Collings curtsied again and exited.

When she was gone, Mrs. Dalton turned a laughing, astonished face to Lady Ogden. "Pray, what was that about? You appear in a perfect flame, Charlotte!"

"You may well ask, Amarys!" Lady Ogden pressed tight her lips. She could not quite repress her feelings, however, and she beat the heels of her hands together. "Awful woman! Ill-bred, venomous, spiteful!"

Mrs. Merriweather directed a smile of apology at Mrs. Dalton. "Would you mind it very much, my dear, if I spoke with my niece in private?"

"Of course not." Mrs. Dalton tactfully withdrew and closed the door, leaving the other two ladies alone in the drawing-room.

Lady Ogden drew in a deep, shuddering breath. She discovered she was shaking. "That insufferable tattle-monger! I came very close to losing my good sense!"

"Your good sense wasn't at risk, but your temper certainly was," retorted Mrs. Merriweather with a small chuckle.

"Yes, quite true," said Lady Ogden ruefully. She sank back down beside her aunt and clasped her hands tightly together. "I simply cannot bear that smiling, false solicitude. The same as what my poor mother endured! She was too genteel to give well-deserved set-downs, but I certainly was not!"

"How well I recall! Turkish treatment! You early earned for yourself a reputation for prickly pride, Charlotte. This work today will only reinforce that old opinion. Mrs. Collings will see to it!"

"I care little enough for that! She was always an odious little toad! I cannot stomach such veiled innuendos and insults," exclaimed Lady Ogden. "My father's excesses laid us open to such wretched impertinences, especially during my mother's last illness. The humiliation was not to be borne. I made certain everyone knew it! Dear heaven, I hope *he* will never return!"

"Well, here's a flame! Sir Martin is not likely to return. He'll cling to the rents as long as he can," said Mrs. Merriweather with admirable good sense. She patted her niece's arm consolingly. "As for Mrs. Collings and her ilk, we need not concern ourselves. Dear me, the look on her face! Mrs. Collings will not soon be back, I wager. Not after your blast across her bows! The obnoxious woman thrives on gossip and there is none to be found here."

Her aunt's comfortable assurance dashed like cold water over Lady Ogden, extinguishing her anger. "No, indeed." *No gossip to be found here...*Her body felt chilled and leaden with a feeling of sudden dread. She hoped that Mrs. Collings would not be able to manufacture anything out of her visit that would be listened to by the neighborhood. The particulars of that last infamous house party had undoubtedly been carried up to London by the late viscount's set. Mrs. Collings' half-admission she had heard something in town was proof enough of that. It was to be hoped the old gossip was enough to put to rout any other explanation for her ladyship's interesting condition once it became universally known.

Lady Ogden's ire rose again. "I cannot believe the gall of her! Insinuating and rooting about! I tell you, aunt, she is a menace."

Mrs. Merriweather gently squeezed her niece's forearm. "Be at ease, my dear. There is no way possible for Mrs. Collings or anyone else to guess the truth."

"Mrs. Collings hit on it, all too readily."

"She was fishing. She didn't really believe it. She was merely trying to get a rise out of you, Charlotte."

"Still, aunt." Lady Ogden shuddered, imagining the consequences to her if there was any taint of gossip. *I'm wagering all that I am!* She had staked her honor and her reputation. If her folly was found out, she would become a social pariah, looked down upon as a woman of depraved character. Mrs. Collings would not be the only one of her neighbors who would condemn her. She would be pilloried as a wanton.

"Why, Charlotte, I can feel you shaking! Are you all right? Mrs. Collings' visit must have affected you even more than I guessed."

She said quickly, "I'm angry, aunt!"

"*Of course*, you are! It's only natural. I own, you had provocation! That woman and her poisonous tongue!"

Lady Ogden abruptly felt suffocated. She leaped up and crossed over to tug on the bell pull. "A little fresh air is what I need! I feel positively besmirched after enduring that horrid woman's visit! I know you will understand, aunt. Pray apologize to Amarys for me. Will you mind that I leave you?"

Mrs. Merriweather shook her head. She regarded her niece with an understanding smile. "Go along with you, then. I will see you presently."

A footman responded to her ladyship's summons. Lady Ogden told him to take word to the stables. "Have my mare brought around to the front in a quarter hour and pray send Mills up to me."

"Aye, m'lady."

Not many minutes later, Lady Ogden was seated on horseback. Since Lord Ogden was not accompanying her, and as she had given her word, she took a groom with her. The groom was well-trained and followed along behind, so he was not an intrusion on her reverie. Her aunt had been right, she thought, she had been very disturbed by the visit from Mrs. Collings. She had felt sullied by the lady's conversation until at the last she had become enraged and vanquished the insufferable woman. Yet anxiety and residual anger set up tension in her shoulders. She was impatient of herself. *There's nothing to fear.* Her nervous energy transferred to her mount and the mare cavorted under her.

Lady Ogden gathered her reins a bit tighter. All she wanted was a good ride to blow away the lingering agitation of her spirits.

32

As she put her mare along, Lady Ogden reveled in the breeze that rushed past her face. Now that the dryer summer was upon them, she and the viscount rode together nearly every day. She always took for granted that his company would be available to her. However, all that day business had kept his lordship fully occupied and there had been no opportunity. *It is strange, but I miss him.*

The fleeting admission seemed to conjure him up. She saw the horseman trotting his mount towards her and recognizing the set of his shoulders and the easy way the gentleman sat in the saddle, her heart gave a small leap. She spoke briefly to the groom, who then turned his horse and trotted off. As Lady Ogden rode to meet the viscount, she schooled her features. It would not do to show him such a glad face. She reined in her mare and nodded. "Good day to you, my lord!"

"And to you, ma'am! You are obviously out for a good ride. May I join you?"

"Of course." She was unaccountably pleased to have the viscount's company, and for a few moments, forgot the provocation arising out of Mrs. Collings' visit.

Lord Ogden turned his mount to walk beside hers. He glanced back the way she had come. "Where is your groom? I thought he was with you."

"When I caught sight of you, I dispensed with him," said Lady Ogden. She touched her horse back into a smooth, ground-eating gait. As she expected, the viscount easily urged his gelding to match pace. Despite the comfortable companionship, however, her thoughts turned again to Mrs. Collings.

After a few moments, Lord Ogden spoke across the short distance between their mounts. "You are in a temper."

With a flashing look, she challenged him "Why should you think so?"

The upper portion of his face was shadowed by the curved brim of his beaver, so she couldn't discern the expression in his eyes, but she could see that he smiled at her. "I believe I know you well enough to realize it. Come, what has overset you, ma'am?"

Lady Ogden did not dispute what he had said. It would only make her look foolish. They had become too familiar with one another's moods, she reflected. Her simmering resentment boiled up again and it suited her to tell him of it. "A vulgar, horrid woman! Sir Edward and Lady Thane's sister-in-law, Mrs. Collings, came to call only to dig up what gossip she could. You might remember her – Mariah Sharpe."

The viscount frowned. "I have a vague recollection. One of the Collings cousins, wasn't she? What about her?"

Lady Ogden tightened her lips. Her temper was still riding her, but she said, quite steadily, "She dared to imply there was something scandalous existing between us."

Lord Ogden shot her a crooked grin. "But isn't there, my dear?"

Lady Ogden threw a glare at him, angered by the lazy mockery in his riposte because it belittled the matter. "That is not the point, sir!"

Lord Ogden sobered. "Of course not. I hope you were able to deflect the lady's curiosity?"

"I sent her away with a flea in her ear!"

The viscount gave a crack of laughter. His dark eyes gleamed when he looked at her. "That sounds very like you, Charlotte. Was the lady badly offended?"

Lady Ogden curled her lips in a smile. She suddenly felt a satisfaction that had eluded her before. "Oh, I do hope so."

"Then let us trust that the lady will not return."

"Mrs. Collings is staying at Thane Hall," she said briefly, frowning at her horse's twitching ears. She looked over again at her riding companion. He looked alert, a gentleman used to command, tough and competent. He was a man who could be expected to handle problems. "The lady is on her annual visit, down from London for the summer."

Lord Ogden gave a nod. "I understand you, ma'am. The amiable footing that we enjoy with Sir Edward and Lady Thane will bring Mrs. Collings along in their train."

"Exactly so." She amplified her feelings. "I don't like Mrs. Collings, nor do I trust her."

The viscount shrugged his broad shoulders. "We must armor ourselves against the slings and arrows of the lady's malicious tongue. Shall we gallop, ma'am?"

Lady Ogden acquiesced and enjoyed the remainder of the ride. Though his lordship had not offered any concrete strategy for dealing with the worrisome Mrs. Collings, she nevertheless felt cheered. She let go of her temper and a scarce-understood anxiety and simply let herself be in the present, taking a lively interest in all she saw. At one point, from a rise in ground, the viscount pointed out with his crop the progress that was being made in the repair of the road that wended through the park and led to the gates of Delincourt.

"As you know, it was little more than a rutted cart-track," said Lord Ogden. "The distance involved means it's taking longer than the front drive, but the workmen have been making good progress."

"The approach to the front of the house looks much better. The trees needed a good trim and the front lawn is neater for having been kept mowed," said Lady Ogden. "Delincourt begins to show the beneficial direction of your hand, my lord."

The viscount smiled, looking pleased with the compliment.

When they finally turned their mounts around to return to the manor house, the late-afternoon shadows were well-advanced across the ground. Lady Ogden threw a glance up at the darkening, overcast sky. "We shall have rain before morning," she remarked.

"Yes, and a heavy wetting could slow the roadwork," said Lord Ogden, in his turn looking up and frowning at the sky. "Let's hope we're not in for a deluge."

Lady Ogden agreed. She was relaxed, swaying easily with her mare's motion. Her intemperate emotions had blown away like clouds while in the viscount's company. It was not something she analyzed. She believed she had merely benefited from the fresh air and exercise.

Upon entering the manor house, Lady Ogden went upstairs to her bedroom and rang for her dresser. Mills helped her to exchange her riding clothes for the new deep lilac muslin daydress. The dresser also freshly arranged her mistress' hair, pulling it up in a knot and arranging a cascade of curls. Lady Ogden looked into the mirrored glass at her reflection and smiled with delight. "I look very fine, indeed."

"The lilac turned out very well, my lady," said Mills with equal satisfaction as she gathered up the discarded riding habit.

Over her shoulders, Lady Ogden adjusted the folds of her gray cambric shawl, the one which her aunt had lovingly embroidered and hemmed for her. She glanced at the large black shawl that was tossed carelessly aside on a chair and she made a vow that she would not wear the hated thing again. "Pray get rid of the black shawl, Mills."

"Yes, my lady."

Lady Ogden repaired at once to the upper drawing-room, where she expected to find her aunt and Mrs. Dalton. However, when she entered and glanced about, she saw only her young friend, and she said cheerfully, "Why, where is my aunt? I was certain I would find her here with you, deep in study of the newest fashion plates in the *Ladies' Almanac*, and ready to render her advice with the pattern we cut out."

At her ladyship's entrance, Mrs. Dalton had leaped to her feet. She said quickly, "Mrs. Merriweather said she had some work to finish in the stillroom. I'm so sorry, Charlotte."

Lady Ogden was astonished. "Why, Amarys, you appear overset. What has happened?"

Mrs. Dalton came swiftly forward to catch up one of the viscountess' hands between her own. Her countenance flew twin flags of indignation. "Oh, Charlotte! Before she left me, dear Mrs. Merriweather told me what that horrid woman had the nerve to say!"

"I wish she had not," said Lady Ogden, heat rising in her face. *What had Aunt been thinking?* As her aunt had pointed out, Mrs. Collings had merely been fishing. Appalled, she could only imagine what would happen if Mrs. Dalton guessed that she had been made privy to the actual truth. "I didn't want you to be regaled with such stuff."

"Such an odious female! I wonder that you didn't call for Somerset to toss her out on her ear!"

Lady Ogden shook her head, squeezing her friend's fingers before she gently withdrew her hand from Mrs. Dalton's clasp. "It was very bad. The lady's ill-breeding put me very much out of temper."

"It's small wonder, indeed! I'm surprised you are now so calm."

Lady Ogden slid her arm around the other lady's trim waist and walked with her across the faded carpet. As she sat down at the work table, she gave a reassuring smile and said in a teasing tone, "My humor is quite restored, so you needn't fear that I'll cut up at you."

"As though I fear that!" Mrs. Dalton sat down also but she was not finished airing her views. There was a militant sparkle in her fine eyes. "*Well!* When you put off full mourning and begin having dinner parties at Delincourt again, you must not on any account invite Mrs. Collings!"

Lady Ogden laughed. "I can't very well banish her from my guest list, Amarys. After all, Mrs. Collings is Sir Edward and Lady Thane's sister-in-law. I do appreciate the sentiment, however."

Mrs. Dalton's indignation suffered a check. She looked thoughtful. "Oh, that does make it awkward, doesn't it? And of course, you do wish to stay on good terms with your neighbors."

"Yes, I do." Lady Ogden picked up the pattern-book and opened it, flipping through some pages. "Lady Thane is a dear friend. It would pain me to give her offense."

Mrs. Dalton brooded for a moment before she tossed her head. "I shall show Mrs. Collings only the barest civility. And we shall not become *wondrous great friends!*"

Though amused by Mrs. Dalton's fierce allegiance, Lady Ogden was desperate to turn topic. She thrust the pattern-book beneath her friend's gaze. "Do look at this lovely gown, Amarys! I think it will do very well for you!"

Mrs. Dalton laughed at her. "But Charlotte, it is so extravagant for an evening gown! And quite expensive to make, by the look of it."

"Rev. Major Ledger is coming to dine tonight. Wouldn't it be nice to have something like this in your wardrobe to wear?"

Mrs. Dalton blushed. "I own, I would like that."

"We've all remarked with regret on how Rev. Major Ledger's visits have declined," said Lady Ogden gently. "But I suspect you have most particularly felt the loss."

Mrs. Dalton sighed. "Indeed, I have been surprised at how keenly I have felt the gentleman's absence," she admitted softly. She raised her brilliant eyes to meet Lady Ogden's sympathetic gaze. "I have wondered at myself of late. I had believed myself to have become more prosaic. I did not think I was a silly little romantic anymore!"

Lady Ogden reached out and hugged her friend. "You aren't silly, Amarys."

"I do have a gown that I haven't worn because I thought it too fashionable for our informal dinners," said Mrs. Dalton tentatively.

With a smile, Lady Ogden again reminded her. "Rev. Major Ledger is coming to dine."

Downstairs in the study, the viscount sat frowning over what Lady Ogden had told him about her visitor, Mrs. Collings. It did not suit him that such speculation should be bandied about. Of course, his valet had heard the servants tell of the days leading up to his cousin's demise and Grimshaw had related the sordid details to him. The household and the late viscount's guests were all aware that Henry had visited her ladyship's bedchamber before the accident, so it was legitimately possible in their minds that she was gotten with child. The tale had almost certainly made the rounds of the county, carried as servants' gossip, and had obviously been broadcast in London by Henry's cronies. Yet one of their respectable neighbors, Mrs. Collings, had felt emboldened enough to question the veracity of that tale and dared to hint at a different possibility.

Lord Ogden stared at the locked drawer in his desk, where he had put away the special license that he'd had Rev. Major Ledger procure for him in London. He wished he had the right to protect her ladyship in the manner she deserved.

Of all things, he wanted to quash any such conjecture, but how to do it, he could not see. Damaging speculation might be fueled were it to become known that any stipend made over to Lady Ogden was conditional upon the birthing of a posthumous child. In the mysterious ways of the universe, financial matters inevitably surfaced. It was acceptable that he should provide support for his cousin-in-law, he reflected, but not that it should be contingent upon such bizarre terms. It would beg the question of whether or not he was providing support for his own child. The very fact that those terms existed would always present a risk of scandal.

Then he thought of the original stipend he had meant to bestow on Lady Ogden before their devilish bargain had been struck. "If I was to make that settlement over to her now, before she bears the child," he murmured. It stood to reason that as the titular heir, he would make such charitable provision. When it became common knowledge that her ladyship had already received a stipend – and he would make certain that it did become known – it would go far in undermining any malicious conjecture about who had sired Lady Ogden's child.

Turning it over in his mind, the better he liked it. He swore softly to himself. "I've been negligent. I should have made the provision before this." He castigated himself for not having foreseen that he should have laid the foundation of respectability a little better. Even when his heart had been most hardened against Lady Ogden, he had never wished her to be whispered about and held up to public censor.

Though he had corresponded several times with his solicitor about estate business, it had been some months since he had seen Digsby. It would not occasion comment if he were to have private matters to lay before the solicitor. He rather thought it was time for that gentleman to wait upon him again. The viscount pulled a sheet of writing paper toward himself. Dipping a pen in the inkwell, he wrote to the solicitor of his wishes, requesting that Mr. Digsby come to Delincourt with the requisite legal documents at the earliest possible date.

The hour was growing late when Lord Ogden emerged from the study. He bounded upstairs to change for dinner, climbing the treads three at a time. Rev. Major Ledger was due to arrive presently. He looked forward to the gentleman's agreeable company. It had been too long since his friend had been to dine.

When Rev. Major Ledger had given his first sermon, the church pews were filled from all ranks of the county. The gentry and the professional class, as well as the lower ranks of tenants and townspeople, had wanted to hear their new vicar and take their measure of him. The weeks since had not seen the congregation much diminished. Rev. Major Ledger's calendar had become full of dates for christenings, the declaring of banns, and performance of weddings and burial services; in short, Rev. Major Ledger had been called upon to discharge every duty expected of the vicar of a large parish. He had also enjoyed a flurry of hospitality from his parishioners. His frequent visits to Delincourt and his welcome presence at the viscount's table had inevitably become rarer.

When Lady Ogden next saw Mrs. Dalton, she knew that her friend had taken particular care in her appearance. Mrs. Dalton was the last to enter the drawing-room and drew all eyes. She was wearing a gown of azure blue crape vandyked around the petticoat. Her height and her slender figure made her look like a slim, graceful sylph.

"Why, Amarys, how nice you look!" said Mrs. Merriweather.

Delicate color tinted her cheeks. "Thank you, dear ma'am."

Lady Ogden looked quickly at Rev. Major Ledger. The gentleman's gray eyes had lit up at sight of the elegant young lady. *Amarys has her reward.*

Through dinner and after, Lord Ogden thought several times he had rarely seen his sister in better looks or spirits, and he did not wonder at it that his old comrade-in-arms could scarcely take his gaze off of her. For himself, however, there was but one beautiful woman in the room, one which he believed eclipsed all others in the world.

Lady Ogden glanced again at the viscount. He had been watching her all evening. She felt a familiar flutter of anticipation, the physical low-in-the-belly tug. After she had gotten past the morning sickness, she had been shocked at how much she wanted him, such a strong desire, a greediness even, for his lovemaking. *This all for a man who has never said he loves me.* She unhappily believed she could not give him all of herself. *No, I dare not! It will destroy me.*

But that night, in the searing throes of wicked passion, she came closer than she ever had before.

"LOOK INTO THE MIRROR! Look at yourself, Charlotte!"

"I won't!" she cried, squeezing shut her eyes. It terrified her, what she might see in the curved cheval mirror. He had shaped her into his creature, a creature of passion, a woman she no longer recognized.

"You *will* obey me in this!" He smacked her arse, a stinging pop, harder than he had ever done. It was not a lover's stroke, but a punishment, shocking her, and tears smarted under her lids. She inhaled the pervading musk of arousal, filled her laboring lungs. Their rasping pants did not drown out the sucking, moist noises of their brutish swiving. "*Look at yourself, Charlotte! Look at us!*"

She snapped open her eyes, unable to resist his lordship's will. The silvered cheval glass pitilessly reflected their debauchery, the guttering pale candlelight, the shadowed tumbled bed. With glittering black eyes, Vincent kneeled behind her, his large, calloused hands clutching her hips. He was moving against her, inside of her. The heat of his body was like a furnace. The chords of his neck and powerful arms stood out, as did the contoured planes of his hair-roughened chest and taut abdomen. His hard body glistened with sweat as he zealously swived her with his engorged shaft. Every time he drove into her, the rounds of her arse rippled, her full breasts jigged. She was burning all over as with a fever. A sheen of moisture had popped out on her pinkened skin.

None of it was as startling as her own countenance. The tormented twist in her flushed face, the twin pinpoints of flame in her wide-opened green eyes, was a wonderous, haunting revelation. The sensual, powerful vision in the mirror was a debauched enchantment, seducing her swimming senses – the abrupt dilation of her darkened pupils, the parting of her glistening lips, the lewd vigorous coupling – made witness to their strenuous carnal congress was intensely arousing. She gasped raggedly. Her whole being grew taut, a portent of what was to come. She felt herself hurtling at terrible speed. An anguished cry strained from out of her constricted throat.

"Do you see, Charlotte?" He breathed harshly, rapidly. His contorted face – darkened, fierce – was stretched in savage rictus. He ground out the words again through gritted teeth. "*Do you see?*"

"Yes, yes!" His name was carried on a thin, breathless sob. "*Vincent!*"

She couldn't tear her frantic gaze away. Mesmerized, she watched. Pulsations of passion overtook her captive, ripening body. What she saw happening, what she felt, suddenly and gloriously melded. Her afflicted frame shuddered...shuddered...and abruptly convulsed in a fury of incandescence. She shrieked. She saw no more. She was sent spiraling violently outwards in a tremendous burst of blazing stars.

33

At breakfast, Lord Ogden cheerfully greeted his sister and the other ladies. "Good morning! It bids to be a fair day." His gaze lingered longest on Lady Ogden. He was aware of a pleasant contentment. He felt fully rested and at ease. It was enjoyable to listen to the feminine chatter over the clink of cutlery on the china plates.

Lord Ogden idled over his morning coffee, reading the newspapers. As the three ladies bid him farewell and quitted the breakfast-room, he overheard Mrs. Merriweather address her niece. "Oh, I had forgotten to tell you! While you were out riding yesterday, you had another missive from Sir William, my dear. It looked to be a rather lengthier letter than before. I put it on your desk in your sitting room."

"Thank you, aunt. I will go up directly."

Behind their retreating backs, Lord Ogden discovered that his hand had formed a fist. He loosened his bunched fingers. He reassured himself that he held the upper hand over any overture which Sir William Talley might make to the viscountess. Her ladyship might still be accepting correspondence from the gentleman; but the impudent bastard could hold very little space in the lady's brain after the passionate passage during the night. He felt a sharp tightening of his belly, a pleasant stir in his loins. He had forced her to acknowledge how well they were matched; their carnal congress had ended with her passing out from the glories he had wrought on her. *No, she will not spend much thought on any other man. I shall see to that!*

Unaware of the viscount's fierce determination, Lady Ogden separated from her aunt and Mrs. Dalton, with a word of excuse, and entered her private sitting room. She sat down at her writing desk and picked up the letter. She broke open the wax seal and spread open the crackling sheets, observing that her aunt had been correct. This was no short note but a full-fledged letter. The contents made her stare and she read several of the lines more than once.

...I have reflected many times upon my behavior while I visited at Delincourt and I have concluded, somewhat shame-faced, that my behavior was boorish. I owe you an apology, Lady Ogden.

Though my very dear friend, Lord Henry Ogden, always bade me to amuse myself just as I wished, I should have been more considerate of the sensibilities of the ladies in residence. More particularly, to your sensibility, which demanded and was owed such courtesy and civility as I should have, as a gentleman born, naturally offered to you as your rightful due.

I therefore again offer my most humble and sincere apologies. Perhaps my small tokens will be accepted in that spirit. I trust you shall enjoy the chapbook and music. May I dare to hope that you will look more kindly upon me in your reflections?

Yours, etc. etc....

Lady Ogden let the sheets fall to the desk and sat back in her chair to ponder the surprising tenor of the letter. Sir William had expressed himself well. Against her own better judgement, she was slowly beginning to revise her opinion of the gentleman. He had been consistently respectful in his few communications. He sounded sensible and kind. He had been the only one of Lord Henry Ogden's cronies to offer any word of condolence at the burial service. Perhaps she had misjudged Sir William Talley a little by lumping him in with all the other gentlemen who had disported themselves at Delincourt. What did she know of him, really, since she and her aunt had always exiled themselves whenever the late viscount had brought down his friends from London. *And for good cause*, she tartly reminded herself, when they had always descended like locusts, eating and swilling and amusing themselves with such dissolute abandon.

Perhaps that dawn, her perception of Sir William had been flawed. After all, she had fled from what would have been a rape by her husband the viscount. Perhaps she had superimposed her trepidation onto Sir William.

She tapped one finger on the top-most sheet of the letter. It was possible Sir William was not quite of the same bad cut as the others. *But still, the way he looked at me.* She knit her brows. It was conceivable that all gentlemen were the same, predisposed to sensual predilections and carnal desires. *Sir William, at least, did not ravish me and set me up as his mistress.* The sudden bitter tenor of her ruminations disconcerted her. "How self-pitying," she said aloud. "And quite useless, too."

She decided to discuss the contents of Sir William's letter with her aunt. She valued that lady's opinion and maybe it would serve to bring better order to her own thoughts.

Lord Ogden had ridden out before she left her sitting room, leaving word that he would not return for luncheon. He was going on an inspection of the several projects he had initiated over the space of weeks and months. The steward had accompanied his lordship.

Lady Ogden had a busy day ahead of her, as well. She spent most of the morning with the cook working out menus and discussed the household accounts with Mrs. Tower. She didn't see much of either Mrs. Merriweather or Mrs. Dalton until luncheon, so she had little chance to speak privately with her aunt. Her opportunity finally arose when Mrs. Dalton declared her intention to call at the vicarage, carrying with her some comfits and jellies from Delincourt's larder for Rev. Major Ledger's kitchen. Lady Ogden encouraged the friendly errand and carried one of the small baskets out to the gig. She saw Mrs. Dalton off, waving a good-bye.

When Lady Ogden re-entered the house, she asked for a private word with her aunt and led the way into the drawing-room. Before she had come downstairs earlier, she had tucked the letter into the front of her dress. When she and her aunt had settled onto the settee, she said, "I have Sir William's letter here. I wished for you to read it." She brought out the tightly-folded missive and handed it over to her aunt.

Mrs. Merriweather looked at her in surprise and unfolded the pages. After she had read them, she returned the sheets to her niece. "Sir William pens a fine letter."

Lady Ogden refolded the pages and slipped them back into their hiding place. "I had hoped for a bit more from you than that, aunt."

"What would you have me say?"

"Why, something about Sir William! Is he sincere, do you think?"

"As to that, I am suspending judgement." Mrs. Merriweather studied her niece's perturbed expression. "Does it matter so much to you, Charlette? About Sir William, I mean."

"I don't wish to bear anyone ill-will," she said slowly. "If I can believe Sir William is sincere, then I *should* not think badly of him. Yet I cannot forget that he made up one of Henry's set. Sir William showed nothing of this face then."

"Surely, you know gentlemen will often say things that they sincerely believe, but which their behavior contradicts," said Mrs. Merriweather with a slight shrug. "My dearest, Mr. Merriweather was just such a one. He *swore* he'd come about in his fortunes but he never did."

"That's not the same thing, ma'am. We are speaking of a man's character."

"Yes, well – then consider your father's character," said Mrs. Merriweather tartly. "He was neglectful and mean-spirited towards you and your dear mother. And to me, also, but I shall say nothing of *that*! He was always swearing to reform his ways, was he not?"

Lady Ogden was silenced. It was an unanswerable argument. "Thank you, ma'am. I will think on what you have said." She went upstairs to put away the billet, but Sir William's letter did not leave her thoughts. She wrestled with the dilemma in which she found herself. It was one thing to politely thank a gentleman for a token gift, but quite another thing to enter into private correspondence with one who was not related by blood or marriage. If Sir William was truly contrite...truly sincere. It was conceivable she might gain an agreeable connection. She contemplated the novel idea. She did not have a dearth of friends, after all, and she decided to reply to the gentleman's letter. It took her the better part of an hour, but she was at last satisfied with her response, and she set the letter out in the entrance hall to go in the mail.

Late in the afternoon, the three ladies assembled together in the upper drawing-room to begin stitching up a new dress pattern. Their conversation centered on the project. However, once they had agreed on how to proceed, Mrs. Merriweather revealed she had not altogether been focused on dressmaking. "Sir William Talley, writing you so civil a letter! I can scarcely get over it."

"Yes, indeed," said Lady Ogden with a shrug. "It was rather a surprise."

"Oh, does Charlotte have a beau?" asked Mrs. Dalton cheerfully. "How exciting!"

Much annoyed, Lady Ogden frowned at her aunt. She wished that Sir William's name had not been brought up. "It's not at all exciting. And Sir William is *not* my beau!"

"Sir William Talley! That does sound promising. Have you known him long, Charlotte? I wish I had an opportunity to meet the gentleman," said Mrs. Dalton with mild interest. She did not look up, however. The pattern was for a gown for herself and she was concentrating on pinning it correctly.

"The man is not suitable company for a lady!" exclaimed Mrs. Merriweather.

"Indeed, Amarys, he is not! He was one of Henry's boon companions and-and not at all respectful or gentlemanly." Lady Ogden was struck by her own immediate reaction, as well as her aunt's negative response. She at once regretted the letter she had penned earlier. If she felt such instinctive disfavor toward Sir William, then she had no business entering into correspondence with the gentleman.

Mrs. Dalton glanced up, surprised. Her eyes twinkled. "Oh, I see! Then most likely, he's a terrible rake and almost certainly a gamester."

Upon seeing her companions' astonished expressions, she laughed again. "When I resided with my sister and brother-in-law, we heard all the town gossip. My brother-in-law is regularly in London on matters of business. Poor Daniel! He is truly an estimable gentleman. It pained him greatly to be connected, however remotely, with Henry Ogden and that set. He never divulged to me or my sister any more than generalities of Henry's scandalous progress, so I didn't recognize your correspondent's name."

Lady Ogden made up her mind. She must retrieve her letter before it was picked up by the courier. She made her excuses to her aunt and her friend and got up from the work table. "I have just recalled something

I need to see about. I shall return shortly." However, when she went downstairs, she discovered that she was too late. She shrugged fatalistically. It was not like she had penned any great thing. More than likely, Sir William would merely read it before tossing it into the trash.

She decided to put it out of her mind.

Lady Ogden's letter was not the only one to be carried up to town. Mrs. Collings regularly wrote to her acquaintances, her letters filled with gossip of the limited society in which she found herself during the summer months. She had confided the latest salacious report to her closest bosom-bows – the late viscount's wife was definitely with child. Mrs. Collings' friends filled their days with fashion, social entertainments, and titillating gossip, and it was not long before the interesting tidbit of news reached Sir William Talley's ears.

On that long-ago drunken morning, he had been hit with the brainstorm to use the late viscount's relic as a means to help himself to Delincourt. Ever since discovering her ladyship in the hallway coming away from her lord and the later realization that she could birth a posthumous heir – an outcome he could make sure of himself by virile seduction – he had toyed with the notion of wedding her. The late viscount had often complained of the estate's insolvency, but Sir William had wondered how much of that was true. Lord Henry Ogden had always been well-dressed and he had spared no expense for his carriages and horses. Sir William dismissed the nagging question for the moment. His goal of becoming master at Delincourt and one of the landed gentry was far more important.

Sir William Talley of Delincourt Manor.

It had a fine ring to it.

He'd be stepfather to the heir, exercising complete control over the young heir's inheritance until the little viscount came of age. He'd make certain the whelp prospered and as long as the boy lived, his own future was secure. If Lady Ogden was brought to bed of a female...he could see no pecuniary gain in one and certainly he had no intention of supporting a girl-child. Children were such frail little creatures, he believed; anything at all could happen to cut short a small life.

As for a wife, he had no need of one unless she came with a large fortune. He briefly wondered about Lady Ogden's own finances. Surely, she must enjoy at least a comfortable competence, which upon her wedding would come under her new husband's control. In his imagination, there were no unlucky happenstances to mar his plans. Lady Ogden would wed him, he would have control of her fortune, and she would be brought to bed of a posthumous male heir to Delincourt. The coming years stretched long and golden before him.

Sir William touched the brim of his hat with the tip of his leather crop, acknowledging an acquaintance as he rode in the park. The chestnut hack between his legs moved forward with a pretty action. He was pleased with the world. That very morning, he had received a reply to his letter. Lady Ogden's correspondence was cautious in tone but she had accepted the olive branch he had offered. *Silly woman had believed everything. That damned missive was worth every minute spent slaving over it.* His campaign was going well. The foundation had been laid. He had come into possession of the all-important intelligence that Lady Ogden was indeed breeding. He had only to call upon the lady and then he would know whether the effort he had expended up to this point would be worth it. He coldly believed a woman's resistance could always be overcome with a masterful dominance.

He recalled her ladyship, and her haughty green eyes, on the last visit to Delincourt.. She had given a slight inclination of her head upon the arrival of her lord and master with his friends before she disappeared upstairs with her aunt. She had been either too proud, or perhaps too missish, to preside at table during their revelries. It was a question that had more than once occupied his mind.

Over the evening's deepening card play and drinking, Sir William had made a lazy inquiry of his host. "Her ladyship is shy? Retiring, perhaps?"

Lord Ogden snorted. "Standoffish, more like."

Sir Williams had watched Henry Ogden as he lifted his glass for a mouthful of brandy, only to find he had already emptied it. His lordship looked blearily astonished. He pulled the decanter to him and splashed another measure of brandy into his glass. Sir William shrugged and suggested, "A prideful lady, then."

The viscount had scowled. Thereafter, he frowned heavily over his cards, openly brooding over his crony's observation. His obvious sense of ill-usage grew. Not many minutes later, Lord Henry Ogden had thrown down his cards and pushed back his chair, loudly declaring, "I'm for pricking my wife, sirruhs!" Amidst ribald encouragement, his lordship had lurched up the stairs. Moments later, the crash of a door and loud, raised shouting was distantly heard, sending all the cardplayers into paroxysms of laughter.

Sir William smiled as he remembered. At his instigation, the viscount had abruptly left the comradery of his boon-companions and stormed upstairs to her ladyship's bedchamber. He recalled, too, the prominent bruise on Lady Ogden's face the following day. The viscount had finally acted the man. *Now she is breeding. It could not have worked out better.* He complacently congratulated himself.

In his private opinion, Lord Henry Ogden had been too easy with his lady wife. The viscount should have insisted that she act as a proper hostess. *I'd like the teaching of her.* She wasn't a charming armful, not like the Stonebridge, but she wasn't a mean bit, either. With glimmering fear in her face, with her hair tumbled down about her shoulders, she had been a temptress. He had toyed with the notion of taking her against the wall, but Henry Ogden had been his friend and one found one was born a gentleman, after all. He had thought often and often about that dawn, with the sun barely creeping up, with just enough light to examine her face and the hidden contours of the body so modestly swathed up in the folds of the long shawl and old-fashioned nightgown. He tightened his gloved fingers on the handle of his crop. *By God, I should like to bed her.*

Sir William left the park and guided his mount through the crowded, noisy thoroughfares to a certain back street. Before a small, modest townhouse, he dismounted and tossed the reins and a copper to a loitering boy. "Walk my horse. I will be an hour." He trod up the shallow steps of the townhouse, confident of his welcome.

Sir William, correctly attired in riding coat, a well-tied cravat at his throat fixed with a stickpin, a twilled waistcoat from which dangled a number of fobs and a beribboned quizzing glass, and biscuit-colored breeches, was received by Mrs. Stonebridge in the front parlor. She was a lushly-formed young woman, with blonde curls and limpid blue eyes, and a dimple that hovered in one round cheek. She smiled prettily and held out her hand to him. "Why, Sir William, this is an unexpected pleasure."

Sir William bowed over her dainty fingers, kissing the tips with a practiced air. He straightened, saying dryly, "Is it, my dear? I cannot conceive it could be so when I had your note yesterday, asking that I wait upon you this afternoon."

The lady was wearing a charming and very expensive muslin dress, one of the many which he had paid for. She played with the satin ribbons tied under her shapely bosoms. A little pettishly, she said, "Well, what was I to do? You have not sent the usual billet and here it is, after the first of the month, and I have duns sitting on my dresser top."

"Calm yourself, my plump little partridge. I have it safe here in my pocket," said Sir William and he drew forth the sealed square from out of his coat pocket, handing it over to her. Mrs. Stonebridge practically pounced on it, a tremor visible in her fingers as she opened and quickly made herself mistress of its contents. He watched her with some amusement. "I trust the amount of my cheque is agreeable."

"Yes, of course. How could it be otherwise, sir? You are generosity itself." Mrs. Stonebridge smiled brightly up at him.

Sir William put his hand back into his coat pocket and withdrew a small, glittering circlet. He dangled it on the curve of his gloved fingers. "A token of my admiration, madam."

Mrs. Stonebridge squealed. "Oh, Sir William! It's a charming bracelet." She clasped it at once around her wrist and admired the sparkling little piece.

Sir William tapped the tip of his leather riding crop gently against his riding boot. The sound of the rhythmic motion eventually drew the lady's attention from her avid contemplation of the chip diamond bracelet. After a moment, she raised her eyes to his face, a dawning comprehension whitening her cheeks. He smiled slowly at his convenient. Once he had schooled her, he had begun to derive more enjoyment from their liaison. "Shall we adjourn to your bedchamber, Mrs. Stonebridge?" He waited to see if she would make any objection, but disappointingly, she did not. On one occasion, she had flung at him that he was not half the lover that Lord Henry Ogden had been.

She had not been impertinent again.

Sometime later, a satisfying time spent slaking his twin appetites, Sir William lounged sated against the tumbled pillows. Lazy thoughts wended like mist through his saturated brain. From under half-closed eyelids, his sleepy gaze meditated on the abandoned riding crop, lying where he had tossed it aside on the rumpled bedsheet. The prideful Lady Ogden...yes, he rather thought he'd enjoy the teaching of her. His musings of Lady Ogden were peculiarly stimulating; his greedy pego twitched and stirred.

"Eros, I am thy servant," he murmured.

Sir William caressed the plump femininity beside him. Under his hand, the lush curve of warm, bare flesh shuddered. He turned his head, a pleasant sight coming into view, the blood-red crisscrosses of raw welts he had raised on her ample, white buttocks before he fucked and spent himself in her pussy.

Her twat quivered, just so, not so many minutes past.

A strong rush of fresh lust shot to his loins. Softly he laughed, agreeably surprised, and looked down at his fully-aroused pego. He gave the standing tool an experimental tug and the flat crown wept. "Why, I can do it again." Going up on his knees, he grasped and spread the halves of the plump, well-disciplined arse. His thumbnails grazed the exposed depression; she reacted like she'd been touched by a hot brand.

"No, no."

"Yes, yes, there is time. My horse will keep. The hour is not yet up." He was already breathing heavily. His hands firmly splayed her scourged buttocks. He pressed the broad knob of his stout plugtail into place and bore down against the resistant, tight rosette of her back way. The fat head popped through. He grunted, in relish. He liked his pego pinned in her tail. *The dry plugging of her ruddy puckered dimple, the clamp of her bunge!*

A sharp, bitten-off screech was wrung from the pretty creature, but no matter. He had bought and paid for the privilege of bedding her in any way he chose. He had curled his fingers cruelly into her abraded flesh, arresting her recoil. The well-flogged pulchritude inflamed him. "Ah! Such a riveting sight! My swollen whore pipe buried in your pretty tail!"

The fearful whimpering was music to his ears. He recalled how she had wept while he flogged her and the inevitable rush of power racked his loins. He hawked and spit on his throbbing tool to ease its dark passage. Grunting again, making short work of his mounting, he forced his jutting pego deep, shoving until his hairy ballocks pressed against her trembling bum.

Breathing more rapidly yet, his voice thick with lust, he announced, "Mrs. Stonebridge, I'm going to bugger the price of that bracelet out of your arse."

34

An unexpected visitor arrived in the neighborhood. The gentleman came in a hired post chaise and was accompanied by his valet. He took rooms at the inn next door to the smithy in the village. His identity was well-known and word was quick to spread. Speculation ran rife. Whatever could the gentleman be doing there again, just months after the death of the unlamented viscount.

The gentleman gave orders to the driver for the equipage to be taken to the stable, where the horses were to be stabled and baited after the journey. He paid the charges and gave some extra coins to the man. "See about hiring a smaller vehicle from the landlord," he drawled. "I shall want it within the hour." He entered the inn and went at a leisured pace upstairs to his rooms, where his valet awaited him.

When he returned to the inn yard, the unbuttoned front of his long greatcoat revealed that he had changed his raiment. He climbed up into the rented gig behind the waiting horse, slapped the reins, and drove off to make his way over the road to Delincourt Manor.

It was a quiet afternoon. Lady Ogden's head was bent over some fine needlework and Mrs. Merriweather was playing solitaire. Lord Ogden stood at the fireplace, stoking the fire. He had just risen from his chair, setting aside a book he was reading. Mrs. Dalton had minutes before quitted the drawing-room to go up to her sitting room to write some letters. She was a faithful correspondent and set her pen to paper every week.

The door to the drawing-room was opened and the butler entered. Somerset's expression was impassive. "Sir William Talley has called, my lord."

Lord Ogden straightened from his task, making a sharp pivot. Behind his shoulder, he heard Lady Ogden utter a soft exclamation. He cursed inwardly that he had turned so quickly. He wished he could see her expression – was she pleased or simply surprised by the gentleman's visit. Another swift thought occurred to him, one which he found particularly unpalatable. Perhaps she had invited Sir William to Delincourt as a guest. Lord Ogden kept his expression impassive. He calmly laid aside the heavy, iron fire tool. "Send the gentleman in, Somerset."

"Very good, my lord."

Lady Ogden was astonished. She hastily composed her expression, not wanting to be caught staring in surprise. Sir William's last correspondence had been pleasing, but she had never expected that he would come to Delincourt. She wondered whether her perceptions of the gentleman would be any different. On past visits, she had thought him overbold and hedonistic; now, she still had reservations but was willing to make allowances.

Lord Ogden turned away from the fireplace, angling himself so that he could see his cousin-in-law. Her ladyship was sitting in her chair with her tranquil gaze fixed on the doorway. She had allowed the lawn handkerchief she was hemming to drop to her lap. Her expression revealed nothing more than mild civility. The viscount tightened his lips. He could catch no inkling of what thoughts might be revolving behind the calm in her eyes.

However, Mrs. Merriweather had visibly reacted. Her placid demeanor had vanished and she had pursed her mouth. She sat very upright in her chair, her gaze also fixed on the entrance to the drawing-room. There was not a shred of welcome in that lady's countenance and since the viscount knew her to be of the friendliest nature, it was most telling.

Lord Ogden waited with interest for his first glimpse of one of his cousin's closest cronies. *Sir William Talley.* The self-same gentleman who'd had the effrontery to correspond with the woman who graced his bed. It mattered not a whit that it was actually her bed – the principle was the same.

Sir William Talley stepped across the threshold into the drawing-room with a confident air. He did not seem to mind the three stares that were directed at him, but merely acknowledged them with a faint lift of his brows. His self-assurance was such that it would never occur to him that his appearance was lacking in any way.

Lady Ogden saw that Sir William looked just as she remembered. His appearance was just as meticulous and fashionable. His hair was swept back and pomaded. The fit of his superfine coat over his shoulders was superb and his twilled silk waistcoat was artistically worked in large flowers. The pantaloons he wore were a clear biscuit in color and were smoothed into a pair of gleaming black Hessian boots.

Sir William bowed. "Lord Ogden. Lady Ogden. Mrs. Merriweather."

"Sir." Lord Ogden bowed. Lady Ogden had risen from her chair and she curtsied. "Sir William." Mrs. Merriweather did not rise. She gave only a frosty nod.

The civilities thus concluded, Sir William addressed the viscount. "I am glad to find you at home, Lord Ogden. I wished to make your acquaintance and, of course, pay my respects to the lovely Lady Ogden."

Sir William smiled over at the lady, directing a second bow to her. He ran his gaze rapidly over her ladyship, his experienced eye discerning hints of her figure beneath the lines of her dull-colored daydress. She did not appear particularly round of belly; he hoped his information was not in error.

Lady Ogden inclined her head and sat back down in her chair, picking up the piecework again. She set a small, neat stitch. She pretended her attention was fixed on her needlework, but in actuality she was burning with curiosity. She wanted to unobtrusively observe the meeting between the two gentlemen.

"I understand you were a friend to my cousin," said Lord Ogden in a neutral tone. His expression was unreadable. He did not sit down nor gesture for the visitor to avail himself of a chair. Instead, he clasped his hands behind his back. He held his shoulders very straight and took up a wider stance.

Stealing a glance at him from under her lashes, Lady Ogden thought his lordship's bearing was remarkably formidable. She was surprised by his standoffish attitude, for he had never behaved in other than a friendly fashion before upon receiving a caller. She noted that Sir William's amiable expression had wavered. He cast a glance in her direction, but she pretended not to see, bending her head over her stitching.

Sir William decided to ignore the viscount's bad manners. "Yes, indeed. We were exceedingly close."

The two gentlemen had been examining one another. Neither liked what they saw. Lord Ogden quickly sized up the other man, cataloging the gentleman's appearance with a jaundiced eye. The tight-fitting coat was cut so narrow that it obviously couldn't be gotten into without help. The silk twill waistcoat was flashy, with several fobs and seals and a quizzing glass dangling on a ribbon. The heavy-lidded, pale blue eyes, the deep lines of dissipation marking the pallid countenance, the languid air - all confirmed him in his first, critical impression. His lordship's lip curled. *Fop, gamester, perhaps worse.* However, he did not make the mistake of believing there was not muscle underneath that neat coat. Sir William in all probability was a frequent visitor to Gentleman Jackson's boxing saloon or some other sporting gymnasium.

As for Sir William, he saw a well-set up fellow taller than himself, obviously of a virile and vigorous physicality. The face and hands were unfashionably tanned and the short, curling hair was carelessly brushed back. The viscount's clothing was dated in color, but was of a neat, spare cut that stamped his lordship of the military set. His visage was almost savage with its sharp cheekbones and the blade of nose rising proudly above firm-held lips. The dark eyes were cold and penetrating. His lordship looked competent and, in a lower society, would have been called 'a tough customer'.

Sir William detested his lordship on sight. He showed his teeth in an insincere smile. "As I said, I was an intimate of your cousin. If I may be permitted to say so, the two of you do not favor each other."

Astonished, Lady Ogden looked up from her stitching. Alarm shot through her, causing her heartbeat to speed. She was shocked and dismayed by Sir William's observation. She had been got with child by a man that bore a strong resemblance to the last viscount; it was the bedrock of her fraud. "But they are very like!"

Sir William gave a deprecating laugh. "I beg to differ, my lady. The gentlemen do not favor at all. Oh, perhaps a little in their features and general build, but otherwise I think not."

"But how can you say so, Sir William?" exclaimed Lady Ogden. "They are cousins!"

"My dear, you forget yourself," murmured Mrs. Merriweather. "The light in here is not at all adequate for such close stitching. Perhaps you should take it elsewhere."

Lady Ogden caught herself up at the cautioning note in her aunt's voice. The lady's quick shake of the head further warned her that her agitation was out of place. She bit her lip, realizing how nearly she had exposed herself. If her disquiet had been noticed by the two others in the room, it must surely have roused closer scrutiny. However, the gentlemen were not looking at her ladyship. Instead, their gazes were locked together.

Lord Ogden smiled but he set his jaw. He disliked the way the gentleman so easily insinuated insult. "You mean, I am a sunburned soldier without polish while my cousin, Henry, was a gentleman of fashion."

"Something like that," agreed Sir William. He lifted a hand, as though forestalling the other's possible umbrage. "I rarely voice sentiments which must of necessity wound another, I assure you. And never with your lordship's own candor. I trust I have not offended you, my lord."

Lord Ogden did not hide his contempt for the gentleman's scarcely-hid superciliousness. His gaze traveled over the gentleman. "You haven't offended me. I'd rather be a battle-hardened soldier, having performed my duty with honor, than a wastrel of weak character."

Lady Ogden gasped. Her amazed gaze flew to the viscount's cold countenance. His eyes appeared almost black. His face was expressionless, but a tight-lipped smile played over his firm lips. She had seen that expression before. *He is in a rage.* It leaped to her startled mind that his lordship meant to push their visitor into some sort of confrontation.

Sir William stiffened. His pale eyes glittered. "You are very direct, indeed, my lord. I must protest. I find you insulting."

Lord Ogden's response was exceedingly clipped. "Henry was my cousin. I shall speak of him as I choose."

Sir William's angered expression slackened to blank surprise. He blinked, making a rapid mental adjustment. "Yes, of course. For a moment, I thought –" He broke off, frowning.

"You thought what, Sir William?" Lord Ogden raised a dark brow. His voice was turned faintly satirical. The dangerous smile still curled his tight-lipped mouth.

Sir William shook his head, his own smile slipping firmly back into place. "It was nothing, my lord. Merely, I believe your judgement of my poor, departed friend to be rather harsh. But as you say, he was one of your relations. Who better to judge? I am reprimanded, my lord."

"Yes." Lord Ogden did not say anything else. He did not move. He simply looked at the gentleman. His physical stillness was most disquieting to one used to a livelier company. There was a long silence, growing more uncomfortable for at least the one party.

Sir William fidgeted a little, shifting his weight from one foot to the other. The clock inexorably ticked away. Lady Ogden switched her narrowed gaze from one gentleman to the other and back again. She found she kept holding her breath. She felt suspended, awaiting she knew not what. However, she did not break the tense silence. That was left for Sir William to do.

The gentleman cleared his throat. "Well, I must take my leave, my lord. I don't wish to keep the horse standing too long. I merely wished to make a courtesy call. I'm staying a few days in the district, you know." His pale blue eyes flickered in Lady Ogden's direction. "Perhaps a few weeks. I scarcely can tell."

Sir William's inference that his plans were dependent upon her ladyship was plain. A faint flush rose in the lady's face. Lord Ogden was not amused. With a chill in his voice, he said, "I trust you may find your own way out, sir."

Sir William's dissipated countenance tightened with annoyance. He appeared deeply offended. He favored the viscount with a resentful glance and a shortened bow. "Indeed, I am very familiar with Delincourt Manor." With that parting shot, Sir William strode out of the drawing-room, leaving the door standing open. Without in the entry hall, he uttered an angry demand for greatcoat, hat and gloves. Moments later, the swift staccato of his boot heels hastily crossed the marble floor, followed by the crash of the front door.

With the gentleman's abrupt withdrawal from the room, the viscount and Lady Ogden had stilled as though in tableau. At the noisy bang of the front door, they each stirred and exchanged a weighted glance.

Mrs. Merriweather had been forgotten during the unpleasant exchange. The lady rose to her feet. "Well! I believe I shall take myself off to work in the stillroom and recover my equilibrium. I'm feeling quite overset by our unexpected caller." As she walked past Lord Ogden, she bestowed an approving smile upon him. "Very well done, my lord."

Somerset stood aside for Mrs. Merriweather's exit, then came into the drawing-room. The impassivity of his expression was compromised by a betraying quiver in one cheek. "My lord, is there anything that you wish me to do?"

"No, no, nothing at all. Wait, perhaps a glass of wine would not come amiss. Our visitor left a sour taste in my mouth." Lord Ogden turned his head and made polite inquiry. "Will you join me, ma'am?"

"Yes, that will be pleasant," said Lady Ogden quietly. "And perhaps we may have a few of Mrs. Tower's excellent biscuits, too." Worry was evident in the butler's old eyes and she smiled reassuringly. Sir William had always participated with enthusiasm in the late viscount's raucous house-parties. The gentleman's unexpected visit, bringing with it disagreeable memories, must have come as an unlooked-for and unwelcome surprise to the family retainer. It could scarcely have been otherwise, for those had been her own feelings. Despite the respectful tone of the gentleman's recent correspondence, Lady Ogden had found that she still could find nothing in his face or his person to like.

The viscount nodded dismissal. "Thank you, Somerset, that will be all." The butler bowed and retreated, shutting the door behind him.

Lady Ogden silently folded up her piecework and set it aside on the occasional table. She did not know what to expect from the viscount. She had earlier thought him to be exceedingly angry and she braced herself for questions and recriminations. She had not forgotten Lord Ogden's extraordinary reaction when he had learned of Sir William's small gifts to her. Now the town gentleman had all but declared that he was settled in the neighborhood for the sole purpose of furthering his acquaintance with her!

"So that was one of Henry's boon companions," remarked Lord Ogden in a considering way. He threw her a glance. "I confess I was not particularly impressed by the gentleman. Was Sir William always such a pompous twit?"

Lady Ogden chuckled and relaxed. His lordship's reasonable tone reassured her. She was glad that the gentleman's surprising visit was being taken in stride. The viscount's open antagonism toward Sir William had alarmed her. However, she saw now how foolish her fears had been. *Ridiculous! Why would he push a quarrel on Sir William?* "I can say in all fairness that he was much the same. However, the gentleman was more courteous than I have ever seen him."

"You don't say!" Lord Ogden could not imagine a worse showing on Sir William's part. The man's assured air had all but deserted him under the pressure of his own personality. He had routed the object of Lady Ogden's interest without impairing his own dignity and he felt smug satisfaction "How did you bear with him, then?"

She gave a tiny shrug. "We did not. My aunt and I never presided over Henry's parties. We always stayed above-stairs, spending our days and evenings in the upper drawing-room until all of the gentlemen were gone away again."

Lord Ogden was given a further glimpse into the unhappy life that his cousin-in-law had led during her marriage. She implied that the late viscount's house-parties had been more than the stuff of outrageous congeniality. He could think of only one reason for the lady to have exiled herself from presiding over the entertainment of her lord's guests. She must have feared intolerable insult. The irony did not escape him, but he brushed it aside. Roughly, he asked, "Were you ever importuned?"

She shook her head. Her eyes steadily met the demand of his heated gaze. "Not in the way you mean. But the way we were addressed, with such disrespect and lack of common courtesy! The sly, insinuating *things* that were said. It was not to be borne."

"Surely my cousin did not stand for this!" He saw the curl of her lip and, suddenly, he understood. The company was merely following the example set by the late viscount. "Despicable of Henry," he said briefly. She made a gesture, indicating that she wished to be done with the subject, and he obliged her.

"Arthur is smitten with my sister," he remarked, turning to a subject of import that had been lately on his mind. "I suspect Amarys is not indifferent to him."

"Yes, that's true." Lady Ogden eyed her companion. "Do you mind it?"

Lord Ogden shook his head. "No; I cannot think of a better man for my sister. Arthur is also well-situated. He has invested in 'Change and he has the living. I'm fond of Amarys and I would like to see her happily settled. He will be an admirable husband to her."

"I'm glad. I should like to promote the match."

"Yes, do so."

Lord Ogden picked up the fire tool and prodded at the slow-burning fire. Lady Ogden picked up her hemming and set her fine stitches. It was a very prosaic, marital-like end to their conversation. Neither of them realized it.

The ladies had assembled in the drawing-room and waited on the viscount to join them before going in to dinner. Their easy conversation was general until Mrs. Merriweather mentioned the visitor. "Sir William Talley, coming here! All the way from town! My dear, I was never more astonished."

"Yes, I cannot imagine what the gentleman was thinking," said Lady Ogden, her light tone dismissing the importance which her aunt had attached to the gentleman's call.

"Can you not?" inquired Mrs. Merriweather with uncharacteristic sarcasm. "Come, where *have* your wits gone? The man has plainly come to court you."

Lady Ogden frowned, embarrassed and annoyed that the topic was being discussed in front of the viscount's sister. Besides, she had a lively dread that the viscount would enter the room and overhear the conversation. She didn't know why she felt that would be calamitous. After all, she had already dismissed her previous fears as being fanciful. Looking back on it, she couldn't imagine why she had thought such a thing. The viscount had not forced a quarrel. Nevertheless, she didn't want to be caught talking about Sir William in such a context. "You are being nonsensical, aunt."

"Hah! I wasn't born yesterday, my dear Charlotte!"

"Sir William Talley! I regret I was not downstairs when he called," said Mrs. Dalton. "You have given me the liveliest curiosity to meet the gentleman."

Mrs. Merriweather exclaimed, "My dear, you don't know what you're saying!"

"Oh, I don't know." Mrs. Dalton smiled impishly, her eyes alight with laughter. "I have long wondered what a rake and gamester might be like."

"I doubt you would have been impressed," said Lady Ogden quickly. The gentleman was one of Henry's drunken, loutish London friends, whom she had originally regarded with detestation. Yet over the intervening months since the death of the late viscount, Sir William had begun to present himself as a man of more substance. Upon seeing Sir William again, she could not like him any better than before. Her opinion of the gentleman had not changed and her instinctive urge to guard her young friend from the sort of attentions that Sir William was certain to lavish upon such a lovely and charming lady was all that was needed to crystallize her own thoughts. *I shall seek no friendship there.* Responding to his letter had been a mistake; not retrieving it before it was posted had brought Sir William to the neighborhood where he had taken up rooms at the local inn.

She made up her mind to send a note to put an end to the acquaintance.

"How did my brother receive the gentleman? I would not think he would be best pleased to meet one of our cousin's intimates."

Lady Ogden and Mrs. Merriweather exchanged a glance.

"Oh, you must tell me! I can see that something happened," said Mrs. Dalton.

"Nothing *happened*. I merely gathered that his lordship did not like Sir William. Isn't that right, aunt?" said Lady Ogden quietly.

"Quite right," agreed Mrs. Merriweather.

Lady Ogden recalled her conviction that the viscount had been put into a towering temper as a result of Sir William's supercilious insults. "I'm quite sure neither man liked the other."

"I'm not surprised. They are not of the same kidney. Lord Ogden is superior in every respect," said Mrs. Merriweather firmly.

"You have complimented my brother, ma'am, and I thank you for it," said Mrs. Dalton warmly.

The viscount entered the drawing-room, putting an end to the conversation. "I apologize for my tardiness, ladies. Shall we go in to dinner?"

Lady Ogden engaged in lively conversation with her table companions. However, her mind kept turning over what her aunt had said. It was true, she reflected. She had seen the labors the viscount had put himself to with the estate. The improvements had begun to take shape, most particularly in the results from the repairs his lordship had ordered to be made to the tenants' cottages. Through the grapevine that ran through any estate, she had heard that Lord Ogden was universally regarded as a good landowner. His lordship had been rewarded with the pleasing intelligence that new families had applied for two of the deserted crofter farms, having been sent word by their relatives of the new viscount's good reputation.

Lady Ogden recognized there were many things to admire and respect about the new master at Delincourt. It was a very short step, indeed, to feel a softening in her heart for him.

And that terrified her.

35

The following morning, Sir William returned and sent in his card. Lady Ogden thought of denying him, then reconsidered. There could be no better time to make clear to Sir William that she believed their renewed acquaintance was a mistake. It would be an uncomfortable conversation, she thought, and perhaps less embarrassing if there was no one else to witness it. "Send in Sir William, Somerset."

"Very good, my lady."

Lady Ogden was at a loss in how to start such a conversation. The gentleman's opening gambit made it more difficult. Sir William entered the drawing-room and bowed. "Lady Ogden, I'm happy to find you at home to callers."

"Sir William." She curtsied and sat down on the settee."

"I bear an offering, my lady." Sir William advanced and held out a slim volume to her.

Mindful that she was about to end their association, but still uncertain how she should proceed, she hesitantly accepted the book. She turned it over and read the inscribed title; it proved to be one of Lord Byron's works. She looked up at Sir William, wondering whether he meant to imply anything by giving her one of the scandalous poet's works. She was sure of it when Sir William quoted Lady Caroline Lamb's much-publicized opinion of her former lover.

"Mad, bad and dangerous to know," said Sir William, flashing a smile as he placed a hand over his heart.

The inference was plain. *Why, Aunt is right,* she thought with astonishment. *It's not friendship that is meant here!* There was not a doubt left in her mind. She tried to hand the book back. "Sir William, I cannot accept this gift from you."

He brushed aside her objection with a shrug of his shoulders. "It's but a trifle, my lady." He sat down on the settee, angling his body toward her.

"Nevertheless, I cannot accept it. In fact, I was wrong to accept anything from you." Lady Ogden drew in a breath. She was determined to extricate herself from what she perceived at last was an enormous, ill-conceived connection. "I must explain that any friendship between us is not possible."

Sir William plucked the book from her outstretched hand and tossed it aside. He pulled both of her hands into his own. With earnestness in face and voice, he said, "I have been thinking of you. You have a pull on me which I cannot deny. In truth, you have bewitched me."

"This is absurd!" Lady Ogden attempted to free her hands from his firm hold. He was sitting beside her and she discovered she was at a disadvantage. She was in effect trapped, unable to jump up from the settee and put distance between them.

"I wrote to you. I laid myself prostate at your feet in abject shame and humility. I have come to realize the rare prize you are. In short, you have persuaded me to become a better man."

"*What?*" She ceased trying to pull her hands away and stared at him in sheer amazement. "What are you saying?"

"I'm saying that I wish you to become my wife."

While she was still staring at him, he leaned in, lowered his head, and took possession of her mouth. An instant, she was immobile with shock. Then she reared back, turning her face away from him. She tugged again at her hands. "Let me go!"

The gentleman appeared impervious to rebuff. He raised her hands to his lips and kissed them. "You don't know how enamored I am of you! Oh, my dear! Give me the right to take care of you! You shall want for nothing."

"Just let go of me!" She was adamant and at last he seemed to realize it

Sir William released her hands. She whipped them back. "My apology, dear ma'am! I have frightened you with my ardor. Through our correspondence, I had sworn we had formed an intimate attachment."

Lady Ogden dashed the back of a hand across her lips. She felt besmirched. "*Intimate attachment!* No such thing! How dare you, sir!"

"Perhaps I have been too precipitate," said Sir William. He studied her indignant expression and appeared to come to a decision. As he got up from the settee, he said, "I must give you time to reflect upon the advantages of my offer. I shall take my leave of you now."

Lady Ogden sprang to her feet. "Sir William! I tell you that it is impossible!"

"I do not recognize that, my lady." Sir William bowed and sauntered out.

Lady Ogden stared after him in consternation. A few seconds later, she heard the unmistakable sound of the front door being shut. She still could not quite believe what had just happened. She had failed miserably. Rather than put a stop to the gentleman's acquaintance, she had been made the object of his expression of ardor. "What am I to do now?"

Before she had recovered from her dismay, the viscount strolled into the drawing-room. "I understand from Somerset that Sir William called on you again."

"Yes." Lady Ogden tried to pull herself together. The gentleman's visit had overturned her equilibrium. *He made me an offer!* She was heated and flustered, not at all like her usual self. Sir William had completely destroyed her poise.

"You appear a little flushed, my lady," observed Lord Ogden.

She turned away from the viscount and attempted to compose herself, pressing her palms against her betraying cheeks. "Do I? Perhaps I-I stood up too quickly."

"I think Sir William put you to the blush. Did he kiss your hands and make big sheep's eyes at you?"

The trace of mockery in his voice served to steady her. In fact, it angered her. She turned around, mistress of herself again. "You are in a strange mood, my lord."

Lord Ogden raised his dark brows, a satirical smile coming to his face. "Am I, indeed? Perhaps the boot is on the other foot, my lady."

She flounced away from him, uttering an incoherent exclamation, and he laughed.

His lordship's gaze was drawn down to the small book laying on the carpet. He bent to retrieve it. "What's this?"

Lady Ogden realized at once what a spot she was in. She had forgotten Sir William's gift. It had been hidden behind the fall of her skirt, but when she moved it had come to light. She was appalled. *Byron's work!* She recalled with perfect clarity with what chilly reserve he had examined the psalm chapbook. A work by the scandalous, decadent poet was infinitely worse. "Oh, no, give it to me!" She stepped toward him, throwing out her hand as though she meant to grab the slim volume from him. "It is nothing! Pray give it to me."

Lord Ogden read the book's gilt title. He lifted his eyes and looked at her. The darkness of his heated gaze arrowed straight at her. She could not help the shudder of apprehension that ran through her. "Lord Byron." He smiled but there was an edge to it. "It seems that I have underestimated Sir William. He is obviously an ingratiating fellow. I was not aware that you had a taste for lurid poetry. Is this why you receive him alone, my lady?"

"It's not what you think," said Lady Ogden in a low voice.

"You would be frightened by what I think," snapped Lord Ogden. He tossed the book onto the settee and strode up to her. He grasped her wrist with bruising fingers. She was amazed by the strong emotion that she could see had been aroused in him. "Did he make intoxicating love to you?"

"Pray do not be ridiculous!" Her heart was beating fast. She did not know what he might say or do if she admitted that Sir William had kissed her. The prospect alarmed her.

It looked as though he would say something else. But instead, he tightened his lips, biting back whatever it was. Then abruptly, he released her and stepped back. There was patent anger in his controlled inflections. "This is neither the time nor the place for this discussion."

"We will not discuss Sir William at all, my lord!" she said defiantly.

He looked at her, thin-lipped. A betraying tic jumped in his jaw. "You are correct." There was an unmistakable threat implicit in his roughened tone. She was sensitive to it and it made her anxious. He ran his deliberate, fiery gaze over her figure, seeming to strip her of her clothes. A fierce blush flamed her face. She shivered, whether from dread or anticipation, she did not know. His conduct belonged to the dark, overwrought passion of the night. *My God, we are in the drawing-room! And the door stands open!*

Lord Ogden reached out to snag one of her hands. He turned it over and pressed a burning kiss into her curling palm. His teeth nipped the soft flesh at the base of her thumb, making her gasp. When he let her go, she whipped her hand back and clasped both of them at her waist in a protective gesture. She was breathing quickly. The color fluctuated in her face. His shocking sensuality left her quivering with a strange fluttering panic.

In a low, hard voice, he said, "No other man's name shall be on your lips – *but mine!* Until tonight, madam." He bowed and left her.

Upon the return to the inn, Sir William coldly calculated what his chances were with Lady Ogden. If he knew women, and he thought he did, more than once she would recall his show of ardor, perhaps even with a sense of wonderment. A country-bred, unsophisticated woman most certainly would count it as a feather in her cap that she had captivated a town-buck such as himself. He would wait a day or two, giving time and the romantic timbre of her own simple mind to work on his side before he returned. Sir William gave a self-satisfied smile and flicked the tip of his whip at the trotting horse between the traces. He'd have the widow and Delincourt yet.

36

Sir William adhered to his strategy. When he called again at Delincourt, he was not surprised that Lady Ogden did not receive him alone. He had measured her character. Much could be determined in how a woman responded to a gentleman's kiss and she had not. He had concluded she was of a prudish nature. She would naturally be careful of her reputation. It was tiresome to have to make up to Mrs. Merriweather, who was obviously her niece's chaperone. However, he deemed it a necessary irritation. It was pleasanter whenever the viscount's sister, Mrs. Dalton, was also present. She was attractive and blonde, but a bit statuesque for his taste; however, he could forgive her that fault when she smiled and chatted away, her easy manners quite different from Lady Ogden's wary reserve or Mrs. Merriweather's chilly front.

He smiled and bowed and generally showed himself to be a man conducting a serious courtship. He even began showing at the local church. He always made it a point after the service to go up to Lady Ogden and greet her and to courteously tip his hat to the other two ladies and the formidable viscount.

Sir Edward and Lady Thane observed these encounters with disapprobation. They knew of Sir William Talley, recognizing him as one of the late viscount's wastrel friends. "That fellow!" muttered Sir Edward. He and his lady wife never accorded Sir William more than the most distant of bows.

Mrs. Collings was not of a religious bent, but she grew bored with her own company and there was fodder for gossip at any church. When Mrs. Collings accompanied Sir Edward and Lady Thane to Sunday service, she generated attention. The lady's dashing attire, a cutaway pelisse over a very fashionable dress and an extravagant bonnet with four ostrich feathers, aroused much interest. However, it was the lady's bold approach to Sir William Talley that set off several more astonished comments. Mrs. Collings went straight up to the gentleman. "I am delighted to run into you, Sir William. I am Mrs. Collings. Sir Edward and Lady Thane are my in-laws."

Sir William lifted his eyeglass and looked at her through it. "Er, Mrs. Collings, did you say?" Mrs. Collings at once claimed a previous acquaintance with him in London, reminding him of a certain fashionable party, and he laughed and agreed that they had met. Dropping the glass, he bowed over her gloved hand. Mrs. Collings rewarded him with a simpering smile. He suavely returned her smile. "We will meet again, I feel certain."

As Lady Ogden and her companions neared, he excused himself to Mrs. Collings and stepped forward to intercept them. Sir William insisted upon giving his arm to Lady Ogden to escort her along the flagstone path toward the carriages. The gentleman's insistence was such that Lady Ogden felt to refuse would create a scene in front of her neighbors. She cast a wild glance of appeal at Mrs. Merriweather and Mrs. Dalton. They easily interpreted her ladyship's mute entreaty. Though Mrs. Dalton would have liked to speak a little longer to Rev. Major Ledger before she left, she did not hesitate to set aside her own interests.

"Come, Mrs. Merriweather!" she said, linking arms with the elder lady, and the two followed the couple in faithful chaperonage.

Lord Ogden stayed behind to convey a word of praise to his friend for the sermon. Rev. Major Ledger gracefully accepted the compliment, but he was more interested in watching the visiting gentleman's progress. "Who is that flashy cove?"

Standing beside Rev. Major Ledger, Lord Ogden did not have to ask him to whom he was referring. His own gaze followed the receding party. He said grimly, "That is Sir William Talley, one of my cousin's bosom-bows. He wages a campaign with Lady Ogden."

Rev. Major Ledger raised his brows. He cut a glance at his lordship. "Does he, indeed? You greatly astonish me. Have you barred him from the house?"

Lord Ogden's stern, hawkish visage grew still more forbidding. "I have thought of it, believe me. But I have no cause other than my dislike. As long as the ladies give him leave to call on them, I can do little."

Rev. Major Ledger reminded him of an indisputable fact. "You have the advantage, Vincent."

"Yes, but I don't think she knows it," retorted Lord Ogden. He added irritably, "I must go or next I will find that jumped-up popinjay taking my seat in the carriage!"

Rev. Major Ledger laughed. "I've no doubt you'll give him short shrift!"

Upon returning to Delincourt, the ladies put off their bonnets and pelisses and gathered in the drawing-room for a quiet afternoon of conversation over their stitchery. Lady Ogden spoke of her frustration to her aunt and Mrs. Dalton. She had tried to discourage Sir William's determined assault on her defenses, but to no avail. He seemed deaf to her expostulations and took her consistent rejection of his offerings and invitations in stride. His latest maneuver of waylaying her at church services was the most difficult tactic to defend against. "I can't very well snub the gentleman as I wish! Not on the church steps! Not without starting a brew of gossip."

"Sir William drives out to Delincourt nearly every day," observed Mrs. Merriweather. She shook her head in disapproval. "He's obviously laid siege, my dear. The gentleman seems quite determined."

"Yes, he hounds me relentlessly. I don't know why," exclaimed Lady Ogden. "I'm a widow with no portion! And I've made it plain that I've no interest in his civilities!"

"He brings posies tied with ribbons. He asks for the privilege of driving out with her, only to have his offer firmly refused," said Mrs. Dalton cheerfully, addressing Mrs. Merriweather around her ladyship. "What a dim fellow he is!"

"He lavishes me with compliments," said Lady Ogden with gloom.

In a confiding fashion that tickled Mrs. Merriweather, Mrs. Dalton said, "His armor is thick. Lady Ogden's rebuffs bounce off without a dent being made in his affability."

Lady Ogden groaned. She said despairingly, "I don't know what else to say to him."

It was unfortunate that the viscount entered the drawing-room in time to hear her lament. "You're speaking of Sir William?" Lord Ogden's observation was caustic. "The gentleman behaves like an untrained pup. I trip over him wherever I turn. He is constantly underfoot!"

The ladies shared speaking glances. The viscount's scowling expression was reason enough to introduce a new subject and Mrs. Merriweather had the happy notion of mentioning that it was the season for grouse-shooting. Lord Ogden's expression at once cleared. "I hope to get up a shooting party this week, in fact. Sir Edward, Rev Major Ledger, Mr. Kelton, possibly a few others. We'll have grouse for the table, I promise you."

Mrs. Dalton dared to quiz her brother. "Not Sir William?"

Lord Ogden's brows lowered over his eyes as he looked darkly at his sister. Then he gave a reluctant grin and said, quite mildly, "No, not Sir William."

Somerset entered to announce a caller. He said woodenly, "Sir William, my lord. Shall I show him in?"

Lord Ogden scowled. "Are we not to have a moment's peace without that fellow showing his front? I will be in the study. I have ledgers to look over." He at once quitted the drawing-room.

Lady Ogden sighed. She shared the viscount's sentiments, but nevertheless she felt constrained to show a civility which in truth was beginning to wear thin. However, Sir William did not deserve outright discourtesy even if he was proving himself to be a pest. "Pray show the gentleman in, Somerset."

"Very good, my lady."

"Whatever you do, don't invite Sir William to dine with us," warned Mrs. Merriweather *sotto voce*.

With a speaking glance, Lady Ogden rose to her feet as Sir William was ushered in. The gentleman bowed and she dipped a curtsy. "Sir William."

"Lady Ogden, I trust you are well."

"I was able to sustain the carriage ride home from the church, sir, if that is your meaning," said Lady Ogden tartly. The gentleman had an annoying habit of expressing an over-solicitude that set up her back. She was not such a poor creature as he seemed to believe, she thought with indignation.

Sir William chuckled. He turned his suave smile on Mrs. Merriweather and Mrs. Dalton, but he addressed himself to the elder lady, his smooth tone laced with a hint of mockery. "I hope you do not find my visit too *de trop*, madam."

Lady Ogden stiffened. She had never been able to abide disparagement of her family. Her hackles rose. The gentleman should have ignored what he had obviously overheard. Instead, he had made a point of it to embarrass her aunt. She had no need to go to her aunt's defense, however.

"As a matter of fact, you are *de trop*. You will excuse us, of course," returned Mrs. Merriweather, two spots of color in her face. "Somerset, pray show the gentleman out."

Sir William raised his brows. He looked over at her ladyship.

Lady Ogden said coolly, "My aunt is correct, sir. Somerset will show you out."

Sir William was discomfited. He could not remain in the face of such a firm repulse, especially when the butler was standing behind him and holding the door for him. He bowed but inwardly seethed. He had thought to crush the old bag but she had proven more resilient than he had thought. He had also underestimated Lady Ogden's fondness for her aunt. Judging from the viscountess' frosty expression, he had badly miscalculated. It was indeed time for a strategic retreat.

"My pardon. Perhaps there will be a better time to call." Sir William left the drawing-room. The impassive butler pulled shut the door and motioned for the footman to hand over the gentleman's hat and gloves.

Sir William was still standing in the entrance hall, pulling on his driving gloves, when Lord Ogden stepped out from the study. "A moment, Sir William." Lord Ogden gestured toward the open doorway from which he had emerged. "Pray join me. I haven't had a good opportunity to speak much with you."

"Of course, my lord." Sir William entered the room and sent a curious glance around. The ground-floor study was a room he had never had occasion to enter and his impression was not favorable. He thought it cramped and oddly-shaped, crowded by a massive desk, a few upholstered chairs, a side table on one wall, and bookshelves. He sat down in a wingback, crossed his legs, and perched his hat on his knee.

The viscount shut the door. He walked forward. In front of the side table, he paused. "A drink, sir?"

"Brandy if you have it."

Lord Ogden lifted a decanter and poured a measure into a glass.

Sir William eyed the viscount as he accepted the wineglass. He'd noted that his lordship had not poured a glass for himself. "It occurs to me that this is not a purely social invitation, my lord."

Lord Ogden bowed. "You are correct." He sat down in the opposite wingback and contemplated the other man "I've noticed of late that we have the pleasure of your company here at Delincourt nearly every day. Your attentions toward her ladyship have become unmistakable."

Sir William tasted the brandy in the glass and he nodded his approval of the vintage before he replied. "Through our correspondence, the lady and I have formed an attachment."

"The devil you have!" exclaimed Lord Ogden.

"Ah, you seem inordinately concerned for the lady, my lord," said Sir William, raising a thin brow.

Lord Ogden didn't trust the gentleman. He was jealous, but he had known he would look ridiculous if he said anything to Lady Ogden. He knew also that he could not endanger the carefully cultivated indifference that he and Lady Ogden presented to the world at large.

Lord Ogden realized how narrow the ledge above the precipice. He risked exposing more than he wanted if he was to successfully throw an obstacle in the gentleman's way. *Careful, careful.* He must not act in any way other than what could be readily explained by society's standards. "The lady is my cousin's widow. Lady Ogden and her aunt are under my protection."

"Ah, yes, the esteemed Mrs. Merriweather," murmured Sir William. He was still smarting. "The diligent chaperone. One of those faded ladies, the hanger's-on found in every household, who can always be counted as a nuisance, do you not agree?"

Without a flicker of change in his expression, Lord Ogden stared at the gentleman. *You sodding bastard.* He had grown to be rather fond of Mrs. Merriweather and though it galled him, he ignored Sir William's cruel observation. Instead, he voiced the natural concern of a male relative for a dependent when faced with a possibly disadvantageous situation. "Lady Ogden kept me fully apprised of your correspondence. I permitted it, for you were kind enough to condole with her. But you go too far with this spurious claim, Talley. Her ladyship would have told me of any attachment before this."

"Are you certain of that, my lord?" asked Sir William with a slow, broadening smile.

Lord Ogden returned the smile, but he felt far from amused. "Perhaps you do not know this, Sir William, but my cousin left her ladyship very behind in the world. Lady Ogden must apply to me for all of her support, so yes, I do believe that she will inform me if she wishes to change her circumstances." He had the satisfaction of seeing the smile wiped from Sir William's face.

"Are you certain of this? Lady Ogden does not enjoy an independent competence?" demanded Sir William.

Lord Ogden was enjoying himself at last. "Quite certain. This is the reason I've taken it upon myself to speak to you, sir. If you have it in mind to proffer a suit of marriage to my cousin-in-law, I wish to ascertain that you will be able to support her in a reasonable fashion."

"Why, I don't know what to say, my lord. It's early days to be talking of a suit!" Sir William gave an unconvincing laugh. He set down the wineglass on an occasional table. "I shall take leave of you now, my lord. I shall not take up any more of your time."

"Of course." Lord Ogden politely saw Sir William out, for once feeling charitable over the gentleman's visit.

When Sir William set forth from Delincourt, he allowed the horse to fall into a walk, unlike the smart pace he usually required of the hired nag. His interview with the viscount was an irritant to his restless thoughts. He had suffered another check. He had to concede that he had made an error in his assumptions. He had to readjust his thinking, for which he needed privacy alone with his thoughts. He scowled over the unwelcome information that had been told him. The tidy courtship he had envisioned had met with an unexpected set-back. It was certainly daunting to learn that her ladyship was penniless, but perhaps that had been the viscount's intended effect.

Whatever Lady Ogden's fortune, he told himself, he had to keep his eye on the main prize. *Delincourt.* Her ladyship's lack of a competency was a minor detail beside it.

Sir William slapped the reins, setting the horse to a trot. The fellow was trying to scare him off, he decided. The viscount could see which way the wind was blowing. He had said as much by acknowledging that her ladyship had been receptive to Sir William's correspondence and visits. The upstart was merely looking after his own interests. His position would be destroyed if Sir William succeeded in his suit with Lady Ogden. The fellow would have no alternative but to return to the army, reflected Sir William, and good riddance to him. He was more determined than ever to have the widow and Delincourt Manor.

After Sir William's ignoble rout, Lady Ogden and her companions decided to pay a long-overdue social call to Thane Hall. Upon their arrival, the three ladies were given a warm welcome by Lady Thane. Her sister-in-law's greeting was tepid. However, Mrs. Collings was glad to have visitors even if they were from Delincourt.

Lady Thane addressed Lady Ogden but included the other two ladies with her smile. "Your timing could not be better! I was just about to send a note to you! I wish to invite you to a dinner party on Thursday next. Do you think you will be available? What of Lord Ogden?"

"I can't speak for his lordship, only for myself. I should like it very well." Lady Ogden looked inquiringly at her companions.

Mrs. Merriweather nodded at once. "We should be delighted, Lady Thane."

"I shall be honored," said Mrs. Dalton, smiling. "And unless he is very much more unsociable than I imagine, my brother will be happy to accept your invitation."

"I'm glad to hear it. I will be sending out invitations to Rev. Major Ledger and a few others. But come! Sit with us and take tea."

Lady Thane chatted happily with her guests over the tea. Mrs. Collings was swift to become bored with local events and the concerns shared by the others. Within a short time, she had steered the conversation to things of more interest to her. The newest fashions and the latest *on dits* from the tabloids were her bread-and-butter. Deep in their own side conversation and fast becoming better acquainted, Lady Thane and Mrs. Dalton paid little attention. Lady Ogden and Mrs. Merriweather were civil, but could scarce drum up much interest when Mrs. Collings began to talk of London and all of her doings in that great metropolis.

"By the by, in London I heard the most scintillating tidbit, Lady Ogden! It was concerning one of the late viscount's bosom bows. Quite entertaining!" Mrs. Collings tilted her head, her eyes glittering, and smiled at her ladyship. "I am persuaded you are well-acquainted with him – Sir William Talley. He is presently staying in the neighborhood. I spoke to him at church only this morning, in fact. I believe you did as well, did you not?"

"I am acquainted with Sir William," agreed Lady Ogden. It was clear to her that Mrs. Collings was envious that Sir William had displayed an interest in herself and she wondered at it until she recalled how self-centered the woman could be. She exchanged a glance with her aunt. She was unsurprised when Mrs. Merriweather rolled her eyes.

Since his arrival, Sir William had called often at Delincourt. Lady Ogden wondered how long it had been before that bit of news had come to Mrs. Collings' ears. At least the tedious woman would never hear of Sir William's extraordinary offer of marriage, she thought, since she had only confided that incident to her aunt and Mrs. Dalton.

"Well! My dear, it is reported that he has taken up with Mrs. Stonebridge!" said Mrs. Collings in thrilling accents.

Lady Ogden raised her brows. She was surprised by the lady's anticipatory tone. "Indeed? I'm not acquainted with the lady."

At last becoming aware of the trend of her sister-in-law's discourse, Lady Thane broke off with Mrs. Dalton. She hastily interjected. "Lady Ogden is not interested in such stupid reports."

"Surely you know of her! I'm persuaded you must!" Mrs. Collins' smile was pure malice. "It was common knowledge that she was the late viscount's mistress!"

There was a shocked, startled silence. Lady Ogden and Mrs. Merriweather stared with disbelief and anger at Mrs. Collings. The lady's shrill exclamation had carried to everyone. Mrs. Dalton's fine eyes widened. Lady Thane gasped at her sister-in-law's appalling reveal. "Mariah!" Under Lady Thane's amazed remonstrance, the lady's gaze flickered. Her penchant for gossip and her dislike of Lady Ogden had pushed her beyond what was acceptable.

Lady Ogden felt blood rush to her face, heating her cheeks. Of course, she had suspected that her husband the viscount had set up a mistress, but she'd never been certain. Henry's mistress...Sir William Talley...It was a sickening blow. If she had not already realized that she had erred in setting up a correspondence with the gentleman, her eyes would have been fully opened by this intelligence. *What a fool I was!* The revelation made by Mrs. Collings had made even a bowing acquaintance with Sir William Talley impossible. As for the messenger, she had no mercy. Her tone was cold, incisive. "I do not concern myself with common gossip, uttered by those with common minds!"

Mrs. Collins gasped. Her face reddened. Her mouth opened and closed like a fish out of water.

Mrs. Dalton gave a gurgle of choked laughter, which she swiftly covered with a cough behind her hand.

Mrs. Collings was affronted. She found her tongue. "Well! I suppose I must know how to take that! I must tell you, Lady Ogden, I am insulted!"

"You are well-served, Mariah!" exclaimed Lady Thane.

The lady's wrathful interjection was barely noticed by the viscountess and Mrs. Collings, who stared at one another with antagonism. Lady Ogden was set to utter a scathing rejoinder when she felt the warning nip of her aunt's fingers on her forearm and she pressed her lips tight together. She was thankful for her aunt's intervention. If she let free all the fury pent up inside of her, she could very well damage her relationship with the Thanes.

Instead, it was Mrs. Merriweather who took the initiative. She turned to her hostess. "Lady Thane, I see by the clock that we have overstayed. Pray do forgive us! The tea was delightful, but we really must be going."

All of the ladies immediately rose, taking polite leave of one another. Mrs. Collings alone declined to be civil, sharply turning her back. Lady Thane walked with her guests from the drawing-room to the front door, murmuring a mortified apology. "I'm sorry! I wouldn't have had it happen for the world!"

"There is no blame attached to you," said Lady Ogden, giving her friend a quick hug.

37

The next afternoon, Sir William called again at Delincourt. Somerset informed Lady Ogden that he had put the gentleman in the front parlor. The butler was aware that her ladyship had sent a communication by a groom to Sir William that very morning. "Shall I show in the gentleman, my lady?"

At the butler's unmistakable air of disapproval, Lady Ogden raised her brows. She could not rebuke the old family retainer, however. The visit was unexpected. She considered what she should do. She did not want to be alone with Sir William, but she did not have a chaperone readily available. Lord Ogden was out shooting with his friends. Her aunt was at the other end of the manor, busy with a project in the stillroom. Mrs. Dalton had decided to take a long walk and was not yet back from it. Lady Ogden wished that she had accepted Mrs. Dalton's invitation to join her. Reluctantly, she decided not to put off seeing the gentleman. "Pray send Sir William in, Somerset. And send word to my aunt to join me. You will find her in the stillroom."

The butler's expression was wooden. "Yes, my lady."

Lady Ogden waited for the gentleman to enter. When he did so and they had exchanged the usual civilities, she said, "This visit surprises me very much, Sir William. You are forward, sir, after my note to you this morning. I have made my feelings clear. It was a mistake to renew our acquaintance. There can never be anything between us."

"Yes, I am forward, but I cannot and will not hide what is inside of me." Sir William managed to possess himself of one of her ladyship's hands. He bowed over it, pressing his lips to her fingers. He straightened and smiled at her, retaining her fingers in his clasp. "You perceive me, your devoted servant."

She retrieved her hand as soon as she could and moved away, putting distance between herself and the gentleman. "This will be the last time that I receive you, Sir William."

Sir William struck a heroic pose, a hand to his breast, sliding one foot forward of the other. "Lady Ogden, surely you can appreciate my sincerity. Have I not corresponded with you? Have I not proven something of my devotion?" Her ladyship didn't react to his thrilling rhetoric with maidenly blushes, but instead appeared rigid and cold. He was irritated. It was no wonder Henry Ogden had looked elsewhere. It must have been like bedding an icicle. "Believe me, I have often and often thought of you since Henry's demise."

That much at least was true.

He made another elegant bow, his hand still pressed to his breast, even as his gaze ran over her. She had moved into a patch of bright sunlight coming in through the window and he could discern her silhouette through the thin fabric of her muslin dress. The viscountess was definitely gravid and he felt acute distaste. However, one must button up one's aversion and press on for the prize, he told himself. He had to get past the woman's prickly defenses. However, the next words out of her ladyship's mouth showed him that the task might prove more difficult than he had anticipated.

With a bright, glittering glance, Lady Ogden said, "I'm told that you are acquainted with a Mrs. Stonebridge."

Sir William straightened, abandoning his pose. *Damn the gossips,* he thought dispassionately. It was extraordinary that such news had made it so deep into the country and reached her ears. He must surmount her prudish notions. He spread his hands in a deprecating fashion and offered his most winning smile. "My dear ma'am, the lady of whom you speak is a member of the same social set which Henry and I enjoyed. I am acquainted with Mrs. Stonebridge, yes, but there is nothing in that."

Lady Ogden did not appear to believe him. "I have heard you are more than acquainted with the lady."

Sir William set his teeth, pushing back his impatience. It surprised him, this intransigence of hers. All of his past impressions of her had been fleeting ones as she whisked herself out of sight, so that he had thought her to be of a retiring nature, a provincial creature of little significance. But lately, he had reason to call into question his previous assumption. She had been surprisingly resolute in refusing his overtures. "Lady Ogden, there is no reason for this-this..."

She raised her brows. "Yes, Sir William?"

He smiled again, and deliberately, he insinuated that she was acting from a base jealousy. "...*unwarranted* suspicion. I am indeed acquainted with Mrs. Stonebridge, but that is all it ever was. Many times, I met her in my poor friend's company. I cannot conceive why we are even speaking of the lady."

Lady Ogden's color rose. "You mean, this woman was my late husband's mistress, do you not?"

Sir William was astonished and disapproving of her ladyship's frankness. He made a short bow. "I'm unused to such open conversation as this in polite society, madam."

He studied her face, and seeing perturbation plainly writ on her countenance, he decided that a show of frankness on his own side would not come amiss. "I'm sorry, this news has obviously distressed you. However, now that you know so much, I feel compelled to tell you the whole truth. The lady was naturally distressed to learn of Henry's death, which news I carried to her as both a duty and a compassion. I have spent some time lately in the woman's company. I've also endeavored to provide what little financial trifle I could spare for her succor, for she was left in desperate straits." He shrugged and spread his hands again. "Henry had not left the lady even a farthing."

Lady Ogden caught her breath. She turned away, not willing for her expression to be read too closely. She feared her bitterness would swim too near the surface. *How well I know! Henry's stinginess, his mocking behest to me!* She tightened her lips. The woman's circumstances were pitiable, but the fact was that *she* had been the legitimate wife and *she* should have been the one provided some form of support upon the death of her husband the viscount. No such expectations could possibly have been harbored by the viscount's mistress. Behind her, Sir William was echoing some of her agitated reflections.

"Of course, Mrs. Stonebridge had no right to expect any more out of the arrangement."

Lady Ogden swept back around. She was trembling, angered with her late lord, angered at her own naivety. With bare restraint, she retorted, "I should say not."

Sir William made a slight bow. "I trust I have related all that needs to be explained."

Lady Ogden stared at Sir William. She couldn't very well lash out at the gentleman for setting up this female, this Mrs. Stonebridge, as his own mistress. It was none of her affair. She supposed the woman had to make harsh choices to survive. However, she was not so naive to believe such a decision had not been unduly influenced by Sir William Talley when he carried to Mrs. Stonebridge the news of her lover's death. *Taking advantage of Henry's cast-off. It's just the sort of thing one of Henry's amoral friends would do,* she thought contemptuously. Suddenly, all of her questions were at an end. She knew that Sir William had done just that. He had Mrs. Stonebridge in his keeping. Yet he was here, in her drawing-room, making up to her. *But for what purpose?* She had a ready answer come to her for that, too. It became stunningly clear. *He is here for Delincourt and I am the means to take it.*

She saw so much now. It was all so clear. Her aunt had been wrong. Sir William was not courting her for herself, but for Delincourt. His letter, his gifts, his extraordinary declarations of devotion were all lies. *Vincent never offered me Spanish coin. He was straight-forward in his intention to bed me. The bargain wrought between us is at least an honest one.*

Sir William believed she had come from her husband's embrace, that dawn morning in the hallway. He had guessed, or heard rumor, or perhaps merely hoped, that she was with child. Then he had come down to Delincourt to make sure of it. He was a gamester. He was willing to wed her, gambling that she was carrying Henry's heir, so that he could stepfather the infant viscount. At one stroke, he would remove the heir-presumptive and become master of an estate, no matter that it was an encumbered property. It was a despicable plan, and she could not bear another moment in the gentleman's company. "I must bring this visit to a close, Sir William. My aunt is waiting for me."

Sir William was taken aback. "My dear Lady Ogden!"

The door opened and Mrs. Merriweather stepped in. "There you are, my dear! I was just coming to find you." She saw that her niece was not alone and her cheerful smile dimmed as she recognized the gentleman. Her faded blue eyes were chilly as she advanced forward a few steps. "But I see that we have a visitor."

Sir William bared his teeth as he sketched a bow. "Mrs. Merriweather, always a pleasure."

Mrs. Merriweather gave a short nod. "Sir William."

"Sir William was just taking his leave, aunt."

"Well, we shall not keep you, sir."

In the face of such discouragement, the gentleman could not remain and he had no recourse but to bid the ladies adieu. "Lady Ogden, Mrs. Merriweather."

When the door was shut behind the departing gentleman, Mrs. Merriweather turned to her niece. "Well! I know now why you sent for me. But I wish you had waited until I had gotten here before you saw that man."

Lady Ogden took a restless turn about the room. "Content yourself, aunt. You came in good time. I have told Sir William that I shall not be receiving him again."

"My dear, I am very glad to hear it! I *could* not like him, even if he did write such a good letter."

"I own, I was taken in for a short time. But Sir William has shown his true colors. I have his measure now. He doesn't want me, but Delincourt. He believes that I would have him and that my child would give him the right to help himself to the estate monies."

"My dear Charlotte! I stand amazed! Such a diabolical deception."

"Diabolical, indeed." The distaste Lady Ogden felt underlaid her next exclamation. "Aunt, he practically admitted that he has made Henry's cast-off his own mistress!"

"Then Mrs. Collings was right! How distressing for you! So, Henry *did* have a mistress! Not that I doubted it for a minute, mind you, but still, to hear it first from that *awful* woman." A sudden thought struck Mrs. Merriweather, and she demanded, "Whatever was Sir William thinking, talking of such things to you? What indelicacy of mind!"

Lady Ogden gave a rueful laugh. She was remembering the gentleman's brief, shocked expression and in retrospect it was somewhat amusing. "I fear it was I who was indelicate, aunt. Indeed, Sir William was taken aback that I should speak of Henry's liaison or repeat what Mrs. Collings said about this Mrs. Stonebridge."

For a moment, Mrs. Merriweather simply stared at her before shaking her head. "I'm at a loss, Charlotte, truly I am! I really don't know what to make of modern manners. A lady broaching *such a subject*, and *especially* to a gentleman! In my day, the conventions were strictly abided by and woe to those who did not. Why, only think of Lady Caroline Lamb! Tossing aside the rules of society, and for what? *A poet! Byron!* Such hoopla I hope never to hear again! I never *could* stomach the man's poetry!"

"Ah, but like the poor, mad Lamb, I am hardly living a conventional life," murmured Lady Ogden, a hand lightly smoothing the fabric of her dress over her rounding belly.

At the reminder of her niece's unusual situation, Mrs. Merriweather's countenance colored. She said hurriedly, "Never mind! We need not go into all *that*, Charlotte. I'm just glad we shall see no more of Sir William. Have you told Somerset that he is to deny us in future?"

"Not yet, but I intend to do just that." Lady Ogden gave a wry smile. "I have a feeling that his lordship will not mind it in the least."

"What won't I mind?" asked Lord Ogden, who had opened the door and come into the drawing-room on the echo of her statement.

Lady Ogden was disconcerted by his lordship's sudden appearance. "Oh, you are back!" She saw that he had changed his raiment since she had last seen him when he had gone out grouse-shooting. He looked devastatingly attractive in the neatly-cut bottle-green frock coat, worn over a twill tan waistcoat and dark trousers. His crisp, curling hair was brushed back; a few droplets of water clung to the black strands, hinting of his recent ablution. All of a sudden, she had a mind's-vision of him, stripped to the waist and washing in the water basin, splashing water into his face and onto his broad, muscular chest, the muscles rippling with his vigorous movements. Her cheeks grew heated. *My mind is strangely disordered. Why do I think of such things?* "How-how was the shooting, my lord?"

Mrs. Merriweather was not to be deterred by the bagging of birds. Before his lordship could respond to her niece's query, she announced with satisfaction, "We have seen the last of Sir William."

"Have we, indeed?" Lord Ogden turned his interested gaze on his cousin-in-law. She looked unaccountably flushed. He raised his brows. "What's this, my lady?"

"Yes, I've decided that Sir William is no longer welcome at Delincourt," said Lady Ogden. She tilted her head with a quizzing smile. "Have you any objection, my lord?"

"Not the least in the world, ma'am," said Lord Ogden promptly. "The man's company was merely tolerated. I've never sought a friendship there."

"Why ever didn't you say something of this before?" asked Lady Ogden, much surprised by his lordship's decided response, though she didn't know why she should be since Sir William was one of Henry's cronies. She had seen at that first meeting the gentlemen's mutual dislike of one another. She should be more surprised by the viscount's forbearance. "You could have made your wishes plain and I would have denied entrance to Sir William long ago."

Lord Ogden smiled. He made a courteous bow. "I believe I once told you that you could invite whomever you liked to Delincourt."

Warm color flooded her face. His lordship had shown a respect for her that was both unexpected and astonishing. He was making a habit of throwing her surprisingly off-balance, she reflected, and he did not even know it. "Thank you, my lord."

The viscount bowed again and tactfully turned to engage Mrs. Merriweather in conversation. Lady Ogden sat down in a nearby chair and began to arrange her shawl to best advantage, thinking about the viscount, something which she knew she did much more often than was good for her. Lord Ogden reached out and brought a fold of the shawl over one of her shoulders. She nodded in thanks and smiled up at him. It was an unintentionally intimate moment. Their gazes held for an instant, despite Mrs. Merriweather's presence.

Mrs. Dalton walked into the drawing-room, saying cheerfully, "I came in through the back entrance and I heard from Cook that we are to have spitted, roasted grouse for dinner. Well done, brother!"

"Yes, our shooting party was successful. We each bagged enough birds for our separate households," said Lord Ogden, breaking away from Lady Ogden's green eyes and turning toward his sister. "You look very becoming, Amarys. Your cheeks are turned rosy from the outside air."

Mrs. Dalton smiled, but she could hardly be expected to do more than acknowledge a brother's compliment when something else was exercising her mind. "I suppose then that we shall not see Rev. Major Ledger this evening," she said regretfully. "He will be feasting at his own table."

"On the contrary, he expressed himself eager to join us. He left only to take home his birds and to change out of his hunting clothes before he will return," said Lord Ogden, smiling at his sister.

"We all do so enjoy Rev. Major Ledger's company," said Mrs. Merriweather. She turned her gaze to Mrs. Dalton and said teasingly, "Do we not, Amarys?"

The lady blushed and softly agreed, while Lord Ogden grinned at her.

Lady Ogden felt the tug of a smile on her own face. The circle of those standing about her, along with Rev. Major Ledger and a few others, had formed a vital connection to her life. An unconventional, harrowing detour in her existence had brought her to this place and this moment. In many ways since, her life had become richer, fuller. She hugged herself within the folds of her shawl. She had a fierce, exultant longing for the child she carried. It no longer represented a means to an end. She looked at the viscount. *Ravisher...seed-bull...lover.* An unexpected warmth suffused her. No, she could not tell him what she suspected was taking place in her heart. He would never believe her.

38

Lady Thane had high hopes for her *soirée*. Most of the invitations she had sent out had been accepted, only a very few declining due to illness. The moon hung full, unobstructed by clouds, shedding its white light, and making travel on that Thursday night easy for her guests.

Unlike smaller houses in the neighborhood, Thane Hall could boast of a small ballroom. The dinner-party had evolved since Lady Thane had initiated her plans; her sister-in-law Mrs. Collings had seen to that, and if the full truth was to be known, Lady Thane had been put on her mettle. She had wearied of Mrs. Collings' stories of the rarified social circles that lady was used to and her laments at the provinciality of the entertainment to be had in the country. Instead of being a mere gathering for a convivial dinner, the evening was to consist of music and dancing, followed by a supper, and there was even a small cardroom for those so inclined.

Lady Thane stood just inside the small ballroom, receiving her guests. Mrs. Collings was beside her, graciously nodding to the arrivals as though she was the hostess. Sir Edward was not one for remaining long with his wife and sister-in-law at the open doorway of the ballroom. He alternately bounded out to meet some of the incoming guests on the landing or after they had greeted Lady Thane and Mrs. Collings, ushering them personally into the ballroom, all with a good deal of laughter and welcoming words. He enjoyed entertaining and he took a good deal of pride in his wife's ambitious arrangements for the evening.

The party from Delincourt arrived and with his effortless *bonhomie* Sir Edward stepped forward to meet them. He thrust out his hand to the viscount. "Ah, Vincent! It is good of you to come, my lord. Lady Ogden,

Mrs. Merriweather, Mrs. Dalton! I am glad to see you! Come in, come in! Lady Thane is just inside the door there."

Lord Ogden grinned as he shook Sir Edward's hand. "Thank you, Ned. The ladies and I have looked forward to this evening."

"No more than I have. I like nothing better than having all my neighbors disporting themselves at Thane Hall." Sir Edward spotted another welcome guest approaching them. He detained the viscount by a hand on his lordship's elbow. "There is Mr. Kelton, coming up the steps. You'll want to speak to him, of course. Mr. Kelton, you are most welcome, sir. Here, both of you, come apart a moment. I have something to put to you."

Lady Ogden, her aunt, and Mrs. Dalton moved forward to greet their hostess, leaving the gentlemen behind. Lady Thane warmly greeted the three ladies, while Mrs. Collings vouchsafed only a chilly nod. "My dear Charlotte, you are in such good looks. I am glad you've put off your blacks! Mrs. Dalton, such a lovely gown. You quite eclipse us all. Mrs. Merriweather, you are always welcome." Lady Thane explained about the dancing to Lady Ogden. "I know you do not yet dance, Charlotte, but there will be the music and much enjoyable conversation. And the supper later, of course."

"It sounds delightful, Sarah." Lady Ogden looked past her hostess into the small ballroom, which was already crowded with guests. "Why, it appears that the entire county has come tonight!"

Lady Thane laughed. "Almost, yes. We will be packed back to back and elbow to elbow, I fear." She was still speaking to the Delincourt party when she had her first inkling that her *soirée* was not to run as smoothly as she had anticipated.

Sir William Talley sauntered through the open front door. He gave his hat to an attentive footman in the entrance hall and walked up the stairs to greet his hostess. Astonished and disbelieving, Lady Thane was rendered speechless by the gentleman's uninvited appearance. Mrs. Collings stepped into the breach, all affable cordiality as she held out her hand. "Sir William! So good of you to come! I had hoped you would."

He smiled and bowed over her hand. "My thanks again for the invitation, Mrs. Collings."

Lady Thane drew in her breath sharply. A spot of color rose in each smooth cheek. She was generally a kind, patient woman, but it made her furious that her sister-in-law had put her into such an untenable position. She still could not quite believe it. Her expression was unguarded; indignation warred with indecision in her countenance. All who witnessed Sir William Talley's arrival had no difficulty in perceiving that it had been totally unexpected.

Mrs. Collings turned to Lady Thane. She gave a satisfied smile, preening over her triumph. "I met Sir William when I was in the village yesterday. I told him that we were having a little assembly tonight and I insisted that he must come." Lady Thane was still staring at Sir William with what Mrs. Collings thought to be a rude gaucherie.

Sir William raised his brows. He looked from Mrs. Collings to Lady Thane. "But I would not wish to intrude, my lady, when we have only the slightest of acquaintances."

Lady Thane was put on the spot under the eyes of all present. She could read the consternation in the faces of Lady Ogden and Mrs. Merriweather. Mrs. Dalton merely looked pensive. Suppressing her inclination to speak sharply to her sister-in-law, Lady Thane felt she had no choice. Good breeding dictated she endorse her sister-in-law's invitation. "Of course, you will not be intruding, Sir William."

Lord Ogden and Sir Edward, who had lagged behind to speak to Mr. Kelton upon his arrival, came up in time to hear something of the conversation. Sir Edward muttered an exclamation under his breath.

Mrs. Dalton struck in. "Lady Thane was just reminding us of her delightful plans for our entertainment, brother."

Lord Ogden had overheard enough to realize the predicament in which the lady found herself. He smiled sympathetically and addressed her. "Naturally, we are looking forward to the evening, dear ma'am." Lord Ogden nodded to Sir William, unsmilingly acknowledging the gentleman's presence.

Sir William turned aside from his reluctant hostess and Mrs. Collings in order to bow and say a few civil words to Lady Ogden and Mrs. Dalton. He did not attempt to include Mrs. Merriweather in his greeting, an obvious oversight which did the gentleman no good service in the eyes of any of the ladies from Delincourt.

Lord Ogden took for granted that Lady Ogden was well-protected from the dandified London gentleman by his sister and Mrs. Merriweather. In company with Mr. Kelton, he passed into the ballroom, remarking, "A fine evening is ahead, Mr. Kelton. I trust you are up for the dancing, sir?"

"I believe I am said to have a good toe, my lord," said Mr. Kelton.

When Sir William offered his elbow to Lady Ogden, she lifted her brows and deliberately turned to address her aunt and Mrs. Dalton. "Listen to that music! Let us go in."

"Yes, indeed," said Mrs. Dalton, slipping her hand around the viscountess' elbow. "Mrs. Merriweather, do you join us?"

"Of course." Mrs. Merriweather, taking her place at her niece's other side. The three ladies stepped into the ballroom, ignoring the gentleman. Sir William was left to follow behind them, the set smile on his arrogant face covering his angered humiliation at being so directly cut by her ladyship.

Lady Thane drew her sister-in-law apart from the rest and said in a low tone, "Mariah, how could you invite Sir William?"

"Why, whatever do you mean? Your numbers at dinner were going to be uneven. I simply made an improvement," said Mrs. Collins, making a show of opening her fan and slowly waving it.

"After what you told Lady Ogden! Sir William's presence will be an insult to her ladyship's sensibilities!"

Mrs. Collings tittered. She snapped shut her fan. "My dear, how very odd of you to take on so! Sir William is a fine gentleman. His inclusion will add a certain cachet to what would otherwise be a rather dull evening party. As for Lady Ogden, it will be no fault of mine should she take offense." Mrs. Collings moved away into the ballroom, her goal to speak to the viscount. His lordship was the highest-ranking gentleman in attendance and she was determined to claim his attention. She was most certainly due a dance with the viscount and if she could manage an invitation from him, she would partner his lordship at dinner.

Lady Thane was left seething, but she was forced to put as good a face on the situation as best she could. It did not help when her beloved husband stepped close and asked in a low, demanding tone in her ear, "Whatever decided you to invite *that* fellow?"

"It was not my doing, sir! You must have heard! Your sister-in-law took it upon herself to even my numbers!"

"Not without your encouragement, I'll wager. Mariah would not behave so forward!"

Lady Thane sent a blistering glance at her husband. Sir Edward was very much startled. He was not used to such fiery looks from his gentle-natured wife. Lady Thane swept away to attend her duties as hostess, making certain that ladies would be paired with suitable gentlemen for the dancing and, later, for the supper.

Rev. Major Ledger had already arrived and he quickly made his presence known to the ladies of Delincourt. He appointed himself as their gallant, attending to their comfort by finding empty chairs against the wall where they could watch the dancing and talk with their neighbors and fetching glasses of punch for their refreshment.

"You are mightily accommodating," remarked Lord Ogden to his friend. "I never took you for a desperate flirt before."

Rev. Major Ledger laughed. "I'm happy enough to fetch and carry," he said with good-natured, unimpaired humor. He grinned at Lord Ogden. "No one expects a man with a bad leg to caper about on the floor. Unlike you, Vincent, I don't have to do the pretty and I can suit myself."

Lord Ogden grimaced. "Yes, damn your eyes. I shall have to stand up with half the women here to remain on civil terms with my neighbors. It's a bloody nuisance." He was disgruntled. There was only one lady that he really wanted to dance with, but her ladyship was not dancing because of two of society's dictates – she was still in mourning and she was in a delicate condition.

"You are the highest-ranking gentleman in attendance. You must do your duty, my lord," said Rev. Major Ledger piously. As he walked away, the viscount muttered something slanderous about his friend's antecedents and the vicar was set to laughing.

Rev. Major Ledger settled into a chair beside Mrs. Dalton and the two fell into what appeared to be a conversation of all-consuming interest. Mrs. Dalton was naturally solicited several times by other gentlemen to partner them onto the floor, invitations which she accepted with pretty manners, but she invariably returned to her chair and turned again to the enjoyment of Rev. Major Ledger's company.

Later, Mrs. Dalton and Lady Ogden made a slow promenade around the ballroom, her ladyship having expressed a wish to leave her seat for a bit of exercise. As they walked, they greeted all of their acquaintances who were not then on the dance floor. Lady Ogden commented that it was a good turn out that evening. "Sarah must be very well-pleased. The evening is quite a success."

"Yes, even with Sir William's unexpected appearance. That sister-in-law of hers! I felt for her, poor thing."

"At least Sir William seems to be behaving himself. I must say, I'm astonished. I don't think he has neglected a single lady this evening," said Lady Ogden, observing the gentleman disporting himself on the floor, partnering a flushed matron.

"Except for us," said Mrs. Dalton with a roguish smile.

Lady Ogden laughed. "Yes, but I'm not surprised. We dealt an insult to his pride."

"Yes, it was very bad of us." Mrs. Dalton's gaze went across the ballroom to linger on the smiling gentleman who had commanded so much of her attention. Rev. Major Ledger was just then in conversation with Mr. Kelton. Her cheeks turned rosy. "Charlotte, I must speak privately to you!" She halted near the open doorway of the ballroom and she gestured toward it. "Will you come with me?"

"Why, of course."

The ladies stepped out of the ballroom and went apart into the small parlor that had been set up as a cardroom for any guests who grew tired of the dancing. It was empty as no one had yet taken advantage of its entertainment. Lady Ogden closed the door and turned to her companion. "What is it, Amarys?"

Mrs. Dalton's eyes were shining like stars. "Oh, Charlotte, if only Rev. Major Ledger and I had not been interrupted! He-he was about to say something of the utmost importance!"

"Do you believe he was about to declare his feelings for you?"

"Yes, yes, I do!"

"I'm so happy for you, Amarys!" Lady Ogden hugged her friend. Mrs. Dalton laughed, returning the swift embrace. Lady Ogden stepped back, still smiling. "I had hoped you would make a match of it! Rev. Major Ledger will make you a charming husband."

The color fluctuated prettily in Mrs. Dalton's cheeks. "Yes, I think so, too!"

"You must go back in at once and give the gentleman every chance to express himself," said Lady Ogden, turning to open the door again.

Mrs. Dalton agreed and stepped past her. Mrs. Dalton paused outside the parlor, surprised when Lady Ogden did not follow her. "Aren't you coming with me?"

"I think I shall stay here for a little while and enjoy the quiet," said Lady Ogden. Her friend returned her smile, perhaps with more understanding than her ladyship was aware of, and quietly shut the door behind herself.

After Mrs. Dalton had left her, Lady Ogden sat down in a chair, content to be alone for a few moments while she thought deeply about the viscount. When the door opened, her thoughts were so focused on Lord Ogden that she looked up, expecting to see the viscount. It was a shock that it was not his lordship who entered the parlor. "Sir William!"

"Lady Ogden." Sir William closed the door and bowed to her. "I saw Mrs. Dalton exit and I thought to avail myself of the opportunity for a private word with you."

Lady Ogden rose from the chair. She did not want to be alone in the same room with him. She would make her exit at once. "I have nothing to say to you, sir. Nor can I imagine that there is anything which I wish to hear from you."

Sir William threw up a hand, advancing toward her. "You must see how it is, Lady Ogden! You have been much in my thoughts these past few months. Even before the dreadful loss of my dear friend, Henry, I had admired you."

"What nonsense!"

"You were right when you accused me of being too precipitate. My excuse must be that I was anxious to assure you of my devotion."

"Sir William, believe me when I say that I don't wish to hear anymore," said Lady Ogden. She gestured with her hand toward the door, letting him know that he should move out of her path. "You must excuse me. I will return to the ballroom."

His gaze dropped to her rounded figure before rising again to her face. "Ladies who are in a delicate condition are notoriously emotional. My reputation and my past actions have done me damage in your sight. But it's all in the past, I assure you! My only desire is to wed you and to be a good father to Henry's heir."

Lady Ogden was amazed by the gentleman's brazen falsehoods. *Does he honestly take me for such a fool?* It was not she, but Delincourt that he desired. She knew it now. As long as Henry's heir was alive and under-age, she thought, Sir William would have free rein at Delincourt. As a landed gentleman, even though he would technically be regent only, it would be an elevation in status for Sir William Talley. *If my child is a girl...* a chill touched her. A penniless wife, together with an unwelcome girl-child requiring financial support, was a very different thing than the mother of Delincourt's heir.

Sir William's own thoughts had been moving swiftly. He thought of what she would be like as a wife. Her ladyship's chestnut coloring was not to his liking, nor was her slightly-built figure all that appealing to him. However, the use of the crop would add a certain piquancy to his fucking of her – it made him horny just to consider it. Whether she whelped a male heir or a girl-child, he might keep her for a bit of fun. When he became bored of her charms, he could loan her out to his cronies. It might be amusing, he thought idly. Their circle had on more than one occasion shared a pussy. When the sport finally tired him, as surely it must, he would think of something else to do with her ladyship. A man owned his wife, body and soul. He could do with her as he wished.

Lady Ogden stared into those calculating, pale eyes. *After the legal bond of marriage, he would not need me. All he would need would be control over a male heir.* She realized she would not bet a groat against her own early demise or possibly a commitment to an insane asylum. Such wickedness should not ever have entered her brain. However, Lady Ogden felt the chill truth down to her bones. The gentleman plotted a complicated course. Perhaps he had already deliberated over the desirability of murder.

Lady Ogden shook herself free of her paralysis. She smoothed her hair with trembling fingers. "Pray say no more, Sir William. It's past time that I returned to the company." She moved to go around him toward the door.

Sir William's erotic imaginings triggered his next action. He suddenly reached out and dragged Lady Ogden into his arms.

"Unhand me!" She struggled but his strength was greater. His arms were like tight bands around her body.

He said thickly, "I'll force you to take me, so I will!" He was fully aroused. He'd wanted her against the wall on that dawn. He'd have her now on the nearest card table, and in the process, he'd shame her provincial heart into wedding him. He backed her up, treading heavily on the hem of her skirt, and there was the sound of ripping lace.

Neither heard the door open.

Lady Ogden delivered a stinging slap to the gentleman's face.

39

Lord Ogden uttered a wrathful oath. He brushed past Sir Edward, who was immobile with astonishment. In three long strides, Lord Ogden reached the pair. He wrapped his fingers inside the collar of Sir William's coat. Wrenching that gentleman around, nearly strangling him with his own neckcloth, he sent Sir William staggering back. He at once turned to Lady Ogden. *"Are you alright?"*

"Yes, yes, of course." Two bright flags of embarrassment flew in her cheeks. "No, I am not! I detest being *mauled* about! He has torn the lace flounce of my new gown, too! I must go and have it pinned up." She shot a furious glance at Sir William. "You are no gentleman, sir!"

As her ladyship swept past him out of the room, Rev. Major Ledger bowed. He closed the door with a snap. Then he leaned his shoulders against it and crossed his arms over his chest. His eyes were sleet-gray as he examined the erring gentleman. "You've gone beyond the pale, Talley."

Sir William was fully alive to the disastrous consequences he faced. He'd been discovered in extremely compromising circumstances. The four gentlemen facing him were all looking at him with unfriendly, set expressions. He read condemnation in every stare. The interruption had been untimely. Indeed, he was astonished at his own lack of self-control. His salacious ruminations had led him into impulsive behavior that was very different from his characteristic cold forethought.

Mr. Kelton came out of his stupefaction. "Well, upon my word! Fine takings-on, sir! A lady in a delicate condition, too!"

Sir William flicked a bare glance at the man. He didn't know what the upstart mushroom was doing with his betters. He had nothing to fear from one of the lower orders. It was otherwise with the other three men.

The vicar was standing against the door, barring exit. The cast of his face was stern and his eyes were a turbulent silver-gray. Sir William did not think he looked like a vicar should, meek and obsequious; instead, his was a lean, compelling figure.

His calculating gaze went next to his host. Sir Edward Thane was the stolid, respectable sort that made Sir William sneer. But he thought he could appeal to that gentleman's instinctive dislike of scandal. Sir Edward would not want it known that a sordid incident had taken place in his own house. Surely, he could use that to his advantage in extricating himself from what had become a disastrous evening.

All along, Sir William was acutely aware of the last of the four. The viscount's narrowed, burning eyes, his hawkish nose and set mouth, the tick jumping in the side of his jaw – now, *there* was menace. The viscount had taken a wide stance. He somehow appeared to be coiled. An aura of controlled violence emanated from him. Sir William fancied he could discern the twitch of a predator's tail.

He did not allow his alarmed chagrin to show, however. He flicked a non-existent piece of lint from his sleeve and weighed how best to bluff his way out of what was a nasty situation. He needed to drive a wedge between the gentlemen and dilute their shared outrage. He had a part to play and he aimed it at Sir Edward's sense of respectability.

"Lady Ogden was affected by the heat and she began to feel faint. Naturally, I sprang to her ladyship's support," he drawled, looking earnestly at his host. "As she recovered, Lady Ogden was confused and mistook my intention. Of course, her ladyship is not to be reproached. It's well-known that a lady who is breeding is overemotional."

Sir Edward Thane gave a sharp crack of laughter. He eyed the gentleman with anger. "Doing it too brown, fellow."

"You'll meet me, Talley," said Lord Ogden icily.

Sir William glanced at the viscount, raising his brows. A superior smile was fixed on his thin lips. He felt the stiffness in his shoulders, in the rest of his body. Of all things, he wanted to avoid personal conflict. In his opinion, direct, open confrontation never worked to one's advantage. "On what conceivable grounds, my lord? The lady indulged in a fit of the vapors! It was a trifling misunderstanding. I assure you, there was no harm done nor meant."

"You have insulted the lady, who is my cousin-in-law. She resides under my roof. She is under my protection," said Lord Ogden in clipped accents. "You will meet me, sir!"

Sir William shook his head. He kept his smile firmly in place, but a trickle of sweat slid down his spine. "No, my lord, I will not."

"I say you will!" Lord Ogden abruptly backhanded the gentleman in the face. The sharp crack of bone against bone was loud.

"Bravo!" exclaimed Sir Edward.

Sir William's countenance turned white, accentuating the red blotch swiftly rising across one cheekbone. His mask of urbanity slipped. Enraged, stunned, he couldn't believe that anyone would dare lift a hand to him – *him!* He clenched his fists. He was breathing quickly, shallowly. A bloodless snarl twisted his face. He said furiously, "I will meet you, where and when you will, my lord! By God, I will!"

Lord Ogden gave an abbreviated nod. His eyes were cold. A dangerous smile played over his lips. "At dawn, then."

"You are a peer of the realm. He's a commoner. You have the choice of weapon, my lord," said Sir Edward with formality.

"I've done my share of killing with sword and service pistol. It makes no odds to me," said Lord Ogden with an indifference that struck Mr. Kelton as chilling.

"He's not up to your weight with a sword, Vincent," said Rev. Major Ledger with unruffled composure.

"Then let it be pistols," said Lord Ogden coolly.

A modicum of sanity penetrated Sir William's raging fury. The man he faced was late of the wars, in excellent physical condition, and used to doing battle with a sword. The vicar was undoubtedly correct. He suspected himself to be no match for his lordship with the blade. At the viscount's choice of pistols, a slither of relief went down his spine. He fancied that he could hold his own with a pistol. He'd culped a wafer a time or two at Manton's and considered himself to be a pretty shot.

"Pistols it is, my lord!" Sir William struck a pose. A hand at his breast, placing one foot forward of the other, he said jeeringly, "But I am a gentleman! I do not jaunt about the countryside with a set of dueling pieces."

"I haven't a set," said Lord Ogden, speaking still with that hard indifference. He never removed his cold gaze from his antagonist's sneering face. "Ned? Arthur?"

"Allow me, my lord. I have a set of dueling pistols," said Sir Edward grimly. "They are downstairs in my study. Only give me a few moments to retrieve them."

He pivoted and swiftly made for the door.

Lord Ogden murmured, "What a dangerous fire-eater you are, Ned."

Sir Edward stopped in mid-stride. His head swiveled and his astonished gaze swept around to meet the friendly mockery in his lordship's face. He gave a short, genuine laugh.

Rev. Major Ledger straightened away from the door and opened it for Sir Edward to exit. Then he closed it again and limped forward. With quiet courtesy, he said, "You have none of your friends here. I will second you, Sir William."

"My thanks to you," snapped Sir William, hardly aware of the vicar's words. He was trembling, barely holding himself in check. He wanted to strike that insufferable, disdainful expression from the viscount's face. His fingers twitched beside his thigh. He wanted his crop. He would lift it, again and again. He imagined the force of the blows, envisioned the spray of blood.

Lord Ogden smiled faintly at his former comrade-in-arms. "Thank you, Arthur." He turned his head in the other direction and his straight, dark gaze sought out his neighbor. "Mr. Kelton, will you stand for me?"

The gentleman proudly drew himself up. "It will be my honor, my lord."

At a knock on the door, all of the gentlemen turned their heads, with varying expressions of dismay or caution. The door was pushed open by Sir Edward. He swiftly entered, a long box held tight under one arm, and closed the door again. "A near-run thing! I was almost caught at the top of the stairs by Lady Thane! She was walking past the open doorway of the ballroom, but fortunately she didn't see me and went on by. We wouldn't want to stir up the ladies, you know."

"No, we wouldn't want to do that," agreed Rev. Major Ledger gravely, but a glint of amusement warmed the steel in his gray eyes.

Sir Edward strode across the room, carrying the long, narrow box over to the nearest card table. He set it down carefully on the green baize and opened the case with something of a flourish. "Here we are! A pretty pair that I picked up at Manton's."

Despite the high tension, all of the gentlemen were as one in their mutual curiosity and they angled in for a closer look. Resting in the felt-lined box was a pair of elegant weapons, with ten-inch barrels and finely-worked percussion-locks above curved handles.

"Hair-triggers, of course," remarked Sir Edward with ill-concealed pride.

Mr. Kelton nodded, impressed. He carefully lifted out one of the pistols and caressed the silver mountings decorating the weapon. "A fine pair, indeed, sir."

"How do they shoot, Thane?" asked Rev. Major Ledger, picking up the other dueling pistol. He handled the weapon with casual familiarity, lifting it and sighting down the long barrel.

"True as you could wish. Not a hair's difference between them."

Lord Ogden looked over at his opponent. He raised his brows in a haughty manner. A hard edge to his voice, he asked, "You are satisfied, Sir William?"

Sir William flapped a hand and said testily, "Yes, yes!"

Lord Ogden made the most marginal of bows. Sir William took it to be a slight but he returned the bow.

With a last murmur of appreciation, Mr. Kelton relinquished the pistol into its owner's hands and Sir Edward placed it back into the case. Rev. Major Ogden returned the other to its place. Sir Edward nodded his thanks, and said, "I've been thinking. I suggest the bottom of my orchard for the best ground. It's flat, there's a good range of sight. Fourteen paces, shall we say?"

"Tomorrow at dawn. The orchard," repeated Lord Ogden. "It is agreed?" There was a murmuring of acquiescence. When he looked at Sir William, a flame burned deep in his dark eyes, while a peculiar smile played about his tightened lips. "Pray do not renege on me, Sir William. I would take it in very bad part. I should then feel it my obligation to hunt you down and thrash you with my whip, like the encroaching commoner you are."

Sir William reddened, at once furious and mortified, as his lordship's words struck him on the quick. When he had fastened his gaze on those beautifully-worked and deadly dueling pistols, his battle-ardor had begun to evaporate. Through his mind had flitted the thought to quit the neighborhood that same evening. He stiffened, an ugly scowl marring his handsome visage. "I don't back out of a challenge, I believe! Sir Edward, pray make my excuses to Lady Thane. I will not be staying to dinner." With a short bow directed indiscriminatingly at the company, he yanked open the door and exited the room.

"Kelton, can you notify the local sawbones that we shall require his services on the morrow?" asked Lord Ogden.

"Of course, my lord. I shall attend to it this very night after the evening's entertainment," said Mr. Kelton with stout assurance. "And be sure that I will impress upon him the need for discretion."

Lord Ogden shook his neighbor's hand. "You're a good man, sir."

Mr. Kelton puffed out his cheeks, gratified. He turned to his host and said gravely, "In the interests of discretion, I believe we must return to the ballroom and pretend that nothing has taken place. I regret we must forego the pleasure of a round of cards, sir."

"Good of you. I'll walk with you, Kelton. I want to be certain that jackanapes pompous dandy is gone away, besides," said Sir Edward. He shut the case and picked it up. "I'll just put these away for now. It wouldn't do to have them seen laying around by any of the servants, you know. Rumors would go flying."

"Thank you, Ned. I knew that I could rely upon you," said Lord Ogden quietly. "It's best we keep it all buttoned up between us."

With a rueful grin, Sir Edward nodded. "No, we don't want word to get out. Come along, Kelton."

The door shut behind the two gentlemen. Lord Ogden looked across at his old comrade-in-arms. "Well, Arthur, join me in a brandy?"

"When, do you think, it will finally occur to Kelton to wonder at my role? A vicar willing to participate in an illegal duel! Alas, my reputation." Rev. Major Ledger dropped into a chair beside the card table. "I am fatigued. Another one of your damnable starts, Vincent!"

Lord Ogden poured two glasses of brandy and put one into his companion's outstretched hand. He sat down also. "Forgive me, Arthur. I know how you detest having your piece cut up."

"Damn your eyes," said Rev. Major Ledger mildly. He tasted the brandy, and in a moment, in quite a different tone, he said, "Do not kill the bastard."

Lord Ogden slowly swirled the brandy in his glass, looking down at it. "Do you think I mean to do so?"

"You were in aim's-ace of doing it with your bare hands, only a few minutes ago," retorted Rev. Major Leger. "Thank God, you came to your senses in time."

"There were too many witnesses," murmured Lord Ogden, looking up with a grin.

Rev. Major Ledger made a disgusted sound. "That isn't what stopped you and well do I know it! No, you've got another notion in your head."

"What if I was to tell you that I mean to castrate Tally by blowing a strategic hole through his anatomy?"

Rev. Maj. Leger narrowed his eyes, pensively looking into the distance. "Why, I think I should like to see such a pretty shot."

Lord Ogden burst out laughing. "Yes, no doubt you would! You madman, you know well enough I shouldn't attempt any such crazy thing. It can't be done, not without killing the man, which I *would* like to do, but won't, because I've no taste for fleeing the country."

Rev. Major Leger finished his brandy, set down the glass, and dragged himself to his feet. "Good, for I'm fairly certain that as your vicar, I should counsel you to go soak your head."

"Be damned to you," said Lord Ogden with affection. He tossed off the brandy and set down the glass on the card table. "Let's rejoin the rest of the company. Kelton was right; we mustn't give rise to any speculation."

Together, the two gentlemen re-entered the ballroom. The musicians were still scraping away, but it appeared several guests that were murmuring questions amongst themselves had begun to turn toward the end of the room, where a quartet of ladies faced one another, their hostess among them.

"What the devil?" murmured Lord Ogden.

After having a maid pin up the torn lace flounce on her gown, Lady Ogden had returned to the ballroom. She rejoined her aunt, only to be approached by Mrs. Collings, with her jealous spite and viperish tongue. Mrs. Collings had received a letter from an acquaintance, which had detailed every damaging bit of gossip about Sir William Talley and the rest of Henry Ogden's set that had been floating around London for years. It was a humiliation to have to suffer through the vicious account.

Attacked by Sir William and now this! How beastly the evening has become!

Mrs. Merriweather took strong umbrage on her niece's behalf. She quivered with outrage. Her voice was very sharp. "I believe we've heard enough, Mrs. Collings! My dear niece, perhaps we should join the company at the other end of the room. Lady Thane, pray excuse us."

"Of course, Mrs. Merriweather!" Lady Thane was visibly upset. "Lady Ogden, pray forgive – Mariah has crossed the line! For shame, Mariah! I'm so sorry, Charlotte! That you should be subjected to such horrid gossip!"

Lady Ogden inclined her head, acknowledging her hostess. She stared at Mrs. Collings with arctic disdain, not uttering a word. Fully alive to her surroundings, aware of the curiosity that the confrontation was already garnering in those nearest to them, she did not trust herself to open her lips for fear of saying things that would be later regretted. Already there would be talk. Not for the world would she subject her friend to worse gossip.

Mrs. Collings had indeed gone too far. Even she realized it, but her rancor couldn't let it go. "You should have it all! It's no secret! It's said that last year Mrs. Stonebridge bore the viscount's by-blow. What do you think about that, my lady?"

Lady Ogden swept her skirts back from the pollution of the other woman's hem. Ice glittered in her scornful smile. "I think you are a singularly vulgar, malignant creature! Aunt, I am leaving!"

Mrs. Merriweather's voice was cold. "I'm going with you. We shall collect Amarys at once."

Lady Thane was agonized on her guests' behalf. She was so shocked and mortified by her sister-in-law's behavior that she felt her wits to have been scattered. Her sensibilities were overset. Her carefully planned soirée was crumbling into a disaster and she well knew where to lay the blame. With an effort, she managed to overcome her distress and rise to meet her most urgent duty. "Come! I shall go with you to find your wraps!"

Lord Ogden and Rev. Major Ledger met the ladies as they reached the ballroom door and turned out with them. There was the flurry of departure, of confused leave-taking. Mrs. Merriweather insisted that the evening's entertainment was at an end for the Delincourt party. Lady Thane did her best to ease the decampment of her guests with the least possible obstacle. Through it all, Lady Ogden was like a marble statue, regal and silent.

Sir Edward had come forward to join his spouse in bidding their guests a good evening. While the ladies were putting on their wraps, he stepped close to Lord Ogden, who was standing a little apart with Rev. Major Ledger. Sir Edward murmured, "What has put the ladies into such a froth? Do you think they have gotten wind of tomorrow?"

Lord Ogden shook his head. "No, it's something else. Do not fear; I shall discover what it is about."

Still without a clue as to what was behind their sudden decampment, Lord Ogden and Rev. Major Ledger set off on horseback behind the departing carriage. It was not long before the party split up. After a quick word to the viscount and a touch of his hat, Rev. Major Ledger turned off onto the fork of the road leading to the vicarage.

When they had returned to Delincourt and entered the candlelit entrance hall, Lord Ogden quietly requested his cousin-in-law to join him in the downstairs study. She preceded him into the room, restlessly twisting her hands together in front of herself. He shut the door, and with a gesture, invited her ladyship to sit down.

Lady Ogden shook her head, the set expression on her face making evident that she was not in a conciliatory mood. "I prefer to have this interview standing, my lord."

"Very well. I'm not censoring you. I merely wish to know what was behind our abrupt departure. Sir Edward is one of my oldest friends, after all."

Lady Ogden took an agitated turn about the room. "It was that vicious woman!"

"You are speaking of Mrs. Collings."

"Who else?" Lady Ogden swept around to face the viscount. Her eyes glittered like cut green glass. "She told us more about Henry's mistress. She said the same woman has been taken up by Sir William Talley." She clamped shut her mouth. She could not bring herself to relate all the details of the malicious account. It had been too sordid, ending in that last awful barb. *What if the rumor is true and that woman bore his by-blow!* A pang of anguish struck her heart. The old pain had dulled but it still existed. The vicious attack had cut her where she was most defenseless. She had failed miserably as a wife; she had miscarried her own babes. It was unbearable that some strumpet had done what she could not.

The viscount was silent a moment. "And this distresses you...about Sir William Talley's activities?"

"I care little enough for that!" she flashed.

He guessed she was more upset over the gentleman than she let on, but he let it pass. "Thank you for making things so clear, ma'am. I can meet Sir Edward with right on my side since it was his sister-in-law, rather than one of my own party, who offered the insult."

Lady Ogden suddenly deflated. She passed the back of her hand over her brow in a peculiarly vulnerable gesture. Her mouth trembled. "I'm sorry, Vincent. I did not mean to make a scene."

"It's all right. You certainly had provocation. As I recall, it was Mrs. Merriweather who was so insistent on our leave-taking." Lord Ogden meditatively added, "I don't believe I have ever seen the gentle lady so angry." He had hoped to bring the flicker of a smile to her face, but his effort fell flat. Lady Ogden only shrugged.

The viscount moved toward her until he was close enough to place his hands on her slender shoulders. He pressed a brief kiss to her forehead before he said gently, "Go up to bed, Charlotte. I can see you are exhausted."

Lady Ogden nodded, not meeting his eyes. Her throat was thick with tears. She feared she would burst into horrible sobs if she tried to speak. Without uttering a word, she hurried away and left him alone.

After brooding awhile on the whole evening's debacle and the dawn appointment, he went upstairs. Some minutes later, he entered her bedchamber. He was astonished to find her weeping. Shedding his silk brocaded dressing-gown, he slid naked into the bed beside her. "Why, what's this, my love?"

She hastily dried her cheeks. "It's nothing, nothing but a lowering of spirit, my lord."

He caressed the long strands of her soft hair. "I think I know the cause. It was what Mrs. Collings said to you, wasn't it? You mustn't let such spite upset you, Charlotte."

On a hiccough, she burst out, "She told me that Henry's mistress had borne his by-blow!"

He stilled his fingers as he absorbed what she had said in such a flat, tear-thickened voice. With gathering wrath, he realized the magnitude of the blow that she had been dealt. He could cheerfully strangle the widow Collings himself, he thought savagely, but there was a better way to handle the matter. *I will speak to Ned.* In the meantime, she needed to be distracted and he knew exactly how to do it.

"Never mind, love. I've gotten you with child. And this is how I did it." He proceeded to whisper into her ear the wicked things that sparked her to wantonness, while his hands were busy, preparing her body for their mutual pleasure. She was already shivering when his lips followed the trail blazed by his hands. She arched and pressed herself into him, clutching at his shoulders to pull him closer in her wild need.

"Now! Come to me now!"

He rolled her onto her side. "I don't wish to crush you or our child, Charlotte."

She closed her eyes and his arms cradled her, while her back was warmed by the curve of his big body. She raised her hands to clasp his muscular arms and shifted her top leg over his thigh, hooking her ankle behind his hair-roughened calf. "Vincent," she whispered on a plea.

She felt his hips move close against her backside. His heavy shaft slid home into the dampened cleft of her thighs. She moaned softly. His thick, hard length stretched her, his fullness making her clench around him. She hitched out a breathless sigh. *He calls me 'love'. It means nothing, but I shall pretend.* He began moving deep inside of her; before long, her body began its inevitable shuddering. *Oh yes! In these moments, when I cry out my bliss, I know he loves me!*

Much later, when the firelight was dying, later when at last she laid somnolent beside him, her head pillowed on his shoulder and her slender hand laid on his bare chest, she slept peacefully. Unable to follow her into slumber, Lord Ogden frowned upward into the darkness of the soaring bed canopy.

40

Dawn came too swiftly for Sir William Talley. He had spent an indifferent night in his room at the inn. He had given his valet instructions to waken him at the appropriate hour; he rose and by the feeble light of a smoking tallow candle made his toilet. He chose his darkest coat and wished fervently that it didn't sport such bright silver buttons, which previously had been a detail of pride to him. He swallowed a pint of ale, but he could not make himself get down more than a bite of thick-sliced buttered bread.

By the time Rev. Major Ledger arrived to take him up in a curricle, Sir William was regretting that he had ever set foot in the district. The morning was cool, but Sir William was sweating. Anxious that the starched folds of his neckcloth would be affected by the moisture, he briefly touched his fingertips to the exquisite folds.

Rev. Major Ledger assessed his principal. He noticed the gesture and his laconic observation did nothing to soothe Sir William's nerves. "Better button that coat up over the white of your neckcloth. You'll present less of a target that way."

Sir William obeyed the suggestion with shaking fingers. He had never shot at a man before. He had a sinking feeling, which had been growing, that it was not at all the same thing as culping wafers at Manton's, where no one had been shooting back.

At the chosen ground, Sir William saw that Lord Ogden and his second, Mr. Kelton, had already arrived. Sir Edward Thane and the physician were also present, conferring quietly between themselves. They broke off as the vicar's curricle slowed and stopped nearby. Sir William stiffly climbed down from the carriage. He made himself walk forward. Rev Major Leger snubbed the reins, got down, and limped after him.

Mr. Kelton had seen the two approaching men and he murmured to the viscount. Lord Ogden turned. His lean, browned face was expressionless. He looked as though his features had been carved from stone. Only his eyes appeared alive, and they blazed with a fire that shriveled what little courage remained in Sir William's bosom.

The next few minutes seemed strangely unreal to Sir William's brain. Random observations stood out to him in stark detail. A white mist obscured the earth, so that it seemed he was walking through water. The two seconds measured the distance and marked it with points. The physician turned his back on the proceedings. Numbly, Sir William took the pistol in his hand and bent his elbow, bringing the pistol barrel up vertical with his eyes. He marched fourteen paces and turned. The white handkerchief fluttered. Of a sudden, his frozen mental state lifted. He looked, and with a startling clarity of detail, across the expanse of ground at his hated enemy. The viscount was smiling. He completely lost his reason then. Instead of deloping as he had intended – deadly purpose in his heart – he extended the pistol and fired.

The shot echoed. The acrid smoke of the discharge thinned. Sir William saw that the viscount was still standing. Long seconds ticked away. A second shot had yet to be fired.

Sir William watched, in horror, as the viscount slowly, deliberately, brought down his arm and sighted his pistol. Flame and smoke spouted from the gun's mouth. He heard the explosion of the shot. A hot, tearing sensation ripped through his shoulder.

Sir William crumpled to the ground. He dropped the empty pistol and clapped his hand over the sluggishly bleeding wound. He could smell the blood. He felt like as to faint, or to vomit, or both. Blinking away black spots that swam before his sight, he watched the physician hurry across the turf towards him, his black bag swinging from his hand.

"You madman, Vincent!" roared Sir Edward, running up. His face was paper-white. "You just stood there, setting yourself up as a target!"

Lord Ogden inspected a scorch mark in his coat sleeve. He said coolly, "It was a near-run thing."

"The bounder meant to kill you," remarked Rev. Major Ledger in a detached manner.

"I believe you're right," agreed Lord Ogden imperturbably. "Damn! I believe my coat is ruined. Grimshaw will have something to say about it."

Sir Edward looked from one to the other, beginning to get an inkling of what it had been like to have gone to the war. He had been secretly a little envious of their shared comradeship, but now he realized how blessed he had been to remain at home, safe from experiences that so hardened a man to the possibility of a violent death.

"A good thing that Sir William was not a better shot, my lord, or it would be you laying on the ground about now," said Mr. Kelton in a gruff, scolding fashion, overhearing the exchange. He was a good deal shaken. It would not strike him until some hours later, when he had fully recovered over a few glasses of brandy, that his tone of voice had not been at all what one should use when addressing a peer of the realm.

"I didn't expect him to be as good as he was," said Lord Ogden, smiling ruefully around at the loose circle of his friends.

The physician had bound up the wounded man in a rough-and-ready fashion and helped Sir William to stand. "There you are, sir. As neat and tidy as you could wish." Sir William was too much in shock to do more than nod.

Sir Edward retrieved the pistols and carefully placed them into the case. He strove to strike the proper note of nonchalance to match the viscount's and Rev. Major Ledger's coolness. "I shall have to clean these first thing, of course. But come back to the hall with me, all of you! A good, hearty breakfast is needed after such work, heh?"

"You-you must hold me excused, Sir Edward," said Sir William with a fixed, strained smile.

Sir Edward looked surprised. "Well, naturally – I mean, it is understood." It was obvious that he had not meant the invitation to include the defeated party. With a curl of his lip, Sir William turned his back and tottered to the curricle that had brought him to the appointment. The other gentlemen silently watched his retreat. Rev. Major Ledger sighed and shook his head. His responsibility to his former principal was clear and he was not one to shirk his duties.

"I shall join you once I have returned my charge to the inn," said Rev. Major Ledger. He walked away from the rest of the party to climb into the curricle, the carriage lurching under his ascent, and untied the reins. The shaken, wounded gentleman had reached the carriage, but instead of getting up into the carriage, he had sagged against the side of it. Rev. Major Ledger called out impatiently. "Up with you, Sir William. Doctor Manning, have you bound up the wound sufficiently? I don't want the gentleman bleeding all over the seat of my curricle."

"Be damned to you, vicar!" snarled Sir William. He pulled himself up and sprawled onto the leather seat of the curricle, an ordinary action that left him breathless from effort.

"As a man of the cloth, I shall not bandy words with a confirmed sinner," drawled Rev. Major Ledger. He gave the office to the horses and the curricle jerked forward.

Lord Ogden threw up his hand and called out. "Hold a moment, Arthur." Rev. Major Ledger obligingly stopped the team and waited. Lord Ogden strode over to the side of the carriage and stared up at the wounded gentleman. Again, there came the fierce, burning light into his lordship's narrowed eyes, while his face was touched by that same queer, chilling smile. "Sir William, you will recall what I said to you before our meeting upon the field of honor. I shall repeat it, with a caveat. If one word of scandal should ever attach to Lady Ogden's name, I will hunt you down, and I will thrash you with my whip. You will bear the stripes all your remaining days. Do you understand?"

Meeting the viscount's fiery gaze, Sir William's complexion turned pasty. He gave a jerky nod. "I perfectly take your meaning, my lord."

Lord Ogden stepped back from the curricle. Matter-of-factly, Rev. Major Ledger again gave the office to his horses. "Walk on."

Sir William quitted the neighborhood before noon. His baggage was secured onto the top of the hired post chaise. The injured gentleman hauled himself up into the chaise, followed by his wooden-faced valet. The step was put up and the door was shut and the driver gigged the horses. Sir William did not set out to return to his lodgings in London. Better than anyone, he knew how swiftly gossip could rise up and spread. If he showed his front in town, his arm in a sling, and took to his bed until he recuperated, rumors would run rife. He couldn't keep his cronies and acquaintances ignorant of his condition. He doubted that his manservant would keep such a juicy tale to himself. For that reason alone, he did not intend to let the man out of his sight. He even toyed with the idea of letting his valet go but discarded it; the man was too valuable in the dressing of him. He was disgruntled. He foresaw that he would have to resort to bribery.

Sir William wanted no word of the duel to get out. The outcome of the affair of honor rasped against his pride, but more importantly, it was in his best interest to keep silent. Lord Ogden's cold, ruthless demeanor had engendered a chilled terror in him. He had complete faith in that gentleman's keeping of his word; his lordship would hunt him down and whip him if there was one whisper of scandal impugning Lady Ogden's fair name. Sir William writhed inside. The possibility of himself, one who enjoyed applying the crop to others for sexual release, being made the object of a public thrashing...It would not – *could not!* – be borne by one of his stamp.

Sir William made the decision to rusticate at one of the less popular watering places. After all, such obscure destinations existed for the recuperation of the infirm. It sounded just the thing for someone in his weakened state.

After the gentlemen had enjoyed a hearty breakfast, Rev. Major Ledger and Mr. Kelton took their friendly leave of Sir Edward, but Lord Ogden requested a private word with his host. Sir Edward was puzzled and perturbed by the viscount's suddenly grim visage, but he was very willing to acquiesce and ushered his childhood friend into his cozy study. After several minutes behind the closed door, the two gentlemen emerged and Lord Ogden finally took his leave.

The front door was scarcely shut behind the viscount before Sir Edward bounded up the two flights of stairs to his wife's dressing room. Lady Thane was surprised to see him, but after taking one look at her husband's face, she quietly dismissed her dresser. "What is it, Ned?"

Sir Edward impatiently pushed back the heavy lock of hair that always fell forward over his broad forehead. "I have just come from an uncomfortable interview with our neighbor."

"Are you speaking of Lord Ogden?"

Sir Edward snorted. "Lord Ogden! Yes, indeed, for he was every inch on his high ropes, let me tell you! No, that is unjust. Vincent didn't nab the rust, but he must have been the devil of a fellow when he was a major, for I certainly felt much like a callow subaltern called to book."

"I don't understand."

"He wished to speak to me about last night, when Lady Ogden and Mrs. Merriweather took offense at something my sister-in-law said to them and then left with Mrs. Dalton in such a bang. I still cannot believe that Mariah could have so insulted Lady Ogden! Vincent must have been mistaken." Sir Edward saw that his wife's expression had altered. "But what's this? What do you know that I don't, my dear love?"

Lady Thane sighed. "I overheard what was said, Ned, and it is too true! After our guests had left, I taxed our sister-in-law over her role in what had happened, but she was unrepentant. She was cruel, Ned. She told Lady Ogden all the worst town gossip about Henry Ogden and that set. She'd already revealed, on a previous occasion, that the late viscount had a mistress in keeping, but last night she repeated a horrid rumor to her ladyship's face that the woman had borne the viscount's by-blow."

Sir Edward's face reflected amazement, then reddened. "Vincent said that my sister-in-law had offended in an unpardonable fashion, but he did not tell me the particulars. I'm glad he was gentleman enough not to have done so! What a malicious thing to say! How could Mariah have behaved so badly?"

Lady Thane said quietly, "My sister-in-law never liked Charlotte. Whenever she visited her cousins, the Collings, she was often cruel and cutting with her words. She taunted Charlotte without mercy over her unfortunate situation, most particularly at the time of her mother's death."

Sir Edward was appalled. "My word! We all knew one another. My brother is wed to Augusta Collings. Yet I had no notion of this history. Why did I never know it?"

"Why should you? Mariah naturally did not advertise her cruelties. Poor Augusta, that her brother should have wed her! I never knew the whole, only what I saw and heard myself, and what confidences that were told to me by Charlotte." Lady Thane made a small, helpless gesture.

"We were such fast friends as girls. I had hoped to re-establish that comfortable relationship."

"It's a wonder Delincourt is on terms with us at all," responded Sir Edward angrily. He fell silent, his thick brows drawing down. After a minute or two, he added quietly but in a harsh timbre, "I was glad when Henry Ogden died and Vincent came into the title. I felt certain of being on good footing with all of my neighbors at last. Now, my sister-in-law has put all the good at risk with her viperous tongue." He looked down at his wife with troubled eyes. "Has Mariah ever ill-used you, my dearest?"

Lady Thane dropped her gaze. "She is our sister-in-law." She felt a strong, warm hand laid upon her shoulder and the gentle squeeze of his fingers. She looked up to meet her husband's contrite gaze. Sir Edward said, "I am sorry. You will not be asked to bear such bad company any more. I shall see to it."

Sir Edward was a man of his word and he did not put off the unpleasant task. He immediately returned downstairs. Before he entered his study, he turned to his butler and demanded to see Mrs. Collings downstairs at once. He rolled a choleric eye, for he knew his sister-in-law very well. "And if Mrs. Collings is so foolish as to put me off because she has not yet finished her toilet, pray tell her that I will drag her downstairs in her wrapper, which will very much damage her dignity!"

In a very short time, Mrs. Collings swept into the study. "What is this summons, sir?" she asked irritably.

The door was shut by a grim-faced Sir Edward with something of a snap, and from behind it rose and fell a shouting match, which garnered much interest from the butler and footmen stationed in the hall.

The door was opened with a swift jerk and a red-faced Mrs. Collings emerged in a flurry of skirts. "I will be glad – glad, I say! – to go back to town! Your brother and my sister-in-law do not treat me so ill as you! I will pack my things at once!"

"And there you will remain, if they can stand you," roared Sir Edward at his sister-in-law's retreating back as she hurried up the stairs. He turned to his butler. Uncharacteristic wrath crackled in his voice. "Have the carriage made ready. Mrs. Collings will be departing for London as soon as her trunks can be brought down! The lady will not be returning – ever!"

The word spread swiftly through the house. Sir Edwards, that easy-going gentleman, had rung a rare peal over his sister-in-law's head and she, being of uncertain temper and sharp-tongued, had pushed him too far. Sir Edward had banished Mrs. Collings permanently from Thane Hall.

Lady Thane shed a few glad tears, dried her eyes, and serenely went along the passage to wish her terrible sister-in-law a safe trip.

41

Mr. Digsby arrived from London. The solicitor brought with him the documents concerning the financial support for the viscountess, which his lordship had requested. Lord Ogden read over the terms set out in the solicitor's fine copperplate and was pleased. The document conveyed exactly what he had wanted, that Lady Ogden would have received a respectable stipend regardless of the birth of a posthumous heir. It would not be an unusual gesture, whereas making allocation solely for a posthumous birthing might appear suspect. This must surely put to rout any speculation that his sole intent was to provide support for his own child, he thought. "You have two copies ready for signature, one for me and one for Lady Ogden?"

"Yes, my lord."

"Very good. Then I shall send for her ladyship." The viscount pulled on the bell-pull and when a footman entered the study, he related his request. The footman bowed and withdrew, shutting the door again.

Lord Ogden walked to the window, clasping his hands behind his back. He looked out onto the garden, noting that the well-tended beds were in full bloom. He smiled, anticipating her ladyship's gratitude towards him. He spoke over his shoulder. "I should like you to explain the details to Lady Ogden."

"Certainly, my lord."

Minutes later, her ladyship entered with a soft brush of skirt across the carpet. Lord Ogden turned. He watched her approach, taking in her appearance with appreciation, liking her in the deep lilac daygown. He had taken note that she had put off her blacks in favor of the more becoming, subdued hues of half-mourning and he approved. Her ladyship greeted the solicitor and seated herself in one of the wingchairs facing the heavy mahogany desk, looking curious over the unexpected meeting.

Lord Ogden remained standing at the window. It struck him that they had done this before. It had begun this way in very similar circumstances, but on a cold winter's day. So much had happened since that day, he reflected, so much had changed. Lady Ogden seemed to have a softer look in her eyes whenever she looked at him. He thought about the special license that was locked in his desk. With deep satisfaction, he contemplated the future. It appeared incredibly bright to him.

"I have here two identical documents, which Lord Ogden wished me to draft some months ago. Before I read the whole, I shall touch on the most pertinent points before us today. An annuity of L2,000 if the viscountess is delivered of a healthy child, an annuity of L1,000 if she is delivered of a stillborn or suffers an early loss of the babe." Mr. Digsby proceeded to read the brief paragraphs and when he was done, he cleared his throat. "If I might have your signatures, my lord, my lady?"

Mr. Digsby waited until the documents had been signed. He sanded the sheets and handed a copy to each party. The solicitor gave a prim smile. "I am glad this amicable business is concluded, my lord. Is there any other way I may be of service?"

"No, Digsby. I believe that will be all for the moment."

"Then with your permission, my lord, I shall withdraw."

The viscount nodded, but he barely glanced the man's way as the solicitor bowed and walked to the door. His gaze was settled on her ladyship, whose tension-filled figure had captured his attention for some minutes. She had listened quietly to Mr. Digby's explanation, her hands clasped lightly in her lap; but of a sudden, she had leaned forward, her lips slightly parting, while her eyes had remained intently fixed on the solicitor. When bid to sign after himself, she had risen gracefully from her chair, stepped forward, and silently taken up the pen to place her signature on the documents. He had no notion what had so riveted her attention, but he felt a prickle of unease.

The door closed behind the solicitor. Lady Ogden whirled on the viscount. She was pale with anger. Her green eyes flashed and her fists clenched at her sides. "You cozened me! When I came to you – begged you! You could have told me then what you intended."

Lord Ogden was stunned by her fury. He could not understand it. His uppermost concern had been to protect her reputation from gossip. He pointed up the purity of his intent. "I thought to shield you from ill-wishers like Mrs. Collings."

"What do I care for that? I care only that you *tricked* me!" She nearly choked on the word, her frame shaking from the galling knowledge. "My God, what a fool I was! What a fool I've been! All these months, letting you bed me! And for what? A chimera wrought out of my fearful imagination! Well, no more, my lord! No more!"

Lord Ogden stared, disbelieving, at her ladyship's pale, set face. Pain lanced through him. He instinctively struck out, speaking harshly. "You possessed all my love, Charlotte. But instead of accepting an honest man's heart, you chose pecuniary gain. Then you made the devil's own pact to secure your comfort. So be it! You will continue to yield to my embraces! The bargain is not satisfied until your confinement. Then you will bear my child! Not Henry's get, but *mine*!"

Lady Ogden whitened. She made an angry, incoherent exclamation. "Cruel, cruel! How can you reproach me in such a way? How you must despise me!"

"*Despise you?* You do not know the half of my feelings!" The viscount stopped short and clenched his jaw. He feared in the white-heat of his anger, he might betray more than he wished. *She cannot know – not now! – what I feel for her. It would be a weapon in her hands.* His lips felt stiff as he forced calm upon himself. "Make no mistake, my lady. It *will* be my child!"

Lady Ogden gave a scornful laugh. "Whoever else's child would it be, my lord? Do you suspect me of taking another lover to my bed? Sir William, perhaps?"

The viscount stood facing her, his fists involuntarily clenching. The very suggestion that she could lay with anyone beside himself inflamed his brain. The rapid rise and fall of his chest emphasized his wrath. "I should strike you for those words. Your insolence is intolerable!"

Her eyes dilated. She caught her breath. *"Oh, dear God!"* She shrank back from him as she uttered the whispered prayer. A hand fluttered up to the column of her slender white throat. Her other hand rose in a warding-off gesture.

Of a sudden, he had a vivid recollection of a livid bruise staining one delicate cheek. His cousin had hit her. She had confirmed it had not been the first time. Ugly certainty slammed into him. *And this is what she thinks of me!* In that moment, he hated her. Impotence was like bile in his throat. *"Damn you!"*

Lord Ogden turned on his heel. He strode to the door and wrenched it open. He exited, slamming shut the door behind him.

Lady Ogden dropped down onto a chair. Her head swam with a maelstrom of emotion. The rapid thudding of her heart made her breathing labored. At what she took to be his lordship's cruel reminder of her miscarriages, an ache of anguish had blossomed under her breastbone. She had wanted to wound him and it was at his pride that she struck. It had been a terrible mistake. She felt sick. She hastily pulled out her handkerchief and pressed it to her lips. *I shouldn't have...fool, fool!* He had looked murderous. Through his eyes – glaring hotly at her through his eyes – was her late husband, the brutish man who had struck her in the face and tried to force himself on her that last fateful night.

When Lady Ogden recovered some of her equilibrium, she did what any rational woman in her position would do. She fled upstairs to the safety of her own apartment, the parchment crushed tightly in her hand. The mistake she had made in how she had confronted the viscount...she shuddered. She did not wish to be discovered by her aunt or Mrs. Dalton in such an agitated state. She didn't want to be forced to search for explanations, explanations that couldn't be made.

In the privacy of her sitting room, she slowly read the terms of the document to be certain she perfectly understood them. The base bargain she had struck need not have existed, it was true; but the rest of their pact had taken on a better form, having been underpinned by a legal document. *A barter, indeed. My virtue for my future,* she mocked herself, not for the first time. The smallest annuity, which was to have been hers regardless of the birthing of an heir, she brushed aside as the irrelevancy it was. She had been shocked, yes, and felt horribly betrayed to learn of his lordship's duplicity. However, matters had moved far beyond that point. She was breeding. She tasted fresh bitterness. The heir presumptive had obviously gambled that he could bed her with impunity, satisfying his carnal lusts, without forfeiting Delincourt; but, he might yet be dispossessed, and by his own seed. The fierce irony was not lost on her. A wild laugh, ending on a sob, broke from her. "I must pin all my hopes on the largest prize!"

The significance of being in possession of such a remarkable legal instrument was not lost on her. It bore Lord Ogden's firm, scrawling signature as well as her own. His lordship could not go back on the terms even if he wished to do so. *Two thousand per annum!* It was the attainment of a long-held dream, that guarantee of financial security for herself and her aunt, yet somehow, she tasted only ashes. She folded the parchment and locked it away in her dressing-case.

Mrs. Merriweather was not unnaturally curious about the solicitor's visit and why her niece had been closeted with the viscount and his man of business. After Mrs. Dalton went off to write her weekly letters, she taxed her niece about it. "What has happened, Charlotte?"

"It's easily explained, aunt," said Lady Ogden shortly. She was still upset over the muddle of her life. Simmering anger colored her reply. "His lordship had documents drawn up which required his signature and my own."

Mrs. Merriweather was startled. "My dear! Has this to do with an annum for your support?"

Lady Ogden gave an embittered laugh. "Yes, indeed! I have been awarded an annum of L750, regardless of whether I produce a posthumous child by the end of my mourning."

There was a brief silence as Mrs. Merriweather regarded her niece with puzzlement. "I don't understand. The viscount has thought better, then, of his initial refusal to add to your support? I thought there was no provision made for that circumstance."

"Why, it is understandable enough, ma'am. His lordship meant to offer support to me before we struck our infamous bargain. I need not have prostituted myself at all!"

Mrs. Merriweather winced and her countenance crumpled. "Oh, Charlotte!".

Lady Ogden was at once ashamed. Her unrestrained outburst had visibly distressed her aunt. "Forgive me, aunt. I should not have spoken so frankly. I must tell you the other terms, which are really quite generous! I shall have L2000 with the birth of live issue."

She had the satisfaction of seeing the older lady's face lighten. "Charlotte! I'm so pleased for you! Such wonderful news! An annum of L2000!" Mrs. Merriweather marveled over it. "Why, it's a veritable fortune! I'm persuaded we shall be very comfortable." Her face was lit by a beaming smile. "You see, it has all turned out for the better, after all!"

Lady Ogden gave a half-choked laugh. A strange despair fell over her spirit. "Yes, indeed!"

Lord Ogden stalked up and down the length of gallery. His swift progress carried him in and out of rectangular patches of sunlight. He suddenly swung aside to one of the tall windows and lifting his hand to seize hold of the heavy drapery at one side. His speeding reflections were not happy.

Five years ago, he had failed to make a place in her heart. His precipitate offer had flustered her. She had refused him, displaying considerable agitation, and sent him away, saying that she would see him again the following day. He'd returned in hopes that his renewed declaration would persuade her. But she had again refused him. She had stood firm against all of his impassioned importunities, even his plea that he might be allowed to write to her. What he had not known then, but knew now, was that she had received a declaration from his cousin.

She had not loved his cousin, but she had wed Henry anyway.

In his saner moments, he'd hoped that his devil's pact would give him the time he hadn't had before, that by binding her to him physically, he could make a place in her heart. He'd hoped to persuade her to take him to husband. However, as he had stared at the fury in her face and heard the scornful, bitter quality of her voice, he had finally realized that she would never accept him, on any terms.

He resolutely turned away from the window. He was also pivoting away from the gloom of his ruminations and the dejection of his spirits. "Enough. It is enough."

42

Three horrible days passed. An uncomfortable, adversarial rift existed between Lady Ogden and the viscount. Their easy exchanges had been blighted. A chill civility was maintained, but in actuality, they scarcely spoke to one another unless obligated to by their company. It became an agony to Lady Ogden. She was deeply unhappy and shed a few secret tears. She came to dread being in the same room with the viscount, her overwrought nerves sensitive to what she felt was the ominous atmosphere. If he looked at her, it was with a terrible light in his dark eyes.

Mrs. Merriweather and Mrs. Dalton finally began to notice the undercurrents of hostility. "Why, what is the matter with Lord Ogden?" asked Mrs. Merriweather.

"I think my brother and Charlotte have quarreled," said Mrs. Dalton shrewdly.

"Is that true, my dear?"

"Pray don't concern yourselves." Under pressure, Lady Ogden admitted only to a tiresome quarrel but not to any particulars. She did not air her distressed conviction that the viscount now found her presence intolerable.

On the third eventide, Rev. Major Ledger dined at Delincourt, which was still his pleasant habit whenever his duties allowed. Lady Ogden felt an inordinate relief. The gentleman's company was always agreeable and that evening the more so since the viscount seemed peculiarly preoccupied despite his old comrade-in-arms' cheerful presence. Lady Ogden was apprehensive; she wondered uneasily what weighty thoughts afflicted his lordship. His lordship's brooding expression was forbidding.

Over coffee, Lord Ogden announced that in two days' time, he would be setting out on a tour of inspection, accompanied by his land steward. "Stockley has naturally given me reports, but I wish to see the other properties for myself."

"Well! I must say I am astonished. Should I take this in bad part, my lord? I have been here not above a month and already you are fleeing!" said Mrs. Dalton with teasing reproof.

Lord Ogden shook his head, smiling fondly at his sister. "My decision does not reflect upon you, I assure you."

Lady Ogden cast a troubled glance at the viscount, but she said nothing. She had a very good notion why his lordship had made so sudden a decision. It had everything to do with their ugly, blazing row. His remark cut like a dagger, though she had no way of knowing if that had been his intention. Sudden misery curled through her. *I have infuriated him. He cannot bear to be near me.*

Mrs. Merriweather was not so reticent as her niece. "Why, here is Rev. Major Ledger just returned to us from his most recent round of duties. He must surely think it extraordinary of you to leave so precipitously!"

"On the contrary, I think nothing of it at all. These great men, you know! His lordship was always such a restive, impulsive fellow," said Rev. Major Ledger, lurking amusement in his eyes. With a vein of light mockery, he added, "Let him go and shake out his fidgets!"

Lord Ogden discerned in his friend's gaze a knowing expression. A reluctant smile curved his lips. "Have I affronted you, Arthur? Do you wish to go with me in Stockley's stead? But say the word!"

"No, no, my lord. You will be too caught up in your personal business to be good company," said Rev. Major Ledger, shaking his head.

Lord Ogden cracked a rueful laugh. "You are very right! Very well, then. I shall take Stockley. Grimshaw comes, too, of course." The significance of what he had said was not lost on the company. All looked at him with varying degrees of surprise, but Lady Ogden was more astonished than the others. Since the viscount was taking his valet, it meant a lengthy absence. She was dismayed that the quarrel would have such a bad result.

"Oh, Vincent, no!" exclaimed Mrs. Dalton. Rev. Major Ledger raised one eyebrow, but he did not say anything. He merely looked thoughtful. Mrs. Merriweather asked, "But how long will you be gone, my lord?"

"I don't know, ma'am. I cannot say. A fortnight, possibly more." All the while, Lord Ogden was very aware of the silent lady who sat nearby. She had not uttered a word since he had declared his intention. He felt forced to acknowledge her presence. "Lady Ogden, I trust that you are not as dismayed as my sister and Mrs. Merriweather by my decision?"

"Of course not, my lord," she said composedly. "I understand that you have put off this business for some time."

The viscount bowed. He was not high-minded enough to resist a little dig at her; they both knew why he had delayed so long at Delincourt. With biting irony, he said, "Quite so." A slight flush sprang into her cheeks. He saw it at once and felt ashamed of himself for baiting her, especially in company. *Badly done, Vincent. Badly done.* He had not gotten over the disastrous interview, but he would not allow his exacerbated feelings to excuse his reprehensible conduct. He turned away to address a jesting remark to Rev. Major Ledger.

Stricken, Lady Ogden did not know where to look. She already knew, beyond a shadow of doubt, that his lordship was still furious with her; his smoldering demeanor and subsequent actions had made it plain. She also had been consumed with anger. She had struck out to wound. But she was haunted by regrets. Their heated discord had left a vast breach between them. Since then, he had not visited her bedchamber and the dreadful significance of that had not escaped her.

Despite the ill-feeling between them, it had nevertheless surprised her when the viscount did not come to her chamber. Even when they did not indulge in carnal congress, he seemed to like to sleep with her in the same bed. When he did not come to her chamber the next night either, she was astonished. She had jumped to an unwelcome correlation.

All these months, letting you bed me. Well, no more, my lord! No more!

She had hurled the terrible words at him, but she had not thought he would pay heed to them. She had assumed the duality of her life would remain unchanged. What passed in the realm of the night, in her bedchamber, was entirely separate from the conventional turn of the day.

She had been confident of his insatiable, dark desire for her. She had anticipated a ferocious, lusty assault launched against her puny defenses. *He enjoys being in my bed too well to stay away.*

Yet a third night had passed, alone in her cold bed. Another sleepless night, one in which she had dampened her pillow with hot tears. The viscount had not come, and her one certainty about their unseemly relationship had been shaken from its moorings.

Lord Ogden's lengthy tour meant an even longer absence from her bed. She did not know what to make of it; her own conflicted feelings upset her. Not for the first time, she admitted she did not have the key to the understanding of him. Worse, she no longer understood herself. Though she was aware of a bruising about her heart, she would not listen too closely to what it was saying to her.

The day before Lord Ogden was to leave on his journey, Rev. Major Ledger called at Delincourt and requested a private interview with his lordship. The viscount rather thought he knew what his friend had come about, but he would wait for Rev. Major Ledger to offer explanation.

"Send him in, Somerset." Lord Ogden folded a letter and pressed his signet into a drip of hot wax to seal it. When Rev. Major Ledger was shown into the ground-floor study, he rose to his feet. "Arthur!" He rounded the desk and strode forward to shake hands. "I'm glad you've come."

"I could not let you go without speaking with you," said Rev. Major Ledger, smiling.

The viscount addressed the butler. "Somerset, some of the best brandy, if you please."

"Very good, my lord." The butler stepped back and pulled the door shut.

Lord Ogden gestured toward the wingback chairs angled in front of the fireplace. It was August and no fire burned behind the iron grate. Instead, the long windows had been opened and fresh air eddied into the room. "Pray be seated, my dear fellow." He heard the door open again and turned. "Ah, Somerset, there you are! Thank you, that will be all. Arthur, will you take brandy?"

"If you will join me."

"Of course." Lord Ogden poured brandy for each of them. He gave a glass to his friend and took the other wingback chair. Lord Ogden sat at his ease, warming the wineglass between his hands. Then he slowly sipped the brandy. He was content to let his friend speak his mind in his own good time.

After tasting his own brandy, Rev. Major Ledger sat aside his wineglass on the small table situated near his elbow. He looked over at the viscount and with unusual diffidence cleared his throat. "You must wonder why I've asked for this interview, my lord."

"Oh, well, if you are going to 'my lord' me this and 'my lord' me that, then I cannot promise to hear you out," said Lord Ogden, covering a false yawn with his hand.

Rev. Major Ledger glowered at him. "Damn your eyes, Vincent! You were always a trying fellow, at best."

"That's much better," approved Lord Ogden, grinning at him.

Rev. Major Ledger cleared the annoyance out of his expression. He reverted again to his formal manner and uttered his much-practiced petition. "During these last weeks, I have come to appreciate the manifold qualities possessed by Mrs. Dalton. She is a lady of whom no praise can be too high. I request your permission to pay my addresses to your sister, my lord."

Lord Ogden's brows flew up. He eyed his companion. "Well, I can't say that I am surprised! Though I do find your declaration to be peculiarly bloodless. What am I to make of that, sir?"

Rev. Major Ledger's correct demeanor crumbled. In quite another voice, he said with quiet intensity, "I love her, Vincent. I wish to make her my wife."

Lord Ogden smiled. "Ah, much better! Now you sound like a sensible fellow. Have you spoken to Amarys?"

"Of course not! What a forward fellow I would be if I did not apply to you first. You are the head of your family and Mrs. Dalton's brother."

"As the lady's brother and your very close friend, I suggest that you not waste any more of my time and at once go in search her." Lord Ogden's smile deepened. "She was walking in the shrubberies not ten minutes ago."

Rev. Major Ledger's eyes flickered at the nearest window. "Was she, indeed? Then I shall instantly take my leave of you."

The gentlemen stood up, sharing a grin. They grasped tight one another's hands. Lord Ogden expressed his sincere sentiments. "I already consider you to be my brother. I shall be glad to call you such in truth."

"Thank you, Vincent," said Rev. Major Ledger with equal sincerity and some emotion. He bowed and left the room with a quick, halting step.

Lord Ogden went to a window overlooking the gardens and waited. Within a short time, he witnessed the meeting between Rev. Major Ledger and his sister. They exchanged a few words. Rev. Major Ledger raised one of his sister's hands to his lips and then the pair walked off together, arm in arm, and smiling. Lord Ogden was pleased. "I wish you all of the happiness which you both so richly deserve."

The door opened and Lord Ogden turned. Somerset entered the study to inform his lordship that Mr. Kelton had come to call. Lord Ogden felt an expansive *bonhomie* toward his fellow man. "Capital! Send in Mr. Kelton at once."

"Yes, my lord."

Lord Ogden warmly greeted his caller and invited Mr. Kelton to sit down. He turned to the brandy decanter and poured a measure into a glass. "I hope you will join me in a brandy, sir."

Mr. Kelton bowed his acquiescence before he took a chair. "Thank you, my lord. A glass will not come amiss. It's a day for celebration."

"Indeed, it is," murmured Lord Ogden, again glancing out the nearest window. At the sight of his old comrade-in-arms and his sister, caught up in embrace, a smile lit his face. He handed the wineglass to his visitor before also sitting down. He observed the gentleman's jovial expression. "What is it you are celebrating, Mr. Kelton?"

After an appreciative taste of the brandy and bestowing a compliment on it, Mr. Kelton swiftly explained what was behind his genial visit. "Sir Martin has sold the Grange to me at last, my lord! I'm to be a permanent neighbor to Delincourt Manor."

Lord Ogden was genuinely pleased. "I'm glad to hear it, Kelton! Your pleasant society will be an advantage to all the county."

Mr. Kelton reddened with pleasure. "I thank you, my lord. That's most kind of you, indeed it is!" He tossed off the last swallow of brandy and regretfully put down the empty glass. "There is only one cloud to my happiness and that's why I have called upon you. I hope that Lady Ogden will not take the news too amiss. It must surely cause her ladyship some dismay that her family home has gone to me. I'm not a great gentleman, after all."

Lord Ogden flashed a smile. "I don't think it, Kelton. Her ladyship is a practical female. She will think it splendid that a good man has taken over the management of the Grange." Lord Ogden set down his wineglass. He stood up and gestured at the closed door. "Come! You will see that I speak the truth when you make your greetings to Lady Ogden."

Mr. Kelton puffed out his cheeks as he got to his feet. He bowed, somewhat at a loss to express his utter gratification. He said gruffly, "Very good of you to say so, my lord. But I shall not stay, not today, for I have an appointment. Indeed, my detour to Delincourt will leave me pressed for time. I only stopped to give you the news. I must be off now."

"I'm glad you did come. I might have missed you otherwise." Lord Ogden accompanied his visitor from the study and waited while the gentleman was handed his hat and crop by the footman. Then he walked with Mr. Kelton out of the front door, one hand resting in a friendly way on the other's shoulder, saying, "I am setting out for a tour of my holdings with my steward. I'm wishful to see what state they are in and what must be done to bring them into shape."

"Ah, indeed, my lord?" Mr. Kelton's horse was tethered at the front post. The stocky gentleman trod down the shallow steps and loosed the rein. Mr. Kelton mounted his horse and looked down at his lordship. "When you return, I hope you will share anything you believe might be of interest to me. I have enjoyed our past conversations."

"I shall do so, most assuredly. I've also derived much from our happy association, Kelton." Mr. Kelton raised the tip of his crop to the brim of his hat in acknowledgement, setting heel to his mount. Lord Ogden raised a hand in farewell before turning and going back inside.

Rev. Major Ledger and Mrs. Dalton eventually emerged from the shrubberies and together sought out the rest of the occupants of

Delincourt. Lady Ogden could see at a glance that something of moment had happened and though she guessed what it was, she waited with baited breath for the announcement.

"Mrs. Dalton has accepted my suit. We are to be wed," said Rev. Major Ledger. He appeared somewhat dazed by his good fortune. Mrs. Dalton softly laughed and her fine eyes shone like stars.

"Oh, I'm so glad!" exclaimed Lady Ogden, her eyes glimmering with sudden tears. Emotion caught at her throat. It astonished her and she told herself that it was only because she was so happy. She moved forward and embraced her friend. "My dearest Amarys!"

"Well! A wedding! How perfectly wonderful," said Mrs. Merriweather. She beamed a smile at the young couple. "I'm very happy for you, sir, very happy indeed!"

"Thank you, ma'am."

Lord Ogden flashed a grin as he took his sister's hands in a gentle hold and leaned forward to kiss her on one blushing cheek. "I couldn't be more pleased, Amarys. I wish you and Arthur much happiness."

In her turn, Lady Ogden congratulated the newly betrothed couple. A sad reflection crossed her mind, that at least one party would have a joyful future. She could not see much chance of it for herself. Her relationship with the viscount was one of dishonor and expediency. There could not be a felicitous conclusion. *He will cast me off in favor of a new mistress. And one day, he will wed a virtuous lady. After our affair, I must count myself fortunate to retain a shred of reputation. If I ever wed again* – but here, her depressing thoughts stumbled to a halt.

Lord Ogden was gone for a fortnight. Upon his return, he expressed himself well pleased with the findings of his journey. "Stockley did as well as might be expected with what narrow authority he was granted by my cousin. I believe two of the properties can be brought into better production so that they will be self-sustaining, making it possible to retain them and within a few short years retire the mortgages. Some of the other minor properties we are agreed will not be income-producing without a heavy infusion of capital. I shall direct Digsby to either sell them or find a renter for them, against such time when we must re-assess what needs to be done."

"That's very good news, my lord," said Lady Ogden quietly. The other ladies swiftly added their agreement and the lively conversation covered her close observation of the returned traveler. She drank in the sight of the viscount, his hawkish face, his broad shoulders and lean physique. He appeared weary, though. A deep bracket was formed between his dark brows and his mouth was set tighter than usual. *I have missed him.* She had not realized how much until he was back and it astonished her.

Suddenly, as though he felt her concentrated gaze, his lordship looked directly at her. Her eyes faltered under the intent look in his keen eyes and sudden heat rose to her cheeks. She wondered what were his thoughts, but she was not left long in suspense. When she went upstairs to retire for the night, the viscount followed her example. A half hour after Mills had readied her for bed, a knock sounded on the connecting door between the bedchambers. Lady Ogden started and gave a nervous gasp. Her heart began to beat a little faster. "Enter."

Lord Ogden stepped into the bedchamber. He was still attired in the frock coat and trousers he had worn to dinner. It surprised her, but then she realized, he was not assuming that he could simply return to her bed without some sort of rapprochement. She was sensible of the consideration he was showing her. However, she felt at a disadvantage dressed in her nightclothes and she pulled her wrapper a little closer around her. "Yes, my lord?"

The viscount made short work of breaking down the barriers between himself and his cousin-in-law. She might have declared herself to be done with him and refuse her bed to him, but he would not allow things to end in such a rancorous fashion. "I have uttered things that I regret, ma'am, and for that, I am sorry."

Lady Ogden did not spurn his lordship's overture. She had spent many hours during the viscount's absence in soul-searching questions. She had not been able to answer all of them but enough to know that she wanted to mend the miserable distance between them. "I also was guilty of hasty words, my lord."

Accord was tentatively found and accepted between them.

43

His lordship pleasured her well.

He was tender and thorough, driving her mad with his magician's mouth and hands, before he entered her. The heavy thrusts inside of her frantic, thrumming body pushed her over the edge. She took flight, a breathless agony of wonderous release. When she came back to herself, it was to find that she was cradled on her side in the heated curve of his lean body. His sated shaft was still buried within her, where she throbbed from the aftereffects of his friction. The warmth of his breath stirred her hair. "Sleep, love. It's hours before morning." She dropped at once into dreamless slumber.

At the breaking of dawn, Lady Ogden wakened. She had not consciously felt or heard the viscount leave her bed, yet she had somehow sensed the desertion of his sleekly muscled, naked body. He was returning to his own bedchamber. She pushed herself up and brushed her long locks out of her face. Quickly, she got out of the bed and went towards him, holding out one staying hand. "Vincent? Must you go so soon?"

"You know that I must." Heavy regret weighted his words. He knelt in front of her, placing his hands on her waist to gently pull her forward. He kissed the bare skin of her high, rounded belly. Then he laid his head against her breasts. She cradled his head and threaded her fingers through his crisp, wavy hair. She closed her eyes. It was a sublime moment. The peace of it caught her up, stinging at her eyelids. It was borne in upon her, so gradually that she didn't know when she had finally concluded it, that he was not at all the brute she had once thought him. Everything in his character, in his manner, in his strong sense of responsibility, pointed to the contrary. What had once so harshly taken place between them, that which had cemented their outrageous bargain, was the aberration and not a reflection of the true man.

Regaining his feet, he pulled her into his arms. He kissed her with an ardency that curled her toes. Then he set her aside, gathered up his scattered clothing, and left her. She pulled her nightgown over her head and placed her night cap back on, tying the ribbons under her chin. She returned to her still-warm bed. Her pillow bore his scent and she snuggled into it. She could not return to sleep, however. She could not seem to get comfortable. She tossed and turned for some time before she finally got out of bed. The dawn had given way to full morning. Her wrapper was near at hand and she slipped into it over her nightgown.

Lady Ogden tugged the bell-pull to summon her dresser and paced the bedchamber until she heard the knock on her door. "Come in, Mills!"

The dresser entered the bedchamber. "Was you wanting something, my lady?"

Lady Ogden's brows creased. She felt restless, strange, a nagging pain in her lower back. She hoped a leisurely early-morning ride would work out the discomfiture. "Pray let Cook know that I wish a breakfast tray brought to me. And I'll want my mare in an hour."

The dresser frowned. "My lady, do you think that wise? You're more than seven months gone now. An airing in the gig will be more prudent."

Lady Ogden was impatient of her dresser's overconcern. "I shall not do anything foolish, Mills. Just a light canter."

"But it *is* foolish, my lady! Let me order out the gig."

"Enough, Mills!" snapped Lady Ogden. "I'm fine. Lay out my habit."

"Yes, my lady." The dresser left the bedchamber to do her ladyship's bidding and took the initiative to relay a message of her own. She returned and in silent disapproval, with compressed lips, she set about laying out her ladyship's riding clothes.

An hour later, Lady Ogden went downstairs. The porter opened the front door for her and she stepped out onto the porch, expecting that a groom would have her horse and his own sturdy mount standing ready on the gravel drive. She did not expect to find the viscount also to be waiting in front of the manor. His lordship was dressed in riding clothes and he held the bridle of his gelding in one gloved hand. Lady Ogden tapped her crop against her boot as she walked down the shallow stone steps. She said crossly, "I perceive that Mills exceeded her instructions."

"I don't think so. I'm beholden to your loyal dresser. As the entire household knows, I enjoy riding with you," said Lord Ogden. He gave his rein to the groom and walked over to the side of Lady Ogden's horse. "Allow me to mount you, ma'am."

"Oh, let's get on with it!" Lady Ogden set her foot in his lordship's laced fingers and with his powerful lift went flying up onto the mare's back. She settled into the saddle, gathering her reins. She was vexed with herself. She had been awkward in the mount.

It was Lady Ogden who led the trio at a spanking pace, clattering across the graveled drive before crossing over into the grassy parkland. The groom dropped back and followed at a discrete distance. Lady Ogden was still too cross to indulge in conversation with the viscount, but his lordship seemed content with the silence. After a while, he took the lead and she stared resentfully at his upright back. *He obviously cares nothing for my company. Why did he come?*

Lady Ogden was stricken by a sudden, savage cramping. The fierce pain bowed her over in the saddle, stealing the air from her lungs. When she could draw breath again, she called out. *"Vincent!"*

Lord Ogden checked his mount and slewed round in his saddle. He was alarmed by the twisting of her face and by how she was bent over her horse's withers. "My dear lady! Are you unwell?"

Lady Ogden gritted her teeth. A fresh, pain-washed wave ripped through her lower belly. *No, no, no!* Terror consumed her. *We've ridden only a few miles!* "Get me returned to the house, my lord!"

At a distance, the groom had perceived something was wrong and he galloped up. "My lord! What's to do?"

Lord Ogden ignored the man's alarmed query. The pallid cast of her ladyship's skin, the subtle hastening of her breathing, convinced him at once that her distress was acute and not to be ignored. He reached over and took hold of her slackened reins. "I'm taking you up before me, Charlotte! Do you understand?"

She gave a tight nod.

Lord Ogden leaned over from his saddle and with one strong arm, he snagged her fast. She kicked free of her mount. The mare snorted and shied away, trailing its reins. The groom realized his duty and went after the loose horse.

Lord Ogden heaved her up before him, seating her sideways. The support of his muscular arms on either side held her secure. "Hold tight to me! Don't let go!" She nodded and wound her slim arms around his torso. The viscount kicked the big gelding into motion. She buried her face into his lordship's hard shoulder. The jolting of the galloping horse beneath her accentuated her physical discomfort. She had to bite back more than one cry.

Lord Ogden was sweating. It was one of the most harrowing rides of his life. He did not know what was wrong, but he was certain it was dire. He could hear the tortured sounds that escaped her. He could feel her wracked shudders against him. His heart was thudding in his chest. When at last the manor came into sight, he charged his mount up to the front steps, the horse's hooves spraying gravel. "House! I say, house!"

The noise of his lordship's arrival brought the porter bolting from out of the opened door. The servant's eyes widened. "My lord!" The porter turned, running back through the open entry. *"Mr. Somerset, sir!"*

Lord Ogden got down off of the lathered gelding. He held up his hands, saying peremptorily, "Here, let me help you!" She slid down the horse's shoulder. He caught her with both hands by the waist and supported her for the rest of the way down, but she nearly crumpled when her feet touched the ground. She fell against him, clutching at his coat.

Lord Ogden lifted her into his arms and swung her up against his chest, her long habit skirt spilling over one arm. She looked up into his face, anguish in her eyes, tear-tracks on her ashen face. Fresh alarm lanced through him. He was shouting as he strode up the shallow stone steps and into the main entrance hall. "Send for the physician! Quickly!"

"At once, my lord!" The butler snapped out a series of orders to his minions. "Run, take word to the stable! Send a groom for Dr. Manning. You there, inform Mrs. Tower of her ladyship's indisposition. Porter, take round his lordship's horse!"

Lord Ogden did not hesitate but set foot on the stairs. Striding swiftly, he carried up his precious burden. She was still clutching the front of his coat. The commotion had brought others on the scene. Mrs. Dalton and Mrs. Merriweather had started down and were standing on the landing when Lord Ogden swept past them. The elderly lady followed after him, saying in agitation, "My lord! Was there an accident? Did she take a fall?"

"No, ma'am! I don't know what's wrong!"

Mrs. Dalton was anxious, but she asked no questions. She followed after her brother and Mrs. Merriweather up the last flight of stairs and down the hall. Lady Ogden's woman was waiting at the open threshold of her ladyship's bedchamber. "In here, my lord."

The viscount entered Lady Ogden's bedchamber for the first time through the door from the hall. It didn't strike him then as singular. He merely bore her over to the bed to carefully lay her down. As he lowered her, their gazes clung together. Inchoate emotion thickened his lordship's throat. The poignant, inarticulate communication was broken when the dresser moved forward, forcing him to step back.

Lady Ogden's eyes turned away from him and refocused on her dresser. "Mills! Mills!" It was a plaint from the heart. Tears trickled down her whitened face. "It's the babe!"

Mrs. Merriweather gave a low cry, the back of one hand flying up to cover her trembling lips. Mrs. Dalton put an arm around the elderly lady's shoulders.

Lord Ogden felt as though he sustained a body-blow, depriving him of breath.

"There, there, my lady. Let's have you out of that habit." The dresser briefly turned her head to speak over her shoulder. "You can do no more here, my lord." She looked past Mrs. Merriweather, whose cheeks dripped with tears, to the younger lady. Mrs. Dalton was white-faced but she appeared calm. "Take him away, ma'am."

Mrs. Dalton nodded and curled her fingers over the viscount's rigid arm. "Come away, brother. You are very much in the way. Come, Vincent! You must be sensible! Come away!"

The housekeeper was expected to know about home remedies and basic first aid. Mrs. Tower had at once been summoned by Somerset to attend to her ladyship and she had sailed upstairs in time to endorse Mrs. Dalton's urgent suggestion to the viscount. "Get along with you, milord! There's no call for you to take up the room, tripping up the lot of us. You'll be told when there is something to tell." She entered the bedchamber and shut the door in his lordship's startled, outraged face.

Lord Ogden, his guns spiked, had no alternative but to retreat downstairs. Mrs. Merriweather trailed behind him, twittering anxious speculations and wringing her hands. Mrs. Dalton accompanied her, making soothing noises. Somerset met them at the bottom of the stairs. "My lord, I have taken the liberty of sending for tea. I have also decanted a bottle of your favorite sherry." He gestured at the open door to the drawing-room.

Lord Ogden gave a brief nod. "Thank you, Somerset. That is thoughtful of you." Though suffering from his own anxiety, he was able to feel pity for Mrs. Merriweather's affliction. He turned to the elderly lady standing beside him and held out his arm to her. "Come, Mrs. Merriweather. We shall both do better for some sustaining refreshment."

Mrs. Merriweather nodded, her chin wobbling. "Thank you, my lord."

Mrs. Dalton followed them into the drawing-room, addressing her brother's back. "I could do with a small glass of sherry, I think."

Twenty minutes later, the physician arrived at Delincourt, driving himself in his own gig. He was admitted by the porter and the butler helped him off with his driving coat and took his hat and gloves. Lord Ogden, flanked by the two ladies, emerged into the entry hall. After a brief greeting, Lord Ogden said curtly, "You must go up immediately, Dr. Manning. Her ladyship's dresser and Mrs. Tower are with her." The physician nodded. Carrying his black medical bag, he went quickly upstairs to examine her ladyship.

In the drawing-room, Lord Ogden's nerves were stretched. He had considered himself to be cool-headed under fire, but this was altogether different. The physician's examination seemed to take an inordinate length of time. He waited with scarce-bridled impatience. The precise tick of the mantel clock was a weary repetition in the tense atmosphere. It didn't help that Mrs. Merriweather kept looking at the ormolu clock, and again wondered aloud if it was broken. "For the minute hand has scarcely moved since I last looked at it!"

Lord Ogden muttered a low curse, chafed beyond bearing. "It's not broken, ma'am! As I have repeatedly assured you!"

Casting an anxious glance at her brother, Mrs. Dalton made a determined effort to divert the afflicted lady from making any further irritating remarks. She picked up the teapot again. "Do have some more tea, Mrs. Merriweather. Oh, won't you? Then another biscuit! I really must insist. The cook sent them up especially. They are just the kind you most like!" Mrs. Dalton held the plate of sweets out to the other lady to better coax her.

Mrs. Merriweather tumbled to the lure. She took a biscuit and nibbled on it. After a minute or two, she asked for another cup of tea. "I don't know why it is, but the crumbs keep sticking in my throat."

His lordship stood at the mantel, occasionally using a poker to stab at the burning logs, creating showers of fiery sparks. Now and again, he cast a harassed glance in the direction of the half-open door.

When the physician came downstairs, the butler immediately ushered the professional man into the drawing-room. "Dr. Manning, my lord."

"Dear Dr. Manning! I'm so glad you are here!" exclaimed Mrs. Merriweather, setting down her teacup in haste, rattling it on the saucer. The anxiety on her countenance lightened with hope. "Now we may be comfortable again, I'm persuaded!"

The physician bowed and started on a polite greeting. Lord Ogden waved aside the civility. He put down the iron poker and demanded, "Tell me at once, what is amiss?"

"Lady Ogden has suffered some cramping and bleeding, my lord. But I do not believe her ladyship has lost the child." Mrs. Merriweather was heard to murmur her heartfelt relief. Mrs. Dalton reached over to briefly squeeze her hand, then straightened again in her chair.

The physician glanced at Mrs. Merriweather and he held up a cautionary hand. He directed his next words to the viscount, but he was also addressing the ladies. "However, that misfortune might yet befall her ladyship. Time will tell."

Mrs. Merriweather's countenance fell again into worried lines. "Oh dear, oh dear! I hope it *will* be different this time! Poor, *poor* Charlotte! I do feel for her, for she has already lost two babes. It must positively *prey* on her mind!"

Dr. Manning looked at the viscount. "Perhaps you did not know, my lord, but Lady Ogden has a history of miscarriage."

"We were out riding." Lord Ogden could not bite it back. "Was it that?"

Dr. Manning shook his head. "I can't tell you, my lord. No one knows what causes a woman to fail to carry to term. However, Lady Ogden was not indulging in such exercise when she miscarried in the past, so you must not feel guilty."

Lord Ogden clasped his hands behind his back. All emotion was tightly reined, the tic jumping in his jaw the only outward sign of his inner disquiet. He said crisply, "It's kind of you to say so, doctor. What do you advise for her ladyship?"

"I've told her ladyship to rest and stay off her feet, perhaps for several weeks. When she feels able to do so, Lady Ogden may go about her normal activities." Dr. Manning smiled at the viscount. "I'd recommend that her ladyship forego any vigorous gallops. Once she is recovered, a sedate ride now and again should do no harm. Though I admit, I'd prefer that her ladyship would confine herself to carriage outings."

Lord Ogden inclined his head. The overriding concern he felt for his cousin-in-law's well-being roused his dominant temperament. He was determined to do all in his power to speed her ladyship's recovery. "Lady Ogden will obey your orders to the letter, Dr. Manning. I shall see to it."

The physician was impressed by his lordship's adamant declaration. "May I say, my lord, that your solicitude for her ladyship speaks well of you."

"Lady Ogden is my responsibility," said Lord Ogden tersely.

"My niece is used to being active. Now she is tied to her bed and cannot *do anything!*" said Mrs. Merriweather with fresh distress. "She will be moped to death."

Dr. Manning issued a warning. "Lady Ogden must not be allowed to fall into the megrims. I believe it will be unhealthy for her mental state, given her particular history. You must persuade her to leave her bed and to sit up each day."

Mrs. Dalton stood up and shook out her skirts. "We must take occupation to her ladyship, Mrs. Merriweather."

"Yes, you are quite right," said Mrs. Merriweather, much of the care vanishing from her countenance. She was obviously glad of being given direction. "I shall take my stitchery to her sitting room and keep her company. One of the footmen can bring in her embroidery stand." She frowned suddenly. "It's a dark room for close-work, however. Perhaps instead, Charlotte should be settled on a chaise in the upper drawing-room. Yes, that will be best, I think. Why, we shall be quite merry!"

Mrs. Dalton smiled at the lady's brightening expression. She turned to the physician. "May we go up to see Lady Ogden now? As you have just heard, there are things to arrange."

"Of course, ma'am." The physician bowed as the two ladies left the room. He chuckled. "It appears that Lady Ogden will not lack for care, my lord."

Lord Ogden flickered a smile. "I think you are right." He paid the physician from his purse and held out his hand in farewell. "Thank you, Dr. Manning." When the man bowed and had left him, he clasped his hands behind his back and walked to the window. Frowning, he stood looking out. It had started to rain, a gloomy shower that underscored his inexplicable fear. He was not used to such marked misgivings. It seemed ominous to him, leaving him prey to an uneasiness that he could not shake off.

Upstairs, Lady Ogden was smiling. The sudden invasion of her bedchamber by her aunt and her friend had raised her afflicted spirits. Their cheerful chatter was a welcome relief. She had been awash in melancholia, suffering from apprehension and inchoate fear, her thoughts dwelling on the losses of her babes. "Why, you are so full of plans for me!"

"I shall ask Somerset and Mrs. Tower and Cook to badger you every hour. The management of a well-ordered household cannot be left to chance," said Mrs. Dalton, her solemn tone belied by the teasing light in her eyes.

"Very true! All will go to rack and ruin without my steady hand," said Lady Ogden in some derision. "Somerset will be at the wine, Mrs. Tower will steal the housekeeping money, and poor Cook will burn everything!"

Mrs. Dalton chuckled. "Very good!"

"Poor Charlotte! I know how moped you get!" Mrs. Merriweather leaned forward and patted her niece's hand. She said earnestly, "Rev. Major Ledger must often visit you. It will be good for your soul."

While Lady Ogden was still spluttering with laughter, Mrs. Dalton added her cheerful mite. "When you feel more the thing and the weather permits, my brother must take you driving in the curricle. That will serve to blow out the cobwebs."

"Indeed, it will," agreed Lady Ogden, suddenly yearning for just such an outing, sitting beside the viscount with the fresh air sweeping across her face, absorbing something of his lordship's aura of strength. She would not be so terrified then of what might happen, of the long shadow that her previous history was casting across her mind. *When did I begin to rely on him so?*

"Perhaps Lord Ogden and my niece might also take a turn on the terrace or walk in the gallery," suggested Mrs. Merriweather in a helpful manner.

Laughing, Mrs. Dalton hugged her. "The very thing, ma'am!"

"Shall you have his lordship read to me, too?" asked Lady Ogden, her color a little heightened. She was a little discomposed by all of these plans for herself and the viscount.

Mrs. Merriweather looked surprised. She gently reproved her niece. "Pray don't be nonsensical, Charlotte!"

As gossip so often will, it soon got around the neighborhood that Dr. Manning had been called in to see the viscountess. Several visitors came to call and inquire after Lady Ogden, especially those who had grown to have a closer friendship. Lady Thane was privileged enough to go upstairs and visit with her ladyship in her bedchamber. However, most personages were not so favored and left their cards and kind messages. Rev. Major Ledger was naturally at Delincourt on almost a daily basis and he was often admitted to the lady's private sitting room. His visits appeared to cheer her ladyship. Lord Ogden silently blessed his friend for the enormous good he was doing. After one such visit, he articulated his feelings as he walked outside with Rev. Major Ledger, where the vicar's horse awaited him. He wrung his friend's hand. "Thank you for coming, Arthur. I cannot begin to tell you how grateful I am. Her ladyship goes on better whenever she has talked with you."

"You know I'm ready to do all I can," said Rev. Major Ledger. He did not let go of the viscount's hand, but gripped it tighter. He lowered his voice. "And what of you, old fellow? How are you holding up?"

Lord Ogden's smile flickered. "I wish only for the birth of the child. She will not truly be at ease until then."

Rev. Major Ledger nodded. He gave a final squeeze to the viscount's hand before he turned away to mount his horse.

On a fine day, when the coolness of fall had begun to rustle through the dry, autumn-colored leaves on the trees, Mr. Kelton rode over to Delincourt. He didn't expect to be able to do more than to leave his card, but he was at once shown in to see the viscount.

Lord Ogden greeted the gentleman with outstretched hand. "I'm glad to see you, Kelton. Pray sit down." He waved his visitor to a chair and took one opposite.

"Thank you, my lord." Mr. Kelton settled into the wingback and looked his concern. "I heard in the village that Dr. Manning was sent for some days ago and that her ladyship was taken unwell. I trust Lady Ogden is going along in better frame, my lord?"

"Her ladyship is better, but she is keeping to her private rooms at present. Otherwise, I know that she would have wanted to greet you for herself," said Lord Ogden, smiling at him. "It's kind of you to inquire."

"Not at all, not at all!" Mr. Kelton frowned a little, appearing to be turning over a troubling thought. He nodded to himself and looked again at the viscount. "I had another reason for coming, my lord. My lawyer writes me that Sir Martin has been around to complain. Now the gentleman feels he was cheated when he sold the Grange to me. As you may imagine, I was fair gob-smacked, for I paid a handsome – a very handsome! – price. Indeed, more than I should have, but I wanted the property."

"I'm sorry to hear of this trouble with Sir Martin," said Lord Ogden, his brows knitting. He shot a glance at his visitor. "Do you fear that he will carry his ill-will further?"

"He may try, but he'll catch cold at it," said Mr. Kelton with a snort. "I have directed my lawyer to have nothing further to do with the man, but one cannot take anything for granted. Sir Martin might come to the Grange, thinking that he will bully me instead of my man."

Lord Ogden's thoughts had sped forward and his keen intelligence weighed the likelihoods. He said slowly, "You would not admit him, of course. Sir Martin, being thwarted, might in his frustration turn up here to badger her ladyship."

"That's it, my lord," nodded Mr. Kelton. "I wished to just drop a word."

"Yes, I see. So, you have come to warn me. I do appreciate it, Kelton." He smiled faintly and shook his head. "Let us hope that Sir Martin will not act so foolishly. You are an honorable man, a good neighbor. I trust I may also say you are a friend."

Mr. Kelton puffed out his cheeks. Ruddy color climbed in his face. "Thank you most kindly, my lord. Well, well! Most gratifying, to be sure." With a glance at the mantel clock, he stood up, followed by the viscount. "I must be going. I'm promised to Rev. Major Ledger for tea. A most excellent gentleman. I very much enjoyed the vicar's last sermon. Pray convey my good wishes for a speedy recovery to her ladyship."

"I will certainly do so."

A bulky package arrived at the manor by courier. Lord Ogden glanced at the direction written on the front of it. His sister and Mrs. Merriweather were also in the room and he decided to avoid the teasing, arch comments that were sure to be made to him if he revealed the contents of the package. "Pray put it on my desk, Somerset." The butler bowed and took away the delivery.

The viscount waited until his sister and Mrs. Merriweather had left on a planned errand to the village. Then he carried the small parcel up to the upper drawing-room, where he knew her ladyship to be sitting that afternoon. He had sent away for the special order and he wanted privacy when he gave it to her. He found her situated on a chaise, a large shawl modestly tucked over her legs. Her sewing basket was at her side and in her hands was a piece of fine embroidered linen. He recognized it as a tiny christening dress for her unborn infant. It gave him a feeling that was difficult to assess. He only knew that it warmed him. With a bow, he offered the thick package to his cousin-in-law. "This is for you, madam."

Lady Ogden glanced in surprise at the viscount as she took the parcel. It was unexpectedly heavy and she wondered what could be in it. She used her sewing scissors to cut the strings and she unwrapped the covering of heavy brown paper. Exclaiming in delight, she lifted each of the slim volumes that was revealed. "Why, it's Miss Austen's *Pride and Prejudice*, the complete set!" She looked up, astonished. "My lord! I don't know what to say."

"Say only that you are pleased," he said with his attractive smile. "And I shall be satisfied."

"Yes, I am very pleased! How could it be otherwise? Miss Austen is my favorite author. I knew that her new work had been published in January, of course; but with all that has happened –" Lady Ogden stopped. She thought better about what she had been going to say. *Indeed, much has happened, things that have altered my life.* She said instead, "I have read *Sense and Sensibility* many times since it was published last year in November."

"I discovered as much from your aunt, so I thought you might like a copy of the author's newest endeavor. I wished to relieve the tedium of your convalescence," said Lord Ogden gruffly. He gestured at the books laying across her lap. "I hope the volumes will give you many hours of reading pleasure."

"Thank you, my lord. It was truly an inspired thought on your part," said Lady Ogden. Her face suddenly colored and she dropped her gaze. She added softly, "You are very kind."

Lord Ogden flushed. He bowed and left the upper drawing-room.

44

Just before Michaelmas, Lady Ogden's confinement came upon her. The rise and fall of high-pitched, keening wails coming from her ladyship's bedchamber battered at the viscount's sensibilities whenever he was in his own rooms. *It's my child. She is birthing my child.* The anguished shrieks of Lady Ogden's travails could not be endured and he'd been driven downstairs.

He took haven in the ground-floor study with the admirable intention of going over the expense ledger. Instead, he found himself staring over the desk at the flickering fire. He was too restive to sit for long. He sprang up and began to pace. Soon he wandered over to one of the windows and pushed aside the drape to look outside. His eyes were blind to the oppressive storm clouds and blowing rain. Thunder rumbled and lightening split the sky, but he did not heed any of it, too deep in thoughts that pulled his brows together. After a while, he let the velvet drape fall and returned to his restless pacing.

Lord Ogden had left standing orders that he was to be informed, whatever the hour or his occupation, as soon as anything became known of Lady Ogden's progress. He cast a savage glance at the mantel clock. It's measured ticking exacerbated his temper. "It's bound to drive me mad!" With an oath, he bounded over to the door, wrenched it open, and shouted, "Is there any word?"

A faint, curdling scream originating from upstairs assaulted his ears. He flinched.

He slammed shut the door and resumed his aimless pacing, his hands clenched behind his back. The clock on the mantel inexorably ticked on. He shot it a baleful look. Striding over to the credenza, he opened a decanter and splashed a liberal amount of brandy into a glass. He tossed the brandy back with scarcely a hitch in his breath.

He'd lost count of the wretched hours.

Lord Ogden threw himself into a wingback chair. Rubbing his hands over his face, he felt the sharp stubble on his jaw. He had not been upstairs to his bedchamber to change his attire or shave since her ladyship's labor had begun. He could not bear to be so close to the audible strain of her suffering.

Lady Ogden's labor was not easy. It continued through the black, storm-ridden night into the next day. The viscount's appearance became haggard. His violent repudiation of any sustenance and his refusal to see anyone created concern. Even his lordship's sister was refused entrance. "Vincent? May I come in?" Mrs. Dalton stood at the door, knocking and pleading for some minutes. The door was not opened to her and she did not dare enter after the viscount roared at her to leave.

The bailiff brought the accounts for the year, as was proper since Michaelmas marked the end of harvesting. Somerset took it upon himself to inform his lordship of the bailiff's presence and was told in no uncertain terms what Bartlett could do with the year's accounts. The butler did not demean himself by repeating the viscount's crudity but merely stated that the accounts should be left for his lordship to look over at a later time.

"Beggin' yer pardon, Mr. Somerset. I'll wait a bit." Though Bartlett kicked his heels for some hours in the kitchen, he eventually went away again, morosely shaking his head. It was felt to be a particularly bad indication of the viscount's state of mind that he would not see the bailiff and allow the man to properly discharge his duties. During his short tenure, Lord Ogden had earned a reputation for being rigorously conscientious in performing his responsibilities.

A housemaid voiced what many below-stairs were privately thinking. "Eh, but can ye blame his lordship? A male-child will properly cut him out." She was roundly rebuked by the housekeeper for speaking so pertly of her betters, but no one who heard the housemaid's blunt observation bothered to hide their thoughtful nods.

The upper servants, consisting of Somerset and Mrs. Tower and Lord Ogden's valet, Grimshaw, huddled together in intense conference. His lordship had already spurned the pleas of his sister. Something had to be done. The viscount was not himself. At length, Grimshaw announced he would ride to the vicarage and consult with Rev. Major Ledger, a decision accepted with relief and approbation by the others.

Somerset felt it incumbent upon him to carry the intelligence to Mrs. Merriweather and Mrs. Dalton and he went upstairs to the upper drawing-room, where he could be certain of finding them.

Upon the butler's entrance, the ladies looked up from their close-work, their expressions anxious. "Yes, Somerset, what is it?" asked Mrs. Merriweather quickly.

"I beg pardon for the intrusion. I wished to inform you and Mrs. Dalton that Mr. Grimshaw has taken it upon himself to ride to the vicarage." The butler gave a slight, significant cough. "His lordship might wish to see Rev. Major Ledger."

"The very thing!" exclaimed Mrs. Merriweather, instantly approving. "Surely, it must do the viscount good to see his oldest friend!"

Mrs. Dalton appealed to the butler. "Somerset, you must be able to tell us something! His lordship would not see me, but surely he has spoken to someone?"

"I have been in to take a tea tray, my lady. I shall not repeat what his lordship chose to say to me." Somerset added, his expression wooden, "The viscount threw the laden tray into the corner of the room." Upon the horrified exclamations from the two ladies, the butler bowed and withdrew.

"Oh, it's bad, very bad!" Mrs. Merriweather shook her head, the concern in her face deepening to dismay.

"One might almost say he is unhinged!" exclaimed Mrs. Dalton.

"We mustn't jump to conclusions, my dear. Lord Ogden's title and inheritance are endangered, so perhaps we must excuse his lordship's bad behavior," said Mrs. Merriweather worriedly. "Gentlemen care so much for such things. And rightly so, of course! It's to be hoped that Rev. Major Ledger's visit will prove beneficial."

"Indeed, so we must hope," murmured Mrs. Dalton with a slight crease between her brows. She could not understand her brother's inordinate response to Lady Ogden's labor. Of course, it was only natural that he would be wondering about the inheritance. However, she knew her brother to be level-headed. He had commanded troops in battle. He had survived a forlorn hope. It was therefore puzzling to her that he seemed to have completely lost his mind.

A flurry of activity took place at the manor's entrance. A footman ran out into the downpour to lead the vicar's horse and Mr. Grimshaw's mount round to the stables. The porter slammed the front door, shutting out the blowing rain. Somerset took Rev. Major Ledger's dripping hat and riding crop. The viscount's valet, Grimshaw, who had followed the gentleman inside, helped free him of his splattered greatcoat.

"Where is his lordship? Still in the study?" demanded Rev. Major Ledger, stripping off his wet riding gloves and handing those also to the butler.

Somerset nodded. "He is, sir."

With a quick, halting step, Rev. Major Ledger crossed the main entrance hall. He grasped the brass doorknob, twisted it, opened the door and stepped inside. "Vincent, you bloody madman! You've got all the servants in an uproar. What will you do when it's the birthing of your own heir?"

"– *dear to me.*"

The door was thrust shut, cutting off whatever else the viscount might have said. The porter was digesting the interesting tidbit he had overheard. Grimshaw balefully eyed him. "You'll keep a still tongue, my lad, or I'll break your teeth down your bloody throat."

The porter looked affronted, but he didn't utter a word. Mr. Grimshaw might be a gentleman's gentleman now, but he'd once been a battle-hardened soldier. No doubt Mr. Grimshaw knew something about loosening a man's teeth.

Inside the privacy of the study, the viscount came in for his own rebuke. "Sit down, Vincent. You're making me dizzy walking in circles."

Lord Ogden dropped into a chair. "Then you shouldn't have come," he retorted. Not for the first time, he ran his fingers through his hair.

He dropped his hands and his forearms fell onto the upholstered chair arms. He clasped his hands tight together. Tension had long since settled between his shoulders. He couldn't discipline the apprehensive timbre of his thoughts. Morbid scenarios were running through his brain. By the hour, his inchoate fears had mounted until he was afflicted by tremendous dread. It barely registered on him that his friend was moving about the room.

"Here." A wineglass was thrust under his nose. Lord Ogden straightened and took it. He swallowed most of the wine in a single gulp. The wineglass was pried out of his fingers. "Careful, man! You'll make yourself drunk as a wheelbarrow. When was the last time you ate?"

"I don't know. I don't care. I couldn't choke anything down, in any event."

"Don't be a bloody ass. Making yourself ill isn't going to help her."

At last, Lord Ogden actually focused on his friend. He tried to speak, cleared his throat, tried again, and his somber voice shook. "It's been more than a day. She could die."

The vicar sat down and meditatively swirled his own glass of brandy. "Yes, I've heard childbirth is a dangerous business. I've been about the parish enough to know something of it now. Often there's hemorrhage or childbed fever. The babe could breach or be strangled at birth by the cord."

Rev. Major Ledger's cool voice acted like an acid irritant on the viscount's lacerated nerves. Lord Ogden glared at him. "Shut your bloody mouth! She's not going to die! Not the babe, either!"

"Of course, they're not. So, what is this dramatic turn of yours about?"

Lord Ogden nervously drummed his fingers on the chair arm. He had a good notion of the date the babe should have been born. That was what was plaguing him. He recalled perfectly the very day that he had been informed of her ladyship's quickening. He said abruptly, "Charlotte is before her time."

"Many women are, I believe."

"There must be a reason for it! I've been around livestock much of my life. A mare doesn't drop a foal early without reason and usually it's not a good one." He clenched a hand into a tight fist on the chair arm. "*There must be something wrong with her or the babe.*"

"Vincent, you've got to have some faith."

Like a shot from a cannon, Lord Ogden launched himself back out of the chair and stalked about the room. "I'm going bloody mad!"

"I'd say that's a fair assessment. Now listen to me. No, *listen* to me, damn you!" Rev. Major Ledger was suddenly beside him, grasping his upper arm in a strong grip and yanking him to a standstill. The vicar's gray eyes were fierce. "The way you're acting is going to set tongues wagging, just the kind of suspicious gossip you don't want. Do you think Lady Ogden will thank you for ripping aside the veil of respectability and subjecting her to the censor of the world? *Are* you paying heed to me, Vincent?"

Indeed, he was – his friend's stringent words caught him up, giving him pause. It took all of two seconds, but at last their full meaning penetrated to his suspended reason. He drew his hand down his face. He was appalled at himself. "You're right, of course! Bloody hell, you're right!"

"Good. That's the first sensible thing you've said since I entered this room! Now, you're going to hold onto that glimmer of sanity. I'm going to ring for a cold collation and you're going to eat something, no matter if it chokes you dead."

Lord Ogden was forced into a laugh. "Very well. I put myself into your hands."

Rev. Major Ledger smiled, somewhat ruefully. He let go of the viscount's arm. "Remember you said that, my lord." He limped to the door and opened it. "Somerset! I want you." The butler entered at once; he'd been hovering outside the door in anticipation of just such a summons. Rev. Major Ledger gave short, concise orders. The butler nodded and immediately retreated to carry out the vicar's instructions.

Rev. Major Ledger closed the door. He looked back across the room at his friend. Lord Ogden was again striding back and forth, his hands clasped behind him. His lordship appeared more in control of himself, but his curling hair was unruly and his cravat had been ruthlessly yanked loose. The viscount's dishevelment was completely unlike the fastidious man that Rev. Major Ledger knew so well and he frowned thoughtfully.

When Somerset and a footman entered, bearing laden trays, they quickly placed the platters of meat, a plate of bread and cheese, and the covered dishes on top of the credenza. The butler had also brought in another bottle of wine. He showed the dusty bottle to the gentlemen. "One of the best burgundies, my lord, laid down by your grandfather."

Lord Ogden waved an impatient, dismissive hand. "Yes, yes, thank you, Somerset."

Rev. Major Ledger motioned the butler over and said something in a low voice. Somerset gravely nodded. "Of course, sir. It shall be attended to at once." Without another glance at Lord Ogden or Rev. Major Ledger, the butler and his minion exited.

Lord Ogden grimly attacked the food.

Rev. Major Ledger silently watched him, occasionally pointing out a particularly tender portion of meat or cutting up an apple and handing over the tart pieces. He also kept the viscount's wineglass filled.

Perhaps forty minutes of the clock and Lord Ogden was finished. He noticed that the pounding in his head had receded and the clench of his gut was eased. He had a sense of physical well-being that he hadn't felt in many hours. He narrowed his gaze on his old comrade-in-arms, fully aware that his sulky resentment was stupid. Rev. Major Ledger raised a brow and looked back at him. Lord Ogden said shortly, "Damn your eyes, you were right."

"I'm glad to hear it. My task isn't yet finished, however. My dear fellow, you look as though you've marched quick-time across the Pyrenees! And you reek almost as bad. I told Somerset to send word up to your valet to prepare a bath."

"For God's sake, Arthur!"

Rev. Major Ledger opened the study door and thrust him out. "Up with you, man." Ruthlessly, Rev. Major Ledger drove the grumpy, protesting viscount upstairs to the bedchamber where Grimshaw was waiting with a brass bath filled with hot water. The Rev. Major himself oversaw the bath, recommending that the viscount scrub well between his toes. Lord Ogden threw a sodden, bunched up washcloth at him, which Rev. Major Ledger easily ducked. Inclining his head at the dripping wall, Rev. Major Ledger observed, "Well, I'm glad to see that a bit of manly spirit is still left in you, after all."

"Be damned to you, Arthur," retorted Lord Ogden, quite mildly.

After the bath, Grimshaw shaved the viscount. It wasn't an easy task because Lord Ogden tensed up every time he heard any sound emanating from the direction of her ladyship's bedchamber. The valet finally exclaimed in frustration. "Will you be still, my lord! I've no wish to cut your throat."

Rev. Major Ledger turned half away, his shoulders shaking.

"Oh, you need not hide your laughter at my expense," said Lord Ogden sourly. He rolled his eyes sideways, glaring at his valet. "As you may have observed, I'm already the object of an outrageous disrespect."

Grimshaw had the audacity to make a flourishing bow, the straight razor that was held deftly in his hand sweeping an arc through the air.

"Watch it, man!" exclaimed the viscount, jerking back.

Rev. Major Ledger laughed outright. "I never knew you to run shy of a bit of steel before."

"*Will* you leave off, Arthur?" Lord Ogden turned his fulminating gaze on his valet. "Bloody hell, Grimshaw! You nearly took off my nose! Watch what you're doing!"

"Aye, my lord. Sorry, my lord."

At last, Lord Ogden stood up, freshly shaved and dressed. His hair was neatly brushed. His cravat was impeccable. He lacked only his frock coat and his boots. He looked himself again. However, his dark brows were drawn down across the bridge of his nose and he looked more harassed than pleased.

Rev. Major Ledger got up from where he was sitting. "My work is done," he mocked. "You may bolt back into your hole, my lord."

"Go away, Arthur." Lord Ogden mitigated his brusque tone by holding out his hand. When Rev. Major Ledger took it, he said sincerely, "Thank you for coming."

Rev. Major Ledger squeezed the viscount's hand. Then he limped out of the bedchamber. His halting steps were heard going down the stairs.

The valet addressed his master as he held the viscount's military-cut coat for him. "My lord, Bartlett left the account books."

Lord Ogden slipped his arms into the coat sleeves and waited impatiently for the valet to smooth the coat fabric over the line of his shoulders. He could have shrugged into the coat well enough himself but he was aware that Grimshaw had been anxious for him and it reassured the valet to be able to show such care of his person. "Have the account books sent to me in the ground-floor study. I need some occupation. Have some strong coffee sent to me, as well." He sat down in a chair to pull on his shining black boots.

"Of course, my lord," said Grimshaw with satisfaction.

Downstairs in the entrance hall, the butler helped Rev. Major Ledger on with his damp greatcoat. "It's wonderful how his lordship responded to your presence, sir."

Rev. Major Ledger ruefully laughed. "I didn't offer much in the way of spiritual comfort. I bullied him, Somerset."

"It was just what was needed," said the butler approvingly. He handed over the gentleman's hat and gloves. "A stable boy is holding your horse for you out front, sir."

Rev. Major Ledger sighed and made a wry observation. "Into the rain again! It's much like campaigning, except I shall have a snug fire at the end of it."

The butler permitted himself a prim smile. "Quite so, sir."

From the landing above, a woman's voice called out the vicar's name. Rev. Major Ledger looked up quickly and took a step forward. "Mrs. Dalton!"

Mrs. Dalton rushed down the remaining flight of stairs and swiftly approached him, her skirt fluttering behind her. "I heard that you had come. It was so good of you! You saw my brother?"

Rev. Major Ledger caught the slender hand which she held out to him and bowed. "Yes, I have been with his lordship. He is above-stairs now." He was very aware of the interested observation that was being trained on them by the butler, the footman and the porter. "Let us go into the front parlor, Mrs. Dalton. Then we may speak freely."

"Yes," she agreed. She willingly accompanied him into the front parlor, walking to the center of the room before she turned. He shut the door. Throwing aside his hat and gloves, he approached her. She held out her hands, but instead of taking them, he folded her into his arms. Mrs. Dalton half-laughingly protested, "Your greatcoat is wet!"

He immediately set her aside but slid his hands up her arms to her shoulders. "Forgive me, my dearest! I cannot help myself. If you only knew how I long to make you mine."

She was blushing. "I want it more than anything, too. Just a few days more, my love. Then we will be wed."

Rev. Major Ledger groaned. "It's too long." He framed her face between his hands and thoroughly kissed her. Releasing her, he stepped back. He was breathing rapidly. "I must remember I am a gentleman. It's not the time to indulge in my sentiment."

"No, it isn't," said Mrs. Daltoln, shaking her head, and smiling a little wistfully. She returned to what figured so prominently in her thoughts. "I've been so worried. You must tell me how you found Vincent. His state of mind – he was shut up in the study all day and night! He would not give me leave to speak with him."

Rev. Major Ledger's expression clouded with his own anxiety. He sighed, shaking his head. "You must forgive Vincent. He's in love with her, you know."

Mrs. Dalton nodded. "Yes, so I guessed." She searched his face. "But that's not the full sum of it, is it? Arthur, has my brother said – has he indicated to you –" Under Rev. Major Ledger's clear, unwavering gaze, Mrs. Dalton stumbled to a halt. She was embarrassed by what she wanted to ask, but surely, she could confide her private speculations to her betrothed and be confident of his receptivity. She took a breath and plunged into her wild surmise. "Arthur, is Vincent the father of Charlotte's child?"

Rev. Major Ledger was taken aback. He swiftly recovered and laid a gentle finger across her lips. "We must not speak of it. The child will legally be that of the late viscount."

Mrs. Dalton's eyes widened with astonishment. "Well, upon my word! So, I was correct! I think I'm glad of it, for I did not like my cousin Henry. It will be easier to love my brother's child."

Rev. Major Ledger regarded his love with mixed amusement and curiosity. "Do you not care for the sordidness of it?"

"I'm not so missish. My husband had a mistress, but I quickly got over my heart-burnings."

The startling tidbit from her past lodged in his brain and he really wanted to ask her more. However, Rev. Major Ledger had something of greater import to exercise his mind. It had occurred to him as they spoke and he was beginning to think it might be true. He said slowly, "But how did you know? Surely they did not betray themselves!"

Mrs. Dalton shook her head. "No, not in the way that you mean. However, I saw almost at once how it was. Even though they take such pains to conceal it and, indeed, are often at loggerheads, it became obvious. They love one another and always have done. Then there has been Vincent's recent crazy behavior! I cannot condemn them for giving way to passion after Henry's death. Such nonsense!"

"Then you did not hear any rumors." At the shake of her head, Rev. Major Ledger's gathering concern was put to rest. He had feared the torrid affair had become the subject of servants' gossip and that was how she had come to know of it. Smiling, he caught up her hands. "Such a charming vicar's wife you shall make! Lovely and compassionate!" He placed lingering kisses in the warm palms of her hands, making her fingers curl, and then released her. "Now I must go! We have been closeted together far too long. Come, see me out."

45

Somerset finally brought word that her ladyship had given birth. Lord Ogden felt a slam of dizzying relief. At once, he demanded, "And they are healthy? Lady Ogden and the child?"

"Yes, indeed, my lord."

"Thank God for it." Lord Ogden listened close to a full report from the butler. Her ladyship was brought to bed of a girl. The babe was of a good size and healthy except for some initial trouble with her tiny lungs. His face split into a wide smile. *Michaelmas, Sept.29th, 1813. My daughter.* None would ever know that the infant had actually been born a full three weeks early. As far as the world was concerned, the tiny girl was a full-term babe and legal issue of the late viscount. He lifted the decanter and poured two brandies. He offered one to the butler, whose disciplined face underwent transformation with a surprised, gratified smile. "We have cause for celebration, Somerset."

"Indeed, we do, my lord." The two men, master and servant, clinked glasses and shared the celebratory brandy.

Lord Ogden felt fierce satisfaction. He and his chosen lady had a child. His chest squeezed with a rush of gratitude. *I shall have a care for them always, I swear it before God.*

"Congratulations, my lord." The butler set aside the empty wineglass and made a deep bow. "May I say, on behalf of all the staff, that we are pleased by your lordship's permanent elevation."

Lord Ogden was startled. He realized that the household, too, had anxiously awaited the result of her ladyship's labor. With the birth of a daughter, the important question about his position as heir had finally been settled. Any relief or satisfaction he might otherwise have felt was swallowed up by other emotions. "Thank you, Somerset."

He wanted nothing more than to bound up the stairs to Charlotte's bedchamber and see for himself how she was faring. He wanted to gather her in his arms and kiss her and murmur how much he loved her. He wanted to hold his new daughter. It was with melancholic regret that he set aside the wild wishes. *None of that can be. It would create a very odd appearance. The lady is not my wife.* His restrained emotions threatened to burst their bonds. He feared silence was beyond him. He feared what might proceed from his mouth, that he would give away secrets that were not entirely his own. The ingrained habits of breeding and good manners came to his rescue, however, and he uttered formal, polite words. "Please relay my good wishes and congratulations to her ladyship."

"I shall be happy to do so, my lord." The butler bowed again and walked to the door. Somerset had barely opened it when a footman crossed the threshold and stepped close to whisper into the butler's ear. Somerset asked a low, sharp question. The footman nodded once and hastily retreated.

The butler turned to the viscount, his expression altered in such a way that it alerted his lordship something was wrong. Lord Ogden's heart began to thud. His belly tightened. All of his former agony of apprehension rushed back like the burst of shrapnel overhead. A mighty crack of thunder shook the windowpanes and outside the walls the wind howled. He thought it was fitting of the dreadful moment.

"What is it, Somerset?" demanded Lord Ogden.

The butler's face was etched with worry. "My lord, her ladyship is birthing a second child and it's not going well."

"A second child?" Lord Ogden felt as though he had been plunged into a cold-water nightmare where he could not move or breathe. The ominous spectre of his worst fear was like a gigantic weight upon his chest. He said sharply, "Not going well? What do you mean, Somerset?"

The butler helplessly shook his head. "I'm sorry, my lord."

Lord Ogden clasped his hands tight behind his back. "I do not wish to be disturbed."

"As you wish, my lord."

Lady Ogden was so worn that she no longer cried out but only uttered low, pained moans. The contractions rippled across her belly but little seemed to happen. The physician was worried. Sweat dotted his brow. He didn't say so, but he feared for the mother's life. The others in the room, all women who had some previous experience in birthing, whispered in the background as they went about their business of washing the newborn girl and wrapping her in warm swaddling. Mrs. Tower stood at his elbow and he was glad of the housekeeper's stolid presence.

Finally, a tiny set of wrinkled buttocks presented. "It's a breach," said Dr. Manning grimly. He took up his forceps and attempted as gently as possible to extract the babe. At last, mother and physician together contrived to finish the difficult business. After a cursory examination, the physician handed off the babe to the housekeeper. "It's a stillborn. Now, my lady, you may rest at last."

Lady Ogden gave a deep, tired sigh and her eyelids fluttered. However, she was not allowed to immediately fall into slumber. The women gathered round to help bathe her and dress her in a clean nightgown and to replace the stained bed linens for spotless ones. When Lady Ogden was settled again onto her pillows, she turned her head and fell into an exhausted sleep.

The physician went downstairs to give his report to the viscount. He was astonished at the gentleman's haggard, set expression. But of course, much depended upon this confinement, he reminded himself. "The second infant was a stillborn, my lord. It was a male, less well-formed than the first child. I do not believe, if it had lived, that it would have survived more than a few days."

The viscount nodded. He moved to the window and looked out. He would not show the physician his expression. His voice sounded strained in his ears. "And Lady Ogden? She is well?"

"As well as can be expected, my lord. Her ladyship is worn-out from her labor. She will require care and much bed rest."

"Thank you, sir. You have relieved my mind." A vast, enormous relief cracked open inside of him. The viscount moved to the desk and opened a deep drawer, where he kept his lockbox. With a few short words more, he gave payment to the physician and sent him on his way.

Lord Ogden stood leaning forward with his hands braced on the desk. His head was bowed. His heart thudded heavily in his chest. Wildly divergent emotions surged through him, delighting and paining him by turns. Charlotte and his daughter – joy and thanksgiving. The loss of a son – a surprisingly piercing grief.

In that span of time, a few heartbeats only, it was of little importance to him that a living male would have effectively cut him out of inheriting Delincourt Manor and all else. He had lost a son, as had her ladyship. He tightened his mouth. She at least had the right to a mother's grief, but in the eyes of the world, he had no right to a father's grief. He must hide his feelings, and indeed, must discipline himself to set them aside entirely, but it was not such an easy thing to do. Finally, he could not bear it that there was to be nothing of himself attached to the dead child.

The viscount sat down, dipped his pen in the inkwell, and in his firm, sprawling hand wrote a short note: *The still-born child must bear my cousin's name, of course. I shall take it as a very great favor for the boy to bear my father's name, Titus, as well.* Sanding the sheet, he folded it over twice and sealed it with his signet, pressing it firmly into the wax. Then he requested a footman to deliver the note to her ladyship's dresser with instructions that it was to be given to Lady Ogden at the earliest opportunity.

Lord Ogden heaved a sigh and shook his head hard as though he would empty it of things better not thought. He turned to the year's ledgers which had been left by the bailiff for his inspection. It was a relief to be able to occupy his mind.

Some hours later, Lady Ogden awakened and she was given the viscount's note. It was a short communication, but one which pierced her to the heart. She requested pen and ink from her dresser and wrote a reply. She waited for the ink to dry before she folded the paper. "Mills, bring over the small mirror from my dressing table."

"Yes, my lady." The dresser handed the hand mirror to her mistress and without comment took away the pen and inkwell. Then she busied herself tidying up around the bedchamber, casting a glance now and again at her ladyship.

Lady Ogden peered anxiously into the small hand mirror. She was too pale, but she thought if her hair was brushed and arranged, her appearance would be passable. She dropped the hand mirror to her lap. She must be vain, indeed, to care so much when she knew the viscount did not love her.

Lady Ogden held out the sealed note to her dresser. "See that this is given to his lordship. I have requested the viscount to wait upon me and I wish to be made presentable for his lordship's visit. In a half hour, have the nursemaid bring my daughter to me."

Mills pursed up her lips but she did as her ladyship had asked. It was unusual to have a gentleman who was not a close relation to be invited into a lady's bedchamber, but it was not her place to say so, especially in light of the history between the viscount and her ladyship. She went to put the note into the care of a footman, whose duty it was to carry it to the viscount's hand, and returned to her mistress.

Lord Ogden unfolded the note. He saw that her ladyship had used the same sheet. A short space below his bold scrawl, she had added a few short lines in her graceful hand. *It shall be as you ask, my lord. I wish to inform you that I have decided to name my daughter Elizabeth after my mother.*

The viscount drew in a deep breath and let it out in a long sigh. His own mother's name had been Elizabeth. He could never claim the children for his own, but with her ladyship's gracious action, his parentage was nevertheless acknowledged. He felt humbled. His gratitude was not any lessoned by its quiet, solitary celebration. Lord Ogden very carefully folded the single sheet and put it away in his desk for safekeeping.

The viscountess had also requested that he come up to visit with her in an hour. He would certainly do so, as it suited his own inclinations exactly. He returned his attention to the ledgers but he kept an eye on the mantel clock. Before the slow hands had marked the passing of an hour, there was a quiet knock on the door and a footman entered to inform his lordship that Lady Ogden was ready to receive him. He left his work behind and went upstairs.

Mills had brushed and dressed Lady Ogden's hair, propped her mistress higher in the bed with some extra pillows plumped up behind her back, arranged a shawl over her shoulders, and lastly, drew the bedclothes modestly up around her ladyship's figure. Lady Ogden smoothed the folded edge of the cover with trembling fingers. She could not account for her flutter of apprehension. She wondered how his lordship would handle the unprecedented situation. She decided to take her cue from the viscount and wait for him to speak first.

Lord Ogden was ushered into the bedchamber by her ladyship's silent dresser. His lordship stopped several paces from the bed. His face was nearly expressionless, but there was a burning glow in his dark eyes. It warmed her and some of her nervousness left her. When he spoke, it was to utter a formal, impersonal phrase. "I hope you are well, ma'am?"

"I am well. Pray sit down, my lord." When the viscount had seated himself in the chair that had been set beside her bed, Lady Ogden nodded to the dresser. "You may leave us, Mills. I wish to speak to his lordship privately."

"As you wish, my lady." The dresser stepped out of the room and quietly closed the paneled door behind her.

Lord Ogden waited until they were alone before he turned his gaze back to the lady sitting in the bed. All formality dropped from his manner. He drank in her appearance, observing that her features were fined down to the delicate bone structure beneath her pale skin. She was still beautiful, however, and yet he didn't tell her so, but instead uttered his second uppermost thought. "You look so, so tired, Charlotte."

Lady Ogden gave a small laugh. "As it turns out, birthing is a tiring business." She moved aside a lift of blanket to reveal the tiny, scrunched-up face of a sleeping infant. "Your daughter, my lord. I sent for her to be brought to me. I thought you might wish to meet her."

The viscount swallowed an unexpected lump in his throat. He reached out a hesitant fingertip and feathered it down one miniature cheek. "She is so soft," he said in wonderment. Something delicate and tender unfurled in his chest. He thought he had never felt so fortunate.

"Do you wish to hold her?"

"Of course." Lord Ogden carefully picked up the little, swaddled bundle and cradled her warmth to his chest, and admired the perfection of his tiny daughter for several minutes. The babe yawned. He laughed softly and returned the infant to her mother's arms. "You should name the child after yourself, Charlotte."

"Well enough; she shall be Elizabeth Charlotte."

The viscount regarded her for a moment. "Elizabeth was my mother's name, as I believe you know."

"Yes, I know."

"Thank you, my dear." He bowed from the waist, a hand over his heart. He addressed the most pressing business. "We must have her christened, as soon as possible, and the still-born, too. I shall send word to Rev. Major Ledger."

Lady Ogden nodded. "Yes, that will be best."

The viscount hesitated. "If you have no objections, I should like Arthur to be her godfather."

Lady Ogden at once agreed. "He is dear to you and I have come to value his worth. It's an excellent suggestion, my lord."

"You are generous, Charlotte," he said quietly.

Lady Ogden caught her breath when he lifted one of her hands and kissed the back of it. Then he sat holding her hand in a gentle clasp while he smiled at her. Her heart was full to bursting. She thought she could not bear it for much longer, not without bursting into tears. She gave a tremulous smile. "I've grown fatigued, Vincent. Will you call Mills for me?"

"Of course." Lord Ogden got up from the chair and reached out for the bell-pull to give it a firm tug. "I shall leave you now, my dear." He caressed her hair, then briefly placed his cupped hand on the infant's head. He turned away and walked toward the door. Lady Ogden's suddenly brimming gaze followed his retreating figure until he had left the bedchamber, pulling shut the door behind him. She covered her eyes with one hand, swallowing back a strangled sob, holding her infant daughter curled against her breast with the other.

The viscount returned slowly downstairs. Reentering the ground-floor study, he sat down at the desk and pulled a sheet of paper towards him. After a moment of thought, he dipped his pen in the inkwell and penned a communication which he ordered to be delivered at once to the vicarage. A half hour later, Rev. Major Ledger had arrived and was shown into the study, where he was closeted with the viscount for some little while.

Lord Ogden put his friend in possession of the startling news that the viscountess had been delivered of two infants, the living one a girl and the other a still-born male. While Rev. Major Ledger absorbed how nearly his friend had escaped misfortune over the succession of the peerage, Lord Ogden succinctly explained what he wanted. "I've spoken to Lady Ogden. Her ladyship wishes for the girl to bear her own mother's name, Elizabeth. The still-born shall be named Henry Titus, for my cousin and my father."

"There's no question, Vincent. I shall at once christen the infants. Today, if you wish."

"Thank you, Arthur. It's important to me."

"Believe me, I understand." There was a wealth of meaning in Rev. Major Ledger's voice. Without question, he knew that his friend was laboring under a keen, overriding sense of responsibility and would make every attempt to discharge it with all honor. Recalling the special license that he had procured for the viscount, he cleared his throat. "How is her ladyship and the surviving infant?"

"They are well."

Rev. Major Ledger looked full at the viscount. His clear, gray gaze seemed to penetrate to his lordship's very soul. "What of yourself, my friend?"

"I'm well enough." There was an edge to the viscount's voice. "Lady Ogden and I wish for you to stand as godfather to Elizabeth Charlotte."

Rev. Major Ledger was profoundly affected. He wrung Lord Ogden's hand. "I'm very well pleased, my lord! You and her ladyship could not have made a happier choice, believe me."

The still-born heir was christened, along with his squalling sister, and a day later was laid to rest beside the late viscount. It was not to be expected that Lady Ogden would attend the burial service, being still confined to her bed by orders of the physician. However, Lord Ogden bestrode a steaming horse, his hat pulled low and his collar raised to protect against the chilly drizzle, and rode to the chapel cemetery for the internment of the infant. He escorted the carriage which held Mrs. Merriweather and Mrs. Dalton, who were the only others attending the service. The viscount's eyes were bleak and his countenance was stony as he watched the tiny white coffin lowered into the small hole that had been dug in the damp earth to receive it.

Rev. Major Ledger said a few, simple words and recorded the date of burial in the parish register. Afterwards, he exchanged good-byes with the ladies before they climbed up into the carriage. Rev. Major Ledger squeezed his lordship's shoulder in mute commiseration. With a nod, Lord Ogden acknowledged his friend's unspoken sympathy, then swung up onto his horse.

Upon the viscount's return to Delincourt, he requested that the household be assembled and when all the servants had gathered, he addressed them. "As most are probably already aware, her ladyship was brought to bed of a still-born son. I have become master of Delincourt in fact, and though this is a time of grief, it is also one of celebration for the birth of Elizabeth Charlotte Ogden." He dismissed the assemblage and it was discussed and agreed amongst the servants that his lordship had carried off his duty with proper dignity.

Afterwards, Lord Ogden went upstairs and shut himself up in the private study off of his bedchamber, where he could be assured of not being disturbed. He did not expect the undercurrent of welling sadness for the loss of his son to linger, but nevertheless, he wanted some time to himself. He would allow himself a few moments for grief, then set it aside as something never to be examined again.

He was shocked when silent tears coursed down his face. The abrupt outpour built until the strong surge shook him. A wall had burst as though hit by a fusillade of cannon. A terrible, howling sorrow overwhelmed him for all its muted misery. He was all but crushed, bowed over, his chest heaving in great, ragged sobs. The sacrifices of war were at long last acknowledged. There had been too many comrades who had fallen, whom he'd had to mourn all in a rush, because one still had to survive the ongoing battles. No bullets whizzed about his head this time to counter the onslaught. However, his character and his tricks of self-survival were set. A man did not succumb long to his emotions. Instead, he soldiered on.

The viscount got drunk.

When he eventually stumbled from his private study into the adjoining bedchamber, he fell across his bed. He sprawled facedown, still fully dressed, and dropped into a deep sonorous slumber. Even in his somnolent coma, his black brows were contracted and his hawkish face was carved into a set frown. Every once in a while, his body twitched in distress.

Grimshaw padded into the bedchamber. He had been patiently waiting for the viscount. Of all the house, it was only the viscount's loyal private servant who understood best, and his heart bled for him. The valet eased off his lordship's boots. Then he drew shut the velvet curtain hangings around the bed before he exited the bedchamber.

46

L ord Ogden wakened, bleary-eyed. He gingerly took stock of himself. An enormous blacksmith was clanging away on an anvil inside his head, his gut roiled when he turned over on his back, and he felt stiff and battered.

"Stale drunk, by God," he muttered thickly. Otherwise, he decided he felt remarkably refreshed. The purge of emotion had done something to him. A long-suppressed storm had broken over his head and finally cleared, leaving behind a deep peace that was definable.

He had been blessed with the birth of a daughter. A man could be proud of having a healthy child, but other profound emotions were present that he had never anticipated. Already affection and a protective instinct for his tiny daughter filled him. He had not considered himself to be the sort of man who would be bowled out by a mere scrap of a humanity, but so it was.

He pushed himself up to a sitting position, enduring the dizziness and nausea until it passed. Then he yanked open the velvet bed curtains and levered himself to his stockinged feet. He knew it was barely past dawn and grunted with disgust. Slowly, he crossed to the bell-rope, muttering all the way. "Drunk as a wheelbarrow. Put to bed with a spoon. Yet I still greet the first shafts of day." He tugged hard on the bell-rope. It seemed forever before his valet entered the bedchamber.

"Grimshaw. Good man. A bath, a shave."

"Of course, my lord." Grimshaw crossed to each of the windows and ruthlessly thrust wide all of the drapes. Sunlight streamed into the bedchamber, piercing the viscount's aching orbs. The pain extracted from him a deep groan. The valet made an about-face, turning a deaf ear to his master's audible agony. "Will there be anything else, my lord?"

Lord Ogden looked slit-eyed at his valet. He was incensed. *Prodding me like I was a wounded bear, forsooth!* He was not aware of it when he threw back his shoulders. However, his lordship's straightened posture was not lost on his manservant.

Grimshaw had the effrontery to grin.

Lord Ogden felt a stir of amusement at the man's cheek, but he was not yet ready to indulge in happy displays. He still felt like a jug-bitten bear, after all. Through gritted teeth, he said, "Ale with a sandwich. Here, now."

After forcing himself to drink the bitter ale and eat, he began to feel better. By the time he had bathed and been shaven and dressed, his head still pounded, but mercifully, the blacksmith had quit hammering. Feeling much better, he went downstairs to enjoy a large breakfast with his sister and Mrs. Merriweather. The lively, cheerful conversation at table, which he engaged in and listened to with interest, was all to do with the birth and the upcoming nuptials of his sister to Rev. Major Ledger. Suddenly, it occurred to him there was something else of import. His mellow mood took a dive and his smile faded.

"Vincent? Is something wrong?"

Lord Ogden looked quickly at his sister. He dredged up another smile and shook his head. "It's nothing, Amarys. Merely a bit of business I recalled that I need to address this morning. If you and Mrs. Merriweather will excuse me?"

"Of course, my lord," said Mrs. Merriweather.

Lord Ogden left the breakfast-room and strode to the ground-floor study, still preoccupied with the unwelcome realization. He told himself that he must squarely face it. By giving birth to what was believed to be the late viscount's legal issue, Lady Ogden had secured a L 2,000 annuity and had become financially independent. Her new income was respectable enough to enable her to leave Delincourt Manor. Everything inside him rejected the possibility. He entered and shut the door. In an unhappy frame of mind, he crossed the small room to the mahogany desk and sat down behind. "I could not bear to let her go," he muttered. He had to keep her and their daughter at Delincourt. *Whatever the means I have to employ, I must stop her from leaving me.* Even as it fleeted through his mind, he knew how ignoble a thought it was. Months past, he had thrown aside his honor in a single, terrible act. He could not compromise himself again. His honor, his integrity would not allow it. He must let her ladyship make the choice. He must initiate the income. He could not delay. His sense of fairness would not let him do less. With a sigh, he opened the inkwell.

He penned the necessary letter to his solicitor and enclosed another for the London bank. He requested that Digsby see to the business and come down to Delincourt as soon as possible. He also penned birth announcements, addressed to the largest newspapers in London, and set all of the sealed letters apart to go into the post.

For several minutes, he brooded over endless speculations. He worried at them like a dog gnawing on a meat bone. He had no idea what Lady Ogden would decide to do once she had the means at hand. He snorted in disgust at himself. "I'm acting like the rawest subaltern before a first battle, full of nerves and fears." As a way to divert his mind, he pulled out the expenditure ledger, dipped a pen in the inkwell, and began to record the latest paid bills in the long columns of figures.

While the viscount was closeted in the ground-floor study, Lady Thane came to call. Mrs. Merriweather and Mrs. Dalton were glad to extend a welcome. After their own delightful visit with the lady, they took her upstairs to visit in private with Lady Ogden in her bedchamber. Lady Thane was fortunate enough to be introduced to the infant and she stayed above an hour with the viscountess and the new baby. Lady Thane observed the aura of contentment in her ladyship and was glad to see it. "I am so happy for you, Charlotte."

Lady Ogden lifted her adoring gaze from the sleeping infant in her arms and her face lit with a warm smile for her friend. "Thank you, Sarah. You've no notion! I'm happy for the first time in my life." It did not strike her that what she had said was sad, but Lady Thane was very conscious of it.

The physician had left orders for her ladyship to remain in bed for the usual six weeks after a confinement. However, Lady Ogden could not bear to be idle for so long. She began to take up much of her usual routine. She tired easily and retreated often in the afternoons to nap in exhaustion, but the full management of the household was back in her cable hands. When Mrs. Merriweather expressed doubt that she should have left her bed so soon, she dismissed her aunt's concern for her health.

Mrs. Merriweather was not alone in questioning her decision.

The viscount frowned at her. "Is it wise to go against Dr. Manning's advice, ma'am?"

"I'm already much recovered, my lord."

"I am not pleased. I consider this foolhardy of you."

"Fortunately, I don't have to obey you, my lord. I'm not your wife," retorted Lady Ogden. A disconcerting, hot blush came to her face. She was suddenly breathless. She could not believe she had said such a thing. The magnitude of her self-betrayal shocked her.

"No, you are not my wife," agreed Lord Ogden. "Otherwise, I think I'd beat you."

His lordship's expression was pensive and she wasn't certain that he was entirely joking. "That would scarcely endear your wishes to me, my lord." She curtsied and went away at once, flustered by the intriguing turn in the conversation. She entered with enthusiasm into the newest project that her aunt and Mrs. Dalton had begun. It had the advantage of being one that required sitting comfortably in a chair, so that she could rest while she was employed. The ladies had decided to stitch and embroider a new set of altar cloths for the church. "It's a lovely notion! I know Rev. Major Ledger will be glad of it. For too long, Delincourt has neglected a duty to the parish church."

She ceased to ponder on the future, preferring to put out of her mind any thought of her relationship with the viscount. The purpose behind their carnal liaison had been accomplished. The dynamics had all changed with the birth of her daughter. She did not know where she stood with the viscount now, but she hid a hope deep in her heart.

Lady Ogden knew the birth announcement had been published. She left it as long as she could, but she felt it to be her duty to personally inform her sire, Sir Martin Stockton, of the birth of a grandchild and she penned a short note, in it briefly mentioning the stillborn, as well. Astonishingly, almost in the next post, she received a reply from the baronet. The letter was a thundering denunciation, scathing and vicious.

...I saw the announcement. A worthless female! You could have ousted old Crawford's son and I could have taken up residence at Delincourt as your advisor. A stillborn! What a monstrous fool you are! Stupid, feckless girl!... and so the diatribe went.

The terrible, furious words swam before her eyes. The anguish inflicted by the letter's contents overwhelmed her. A suffocated sob broke from her trembling lips. Lady Ogden dropped the letter to her lap and covered her brimming eyes with one hand. She whispered, "It's so hard to bear...such rancor!"

"Charlotte! Dearest!" Mrs. Merriweather's voice was anxious. "Are you alright?"

Lady Ogden shook her head. Her hand was still tight over her eyes, but tears slipped down her face. She was unable to speak past a lump of misery. She mutely extended the letter in the direction of her aunt's voice. The missive was nipped out of her hand. There was a short silence while Mrs. Merriweather read its contents. Over the elderly lady's shoulder, Mrs. Dalton also read the letter and it was she who gave an incoherent, wrathful exclamation.

Lady Ogden fought to recover her equilibrium. She was ashamed. She did not understand why she was so shaken. *I know what my father is...I've always known.* She wiped her cheeks with her fingers and dropped her hands to her lap, twisting them together. There was a hard knot in her chest. She tried to smile. "Pretty sentiments, are they not?"

Mrs. Dalton rushed over in a fluttering of skirt and sank down at her feet. Her fine eyes glimmered with unshed tears as she laid her hand on Lady Ogden's knee. When she spoke, her warm voice throbbed with compassion. "My dear Charlotte! Such terrible, terrible things to write to you! Pray do not regard it! Pray do not!"

Mrs. Merriweather exclaimed, low and trembling, "Detestable, detestable man!"

"Yes, yes, he is," said Lady Ogden, barely able to control her voice. Her throat began to close again. By this time, she should be immune to Sir Martin's cruelty, but it seemed she was not. Of a sudden, she was profoundly, utterly weary. "Put it on the flames, aunt."

"As you wish, my dear." Mrs. Merriweather looked meaningfully at Mrs. Dalton, who still knelt beside her ladyship. "Amarys, why don't you pour a lovely cup of tea for Charlotte?"

"Of course, Mrs. Merriweather." Mrs. Dalton rose gracefully to her feet and urged Lady Ogden to get up from her chair. "Come, Charlotte! You will feel much more the thing."

"I'm sorry! I'm being such a silly watering pot." Lady Ogden tried to laugh, but it was a pathetic attempt, breaking in the middle.

"Nonsense! The shock of such a letter would throw most people into strong hysterics," said Mrs. Dalton bracingly. She twined the viscountess' arm inside her own.

As the two turned toward the table, where the tea tray had been laid, Mrs. Merriweather swiftly folded the letter into a narrow rectangle and tucked it under the white cuff of her sleeve. She turned her head and stared pensively into the hearth fire. After a few moments, she excused herself to her companions and went downstairs in search of the viscount.

A firm knock sounded on the door of the ground-floor study. Lord Ogden was preoccupied, going over the figures from the last month's tallies again. The dire, inexorable decline in the estate's finances seemed to have slowed, by a barely discernible increment, it was true; but there was enough of a marginal difference that he dared to entertain a lift of cautious optimism. "Enter!"

He looked up as the door opened, expecting a servant. He was surprised when Mrs. Merriweather entered. "Mrs. Merriweather! This is a pleasant surprise."

"My lord." The elderly lady closed the door and trod across the worn carpet. He was struck by the determination on her face, a very different expression from her usual placidness. He leaned back in his chair, setting aside his pen. "May I help you, ma'am?"

"I hope so, my lord." Mrs. Merriweather seated herself on one of the chairs facing the desk. She twitched at her cuff and pulled out a small rectangle and began to unfold it. Lord Ogden could see that it was a letter. Mrs. Merriweather stretched out her hand, offering the missive to the viscount. "I have here a letter from Sir Martin Stockdale to his daughter. I wish you to read it."

Lord Ogden reached forward and took the much-creased letter. He saw at once that the wax seal had been broken. Nevertheless, he hesitated. "You wish me to read a private letter? Does Lady Ogden know of this? Isn't this a breach of privacy, Mrs. Merriweather?"

"A *shocking* breach! My niece has asked me to destroy this letter and I shall do so. The matter is left entirely in my hands, as you see."

"But I don't understand."

Mrs. Merriweather huffed impatiently. "What's to understand? I feel it important for you to know something about the relationship between Lady Ogden and her father. It has never been good."

"I've already gathered that. I've heard before this of Sir Martin's indifference toward his daughter. It's naturally upsetting to her ladyship," said Lord Ogden slowly. He wasn't sure yet what to make of Mrs. Merriweather's offering up her niece's correspondence.

"Sir Martin's mean-spirited insensibility was always difficult for my niece." Mrs. Merriweather gave a nod at the square missive he was still holding. "That's something altogether different. It's a particularly vicious communication, berating her harshly for the stillborn heir. As for Sir Martin's blasted personal expectations – *well!* You will be astonished to learn, my lord, that Sir Martin intended to live at Delincourt's expense!"

Lord Ogden's brows twitched together. He unfolded the sheet and made himself swift master of its contents. He was thunderstruck. His face stiffened with his gathering wrath. He could scarcely believe that a man could spew such choleric ravings at a daughter. *Lady Ogden's sensibilities must have been cut to pieces.* Angered, disgusted, repelled, he tightened his lips. The tic jumped in his jaw. He sought to speak without sullying the lady's ears with the curses that came so readily to his tongue. "Sir Martin is clearly deranged. The violence of his language, his intemperate sentiments – it's no wonder Lady Ogden takes no pleasure in the baronet's communications!" He looked up, narrowing his eyes at the lady. "Why have you given this to me?"

"I believe that you care for my niece."

"Yes, I admit to it," said Lord Ogden, suddenly guarded. At once, his brain was engaged and he did not break his gaze from the lady's resolute face. The extraordinary relationship he had with his lovely cousin-in-law was convoluted. He wasn't about to elaborate. He would shield the privacy of their affair. He would tolerate no brooking of the subject and he would snub any questions from the elderly lady. He disliked the idea of treating Mrs. Merriweather in such a way, but if necessary, he would do so. He braced himself for unpleasantness. He intended to respond only with cold civility. He was so caught up in defense that the explanation for Mrs. Merriweather's extraordinary action eluded him.

Mrs. Merriweather fixed her anxious gaze on his stern face. "My niece will feel obligated to receive her father, my lord. That is, if Sir Martin ever comes here. And to rid herself of his obnoxious presence, she will likely offer him a sum of money." She leaned forward in her earnestness. "Sir Martin is a great bully, my lord. I don't wish my dearest Charlotte to be so beleaguered, especially while she remains fragile in her emotions. Why, she *wept* when she read that- that trash! It's so *unlike* her! My lord, I'm worried about her. She's been through so very much!"

Lord Ogden was surprised, then realized he shouldn't have been, not with what he knew of the lady's character. Mrs. Merriweather had not come to stir into things that did not concern her. Mrs. Merriweather cared only that her niece be protected. He was ashamed of his suspicions of her motivation.

"Set your mind at ease, Mrs. Merriweather. If ever Sir Martin should choose to visit Delincourt, I will not allow her ladyship to be bullied by her sire." Lord Ogden chose not to reveal he had been reliably informed that Sir Martin had returned at least once to the neighborhood in past months. He did not feel the knowledge would be constructive, especially once it was relayed to Lady Ogden, which he believed Mrs. Merriweather would surely do. He returned the letter to her. "I have no use for this. Pray do what you think best with it."

"Thank you, my lord." Mrs. Merriweather inclined her head. She stood up and walked to the fireplace. Without uttering another word, Mrs. Merriweather consigned Sir Martin's despicable letter to the flames.

SIR WILLIAM'S RECUPERATION at the unfashionable watering hole had seemed interminable to one of his restless temperament. There was no real society to be had there. His jaundiced eyes had seen none but superannuated invalids and freakish quizzes. The day finally came, when he experimentally rolled his shoulder, that he experienced only a twinge of pain and a little remaining stiffness.

Sir William decided to return to London. Within an hour of his abrupt decision, he was in a hired post chaise, his luggage strapped on the back. Accompanied by his sour-faced valet, who occupied the seat facing backward, he set forth, bowling along on the road back to town. It was a long, boring journey, requiring two changes of horses and a stay overnight at a rustic inn. He was certain there were bedbugs in the damp sheets.

When at last the post chaise entered the outer environs of London and clattered along the cobbled streets, Sir William was in a foul mood. It was a drab day, gray with cold drizzle. Dray carts and hired hacks and private carriages filled the narrow streets, their numbers increasing, and slowing the passage of his own hired equipage. Sir Willian leaned forward to the carriage window with an impatient gaze. "Get on with it! Get on!" he snarled. Upon arriving at his address, he paid off the driver of the equipage and ordered the valet to carry in the luggage. As he entered his lodgings, he gave curt orders to his heavily burdened valet, who was carrying in all the luggage, and to the dour manservant whose responsibility it was to cook and clean. "I want a shave and a change of clean linens. I want supper served in an hour."

At length, replete from the hastily-prepared repast, Sir William settled back from the table in his private parlor. Behind the iron grate, a coal fire warmed the room. The manservant had removed the covers, leaving an opened bottle of red wine, and silently departed, closing the door. Sir William poured a full measure of the heavy-bodied port and drank deeply from the glass. Then he unfolded the latest edition of the *Gazette*, which he had ordered his valet to run out into the freezing rain to procure for him, and began to peruse the headlines. He swiftly became bored with matters of national interest, and yawned, – it was all about the infernal war – and he turned to the society pages where there were likely items of more interest to him. One such item snagged his instant attention. It was a birth announcement. He sat bolt upright, reading it over and over. "Well, well! The prize was well lost from the beginning."

The toss of the dice had been made and even though he would not have gotten Delincourt, he resented that he had been barred from seeing the gamble through to the end. Of course, in the end, he would have been saddled with an unwanted wife and a puling infant, but that was a minor detail.

Sir William threw aside the newspaper. He stood up, moving from one point to another in his small quarters, drinking occasionally from the wineglass. He was restless. He didn't know what to do with himself. His brain turned this way and that. Lord Ogden's fierce promise of violence kept cropping up in his mind. "Barbaric! The man's a lunatic!" At last, with an exasperated oath, he sat down at his desk to pen a few notes to those who would be interested to know of his return to town. Sir William finished his task and propped the notes on the entry hall table, where the manservant would see them and put them out in the morning post.

He finished the bottle of strong, sweet port wine before he went up to bed.

Sir William's disposition was much restored in the morning. The rumor-mill could be used to his advantage. He didn't want it bruited about that he had lost an engagement, let alone been wounded. It rankled his pride. Instead, he casually put it about that he had been on a repairing lease and allowed his acquaintances to make of it what they would. It was not unknown for one of their social circle to dodge the tipsters by going out of town for a few weeks and his explanation was readily accepted. One of the first to call upon him at his lodgings was Mr. Hadley. As it turned out, the foppish gentleman's mid-morning visit proved to be the least appreciated by Sir William; but he suffered the trial with a pretense of good humor because Mr. Hadley could be relied upon to know the latest gossip.

"You were missed, Sir William. Particularly by Mrs. Stonebridge. You had not left her much beforehand with the bills before you went away."

"I doubt that the Stonebridge is ever able to outrun her duns," said Sir William sourly. He was in the middle of tying his snowy white cravat and so he did not look around. However, he could just see his visitor's intelligent, sly countenance reflected in the corner of the gilt-edged mirror.

"The pretty creature accepted my protection with flattering alacrity." Mr. Hadley's gimlet-sharp eyes watched him. "One wonders, perhaps she was not...satisfied with your patronage, Sir William."

Sir William's smile was bland. Inside, he was raging. *The bitch had wasted no time. The merry arse!* As for the gentleman, what incredible gall to hint that he'd been unable to hold on to his convenient for such a reason – *dissatisfaction, indeed!* With a semblance of indifference, he said, "I had begun to tire of the Stonebridge. Her custom had grown stale before I had ever left town, my dear fellow."

Mr. Hadley lifted a thin brow. "Ah! You found another ladybird during your repairing lease, did you?"

Sir William merely smiled. He finished with his cravat and carefully placed a sapphire stickpin in its snowy center. His valet was waiting with his twilled satin waistcoat and slipped it over his shoulders. Sir William buttoned it and adorned himself with several gold seals and a beribboned quizzing glass.

"It was really too bad of you not to give your *congee* to her before leaving the metropolis. She was left quite frantic," said Mr. Hadley. He smiled gently, pensively. His voice lowered. "So willing to please, too."

"Perhaps I should pay a last visit to the lady and make my apology," said Sir William with forced suavity. Inwardly, he wished for nothing more than an opportunity to set the crop to his former convenient's backside. *She* had dared to leave *him!* He'd whip her until she could not sit down. Nothing would give him greater pleasure. The rising swell of pressure in his loins was unmistakable.

Mr. Hadley's shoulders shook with his amusement. "None of that, none of that! We wouldn't want to confuse the little bird." The gentleman's voice dropped again into a satisfied murmur. "She is so eager, *so very eager,* to please."

Sir William allowed his man to help him into his tight-fitting coat. It was a careful process and he felt the familiar twinge in his shoulder with the exertion, but at last he stood fully dressed. He twitched his cuffs into place. All the while he had conversed with Hadley, the back of his mind had been occupied with the bitterness of his defeat at the hands of the new viscount. The nag of pain in his shoulder was a constant reminder. So was the spectre of fear in his brain. The viscount's savage expression was seared into his memory. His stomach churned and bile burned like acid in his throat. He hated the man. If he could act as a *deus ex machina* without peril to himself, he would do it. And he believed he knew just how to do it. He'd plant the poisonous seeds and hope for the sprouting of a foul crop.

Sir William ran his quizzing glass up and down the silk ribbon. "Ah, Hadley. Is there any recent word about town of Sir Martin Stockdale? Does he still frequent the more squalid gaming hells? Yes? How fortuitous!"

"Why do you ask?"

Sir William shrugged. "One must really make the effort to offer personal condolences for the loss of his son-in-law. Henry was such a dear friend, after all."

"Gammon! No, you've some devilment in mind." Mr. Hadley narrowed his eyes upon a sudden thought. "The birth announcement! I saw it a day or two ago and I wondered. Do *you* think the child was legitimate?"

"Oh, without a doubt. You were there. You saw and heard as much as I did," said Sir William, rather annoyed but not surprised that his visitor had made the immediate connection. *Such a clever reptile, Hadley.* He paused meaningfully. "But who's to say what Sir Martin will believe?"

Raising a thin brow, Mr. Hadley stared at him. "You mean to sic the man onto the new viscount? I marvel at your inventiveness, Sir William. But your motive, sir!"

"It's pure enough. You saw the viscount at the burial service for our poor friend. His lordship seemed to be such a stalwart, respectable fellow, don't you think? I disliked him on general principle," murmured Sir William. He had to play it carefully. It wouldn't do to give even a hint of the true depth of his antipathy. *Not to Hadley. It's not wise to be too open with my dear friend Hadley.*

Sir William smiled to himself, contemplating his clever scheme. It would be enough, it would be enough, he thought. His revenge would be simplistic and devious. All he needed to do was to drop a few poisonous insinuations into Sir Martin Stockdale's ear. "I'd wager that *this* Lord Ogden will feel obligated to provide support for the widow and her child. And by extension, the lady's parent. Sir Martin Stockdale."

"The man will be a gadfly, a leach!" Suddenly, Mr. Hadley's eyes held a malicious gleam as he realized the import. "The viscount will never be rid of him."

"Just so."

Mr. Hadley's shoulders shook. "You're a devil, Sir William."

47

"I miss Amarys already," said Lady Ogden, sipping her breakfast tea. It had only been a week since Rev. Major Ledger and Mrs. Dalton were wed. It was a simple, genteel marriage. The wedding was held in the chapel and was performed by a vicar who had ridden in from the neighboring parish. She'd had tears standing in her eyes as Rev. Major Ledger and his bride exchanged simple gold bands. Melancholia and happiness had filled her; she would never know such blissful joy as the couple before her showed to one another but she was overwhelmed with gladness for them. She and Lord Ogden had inscribed their names as the two witnesses in the register book.

"Oh, yes! Such a cheerful disposition," agreed Mrs. Merriweather. "She looked so very lovely! That gown of white French lace over a satin slip, embroidered with tiny leaves at the hem! And the church bells ringing merrily after the ceremony!"

"A grand extravagance on Arthur's part to pay the ringers," remarked Lord Ogden. "The wedding breakfast was surprisingly well-attended."

"It was to be expected, my lord," said Lady Ogden

The entire party had returned to Delincourt Manor where the wedding breakfast was held. The whole neighborhood was invited to greet the newlyweds and as it was their own vicar and the viscount's sister who had been wed, it proved to be a festive occasion. At the wedding and the breakfast, the bride's blond curls were crowned by a long lace veil hanging down the back. The lady exchanged the veil for a becoming bonnet and buttoned a warm pelisse over her gown in anticipation of the ride in an open carriage. After saying adieu, Rev. Major Ledger had proudly borne his wife home to the vicarage in the curricle drawn by the matched bays, a sleek turnout that he had purchased from the viscount.

"It was a wonderful gathering! I don't believe we have ever been so merry here at Delincourt. Mrs. Ledger looked so very happy when we visited yesterday, didn't she?"

"Yes, she did. I'm very glad for Amarys, aunt. Though I miss her dreadfully, I shan't repine. While Rev. Major Ledger was showing you around the vicarage, she told me how much she enjoys managing her own home. She and Rev. Major Ledger deserve every happiness, and they are not so very far away from us, after all. We will always have them for neighbors."

Lord Ogden shot a swift glance at his cousin-in-law. He wondered if he could take that to mean she had decided to remain at Delincourt. The burning question had never been answered.

"Oh, yes, that is a comfort!" said Mrs. Merriweather. "We will be able to visit them often and I daresay *they* will come to Delincourt just as often. The new altar cloths turned out very well, don't you think?"

Lady Ogden agreed. "I was quite pleased. Amarys told me that everyone commented favorably on the altar cloths when they were used at last Sunday's service. I'm glad that we used some of the gold thread picked out of those old brocades we found in the attic."

"My compliments must be added to all the rest," said Lord Ogden. "The three of you created a magnificent pattern."

Lady Ogden was warmed by the accolade. "Thank you, my lord. It was a labor of love for us all."

The viscount nodded. "It was obvious." He flipped through the day's mail and fished out a sealed missive to hand to her. "You have a letter, Lady Ogden."

"Thank you, my lord." Lady Ogden looked at the written direction and her heart plummeted. She knew that handwriting. She turned the square over and over in her hands, and said slowly, "Why, it's from Sir Martin. Two letters in two months! How favored I am!"

She saw Lord Ogden look over at her aunt and the glance that was exchanged between them. She felt heat rise in her face. It was obvious to anyone with eyes that she was reluctant to open the letter. She was not surprised by the sudden anxious expression on her aunt's face, not when she had been devastated by Sir Martin's last letter. She knew that if it had been up to Mrs. Merriweather, that lady would have wanted her spared from any further communication from her father. However, Mrs. Merriweather hadn't the right to interfere. It was up to her whether or not she continued to accept Sir Martin's correspondence.

Lady Ogden took a deep breath. She was apprehensive as she broke the wax seal and unfolded the crinkling sheet. She perused the letter quickly and her dread lessened. The gist was much as usual, full of plaintive, self-centered complaints of the unfair vagaries of life. *Well, it's not as stinging as I expected.* She continued to read down the close-written, ink-blotched sheet. At one point, she gave a short, angry exclamation.

"Not bad news, I trust?" asked Lord Ogden, raising his eyes from reading one of his own letters.

Lady Ogden glanced up at him, startled. "Not at all, my lord." She refolded the sheet and placed it down on the table. Calm in her face, she picked up her cup and sipped her morning tea.

Lord Ogden politely inclined his head. He thought he knew better than to believe her. However, short of wresting the letter from her, he could scarcely say so. He hoped that should she find herself in trouble, she would find it within herself to confide in him. He smiled indiscriminately at the ladies. "What have you planned for your day?"

"We are darning sheets." Lady Ogden smiled as his lordship blinked in surprise. The housekeeper had pulled together a large pile of household linens that needed darning and she and her aunt had decided that was to be their undertaking for the morning. "A mundane task without glamor, not like the altar cloths."

Lord Ogden laughed. "I fear I have contributed to your chore. Last week, I put my foot through a sheet during the night. However, I doubt it will be worth salvaging."

"Mrs. Tower has already separated out the linens that are too worn to be repaired. The maids will tear them into strips to be used as cleaning rags. Nothing goes to waste."

"Then the inventory must be depleted. Pray make a list of what is most needful for the household and I will advance you the funds to buy replacements."

"Thank you, my lord." The surprised note in her voice was obvious.

"I am not my cousin," he said softly.

The truth of that sent a warm blush rising into her cheeks. She inclined her head in acknowledgement, memories of their tempestuous relationship over several months running riot in her head. She hoped he could not read her mind, but she very much feared, from the glint in his eyes, that he had a fair notion what she was thinking.

"Quite, my lord! One doesn't like to speak ill of the dead, but your cousin was a pinch-penny when it came to Delincourt. We could all have starved and gone about *in rags* for all he cared!" said Mrs. Merriweather roundly.

"Hush, aunt," said Lady Ogden, embarrassed. She believed nothing could be gained by dwelling on what had gone before and her opinion was justified. Her aunt's burst of eloquence had brought a frown to the viscount's face.

After breakfast, Lady Ogden and her aunt went upstairs. Lady Ogden carried the letter with her and put it safely away in her private desk before she went to join her aunt in the upper drawing-room. Several beeswax candles had been lighted in anticipation of their work. When she entered, Mrs. Merriweather was standing at the fireplace, looking down into the crackling fire, her hands extended toward it. She turned her head and smiled. "There you are, my dear. I was just warming my hands. My old fingers work better for a little heat."

"It is getting colder. We'll be seeing snow soon."

Together they walked over to the old table, where the linens were stacked, and seated themselves. They took up threaded needles and began patching and darning. Mrs. Merriweather said, "I could see how unwelcome Sir Martin's latest letter was to you, Charlotte."

Lady Ogden looked over at her aunt with a quick, bitter smile. "Unwelcome! I could barely force myself to open it! Not after that last awful one – the one you burned."

"Oh, don't tell me this one was *worse* than the one before!"

Lady Ogden shook her head. "The language wasn't as rough." She grimaced. "I never enjoy my father's correspondence, but I'm usually able to shrug it off."

"But not this time?" asked Mrs. Merriweather. The wrinkles in her face deepened with worry. "What has the *wretched* man written this time?"

"You know me too well." She threw another smile at her aunt, but it faded. "I'm not quite sure what to make of it, aunt. The part where Sir Martin alludes to the birth announcement in the newspapers, it's peculiar in tone. But then, my father's forceful opinions have always been skewed, have they not? Again, he writes how improvident I was not to have produced an heir!"

"An impertinence, to be sure," said Mrs. Merriweather, still worried on her niece's behalf. She reached over the space between them and patted the younger woman's arm. "Ignore it, my dear! *Whatever* Sir Martin has written, don't take it to heart."

Lady Ogden knit her brows. The contents of the letter still occupied her mind. "Aunt, I dislike how it comes off."

"What do you mean?" asked Mrs. Merriweather quickly, pausing again in her darning.

Lady Ogden laughed a little. "I don't know. I cannot pinpoint why I am left feeling so disquieted. After that last letter, so full of rage and spouting all those horrible things, I began to think my father to be unhinged, capable of anything. Perhaps it's merely drink that inflames his sentiments." She dismissed her foolishness with a shrug. "Otherwise, Sir Martin's writing is very much the same, full of himself, his complaints and grievances. He blames the loss of the Grange to the machinations of Mr. Kelton, if you please!"

"Sir Martin is foolish beyond belief! He attaches no self-blame to himself or to his own choices! He'll never bring himself to recognize his own folly." Mrs. Merriweather shook her head, plying her needle. "I trust we shall hear no more of that! Mr. Kelton is said to have paid a pretty penny for the Grange. Surely, that must be enough to satisfy even Sir Martin."

"So I should hope, ma'am," said Lady Ogden quietly, yet she was disturbed. She shook out a yellowed sheet and critically inspected her neat stitch work. Better than her aunt, she understood how rapacious her sire's appetites were. She wondered how long even a 'pretty penny' would keep Sir Martin in funds. She was certain her father would eventually learn of her increased income. The discovery was inevitable, she thought in resignation, as that sort of thing always became general knowledge, sent out to the world-at-large on the wings of gossip. Perhaps her father had already heard rumors. After all, Sir Martin must still have some ties in the neighborhood and their social sphere was not large. The possibility that he might apply to her for succor was not inconceivable.

"If Sir Martin applies to you, Charlotte, you must not give in to him," said Mrs. Merriweather suddenly, making it obvious her thoughts were running along something of the same lines as her niece's unhappy reflections.

"Apply to me! Why, I hope he will not! I'm of no mind to meet any demands of his!" exclaimed Lady Ogden. The idea had been abhorrent when it occurred to her, but she was shamed that it had also occurred to her aunt. *My father's bad character is always a discredit to me.*

"I'm glad to hear you say so, my dear. You have an obligation to think only of yourself and dearest, sweet Elizabeth now," said Mrs. Merriweather with unwonted force.

Lady Ogden immediately stretched out her hand to clasp her aunt's wrist. She said in warm affection, "And of you, dear ma'am! I must also think of you, just as I've always done and always shall!"

Mrs. Merriweather's faded eyes filled. She blinked back her unshed tears with obvious difficulty. "Dear, *dear* Charlotte! You gladden my heart. Truly, you do!"

A fortnight later, late in November, winter made a strong, blustering show. The season had already seen hoarfrost aplenty and sleeting rain mixed with snow, but this was different. The temperature had been plunging for days, but no one expected the tremendous tempest that sprang up out of nowhere. Cracks of thunder blasted the atmosphere, seeming to shake the earth. The cold wind howled. Stray gusts blew out candles as outside doors were snatched from clinging hands and clapped shut by the violent blasts of air. Eddies of chilly vapor ghosted the draperies where the seams of window casements were not tight. The hearth fires were built high in rooms throughout the manor house to counter the sudden frigidity, yet the breaths of the inhabitants showed white on the air in the hallways.

The icy fury ended as abruptly as it had begun, bequeathing a prodigious, profound silence. The battered countryside was left powdered with a pristine blanket of snow.

The storm brought in its tail an ill harbinger.

The hired chaise bowled up the drive, coming to a stop at Delincourt's front door. A very stout gentleman descended with ponderous care to the frozen ground. A short beaver was jammed down over his sullen brow. He was attired in a brown frock coat, with a knitted muffler wound around his thick neck, over old-fashioned breeches. He climbed the shallow steps, leaning heavily on a thick cane, and rapped the brass door knocker. After a short discourse with the porter, who had opened the door, the gentleman entered the manor house. The footman relieved him of his beaver, muffler and gloves. He gave his card to the impassive butler. "I am here to see Lord Ogden."

Somerset ushered the gentleman into the drawing-room. "If you will wait here, sir. I shall inquire whether his lordship is in to callers." A few minutes later, the butler returned to show the visitor into the ground-floor study, where the viscount awaited the gentleman. "Sir Martin Stockton, my lord."

"Sir Martin." Lord Ogden inclined his head. He ran a curious gaze over his visitor, reminding himself that the baronet might one day become his father-in-law. He was unimpressed, for Sir Martin did not cut a good figure. Through past history, he had formed a negative opinion of the baronet and it was not tempered by his visitor's appearance. In a flash, he decided to treat the visit of his prospective father-in-law as a formal call, rather than a sociable one. He was of no mind to encourage the gentleman to overstay his visit. Made aware of Lady Ogden's difficult relationship with her sire, from what she and Mrs. Merriweather had frequently let drop in conversation and from the letter he had been privileged to read, he believed that the baronet's stop at Delincourt was not a pleasant happenchance for Lady Ogden.

"My lord." Sir Martin Stockton bowed, an action accompanied by the unmistakable creak of a heavily-boned corset. Sir Martin had run to rampant corpulence. The overweight Prince Regent also sported a corset, but he still presented an elegant figure, attiring himself in well-cut coats and clean linen. Sir Martin had not attempted to copy the prince's excellent example. The viscount's nostrils quivered, picking up on the sour odor of the unwashed. Lord Ogden's expression did not give away his distaste for the gentleman's stained waistcoat and careless grooming. Always fastidious himself and disciplined by his military background, he could not help but regard the baronet with disfavor.

"Pray be seated," said Lord Ogden. He did not offer his hand to his visitor for a cordial handshake but seated himself behind the desk. He pointed to a wingback chair situated in front of the massive desk, much as he would direct an employee or tradesperson. However, the gentleman seemed unfazed by the discourtesy. There was no appearance of affront in his expression.

Sir Martin sat down heavily in the large chair. The sturdy seat squeaked alarmingly under his considerable bulk. He leaned his cane against one heavy thigh. Without preamble, he stated, "So. You've housed my daughter."

Through half-lidded eyes, which disguised the keenness of his straight gaze, Lord Ogden studied his visitor. The years had not been kind to the gentleman. Sir Martin's large body reflected too many years of heavy drinking and sedentary habits. The massive shoulders strained the seams of his coat and his bulging belly obstructed his view of the ground, over which he stumped with the aid of his cane. Under a thinning thatch of greasy hair, his small eyes were pressed like black currents into a bloat of jaundiced, coarsened features and massive jowls. *I mislike the sly look in those piggish eyes.*

Lord Ogden gave a nod. "As you say, sir. What brings you to Delincourt?"

"I saw the death announcement for Henry Ogden posted in the *Gazette.*" Sir Martin pulled at his fleshy lip, looking indecisive as he studied the viscount's polite expression. Suddenly, he smiled, the wide stretch of his mouth revealing a yellowed set of blockish teeth. "I wished to offer my well wishes on your elevation, my lord! I also wished to pay my respects to my daughter and my granddaughter. Yes, yes, I read the birth announcement, as well. With a great deal of astonishment, I might add."

"Indeed, sir?" murmured Lord Ogden, all of his senses on full alert. He really did not believe that the old gentleman had come down, all the way from London, and in the cold season, on a congratulatory call. The baronet had an ulterior motive, he was sure of it, which had yet to be revealed. Perhaps Sir Martin hoped that the uncertain weather, a sudden squall of thick snow, would oblige Delincourt to offer him extended hospitality. *No doubt, he'd like to board at someone else's expense!*

Sir Martin laughed. He crossed his heavy, stockinged legs at the ankle. "Poor Henry was not above sharing my company. Indeed, I was well-acquainted with all my son-in-law's set. We enjoyed the same entertainments many times."

Lord Ogden allowed a satirical smile to cross his lips. By that admission, he interpreted the baronet's meaning to be that the two had frequented the same gaming hells. "Did you indeed?"

"Oh, yes, yes. One was always running into his lordship. The late viscount was quite the high flyer, my lord. You would be astonished if I was to tell you what high stakes his lordship enjoyed."

"I doubt it," said Lord Ogden dryly. He had inherited all of his cousin's debts along with the peerage. Debts of honor had to be paid at once and had been the first to be discharged. Vividly, he recollected the outrageous sums he'd had to outlay in order to settle his cousin's gaming debts.

Sir Martin guffawed as at a huge joke. He slapped a beefy hand across his wide thigh. "Aye, your cousin was a rare 'un! His lordship was addicted to town life. Scarcely left London at all, you know. I doubt the viscount spent more than a week or two at a time in the country." The baronet's porcine eyes glittered. "Yes, indeed! I should very much like to have fair speech with my daughter. I'm certain there's a pretty tale to tell, eh? But no doubt you know it already, my lord! An amiable conversation all around, ending in great goodwill, I daresay. A close peek at my granddaughter and I shall be satisfied! No doubt I shall boast of her to all my friends and acquaintances."

Lord Ogden was still smiling, but the quality of it had changed. Any of his former comrades-in-arms would have recognized the chilling trait behind it. In point of fact, Lord Ogden was in the grip of a cold, murderous rage. He knew now the object behind Sir Martin's unexpected appearance. The old reprobate intended to shake him like a tree for a pretty windfall of blackmail money.

The baronet was more than insinuating that there was something peculiar about Elizabeth's birth. Sir Martin would stigmatize his granddaughter as a bastard and with his great dirty paws, the man would drag his own daughter into sordid scandal and social ruin, thought the viscount with fury.

In the back of his mind, Lord Ogden wondered what Sir Martin had done with the handsome purchase price for the Grange. He recalled precisely when Mr. Kelton had told him of the sale and it had not been that long ago. In that short length of time, surely the baronet could not have drunk and gambled it all away! However, as he regarded the malicious, grotesque being seated across from him, he decided in the great scheme of things, it wasn't important.

All that was important was that he had sworn before God that he would always have a care for Charlotte and their daughter. The viscount's resolution sharpened to tempered steel. He would not let their lives to be besmirched and tainted by this malignant creature. *I shall kill him first.*

Lord Ogden did not doubt for a second that any 'goodwill' on his part would not arrest Sir Martin's accursed threat. No, the baronet would keep coming back. In fact, any surrender of monies would only strengthen the cards which Sir Martin was playing. At any time, Sir Martin could carry out his threat of exposure to the censor of the world and be better believed because of the blackmail payments.

All these thoughts rushed like whistling bullets through the viscount's mind in seconds. As he looked across at Sir Martin's satisfied, fat smirk, a cold decision formed with crystal-clarity. *He believes he has me by the throat. But he does not know me.*

Lord Ogden said abruptly, "Lady Ogden and her daughter are not in to visitors. It's best to conclude our business at once, Sir Martin. You will return to London in my carriage, accompanied by my servant. I shall write a directive to my solicitor, Mr. Digsby, who handles my business affairs. I shall send it by the hand of my servant."

As he spoke, he opened his ink-well, pulled a clean sheet to him, and began to write: *Digsby, the gentleman before you, one Sir Martin Stockton, Baronet, you may recognize as Lady Ogden's parent. Sir Martin has vilely threatened Lady Ogden and her child. Remove him. You are naturally shocked but believe me. This is what I wish you to do...*

Thrown off balance, Sir Martin spluttered. "But-but this is extraordinarily high-handed! Indeed, I am not certain I like it, my lord!"

Lord Ogden ignored the interjection. He finished the letter, scrawled his signature and sanded the sheet. Through stiffened lips, he said in a tightly controlled voice, "It will be two days, perhaps three. These things are not managed at a moment's notice."

"I have hired a chaise. I have yet to pay the post-boys."

"It's of no consequence. My butler will pay the post-boys," said Lord Ogden with authority. Folding the sheet and affixing his seal to it, he looked over at the baronet's incredulous expression. "I insist you put up at a hotel, which Mr. Digsby will recommend. I do not wish Mr. Digsby to be inconvenienced by having to search half the city for you, do you understand? If you are not there at the hotel when Mr. Digsby calls on you, then all is cancelled."

"You go too fast for me, my lord! I'm not certain I understand you," said Sir Martin, temporizing. The interview had taken a turn he had not foreseen, the control of it snatched out of his hands, and he did not like it.

Lord Ogden grimly smiled. He said contemptuously, "No, Sir Martin, I bloody well think you do."

The baronet's ruddy face turned choleric. "Now see here, my lord!"

The viscount coldly overrode him. "You will await word from Mr. Digsby at the hotel for the conclusion of our business. At my expense, of course."

Sir Martin's angry expression was arrested. His eyes gleamed as he began to rub his thick hands together. "At your expense, my lord! That is generous, indeed. It is, indeed!"

Lord Ogden rose from behind the desk, holding the sealed missive in his hand, and stalked over to jerk the bell-pull. He waited impatiently and as soon as the footman entered, he said curtly, "Send word at once to the stables to have my carriage brought round. It will convey this gentleman to town. You will accompany him to the address written on the outside of this letter, which you will give only into the hand of my solicitor, Mr. Digsby. Then you will wait for any reply that Mr. Digsby might wish to send back. Is that clear?"

"Yes, my lord."

Lord Ogden turned his head to stare with dislike at his visitor. Sir Martin had already heaved himself to his feet with the aid of his cane. The baronet appeared somewhat dazed by the speed of events. "Are you willing to do everything I request, sir?"

"Indeed, my lord! I shall obey you to the letter," said Sir Martin, regaining something of his former smirking assurance. He managed a credible bow despite his girth and the corset creaked.

The viscount briefly nodded. He clasped his hands tightly behind his back. He thought if he did not do so he might yet attack the despicable excuse of a man and throttle him to death. "Good travels, then."

His narrowed gaze followed the baronet's heavy figure as the man tread ponderously out of the room. *A bullet would be quicker, but I haven't the right of war on my side.*

48

Lord Ogden was infinitely grateful that he'd made the decision to deny her ladyship to the baronet, even before Sir Martin had revealed his terrible purpose. He had not wanted Lady Ogden to be made upset by her parent's visit and he shuddered to think what effect Sir Martin's ugly insinuations would have had on her. He believed in the advisability of truth, but he felt relating this particular truth should be delayed until he had the information he was waiting for in hand.

Lord Ogden would have liked to keep Sir Martin's unprecedented call at Delincourt to himself, but that was impossible. The servants would already be talking and it was only a matter of time before news of her father's visit would reach Lady Ogden's ears.

Over luncheon, the viscount informed Lady Ogden and Mrs. Merriweather of Sir Martin's visit. He said coolly, "Sir Martin called upon me, making a brief stop in what was a short sojourn into the country."

Lady Ogden was astonished. "Why, when was this, my lord?" She was unhappy to learn that her father had come to Delincourt and that she had not known it, but at the same time, she was relieved. It would not have been an easy visit. The prospect of such a reunion made her quake. Yet Sir Martin was her father and she owed a daughter's allegiance to him.

"Earlier today, my lady. I'm sorry if you wished to see him. He had scarcely arrived before he left again." Lord Ogden had rid Delincourt of the baronet so speedily that the very swiftness of Sir Martin's departure saved him from making some explanations that were better left for another time.

"But what was the object of my father's visit?" asked Lady Ogden. Suddenly, she dreaded the answer. Her sire was not a convivial man. He had come for some dread purpose, she was sure of it.

Lord Ogden said merely, "We were not closeted for long. Sir Martin expressed his good wishes for my elevation. He remained not above half an hour before he set forward again. The baronet was...pressed for time."

Mrs. Merriweather had been listening open-mouthed, but at this she was roused to indignation. "What, Sir Martin could not stay long enough to see his blood-relations? I don't count myself, of course, being only related by marriage. But what of you, Charlotte, and our sweet little Elizabeth?"

"Leave it, aunt. Believe me, the slight isn't worthy of comment," said Lady Ogden quietly. She did not meet his lordship's level gaze, preferring that he should not guess just how hard it was to accept this most recent example of her father's painful indifference and neglect. At least, she thought, it appeared Sir Martin had not set up the viscount's back.

Mrs. Merriweather turned her gaze back to the viscount, and demanded, "Did Sir Martin leave a note, my lord?"

"I fear not."

"He could *at least* have left a note for you, dear Charlotte," exclaimed Mrs. Merriweather, becoming even more affronted on her niece's behalf. "It was very rude not to have done so. I'm *shocked* by Sir Martin's ill-bred conduct! Though I don't know why I should be, for it is all of a piece!"

"I'm not at all surprised, aunt," responded Lady Ogden. She could readily believe that her sire had not asked to see her. It never occurred to her to question the viscount further. The explanation was altogether too plain. "My father has never taken an interest in me. It's clear his indifference extends to his granddaughter, as well."

Lord Ogden said nothing more. However, his reflections were not kind towards Sir Martin Stockton. It was obvious to him that her ladyship had no good expectations of the baronet; her pensive expression and the downturn in her mouth told him as much. He promised himself that neither Lady Ogden nor their child would ever experience such neglectfulness from him.

Some days later, the expected letter from the solicitor was brought back by his lordship's obedient servant. The footman had thought himself in high alt to be put up by the solicitor, from whom he had been given a handsome tip, and to ride all the way back from London in a gentleman's carriage. It was a tale with which he would many times regale his fellow servants, basking in their envy.

Unaware that he had inflated the footman's self-worth and thus assured himself of the man's complete and unswerving fealty, Lord Ogden swiftly perused the solicitor's closely worded sheet. Then he started again from the beginning, more slowly. The solicitor had obeyed his lordship's orders to the letter. There was also a very interesting bit of intelligence: *...My lord, it is with great satisfaction that I may report an unexpected bonus. I was able to discover the direction of the gentleman's banker, and having secured a power from Sir Martin, I straightaway drew upon the account. All of the commissions which you laid upon me did not cost your lordship a single farthing. In short, the expenses incurred on behalf of the baronet are paid out of his own funds...*

"The monies Sir Martin had from selling the Grange," murmured the viscount. He was pleased by the solicitor's initiative, which both gladdened him and filled him with relief. The financial drain on the estate, which it could still ill afford, had been fortuitously avoided. "Satisfactory, indeed."

There was a postscript, which did not gratify him. *...My lord, in Sir Martin's ramblings it became clear to me that he was influenced in his actions against her ladyship by one Sir William Talley.*

Lord Ogden dropped the letter to the desk. He leaned back in his chair, a deep scowl etching his face. He narrowed his eyes as he tapped a forefinger on the damning paragraph. The gentleman had dared to defy him, but in the fullness of time, he would make good on his promise to Sir William Talley. He roused himself from his grim reflection. For now, he had a more pressing concern. "It only now remains for me to inform Charlotte what I have done with her father. Oh, *bloody* hell!"

The viscount carefully chose his moment and his ground. At an hour when he knew Mrs. Merriweather would be in the stillroom, he sent a request by the butler for Lady Ogden to wait on him in the drawing-room. "We are not to be disturbed, Somerset."

"Very good, my lord."

Lord Ogden paced while he waited, his hands clasped behind his back. It was an exercise in frustration, since the space between the settee and the fireplace was not adequate to comfortably contain the long strides of a healthy gentleman. He finally contented himself with poking for a bit at the burning fire with a fire tool.

When Lady Ogden entered, it was with a lift of her brows and an inquiring smile on her lovely countenance. "You wished to see me, my lord?"

"Yes, thank you for coming to me." Lord Ogden set aside the fire tool, moving forward to take her hand and lifting her curled fingers to his lips. Retaining her hand in a light clasp, he looked down at her. Her green eyes were clear. He hated the thought of watching them cloud over with unhappiness.

Lord Ogden firmed his resolution. It had become an object to him to shield her ladyship from the adversities of life, but in the present instance, he had no alternative but to convey intelligence that must upset her. He had tried out several openings in his mind, but he could discover no easy way to explain the situation to his cousin-in-law. In the end, with his voice devoid of emotion, he spoke in a simple, straightforward manner. "I was not altogether frank with you about Sir Martin's visit, my lady. I apologize for it and trust that you will forgive me. However, my reasons were valid. If I had it to do over, I would do the same thing. My only object has been to defend and protect what is mine. I could hide from you what action I have taken, but it's my wish to be completely open with you. I daresay you will dislike it, but I hope that you will not condemn me out of hand."

Lady Ogden listened, her gaze pinned to the viscount's lean face all the while. An apprehension grew larger and larger. Her mind tumbled from one impression to the next as he spoke to her. She was bewildered at why she had not been informed before of the particulars of her father's visit. She misliked the dread that slowly pervaded her at his lordship's measured words. He was holding her hand, yes, but even that warm comfort could not mitigate her rising anxiety. However, what was most striking to her was the viscount's strange behavior. He spoke without any discernible expression, without any inflection in his deep voice. She was not used to it. *He is so passionless, so wooden.*

Lady Ogden could account for it in only one way. Dismay and shame hurtled through her. Sir Martin must have come to Delincourt for money. That was the reason his visit had been so short. Her ladyship knew well enough how expensive her father's habits were. With a sinking feeling in the pit of her stomach, she wondered just how much Sir Martin had requested from the viscount. She withdrew her hand from the comfort of his lordship's clasp and tightly folded her hands together in front of her.

"I don't understand. Why wasn't I informed before this?" Lady Ogden searched his lordship's stern visage. "Did-did my father perhaps importune you, my lord?"

Lord Ogden's eyes narrowed, almost in amusement, as he looked at her. "Ah, you know your sire too well!"

Lady Ogden flushed. "I do indeed. I'm sorry, my lord." She pushed aside her mortification and straightened her shoulders. Lifting her chin, she gazed straight into the viscount's eyes. "It's a humiliation to me, but I must bear it, as I have any time these several years! What tune did he ask for, my lord? You may feel free to tell me."

"More than I was willing to pay. More than you would ever be willing to pay, I assure you!"

She quailed at the sudden wrath he revealed. Her imaginations ran riot. Sir Martin must have gambled and drunk his way into severe straits, indeed. In a low voice, she said, "Vincent, you must be frank with me."

Lord Ogden was silent. Anxiously, she watched his lordship's face, and when she saw a tic jump in his jaw, her heart sank. She knew that sign of strong temper. Finally, he spoke. "Sir Martin came to trade, madam. He came to claim our *very goodwill,* in exchange for your good name and that of our daughter. In short, he threatened to broadcast to the world that Elizabeth was my bastard and you were my whore."

Lady Ogden's sight darkened. She felt herself sinking, but something caught her. She blinked. She was unsurprised to find herself swung up into the viscount's strong arms. She made no protest as he gently lowered her onto the settee. She clutched at his sleeve, staring up into his grim face. "Vincent, Vincent, it must not be! *Elizabeth*!"

He sat down beside her and took hold of her agitated hands. "I know, my dear, believe me. The horror struck me with no less force, though unlike yours, my concern was equally divided between you and our daughter." He pressed her fingers reassuringly between his own. "I promise you, I shall keep and protect you and Elizabeth to my dying breath. That's why –" He took a deep breath. "That's why I acted as I did." Lady Ogden gazed up at him with painful intensity. Plunging into his confession, he said, "I took immediate steps to remove Sir Martin."

Lady Ogden snatched her hands away, staring at him in liveliest fear. The sudden racing of her heart almost stole her breath. She choked out, "You did not kill him! No, Vincent, no!"

"I will not hide it from you. That's just what I wished to do – what my strongest instincts urged me to do!"

Lady Ogden was inexpressibly relieved. "I'm so glad! I would not wish you to be taken up by a constable for murder or for you to be forced to flee the country!"

As Lord Ogden regarded her, a grin formed on his face. "All of your solicitude is for me! I'm flattered, indeed! What of your father, then?"

"That vile, wretched creature!" she exclaimed. Fury flashed through her. "Do not speak of him again as *my father*! Sir Martin used my mother abominably. The mortification that she suffered at his hands – that we all did! – she and my aunt and myself! Now this, the worst of all!" She pounded the heels of her hands together. "That he *dares* to threaten in *such* a way!"

"My dearest! You must not carry on so."

The viscount attempted to catch hold of her hands, but she warded him off. "No, Vincent! I shall *not* be shushed! From this hour, I utterly cast him off. I shall give the order that Sir Martin is not to darken the doors of Delincourt ever again!" Still in the grip of her rage, Lady Ogden added fiercely, "I would kill him myself if I were other than a weak woman!"

Lord Ogden gave a crack of laughter.

She turned an outraged stare on him. "What do you mean by this, my lord? Do you mock me?"

"Forgive me, Charlotte! I do not believe I have ever thought of you as a *weak woman*! Indeed, I have respected your strength and your pride in every situation!"

Ignoring his lordship's compliment, Lady Ogden stared fixedly at him. Suddenly, she laid an urgent hand on the sleeve of his coat, tightening her fingers on his muscular forearm through the fabric. "You did not pay him. You did not kill him. So, what *have* you done, my lord?"

Lord Ogden sobered at once. "I've had a letter from Digsby, whom I made my instrument in this matter. He writes to me that Sir Martin is well in his incarceration. He takes exercise in the small walled garden attached to the house. He is well-fed and his every need is attended to by his...attendants." Lord Ogden hesitated, before continuing. "Sir Martin is kept supplied with all the drink he desires."

Lady Ogden stared at him in good earnest, completely amazed. "Incarceration? All the drink he cares for? My lord! What farrago is this?"

"I have suspended the threat, my lady. That is all."

"I see." Lady Ogden thought about what he had told her with gathering wonder. She did indeed see, perhaps more than he had intended. She threw another glance at him. "Sir Martin...was not well when he came to call on you, was he?"

Lord Ogden hesitated. He shook his head, saying gravely, "No, I do not believe he was well. Quite the opposite, in fact. I'm sorry if it gives you pain to hear it, but I do not think Sir Martin will live much longer."

Lady Ogden lowered her eyes. She nodded. "Thank you, my lord. That is well worth knowing." When she looked up again, there were tears glimmering in her eyes. "And thank you for your mercy upon him, my lord. It is well-meant."

He gave an abrupt laugh. "I had thought a bullet would be cleaner, ma'am!"

"So it would, but we mustn't repine," she said calmly. "Sir Martin has what he most desired – no responsibility for his person or for those who are most closely connected with him. Instead, he has his mistress the bottle. You are generous, my lord."

Lord Ogden again took one of her hands, clasping it as though it was a precious thing. Completely counter to his gentle hold, he said harshly, "I meant what I said, Charlotte. I have vowed to keep you and our daughter safe." His voice suddenly altered and was no longer harsh. "My love, pray forgive me for my ruthlessness."

Lady Ogden slowly smiled at him. "The roar of the lion! Yes, I see it now. I do recall your saying that at times it forced difficult decisions." She squeezed the strong fingers that held hers. "I am so *very* glad you have made this one, Vincent."

He had wanted her forgiveness; now, he realized that he had her approval and respect as well. She had submitted willingly and without reproof to his judgment. He was humbled and gratified. The viscount lifted her hand and brought it to his lips. He said quietly, "Thank you, ma'am."

49

As the days and weeks slipped by, Lord Ogden waited to learn what plans the viscountess might have formed for her future. The mounting suspense he felt oppressed him. Other than that single reference over breakfast one morning, she had said nothing. The insecurity clawed at his insides. Now that she had the financial means, he did not know if she intended to remain at Delincourt or if she had decided to make her home elsewhere. The unwelcome subject had not yet arisen; strangely, he feared to broach it himself and berated himself for cowardice. Nor had she inquired about the details of her annuity. He hoped she would come to ask his advice, even to confide in him, but she did not.

Lord Ogden observed that she radiated happiness. Though Lady Ogden was still pale, she had lost the tiredness that had marked her countenance after the long hard birth. A clear-eyed, relaxed look softened her face. He had seen it often after the baby was born. On several occasions, he had been privy as she nursed their daughter and he realized it was particularly during those times that he had seen such contentment in her expression. Though he had hired a nursemaid, Lord Ogden made no objection to her ladyship's outlandish insistence not to rely entirely on the nursemaid but to nurse the infant herself. He was delighted by the unexpected maternal side of her. Besides, it suited him. The more content she was, the more difficult it would be for her to decide to leave Delincourt Manor.

Whatever his cousin-in-law's thoughts were on the matter, he assured himself, it would be weeks yet before she was able to travel any great distance. The physician had recommended six weeks of bedrest for her ladyship and though she had not strictly adhered to that direction, Lady

Ogden's slow recovery after giving birth and the increasingly unpredictable weather reduced the likelihood of any immediate projected journey.

*If she should decide to leave...*He steeled himself. He would do what he thought he must in order to secure his success. He was banking that the strength of Lady Ogden's maternal instinct would keep her at Delincourt. He needed more time to persuade her of the advantages of being wed to him. More than once, he had clumsily begun to express his wishful ambition to her, only to falter and fall silent. He had hoped for some inkling of understanding to enlighten her intellect, even if he was not as blunt with her as he might be.

Though it cost him, he did not go to her bed. He didn't want to risk hurting her. He was ever cognizant of the physician's advice to her ladyship. He knew nothing of such things. He would wait longer before he took her to himself again. There would have to be precautions taken, of course. He'd discipline himself, before he crested, to disengage and spend outside her body. Alternatively, he could tie on an infernal French sleeve, made from animal intestines. Whenever the enjoyable convivial congress was resumed, she could not be gotten with child again, not until the culmination of his long-range strategy, the goal which had sprung full-blown into his mind nearly one year before.

He told himself all of that, and knew even as he thought it that he was lying to himself. The truth was that the affair had ended. It had died a natural death. The birth of a posthumous child had set the capstone. Even taking such precautions, even if he *could* be so disciplined, the odds were good that Lady Ogden would conceive again. He would not risk that, not outside wedlock. He would not risk her reputation, nor his honor, to public condemnation. Looking back, it was a wonder to him that the shocking affair had not been uncovered; but with the silent collusion of his valet and her ladyship's dresser, and with the solemn loyalty of his trusted, all-too-knowing friend, Rev. Major Ledger, the secret seemed to have been kept.

The time had come to woo her ladyship in earnest, but he discovered that he had no notion how to set about it. The rules of courtship had been blasted to pieces by the cannonade of illicit passion. It would be folly to think otherwise; he believed he was not such a fool. Social custom that would have dictated his formal overtures to the lady had been stripped from him; he had no direction and no precedent to rely on. It was an enormous obstacle and he did not know how to overcome it.

Still deep in his dissatisfying reflections, Lord Ogden walked downstairs. He was met at the bottom of the staircase by Somerset. "My lord, Mr. Digsby has arrived. I have put him in the ground-floor study."

Lord Ogden was unreasonably annoyed. He had been about to set off for a good clipping ride in hopes of clearing his brain. Even though he had sent for the solicitor, he was not in a mood to conduct business, however important. Abruptly, he decided not to put it off. He handed his crop, gloves and hat to the butler. "I'll see him. Have the groom walk my horse."

"Very good, my lord." Somerset opened the door for him.

Lord Ogden strode into the room. The door was quietly shut behind him. He greeted the solicitor brusquely. "Mr. Digsby, I'm glad you have come. This must be a short interview, however."

Mr. Digsby had already noted his lordship's riding attire. "Forgive me, my lord. I was not told...that is, I can wait until a more convenient time."

"My horse will wait, Digsby." Lord Ogden threw himself into the chair behind the desk. "This will not."

The solicitor bowed. "Very well, my lord. As your lordship requested, I have brought the document that will establish Lady Ogden's account. I've also brought the monies that you required from the bank, my lord." He pointed to the lockbox sitting on the desktop, earning a nod of acknowledgment from his employer.

"Two thousand annum to her ladyship. That was the figure we discussed, was it not? I just want to finish the business as soon as possible," said Lord Ogden impatiently.

Mr. Digsby cleared his throat. "My lord, with respect, Lady Ogden is due not two thousand annum but three thousand. Her ladyship was delivered of a live child, for two thousand annum, and also a stillborn, for one thousand." He hesitated before he pointed out the obvious. "It is a fantastic figure, my lord. It will be a burden on the encumbered estate."

Lord Ogden did not trust himself to respond at once. An unexpected shaft of grief had pierced his soul. He held his face expressionless. His body felt cast of marble. The stillborn – his firstborn son. He suddenly became aware of the sympathy in the solicitor's expression. The man would have been astonished if he'd had a window into his mind. *Digsby believes me to be struck dumb by the amount.*

The strong twist of emotion was hard to shake off. He finally mastered it and said colorlessly, "Of course you are correct, Digsby. Three thousand. I wish the stipend tied up for Lady Ogden and her children."

"Her children, my lord?" A surprised note sounded in the question.

"I expect that Lady Ogden will remarry, sir," said Lord Ogden, feeling the familiar tic jump in his jaw. He was still uncertain of his ground where it concerned his cousin-in-law and it angered him.

"Yes, yes, of course," said the solicitor hastily. He appeared embarrassed. "Forgive me, my lord. I was not thinking perfectly. I should have thought of that likelihood myself. Lady Ogden is still young. She is now a lady of some means. Her ladyship will naturally be courted."

The solicitor's observation grated on him. That the lady might choose someone other than himself was a real and unpleasant possibility. He did not believe he could trust himself any longer to cover what emotions roiled under his cool façade.

Lord Ogden stood up. "I shall leave you now, Digsby."

"Of course, my lord. I shall have the revised copy readied for your signature as soon as possible."

"When you are finished, you have only to give word to my butler or a footman," said Lord Ogden briefly. "Wherever I am upon my return, a message will be taken to me and I will rejoin you to sign the document."

Mr. Digsby bowed. "I understand, my lord."

Lord Ogden quitted the ground-floor study with his long, brisk stride and retrieved his riding accouterments from the butler. As he walked out of the front door, the crop braced under one arm, he set his beaver hat firmly on his head. He stood on the shallow stone steps to pull on his leather riding gloves, his gaze absently sweeping the approach to the manor house. It was a pleasant sight, even with the lateness of the year. Some care had been given to trimming of the trees, earlier in the fall, and the lawn had been kept cut over the summer months. However, what he saw in his imagination was a busy, noisy London street, filled with carriages, pedestrians, and the dustmen sweeping the walkways. A lady who had been kept buried in the country while her lordly husband had pursued his own amusements in town might well choose to remove to London. For all he could discover, his cousin Henry had neglected her ladyship to a shocking degree. She had never been introduced to polite society or gone to the theater or gone shopping in London's myriad of well-stocked shops.

Lord Ogden lifted his booted foot into the metal stirrup and swung himself up onto his horse. Gathering the reins, he nodded for the stable lad to let go of the bridle. He wished he had the right to give her ladyship all of that and more, he thought, as he set the gelding into motion. Upon his return, he was told that Mr. Digsby was awaiting his pleasure. He sighed, and nodded. "Better to get the business over with."

Lord Ogden waited until late in the evening, after coffee had been served, to summon his cousin-in-law. He glanced around the ground-floor study. They seemed destined always to do life-altering business in the quiet, cramped room.

Lady Ogden entered and walked forward to seat herself. It had been a good day, she reflected. She had been able to accomplish all that she wished without needing to lay down to rest in the afternoon. She knew her full strength was at last returned and it gladdened her. Even as she smiled in a friendly way at the viscount, she was cataloguing in her mind what she needed to discuss with the housekeeper and the cook on the morrow. She had not a single premonition that her tranquility was to be sorely tried.

"You are in good looks this evening, my dear."

"Thank you, my lord." Lady Ogden was pleased by his lordship's compliment. She was wearing a Devonshire brown gown that she had recently made up and she knew that the rich reddish brown looked well on her. Complacently, she smoothed her fingers over her skirt. She flattered herself she had made it appear quite dashing with its bits of ribbon and lace flounces.

Lord Ogden was abrupt. "You will recall the agreement drawn up at my direction. You have earned a L3,000 annuity, Charlotte. You have not asked for it, but I have here the first year's payment."

Lady Ogden was disconcerted. *So that's why Digsby is here.* She had wondered, but it wasn't her place to inquire into the viscount's business. This time it had to do with her and she discovered that it affected her not at all. She was content with how things stood. She had a beloved daughter and she was at Delincourt, which remained her home; indeed, it was more than ever her home. She laughed. "Yes, I suppose I have earned it, at that. I had forgotten about the annuity."

"I have not, however." Lord Ogden opened the strongbox on his desk and drew forth the notes which he had previously counted out and banded with string. He slid the stack of notes across the desk toward her. "Here you are. I can act as your banker, if you like. I can invest for you in 'Change. If you'd prefer to work through Digsby instead, I shall certainly understand."

"Why-why, thank you, my lord," said Lady Ogden, taken aback. She started to reach out her hand but then she drew it back. She looked at the viscount, focusing at last on his formidable expression. *Why is he looking at me so strangely?* She gave an uncertain laugh. "I'm not sure what to do."

"You can afford the rent for a decent abode and staff now. Have you given any thought at all to what you wish to do?"

"Why, no, I haven't," she said slowly. She searched the viscount's face for any hint of what might be running through his mind, but his impassive gaze gave her not even the trace of a hint. However, she was certain she had not mistaken the coolness in his voice. A niggle of doubt wormed into her mind and made her anxious. She placed her hands in her lap and tightly clasped them together as she tried to feel her way. "I suppose I must soon make a decision."

"Not at all. You shall always have a place at Delincourt. I would be loath to see you leave."

An uneasy silence fell, one filled on both sides by unspoken questions.

Lady Ogden looked into the viscount's unreadable, dark eyes. Her brain winged swiftly, apprehension, dread, dismay all hurtling through her. He was giving her nothing upon which to base her response, to release what she longed to say, but which she very much feared would make her look the fool. *He has never told me that he loves me.* He had merely told her that he delighted to make love to her, and at that, the sentiment had been couched in crude terms. The agitated state of her mind grew and was such that she could think of nothing but retreat. *I must have time to think!* Her lungs seemed constricted, her heart thudded; but she refused to allow her clash of emotions show in her manner. She rose from the chair and reached out for the L3000 laying on the desktop. Her fingers trembled when she picked up the stack of bank notes, but otherwise nothing of her inward turbulence was apparent.

"Thank you, my lord. Certainly, I shall give some thought to it, for it is not a decision to be made lightly." She studied the viscount's face again, hoping to discern something – *anything!* In a bid to elicit some response, she added, "Perhaps I shall stay at Delincourt. I do not know. I have often longed to experience a different locale. Perhaps I shall rent a house elsewhere."

The viscount nodded, his face impassive. His gaze dropped; he said coolly, "I'm not surprised, given how close your life has always been. I shall have Digsby make inquiries on your behalf. You have only to write him what you require in an establishment, whether you want to live in the country or in town, etc., etc." He picked up the pen on his desk and rolled it between thumb and forefinger in a restless manner. It seemed to her to be a show of impatience with the interview.

An astonishing realization struck her like a physical blow. Something hard formed in the pit of her stomach. Suddenly, she was shivering – the temperature in the room seemed to have dropped by several degrees. Encroaching ice stuck needle-like slivers into her quivering heart. *He doesn't want me here. I thought - I thought...* Her throat tightened. Despair was clamoring in the darkening depths of her wailing soul. She refused to listen; she *couldn't* listen or otherwise she would come completely undone. She'd obviously been very wrong.

Lady Ogden stared at the viscount, willing him to say something else, anything else, but he was silent. The deadening coldness spread inside of her. *He hasn't asked to come to my bed. He has tired of me at last.* A vast chasm opened beneath her feet. She was certain her face held a bruised expression. Her eyes stung while she struggled not to give way. She drew herself up, undergirded by pride. Through tightened lips, she replied, "Yes, of course. I will be grateful for Mr. Digsby's help. I believe the sooner provision can be made for the move, the better it will be." She caught what appeared to be a flash of anguish on his lordship's face. It was gone in an instant and she did not know if she had seen it at all.

Lord Ogden gave a brisk nod. He threw down the pen on the desk. "Good; it's settled. I will hire a second nursemaid for Elizabeth, if necessary."

"Why, what do you mean? I'm still nursing her."

Lord Ogden raised his brows. He looked coldly at her. "I don't think you perfectly understand. Elizabeth remains with me."

Lady Ogden stared at the viscount, aghast. Her brain scrambled with a cascade of appalled thoughts. She couldn't possibly have heard what she thought he had said. She had obviously misunderstood his lordship's meaning. Surely, his lordship did not actually mean that he would separate her daughter from her. She shook her head and gave a quavering laugh. "It isn't a very good joke, my lord."

"My daughter remains with me."

At his flat statement, her heart beat wildly, madly, in her breast. Panic enveloped her; she felt she was strangling, fighting for air. All of her world was crashing down.

"You must think me unfeeling and cruel, but pray allow me to explain. I have a proposal which I think you might – which I hope you might –" His lordship's stumbling words were never finished.

"Unfeeling! Cruel!" she cried out. "You're a monster!"

Lord Ogden's cheekbones flushed. He stiffened; his tone harshened. "I told you before, madam! You made a devil's pact. You conceived *my* child. She is *my...child*."

"Dear God." She felt the color drain from her face. Terror shivered through her limbs and her whole body began to tremble. Her skin prickled with horror. "Vincent, what are you saying?"

Lord Ogden regarded her, seemingly without a clue as to what his shocking statement had done to her. He shrugged. "It is within my rights to choose to bring up my cousin's legal issue. You are free to go. Elizabeth stays with me."

"No! No, no, no! You cannot be so cruel! You cannot!"

"Then you will sell yourself to me."

"What?" He had figuratively punched her so hard that she reeled back and fell down into the chair. Lady Ogden shook her head, trying to clear her whirling brain of the debilitating dizziness. She was confused, upset, she couldn't think straight. She was certain of only one thing. "I think you're mad!"

"Oh, I don't think so, Charlotte!" snapped Lord Ogden. "I merely want your excessive pride humbled. I want you to grace my table. *I want you in my bed!*"

By the time he had finished, Lady Ogden was breathing raggedly. Her bosom was rising and falling with such rapidity that she feared she would faint. "Is that what this is about? Your-your *obsession* with me? You stoop so low to use my daughter as blackmail? You are as base as my father! That you dare! *That you dare!*"

She jumped to her feet, clenching her fists at her sides. The packet of pound notes was bowed almost in two in her hand and the edges scored the inside of her hooked fingers. Such heated fury blazed through her that she felt she must combust on the spot. "My God, how I detest this room! I've experienced nothing but pain and disillusion here!" She swept out a palm, gesturing toward the fireplace. "It was here you ravished me – here, you tricked me!" She gave a shattered laugh. "I stand amazed by my own stupidity! I tumbled so neatly into your hands. Fool, *fool* that I was!"

Lord Ogden was also on his feet. "I never meant to trick you!"

"All I ever wanted was support, Vincent!"

"It was too late. When I ravished you –!" He made a visible effort. His voice was low. "I could already have gotten you with child."

Incensed, she shrieked, "But you didn't!"

His sun-bronzed features appeared gray, a pallor having risen underneath. His hands closed, opened and closed. "I didn't know that! I had to make provision!"

"If you had never touched me again, I would still have had the support I needed for myself and my aunt. I'd have been *grateful* for L750! It would have seemed a princely sum!" She gave a strangled, disbelieving laugh. It was happening again. She was in a desperate place and her fate was to be decided by this man. Fury burst anew upon her. She threw out her arm in a grand, contemptuous arc. "And here we are, in this hateful, *hateful* room! You think to coerce me again! But no, I tell you – no, no! I will not let you!"

He thrust out an upturned hand toward her. It struck her even through the hot haze of her rage that it was a pathetic attempt at appeal. "No! It's not that! What I meant – what I intend –"

"Despicable! I will see you rot in hell!" She was beyond hearing anything else he might say. It was beyond bearing. She couldn't stand to look at him and she swept around. Her breath was ragged, her pulse raced. All she wanted was to escape. She ran to the door, twisted the brass knob, and wrenched it open.

As from a distance, from some faraway place behind her, she heard the urgency of his plea. *"You must stay. Please."*

"Stay at Delincourt! I'd rather die!"

It was a disaster, a total defeat.

Lord Ogden dropped down into the chair and shoved his fingers through his thick hair. "That did not go exactly as I envisioned," he muttered. In truth, he was shaken. She had snapped like old brittle iron. He had thought she would defy him with a show of that damnable pride of hers. He had expected that he would have to chip away at her defenses before she at last yielded. In short, he had badly miscalculated. He groaned. "I went about it all wrong! I've cut the ground out from under myself. Ah, Vincent, you're a twice-born fool!"

Lady Ogden had rushed out before he could say what he would demand from her. He frowned, a stab of anger hobbling his self-recrimination. He did not believe his terms would be found wanting.

After all, she would have a ring on her finger. She would have the satisfaction of gracing a social position. She would be able to bring up her daughter. She would bear other children. *My children.*

He had not intended to blurt out such a stupid ultimatum. His pride had been struck to the quick. His desperation had been ignited to rage. Suddenly, he had felt every bit as cruel as she thought him. He had not wanted to play the hand he held, but she had opened the game with her decision to leave Delincourt.

Before she had entered the room, he had given himself a stern lecture. It was to be her ladyship's choice. He would only lay out her options. He would accept her decision, whatever it might be, and if it was one that made him unhappy, he would accept it in a rational manner. Instead, he had blundered into a position that was indefensible.

He had made his voice as colorless as he was capable. He'd ignored the ache in his chest, even as he steeled himself against the lively fear in her expressive eyes. He had used what he had considered the winning gambit. He would *make* her listen to him. But then her eyes had blazed with such heat that he had been startled. He had seen loathing in her face.

The furious declaration she had hurled at him ricocheted over and over like whining bullets in his brain. *"Stay at Delincourt! I'd rather die!"*

He had stormed the breach. But he had fallen, bloody and maimed.

50

Lady Ogden rushed upstairs. High fear made her heart pound so loud that she could hear it in her ears. When she reached her bedchamber, she rang for her dresser. She was trembling and breathless. "I must get away. I have to get away!" Her shocked brain was yet preternaturally calm. She knew the things she would need. The L3,000 was a fortune. She also had the remainder of her quarterly pin money. The money was her salvation. It made possible her impending flight from Delincourt. She retrieved her jewel box, which held the precious documents that had been signed by the viscount. She could enforce her support from him with those. She would have to send word to her aunt later from wherever she went. She threw open her wardrobe and began flinging garments onto the bed.

When Mills entered, the dresser gawped at the chaotic scene. Her mistress continued to shuttle back and forth in haste. "My lady, what's this?"

"No questions, Mills. You must pack my things, as well as your own. Inform the nursemaid to have herself and Elizabeth made ready. Give the order for the carriage to be brought up to the servants' entrance. We are leaving Delincourt, now, at once."

"My lady! This is a foolish taking!"

Lady Ogden rounded on her dresser. Her taut nerves were near breaking. She was awash with apprehension; it beat through her along with her rapid pulse. She feared that the viscount would learn of her decampment and stop her from taking her daughter. "He means to take my child from me, Mills! *Do you understand?* He will take Elizabeth from me!"

The dresser made no further protests. In concert with many worried glances, she did everything her mistress had ordered. After packing a small trunk for her ladyship, she went away to her own room, shortly to return with a heavy cloak buttoned over her dress and clutching the handle of a battered portmanteau.

Lady Ogden scrambled into a carriage dress and buttoned over it a warm pelisse. She sent word for her daughter to be brought to her downstairs at the servants' entrance and to be warmly dressed for an outing. She penned a short note and left it where it would be found and given to her aunt. Then picking up the straps of her small, heavy trunk, she left her bedchamber in a whirl of skirts.

At Lady Ogden's urgent command to the coachman, the horses surged forward in a ground-eating canter. She settled back against the seat squab and at last began to think past the alarm and dread. The gazes of her dresser and the nursemaid were fixed on her, reflecting apprehension. *My God, what have I done?* The magnitude of her foolhardiness began to sink in. She hadn't a notion where she would go. She hadn't thought at all beyond her immediate escape from Delincourt. But now her anxious mind berated her for what she had done in her impetuosity.

A flurry of tiny snowflakes brushed against the frosted carriage windows. The hot bricks to warm their feet were already growing cool. Full night was coming on. It would be dangerous to continue driving on at such a pace, especially without the moon to light the way. *I must be mad! I've risked all of our lives!*

She rapped on the trap overhead to shout an order to the coachman. After swaying and bowling along for several minutes, the carriage stopped. She alighted at the vicarage with her infant daughter, the nursemaid and her dresser in tow.

Lady Ogden's arrival was an astonishment to her friends. "Please, please, you must help me! I must get away. He means to take my baby from me!" The vicar and his wife were amazed by her ladyship's agitated assertion. But there she was, her face ravaged by tears, her babe in her arms, accompanied by her faithful dresser and the scared nursemaid.

Making a swift decision, Rev. Major Ledger put a hand on his wife's shoulder. "Do what you can, my dear." He strode with his fast, limping step to the stairs and swiftly mounted the narrow rises, disappearing from sight in the turn of the staircase.

Mrs. Ledger rose to the occasion. With practical level-headedness, she said, "You must not remain standing here! Come into the parlor, Lady Ogden. Your nursemaid must go upstairs with the infant to one of the bedchambers, where there is a nice fire. Such a cold evening!" She turned to her housekeeper, who had been hovering in the background. "Mrs. Tompkins, show the nursemaid to the back bedchamber. And make tea for her ladyship. You may also take a tray upstairs to the nursemaid."

Lady Ogden reacted with irrational panic. "No! Elizabeth must remain with me!"

It took some persuasion on Mrs. Ledger's part to overcome Lady Ogden's fearful protestations that she didn't want to be separated from her child, but Mrs. Ledger was firm in her resolve. "Charlotte, the babe will be better for being warmed by the fireside. Allow the nursemaid to tend to her. You will be better for sitting by a fire, too. Now come, I shall not leave you. We will go into the parlor and be comfortable." She was aided by the dresser, who staunchly declared that she would not leave her ladyship's side and also urged the viscountess to go into the parlor.

Lady Ogden gave way and allowed herself to be led into the cozy room. Mrs. Ledger settled her ladyship on a settee and seated herself beside her. She put an arm around her friend, but Lady Ogden's shoulders were stiff. "Now, Charlotte, you must tell me all about it."

Lady Ogden suddenly beat the heels of her hands together. "I don't know what to do! I don't know where to go!"

"We shall discuss it in a little while," said Mrs. Ledger in a soothing tone. When the tea was brought in, Mrs. Ledger poured a cup, sweetened and with a splash of cream, and served it to the viscountess. The familiar ritual seemed to calm Lady Ogden, who murmured her appreciation. Mrs. Ledger was relieved. She turned to the dresser. "Mills, you must take a cup, too."

Rev. Major Leger opened the door to poke his head inside the room. When he had caught his wife's attention, he retreated from sight. Murmuring reassuringly, Mrs. Ledger left the parlor and shut the door behind her.

Rev. Major Ledger had hastily changed into riding clothes, a greatcoat buttoned over all. "I've ordered the horse brought round. I will ride to Delincourt."

"Yes, you must." Mrs. Ledger moved forward to grasp her husband's outstretched gloved hands and addressed him worriedly. "She is nearly out of her mind. I cannot reason with her."

"She is indeed out of her mind if she thinks Vincent would serve her such a foul trick!"

"Charlotte is not an hysteric!" said Mrs. Ledger sharply.

"No," agreed Rev. Major Ledger with a heavy frown. "I've always found her to be a sensible woman."

"*Something* must have happened! Charlotte is high-spirited but she is not a fool."

"Then Vincent is acting the fool," said Rev. Major Ledger grimly.

"Oh, what could my foolish brother have done?"

He kissed her swiftly. "Do your best to calm her ladyship, my love. I must go to Vincent."

The moon was beginning to rise, breathtakingly beautiful in the cloud-ridden dark sky, when Rev. Major Ledger rode up to the manor, the horse's hooves crunching on new-fallen snow. When he was admitted, he at once demanded an audience with the viscount. He was shown into the ground-floor study, where he discovered the viscount sitting behind the desk, his elbows propped on top of it and his head dropped into his hands. His lordship's attitude was one of abject despair. Rev. Major Ledger snapped shut the door. At the sharp bang, Lord Ogden raised his head and looked toward him.

In the privacy of the ground-floor study, Rev. Major Ledger stripped off his gloves and tossed them aside, along with his hat. He advanced on the viscount, the greatcoat swinging with his hasty step. "What the devil, Vincent? Lady Ogden is bawling her eyes out in my parlor!"

Lord Ogden leaned back in his chair. He said wearily, "So she has gone to you, has she?"

"She claims you mean to take the child away from her."

Lord Ogden drew his hand down over his face. "I wouldn't. I couldn't."

Staring at the viscount, Rev. Major Ledger demanded, "*Did* you tell her that you'd take the child?"

Lord Ogden gave a slow nod. Under his friend's unfolding look of incredulity, he writhed with shame, yet it could not rival the misery that pervaded him even to his soul. He ached with it. "Yes; I did. I badly miscalculated."

Rev. Major Ledger didn't mince words. Wrathfully, he exclaimed, "Jolter-head! Brainless, beetle-headed fool!"

Lord Ogden nodded again. He whole-heartedly agreed with the vicar's unfettered, brutal assessment of his actions. He got up and walked over to the side table, where there was a wine decanter and glasses on a silver tray. "I've made a rare mull of it."

"Vincent, Vincent."

"She said she was leaving Delincourt. I told her that she must bear the consequences. I was attempting to force her to stay," said Lord Ogden in a flattened tone. He lifted the decanter and splashed a measure of sherry into a glass, then gestured in question with the decanter at his friend.

Rev. Major Ledger impatiently waved aside the offer of wine. He visibly reined in his temper in an attempt to bring reason to bear. "Have you ever told her that you loved her?"

Lord Ogden said shortly, "Of course, I haven't." He knocked back the wine in a single swallow. He barely tasted it. He wondered when his numbed senses would return. He hoped it would not be before he was drunk off his head.

"Good God, Vincent, she's a *woman!* She needs flowery speeches. She needs your gentle wooing. She needs to hear the words!"

Lord Ogden poured himself another glass of wine. His hand was shaking. He set down the decanter before it slipped from his grip. He tossed a curt response over his shoulder. "She ripped my heart out of my chest once!"

"You're a man! You survived a forlorn hope, for God's sake! You're not a coward, Vincent!"

The viscount turned sharply about. "But I am! I'm so lily-livered that my teeth chatter!" His friend's astonished expression checked his unmeasured outburst. The rapid rise and fall of his chest could not contain his suffering. Unable to bear it any longer, he tightly conveyed his worst fears. "What if she should reject me again? I *could* not bear it again. Especially now, Arthur! I've fathered a child on her. I cannot lose her. I must not! Nor my little daughter, my little Elizabeth!"

Rev. Major Ledger limped forward. He gripped his friend's shoulder and shook it roughly. "Come, Vincent! You know it isn't the eager fellow who is the bravest."

Lord Ogden grimaced. He knew very well what his old comrade-in-arms was saying. "Instead, it's the one who is terrified, but he does what he must anyway." He looked into his friend's clear, gray eyes. He scowled. He set down the wineglass with some force, sloshing the sherry. "Be damned to you, Arthur! You are too good of a vicar."

Rev. Major Ledger squeezed his shoulder before letting go. "Then you must feel a strange compulsion to increase my living."

"Bloody cheek," growled Lord Ogden, but with a twisted smile.

"Come to her now, Vincent. You cannot let it end like this."

"No, of course not. You're right. I must convince her that I've always wanted her to wife," said Lord Ogden slowly. An idea came into his mind. He walked around the desk and swiftly fished out the key from his pocket and bent to open the locked drawer. He took out the special license and straightened, tucking it into the pocket inside the breast of his coat. "I'll order a mount brought round and go back with you."

"Thank God," said Rev. Major Ledger fervently.

"My dear, I'd like a few words privately with Lady Ogden," said Rev. Major Ledger.

"Of course. Mills, come with me." As Mrs. Ledger passed by her husband, she met his eyes, a question in her own gaze. When he nodded in reassurance, she smiled and exited the parlor, followed by her ladyship's silent dresser.

Rev. Major Ledger stopped the impetuous progress of his friend with a hand on his elbow. "Mind you leave your temper at the door, Vincent." He waited for his lordship's curt nod before he showed him into the parlor. "Lady Ogden, here is someone who desires to have an earnest word with you."

At sight of the viscount entering the room, Lady Ogden leaped to her feet. Her face whitened. Her widened eyes held a hunted look. "You've come to take away Elizabeth!"

"No!" Lord Ogden took a quick step forward. She shrank back, warding off his approach; he stopped in midstride. His heart squeezed at the terror in her green eyes. *I have done this! When I wish only to hold her safe!* He slowly raised his hands, palms open to her. He did not want to frighten her further. "I swear I haven't, Charlotte. My word of honor on it."

Lady Ogden gave a brief nod, acknowledging his oath, but her posture remained defensive. Confusion crossed her face. She warily eyed him. "Then why have you come? For I must tell you, I don't trust your motives."

"You do not know my motives," said Lord Ogden tightly.

She laughed a little wildly. "No! Of course, I don't – when you have told me that I must *sell* myself to you in order to keep my baby!"

"You are a misbegotten idiot, Vincent. How did you *ever* seduce her?" muttered Rev. Major Ledger from where he stood behind the viscount's stiff shoulder. Raising his voice, he said, "Lady Ogden, the man is a blinded fool. However, I dearly love him as my own brother, so I beseech you on his behalf. Despite his stupid, misguided pride, he is a good fellow."

Lord Ogden rounded on him with mingled frustration and anger. "*My* pride? Arthur, you obviously don't know this woman. She has a bloody pike shoved up her arse!"

Rev. Major Ledger slapped an open hand hard against the side of the viscount's head. Lord Ogden yelped and glared at him. Rev. Major

Ledger demanded, "Do I have to break your head? Mind your manners, my lord!"

The viscount's obvious temper and Rev. Major Ledger's visible disgust strongly struck Lady Ogden. A spurt of choked laughter was startled out of her. The two gentlemen turned their heads in concert to look at her, both frowning, obviously not understanding nor approving of her amusement.

Lady Ogden put up fingers to cover her quivering mouth, suppressing another gurgle. "You look like two sulky schoolboys!" She gave vent to a peal of laughter which quickly edged toward hysteria. Abruptly, she started sobbing and covered her face. "Oh, God! Oh, God!"

"Charlotte!"

Strong arms swept around her and she dropped her head onto a familiar shoulder. Somewhere in the distance, there sounded a halting step, the creak of a closing door. When Lady Ogden recovered her equilibrium, she pulled out of the viscount's arms and stepped back. She dashed her hands across her wet cheeks. Angry with herself, angry with him, she exclaimed, "Why have you come? Oh, why cannot you let me be! Why do you torture me so?"

Lord Ogden swung around and strode a few short steps away from her. Over his shoulder, he shot, "I love you!"

"*You love me!*" Lady Ogden was stunned. She made an encompassing gesture, which he couldn't possibly see since his broad back was turned from her. "After-after all this? This is what you say to me?"

The viscount whirled. His dark eyes blazed. "Yes! Is it so incomprehensible?"

Lady Ogden laughed in sheer amazement. "You can ask that! When I recall with what insufferable arrogance you have treated me! How you have trampled upon my sensibilities!" She shook her head in furious bemusement. "My God, I have suffered agonies at your hands. But this last – ordering me to accept your suit so that I might keep my child! You're a madman, Vincent!"

He roared out his frustration. "It was all done – *Damn it, it was all a pathetic bid to win your affections!* Everything I have done, every word, every action – you must see it for what it was! I plotted to keep you close. I thought in time, with the incitement of passion, that you would come to love me! Instead, it was I who became the more ensnared!"

Lady Ogden stared at him, her lips parting.

Lord Ogden waited, his chest heaving. He waited for her ladyship to say something, anything at all, but she merely stared at him as though she couldn't believe her ears. Recklessly, he burst out with all of his pent-up, raw emotions. "Yes, I was mad! I may still be mad, for all I know. But know this, too, my lady! I do love you, most passionately and ardently. I always have. I always shall. As God is my witness, it is the truth! I swear it!"

He snatched the special license out of his breast pocket and unfolded it, holding it up to her. "Look! It is the truth! I had Arthur procure this special license for me months ago! I've always loved you. I've always wanted you to become my wife! Not for some arcane purpose but because I love you! I don't know what else to say!"

Still, she just looked at him. Her green eyes had turned almost blank. Incomprehension seemed to have taken her over. In despair, he thought the shock of what he had admitted about his machinations must have frozen her mind with horror. The viscount realized his fate was sealed. He had wagered his soul and he had spectacularly lost. He knew without a shred of doubt that she could never bring herself to forgive him. "Oh, God."

"Oh, Vincent, you are such a fool," she whispered. "I don't know that I can believe you. Not when you have said nothing until now!"

"Charlotte!" he exclaimed, appalled that she could question his sincerity. "I have sworn it on my honor!"

She shook her head. "Why could you not have told me something of what you felt? It would have made such a difference. How could you be so blind, so foolish? I learned to love you. Indeed, almost from the beginning, my heart began to question my mind. But I could not give in to what I felt, not when I believed you to be indifferent to me."

"Indifferent to you!" It was Lord Ogden's turn to stare with incredulity. "*Indifferent?* I could scarce keep my hands off of you!"

"It's not the same!" It was the age-old cry of women echoing down the corridors of time. "You made me the object of your desire. You taught me the carnal pleasures. You made me into a creature of passion. But not once did you declare that you loved me!"

"But I did! Every time I gathered you to me! With every kiss, with every stroke of my cock inside your sweet quim, pleasuring you until you shook with your beguiling frenzy! That's the way of a man with a woman that he loves."

"Damn you, Vincent." She folded her arms tight about herself and turned away from him. Her brain was awhirl, half-fearing, half-hoping. Her entire being was bursting with an agony of indecision and an alarming degree of unfurling elation. She was trembling with it. She heard the sound of his hesitant bootsteps coming up behind her. Then his hand was on her elbow, cupping it, his fingers gently urging her to turn.

"Please, Charlotte. I beg you to look at me."

Lady Ogden could not find it in herself to resist. She faced him and waited for what he might say next. She wanted to hear it, yet again she did not. She could not make up her mind. She loved him, yes, but his declaration was so late in coming. She did not know whether it was too late.

"You have accused me of caring nothing for you, except for what you gave me of your person. I'm not ashamed of the way I feel about your exquisite body. I don't believe any man could look at the woman he loved with anything but pleasure. But it was always more than that with me."

"How can I know that? How can I know it to be the truth?"

"Surely you recall! I went away to boarding school and then directly into the army. In my absence, the little girl grew into a beautiful woman. When I first laid eyes on you again, I was struck dumb. You teased me gently for my backwardness. I was in love with you from that moment to this. It was always you, Charlotte."

She had never understood him. She strained for comprehension. She must understand if there was to be any hope of happiness. The burning question long in her mind could no longer be contained. "Why did you propose such a wicked bargain to me? What did you hope to gain?"

"I have told you. I wanted to keep you close. I wanted the chance to make you love me."

She searched his dark, burning eyes, his intent face, and found only honesty. "But what if I had not learned to love you? If I had birthed an heir, you would have lost everything. The title, Delincourt and...and me."

"It was a risk I was willing to take." His voice turned harsh again. "I bartered my soul, Charlotte."

She said decidedly, "My lord, you are indeed a great fool."

Lord Ogden drew in a tortured breath. He looked at her with agony in his eyes. In a hoarse whisper, he said, *"Charlotte, if you leave me now, I shall die."*

She at last had the key to him. It was never about Delincourt or perpetuating a fraud. He had never embarked on a fraud at all, but had bared his very self to her. The way he had gone about it had been borne out of old anguish and burning anger, but it had indeed reflected his heart, if only she had been able to read it.

Lady Ogden raised a hand to slide over his rigid jaw, to cup his lean face. "I think you must love me very much, to have risked so much," she said softly. "Since I love you almost as well, I think you should marry me, my lord."

He stared down at her, not daring to believe in the turnabout of his fortune. He covered her hand with his own, nearly crushing her fingers against his cheek. He demanded, "Are you playing with me, Charlotte? If you are, it is a cruel joke."

"Oh, no. I only wished to punish you a little." Lady Ogden smiled up at him. "Let us go home, my lord."

"One moment, madam!" His brows lowered over his aquiline nose. "You love me *almost* as well?"

Lady Ogden sighed in a show of resignation, but a smile teased her lips. "Oh, if you must have it! I love you *very* well."

The viscount's face lit up as he laughed. He caught her up in his arms, making her give a breathless laugh, and then he kissed her. His firm lips were possessive, heated; his tongue sought and found entrance, and she moaned in her throat. She wound her arms around his muscular neck and responded to his ardor, her body pliant against him. *It's been long, so long!* His strong arms crushed her to him, as though he would never let her go, and their bodies fit together like halves of a whole. She was made aware of his banked passion. She joyed in the hardness pressing against her belly.

Then, breathing rather hard, his lordship set her down on her feet and drew her over to the settee. There was still a smoldering look in his dark eyes, but he spoke evenly enough. "We must talk, my lady. If I've learned nothing else – and a hard lesson it has been! – it's about the advisability of truth."

"Yes, we must form the habit of being open with one another," said Lady Ogden, still smiling. With the passionate kiss, her body was left tingling. Any lingering doubts had been laid to rest. *Oh, he still wants me! And I want him!* "I have only one caveat. Let's not bore one another with fits of ill-temper."

Lord Ogden grinned at her. "I will agree to that."

The gaiety was swift to dissipate as each of them, sometimes with hesitation, brought up things which they had rarely or ever discussed. Lady Ogden had kept close one such thing, but though she had often given careful thought to what she would say if it should ever come up, now all of her rehearsed words were abandoned. "You have never spoken of our son."

"I cannot speak of it!" The viscount stood up abruptly, his jerky movement indicative of suppressed agitation. He could not articulate how the loss had become inextricably bound with the deaths of his friends in the war. "Do you think my heart made of stone? Every feeling, every animation of my mind, is at once glad for you and Elizabeth yet plunged into the depths of depression and grief. He was my son!"

"Oh, is it the same for you?" she asked in wonderment. It was a revelation to her that he could harbor such deep feeling for a child he would never know. She was conscious of a squeeze in the region of her heart. "I did not know! Oh, Vincent!" Her eyes filled with tears as she stood up. She held out her hands to him. He quickly went back to her and grasped her fingers tightly in his own.

"My dear Charlotte," he uttered. He lifted first one hand, then the other to his quivering mouth. "I shall mourn him all of my life." She stepped closer and laid her bent head on his shoulder. She felt the gentle weight when he let his cheek fall against her head. His breath stirred her hair, his promise rumbled in her ear. "We shall have other children, my love. We shall have other sons."

"Yes."

They stood thus, their hands clasped together between their warm bodies, their heads touching for a long, long moment. It was sublime, as though they had found their way back after a long, arduous journey. When at last they each stirred and stepped back, they had a better understanding of one another and they shared a faint smile. The strained emotions had exhausted them, but now a peace had been reached.

He again lifted each of her hands to his lips, but this time it was with the rich, full gratitude of healing. "Let us sit, my love."

Lady Ogden willingly sat down with him again on the settee. At last, she was ready to hear all that he had to say and to share all that was in her heart.

After several more minutes, Lord Ogden got up and tugged the bell-pull. At the servant's entrance, he requested that a message be conveyed to the vicar and Mrs. Ledger. "Convey our respects and say that we wish to speak to them."

Rev. Major and Mrs. Ledger came at once into the parlor. They saw that the two were sitting close together on the settee, their hands clasped. Rev. Major Ledger raised his brow. "Do my eyes deceive me? I don't see any mortal wounds."

"We have worked out everything between us," said Lord Ogden without preamble.

"Oh, is it indeed so?" asked Mrs. Ledger, looking close from her brother to the viscountess. "Have you truly ironed out your differences? Have you come to your senses?"

The viscount's black brows twitched together over his proud nose. "Why are you giving *me* such a speaking look, Amarys?"

"Well, you *are* my brother." Mrs. Ledger returned her gaze to her friend. "Well, Charlotte?"

"Yes, it's so," said Lady Ogden, blushing She was very aware that her hand laid in the viscount's calloused, warm clasp. It was a reminder of what else had been decided.

Rev. Major Ledger broke out in a smile. His gray eyes twinkled. "I am delighted! But come, the hour is too late to return to Delincourt. Besides, it's snowing. You will remain the night."

Mrs. Ledger concurred. "You must be tired, Charlotte."

Lady Ogden was willing enough. The turbulent ups-and-downs of emotions had taken its toll on her. "Settling at once into a warm bed sounds perfect." She left the parlor, arm-in-arm with her friend, to be shown upstairs to one of the bedchambers.

Lord Ogden turned to Rev. Major Ledger. "Congratulate me, Arthur. I am to be made the happiest of men."

Rev. Major Ledger raised his brows. "Then you were able to convince the lovely lady of your sincere affections?"

"Damn your eyes," said Lord Ogden without heat. "I was a bungling fool, but yes, all misunderstandings have been cleared away."

"Of course, I felicitate you, Vincent! Let us toast the happy outcome." Rev. Major Ledger limped to the side table. He picked up a decanter and poured out two glasses of brandy, one of which he handed to the viscount. "What do you wish to do about the special license? It's out of date now. Will you obtain another?"

"I have spoken to Lady Ogden. The lady wishes to have a traditional wedding and invite all of our family and friends and so do I," said Lord Ogden, swirling the wine slowly in his glass.

"Indeed! I am astonished, my lord. I had thought you would be all impatience once the lady had consented."

Lord Ogden gave a half-shrug. He looked up to meet his friend's curious gaze. "It will be best this way. There will not be any gossip arising from out of the use of a special license. No one will have cause to believe her ladyship to be breeding."

Rev. Major Ledger nodded, fully in agreement with the viscount's pure motive to shield her ladyship. "Very well, indeed. I shall read the banns from the pulpit for three consecutive Sundays. Then you and her ladyship will be free to wed." He raised his glass in a mute toast and drank from it.

Lord Ogden smiled, but he didn't immediately follow the vicar's example. His emotions threatened to overcome him, so his voice was a bit rough. "You'll wed us, of course, my dearest of friends." He held out a visibly shaking hand toward the other man.

Rev. Major Ledger wrung his lordship's outstretched hand. "Of course, I shall, dear fellow! Try to stop me!"

Lord Ogden laughed. He lifted his glass in the toast. "I am truly the happiest of men, Arthur!"

51

The viscount and his cousin-in-law, Lady Charlotte Ogden, were finally wed. The occasion was well-attended by well-wishers. Lord Ogden's married sisters and their spouses, along with their various offspring, came to stay at Delincourt. The vicarage had its share of visitors, too. A few military men were seated in the pews, who either were on leave or whose wounds had ended their soldiering days, and had known his lordship from his time in the Peninsular Army. Lord Ogden and Rev. Major Ledger both came in for much good-natured raillery and congratulation for their changes in fortune.

Lord Ogden believed there was never a finer or more salutary day upon which to be wed. It was a blustery Wednesday morning in February, one of those days where spring wrestled with winter for supremacy.

A little over a year before, the viscountess had been attired in deep mourning. Traveling in the carriage to the parish church, the bride was buttoned up in a warm pelisse worn over her new bridal clothes. For her wedding, she chose to wear a lovely marigold silk with a lace overdress, a gown especially made up by a fashionable London *modiste*, which she would wear again as an evening gown. She glowed with happiness and everyone who saw her was persuaded that they had never beheld a lovelier bride. Friends and neighbors were of the universal opinion that the wedding was a satisfying outcome. Lord Ogden was much better liked than his predecessor and it was obvious that Lady Ogden had at last gained the happiness she richly deserved.

Lord Ogden watched his lady wife. When her ladyship's eyes met his own, her green eyes glowed. Delicate rose tinted her cheeks. Gladness warmed his whole being. *She is mine at last.* He thought he had never beheld a more beautiful woman.

After the wedding breakfast, to which the entire neighborhood had been invited, and the many, many toasts, Lord Ogden and his viscountess finally made their excuses to their guests and went upstairs. They did not retire immediately, but instead went into the upper drawing-room and sat down together on the chaise. After all of the well-wishes and the crowded celebration, it seemed necessary to catch their breath. For a few moments, they sat quietly together, each in private yet companionable contemplation. The viscount lifted their entwined hands and kissed his lady's slender fingers. Lady Ogden observed, "It was a terrible struggle, but we have made a good bargain between us, my lord."

"Oh, I think so," murmured Lord Ogden, smiling tenderly at his wife.

Lady Ogden took hold of his lapel and leaned into him, her lips catching and clinging to his in a lingering kiss. With a muttered oath, the viscount gathered her into his arms. For several pleasurable moments, the couple indulged themselves in what would have been to anyone witnessing it a shocking dalliance.

At last, the viscountess gently disengaged herself from his lordship's ardent embrace and he let her go with reluctance. She glanced down at the juncture of his powerful thighs. Behind the buttoned fall of his pantaloons was an unmistakable bulge. Smiling to herself, she slid to the edge of the chaise and stood up to shake the wrinkles out of her lovely silk skirt.

Lady Ogden met her husband's dark gaze. His fierce eyes seemed to burn with a furnace of heat. Warmth rose in her cheeks and she felt herself responding to the ardor she sensed was barely leashed. Her every fiber, her every nerve, was vibrating. She sashayed toward the door with a suggestive swing of her hips. She paused with her hand on the brass knob and glanced back under her lashes. "I wish to go riding, my lord. Perhaps half an hour, in my bedchamber?"

The viscount sat like a stunned ox. He surged to his feet, staring after her. "My lady, it's the middle of the day!"

Lady Ogden demurely looked at him over her shoulder. "So it is! So indecent! We shall set all the tongues wagging." She opened the door. "I shall be waiting. Pray do not delay!" She whisked herself through the door and pulled it shut behind her.

Lady Ogden laughed softly to herself as she hurried to her bedchamber, where her dresser was waiting for her. Mills helped her out of her bridal clothes, but Lady Ogden would not let her unlace her short corset. "Leave it, Mills. His lordship likes me in my chemise and stays," she said quietly. She sat down on the bench in front of her mirrored dresser and pointed one toe, regarding her slim leg encased in a sheer pink stocking held up by a ruffled garter and tied with a thin ribbon. "And I think I'll keep on my stockings, too."

"Very shocking, my lady," said Mills with a smile. She swiftly unpinned her mistress' hair and brushed out the chestnut locks. Then she excused herself and left the bedchamber.

Lady Ogden was watching the ormolu clock on the mantel of her fireplace. The clock hands showed it wanted but a few minutes to the half hour, so she got up and moved to stand beside one of the bedposts, curling her hand around the decorative wood.

The clock struck the half hour. A knock at once sounded on the door and Lord Ogden entered. He closed the door and turned the key in the lock. "I am eager to shut myself up with my lady wife for a few stolen hours of lovemaking." He looked across the room at her. His gaze narrowed as he drank in the sight of her. She was an enticing vision. He felt the powerful surge of his thick cock. "Your hair – I didn't expect." He swallowed. "It's unpinned, it's flowing over your shoulders. I've not seen it before in the daylight."

Lady Ogden lifted a hand and threaded her fingers through a lock. "Do you like it?"

"I want to fist my hands in your glorious locks," he said fiercely.

Lady Ogden smiled, her heart thudding a little faster. *I'll tease him, just a little.* She parted the top of the white chemise, exposing her dark pink nipples and blue-veined breasts peeping above the supporting edges of the corset. She palmed her bosoms like an offering. "What of these plump handfuls?"

His intense gaze grew hotter, thrilling her; but not as much as his biting words. "They invite my mouth like ripe berries."

Lady Ogden felt deliciously wanton. Between her thumbs and forefingers, she took hold of the sides of her chemise and slid up the hem to expose her garters. She extended one slender leg and pointed her toe. "My garters are the same pale pink as my silk hose. What think you of that, my lord"

"I want to pull the ribbons off with my teeth!"

She shivered. She was still standing near the bed, clad only in her stays over a nearly-sheer chemise that topped her thighs. What he said next brought a hot blush to her cheek and left her trembling with delicious warmth.

"The light is behind you. I can discern the enticing shadow of your mons," he muttered. "My thick tool throbs with the force of my desire. I ache to explore your hot, honeyed depths."

His powerful, blunt speech stoked her burning body. She was ravenous with passionate hunger, wanting him to possess her. "I-I want that, Vincent. I want you to take me!"

With a crude oath that made her shudder in pleasurable anticipation, the viscount tore off his cravat and dropped it to the carpet. Still holding her rapt gaze, he swiftly unbuttoned and stripped off his upper garments. He started towards her then, his broad-shouldered muscular torso naked from the waist up. Instead of the traditional breeches, he had worn biscuit-colored pantaloons to the wedding. The tight knit showcased his hard thighs and strong legs as he strode forward. An unmistakable bulge fronted his unmentionables, growing larger as she watched. Her breath hitched. She threw up a hand. He stopped in his tracks and growled, "What are you playing at now, my wanton girl?"

"Shall I help you with your boots, my lord?"

He stared at her. Then his dark eyes flashed. She saw a queer smile twist his mouth. In a hoarsened voice, he replied, "Yes, of course."

The viscount sat down on an upholstered chair. She knelt on one knee to take hold of the first boot and tugged to pull it off. She was aware of how closely he watched every move she made and her breath quickened.

"You are an erotic vision." His raw voice shook. "I shall show you no mercy when my prick sinks into you at last."

"I don't want mercy! Give me the strong strokes of your thick cock." She had pulled off the second boot and set it aside with the other. She looked up at him. She reached out and ran her hand down the fall of his pantaloons, where she could feel the press and jump of his thickened shaft. "Take me! Do not relent. Rut on me like a beast, Vincent! Make me *feel* it!"

He reached out with both hands and ran trembling fingers through her silken hair. "I will, I swear it."

When she got up from her knees and straddled his thighs, he audibly sucked in his breath and she knew why. The chemise had risen up her thighs, exposing her private bits to his sight. He put his hands on either side of her slim waist, his thumbs rubbing slowly back and forth just below the bottom edge of her stays. Riffs of heat licked through her with the strong beat of her heart.

He growled deep in his chest. "Do you not wish to remove to the bed?"

"This first time must be a dirty little flyer. I'm already wet for you, my love."

Lady Ogden made swift work of unbuttoning his fall. The turgid, reddened flesh sprang forth into her palms and she stroked the ready prick. She smiled into his half-lidded eyes. *Falcon's eyes...fierce, dark, dangerously heated.* She watched his sun-browned countenance, saw the flush slash his cheekbones. He was breathing harsher. His nostrils abruptly flared. "You're torturing me, wife!"

"Such is my dark intent, my lord!" She reveled in her power, but not for long. He lifted his hands to cup her breasts and his calloused fingers squeezed the soft flesh. The deliberate pressure, the rough tweak of her beaded nipples, made her gasp. A liquid warmth suffused her belly. She shivered with sensual anticipation.

His lids grew heavier, his eyes narrowing to slits, their dark color almost opaque. She could feel the beat of blood in his member while she stroked the velvety-hard length. She watched the tightening of his lean face, watched his half-hooded eyes change to a burning intensity. Her own breath came faster. The act of pleasuring him, feeling the tautening of his muscular flanks beneath her naked thighs, served to increase her own desire. *Ravisher...seed-bull...lover.* She lifted herself to fit his hot, blunt head to the notch of her throbbing pith. Slowly, she pushed down onto his thick shaft, taking him deep, until he was fully seated. Her womb contracted. She felt his hands curl tight on her hips.

He gave a long, low groan. "My God, Charlotte!"

A hitch in her breath, she said, "You must promise me a good tumble in the bed after our ride, my lord."

"I swear it!"

They began to move together, as well-versed lovers do. She clutched his naked shoulders and rhythmically rocked up and down in his lap with the slow thrust of his thick shaft. She could feel how her body was responding. Her skin was prickling with heat. Her heart kicked up and raced. *It's good, so good.* The passion began to spiral, carrying her with it.

He tightened his fingers into her rounded bare buttocks, jogging her a little faster. "That's it, my love! You're a magnificent rider. Give it a good screw, that's a good pussy!"

"Vincent, Vincent." As always, his vulgarities served to incite her ardor. She closed her eyes and dropped her head back on her neck, exposing her slender throat to his trail of hot kisses. Her mouth parted, little huffs of air jerked out in tandem with his urgent rhythm. The familiar warmth at her tightening core began to pulse outwards into her quivering limbs. She was afire, the licks of flame beginning to consume her.

Her bosoms jigged above the supporting arcs of her stays. The viscount grasped a breast and dipped his head forward, opening his lips to cover a budded areola. She shuddered and arched forward into his fierce suckling. "Ah, *ah yes*!" She threw her shoulders back and twisted her spine. At the sinuous movement of her body, he let go of her bosom and groaned. He grasped her tighter to tup her in deep strokes.

"Possess me, burn me up! *Make me feel it!*"

"By God, I'll screw you!" The viscount shoved his shoulders against the upholstered chair back. He straightened his legs and dug his heels into the carpet. His fingers crushed the globes of her arse and forced the gallop on them.

She gloried in the swift surge and retreat of his powerful virility. She was caught fast, bound up, by their lusty swiving. She stuttered out quick moans of pleasure. Exquisite shudders began to take over her body. She gasped out a demand. *"Make me!"* Roaring began filling her ears. But she heard his tight, gritted response.

"I'm so willing to oblige you! My lusty cock relishes your tight sleeve! The lance will master your quim! My mettle will spew thick as bull-seed!"

"*Yes*, Vincent! Talk filthy to me. Love me!"

"Sweetness! I'll adore you to the end of our days!"

By Sarah Roberts

His Sugar Baby

IT Specialist

By Kate Anthony

Action Hero Junkie

By Harper Lewis

Hunted, Beware

Don't miss out!

Visit the website below and you can sign up to receive emails whenever Sarah Roberts publishes a new book. There's no charge and no obligation.

https://books2read.com/r/B-A-ATKL-NAFHB

BOOKS 2 READ

Connecting independent readers to independent writers.

www.ingramcontent.com/pod-product-compliance
Lightning Source LLC
Chambersburg PA
CBHW051521050726
47503CB00014B/289